Praise for

South of Justice

"*South of Justice* is a multilayered, intricate, and suspenseful page-turner you'll want to read in one sitting."

—Diane Capri, *New York Times* and *USA Today* bestselling author of the Hunt for Jack Reacher thrillers

"Past secrets test the bonds of family loyalty and a fledgling love affair. The unwavering strength of the protagonists, their commitment to the truth and to each other will have you cheering for *South of Justice*."

—Melissa Hladik Meyer, Author of *Good Company*

South of Justice

Joni M. Fisher

South of Justice

Copyright @ 2016 Joni M. Fisher

All Rights Reserved. Except for use in any review, the reproduction or use of this work in whole or in part in any form by any electronic, mechanical or other means, now known or hereinafter invented, including xerography, photocopying, recording, or in any information storage or retrieval system is forbidden without the written permission of the copyright holder, Joni M. Fisher, or her estate.

South of Justice is a work of fiction. Names, characters, places, and incidents are the product of the author's imagination or are used fictitiously, and any resemblance to actual persons, living or dead, business establishments, events, or locales is entirely coincidental.

ISBN-13: 978-0-9972575-0-2 (Trade paperback version)
ISBN-13: 978-0-9972575-1-9 (eBook English version)

Original Cover Design by Damonza
Interior Formatting by Author E.M.S.

To Maury L. Fisher for giving me roots and wings.

*And to Caryn Louise Cook Frink.
Best. Friend. Ever.*

ACKNOWLEDGMENTS

Deep thanks to critique partners from Kiss of Death and the Tampa Area Romance Authors who encouraged, corrected, and occasionally laughed at my flailing transition from non-fiction to fiction writing. Giant thanks to my editor, Maureen Sevilla. Special thanks to authors: Jamie Beckett, KD Fleming, John Foxjohn, Donna Kelly, Mary McGuire, Melissa Hladik Meyer, and Carol Post for their unflinching, wise advice. Special thanks also to brave beta readers: Dawn Anderson, Kim Addington, Doris Arrington, Cyndi Boswell, John M. Esser, Carol Faulkner-Davis, Maury L. Fisher, M.D., Bev Fortenberry, Caryn L. Frink, Terri Johnson, Audrey Nettlow, Carol Speyerer, Michael VanDoren, Ph.D., and Martha Walker for taking my long journey to publication as seriously as I do.

South of Justice

. 1 .

September 17, 2008

Terri Pinehurst believed that happiness, like respect, had to be earned. Being named the keynote speaker at this year's conference of her peers felt like earned respect. The last time she felt sheer happiness, well, that was a few years ago at this hotel. Fleeting happiness at best. But still. She hoped none of the New York Marriott Marquis staff recognized her, especially that kind bellman who hauled her to her room on a luggage cart after an epic bridesmaid's party.

Too caffeinated to sit still, she had an hour to kill before her address, so she headed away from the conference ballroom in search of a ladies room to freshen her lipstick and tame her hair.

"Terri Pinehurst!" a deep voice called from behind.

She flinched then spun around. Justin Cook, her smart and funny flirt of a study partner from grad school, grinned back at her. "Justin!"

He greeted her with a hug. "So great to see you! Hey, I'm moving to New York to be closer to relatives."

For a moment, she forgot how to breathe. "What about your practice out west?"

His smile dimmed by half. He glanced at his hands, twisted his wedding band, and peered up at her. "We need to be near Poughkeepsie to take care of my wife's father. The sooner, the better. I should have called you, but I wanted to tell you in person."

"You're married?"

"Don't be shocked. I got a life."

"So you're here to make contacts?" She aimed for a casual tone.

Justin nodded. He was bulkier in the shoulders than she remembered.

"I'll introduce you around at the mixer after the keynote speech." If she had been in solo practice, she would have hired him on the spot, but she had partners to consult first.

He picked up her left hand. "I thought for sure you'd be married by now."

She sighed. In the eight years since graduation, she had built up the practice her father brought her into, hiring partners, doing her job, managing the business. Her pals called her the queen of delayed gratification, because she put her long-term goals first, which meant putting off her love life until later. Always later. Besides, as busy as she was she didn't have the energy to get out to meet men.

Justin released her hand. "I'm sure your business is going strong, but you need more life in your life. Marriage is wonderful." His enthusiasm lit up his eyes.

"Marriage looks good on you." If she ever got married, she'd resent having to move her practice and start over. Did his wife appreciate the sacrifice he was making to start his business over? Poor Justin.

"How will I find you?"

During her father's generation, this was a male-dominated field. By far, she wouldn't be the only woman attending, but as keynote speaker she would be the most visible. "It will be easy."

His gaze ran up and down her body while he backed off toward the conference room. "Red hair, green suit. Looking good, Pinehurst."

"You too, Cook." She checked her jacket pockets. ID badge, lipstick, pepper spray, car keys, and cash. She strolled down the corridor and around the corner for a restroom.

Up ahead a large, broad-shouldered man in a tuxedo and cowboy boots leaned one arm on a doorjamb. Terri eyed his fine physique and had passed him before she noticed the sign above him. *Ladies*.

He spoke to the door. "Come on out, please." His Southern accent sounded almost foreign in the heart of New York City. Maybe the boots weren't a costume, like the 'all hat, no cattle' men who wanted to impress women by play-acting a lifestyle.

She sized him up. Thirtyish. Six feet, two hundred pounds. Short reddish hair. Clean-shaven. Broad shouldered. Whatever his drama was, he needed to take it elsewhere. With one hand in her pocket on her pepper spray, she would ask him nicely to move out of the way. If he turned aggressive, he'd immediately regret it.

Aramis aftershave wafted from the large stranger as she tapped his firm shoulder.

Startled, he turned. The combination of his size, the aftershave, and his handsome face hitched up her heart rate, then he aimed his green eyes at her. "Please, help me."

She couldn't look away. Maybe it was the suggestion from an old friend that put her in the frame of mind to think of romance, but something about this man woke up her body and clouded her mind.

A whimpering sound carried from the bathroom to the hallway.

The man scowled. "Ma'am, there's a young lady in there I'd like to talk to. Would you please coax her on out?"

"Why did you call me ma'am?" Her tone came out sharper than intended.

He sucked in a quick breath and straightened to his full height as if bracing for a slap. "Good breeding."

His charm relaxed her. "It's Miss."

He smiled at her while his pupils widened.

Great, Mr. Charmer has his girlfriend crying in the bathroom and now he's eyeing me. "You're not from the city are you?"

"I work in the city. Today, I'm attending a friend's wedding." He nodded toward the noisy ballroom.

"Is that the *bride*?" Terri nodded toward the restroom.

"No."

"Okay then, are you the reason she's crying?"

"Absolutely not."

"You'd say that even if you were." She squinted at him. "No promises."

The charmer stepped aside and opened the door.

Terri stepped through the doorway and eased up to the long granite ladies room counter. Leaning over the sink to apply lipstick, she sneaked a peek in the mirror of a long, lean beauty sitting on a cushioned bench. The way the young woman's head hung, her abundant, brown curls obscured her face. From her deep teal designer sheath dress, down her long, athletic legs, to her sparkling designer heels, the weeping beauty could have been a woman wronged or a spoiled drama queen not getting her way.

"I just met a gorgeous, well-mannered man outside," Terri ventured.

The young woman raised her head, causing hair to part and tumble down her shoulders and back. Her face glistened. Two thin streaks of brown mascara ran from the outside corners of her eyes halfway down her cheeks. She opened her eyes, revealing irises the color of predators—lions, owls, tigers, leopards, and hawks. Amber was rare in humans. Terri plucked a handful of tissues from the counter while she tried to assess the beauty's age. Eighteen? Twenty? No wonder Mr. Charmer was staking out the bathroom. He had to be ten years older than her.

"He asked me to invite you outside to talk." Terri sat beside her on the tufted bench and handed over the tissues.

"Thank you." The young woman dabbed her eyes, missing the lines of mascara, then she blew her nose.

"So why are you crying?"

"Disappointment." Her bottom lip quivered.

Having witnessed the attention-getting pretend weeping that turned men into putty over the years, Terri judged this as genuine grief. The fact she was crying in private spoke volumes.

"Did someone break your heart?"

She nodded. Her eyes welled up, threatening more tears.

"On purpose?"

The girl shook her head and let out a shuddering sigh.

"Is it that man in the tux outside?"

The young beauty stood, unfolding gracefully like a great Blue Heron, much taller than expected. She strode to the sink and wet a paper towel. "No. Blake is one of the kindest men I've ever met."

Confused, Terri looked up at her. It felt wickedly selfish to hope that the gorgeous man outside was just this girl's friend or brother trying to comfort her, but Terri hoped so nonetheless. "Is Blake your date?"

The tall beauty removed the mascara smears from her cheeks. "No. We're both friends of the groom."

"And you're in love with…?"

"Vincent Gunnerson. He's Blake's partner."

"Partner?" Oh, not another handsome gay man. What a waste. *I certainly can't let her wait around for that to change.* "That must be quite…a shock."

The beauty snorted and addressed Terri's reflection in the mirror. "Not that kind of partner. They're co-workers."

Buoyed by the news the young woman had no claim on the hunk in the tux and that he was straight, Terri stuck out her hand. "I'm Terri Pinehurst."

"I'm Nefi Jenkins."

A suggestion of recognition tickled the back of Terri's consciousness. The name Nefi was quite unusual. She'd heard it before, but when? Perhaps this girl was a rising tennis star, or singer, or ballerina. To have such an expensive wardrobe at her age meant wealth from somewhere. Her Louboutin's closed-toe glitter pumps cost $700. Terri knew because one of her partner's wives owned a pair.

After they had shaken hands, Terri asked, "So what are you going to do?"

"Dig a hole and die in it." Nefi sounded like she meant it.

"Please, not in those shoes."

A corner of Nefi's mouth tugged upward for a moment.

Terri felt a big sister kind of protectiveness for Nefi because she had once cried like this in a restroom over a man. "The way I see it, you have a choice. You can hide from the world every time you're disappointed or hurt, or you can master your feelings and go back to the party."

Nefi spoke softly. "I waited six years to see Vincent."

Six *years*? "Why?"

Her long fingers stroked a shot bead chain that hung on her neck and disappeared under the collar of her dress. "He's older than me. I turn twenty-one next month."

So this began as a teenage crush. "And you thought he'd wait for you to grow up?"

Nefi closed her eyes and nodded.

Terri had once been that naïve and full of hope in a relationship that ended in crushing pain and disillusionment. Was Nefi *that* innocent or had Vincent misled her? Terri was not above shaming this Vincent character if he had. Some men fooled even older, more experienced women.

Don't judge. Get the facts. "Why did you think he would wait for you?"

"He gave me his dog tags." Nefi sniffled. "I was waiting for him."

How could a girl be almost legal age in America and so unworldly? *Uh oh.* "Not that it's any of my business but did anything else happen between you two?"

"No sex if that's what you mean."

Terri sighed. So this guy gave her his dog tags. Oh, the unintended consequences of a good deed.

Nefi dabbed tissues on her eyes. For a moment, she stared at her reflection in the mirror then her eyes closed.

Favoring logic over emotion, Terri decided to nudge Nefi toward considering a healthier perspective of her situation. "You know there are six billion people in the world. Let's say half of them are men. I'd bet most of them would be thrilled to go out with you."

Ever so slightly Nefi raised her chin. "Maybe the boys and the old men."

"So maybe one *billion* in dating age range. Roughly equivalent to the entire population of China." Terri stopped when she realized she was babbling.

The air conditioner *whooshed* gently overhead. Voices in the hallway carried through the doorway.

"I can master my feelings. I refuse to miss this party because Vincent brought a date." Nefi straightened her spine and pulled her shoulders back. Her posture reminded Terri of a rehabilitated eagle the moment it hopped from the open cage door onto the grass and recognized freedom.

"Atta girl." Though it could ruin any chance she had with Blake, she said, "In my opinion, the hunk in the tux must be some kind of friend to wait outside a ladies' room for you."

Nefi seemed to be examining Terri. After a moment, she asked, "Blake?" as if she had never considered him anything but a friend, as if she had not noticed he was a hunk.

"It seems to me that *Blake* cares for you." At the risk of sounding desperate, she whispered, "But if you aren't interested in him, please, please, introduce me."

Nefi laughed. It was a joyful sound.

What a mess. Blake paced outside the ladies' room.

Twenty minutes earlier, he had made a complete fool of himself. His brothers often told him weddings put women in a romantic mood. With that in mind, and two flutes of champagne in hand, he decided to make himself available for conversation and dancing.

Finding a woman unaccompanied, he braved the best conversation-starter he could think of. "It's a crying shame to see a lovely woman sitting all alone."

In the dimly lit ballroom, the beautiful young lady immediately stood and hugged him. When she released him from the hug, he assessed her with a quick look-see. *Guess my brothers got this right.*

"I'll take that as an invitation." He sat in the chair to her left and stared back at her. She had long brown hair hanging in loose curls to her waist, a fresh face, and great legs. Friendly as a Walmart Greeter, too.

She smiled at him with a look of expectation that put him ill at ease.

"Are you family or a friend of the bride or groom?" Blake asked, struggling for conversation.

"Friend of the groom." She smirked.

She was toying with him. It was a stretch of the imagination that the groom, Ruis Ramos, had friends his little sister's age, but Blake decided to play along. "Me, too. Are you here alone?"

"My aunt and uncle came with me." She nodded toward the empty chairs to her right. A beaded purse left unguarded at the table sparkled in the candlelight.

"So make my day. Tell me you're over twenty-one."

"Next month."

A cartoon plane on fire—spiraling toward the ground—played in his head. Blake set one flute of champagne out of her reach. He took a sip from the other one.

She smiled. "Congratulations on joining the FBI."

Huh? How did she know? "Ah, thank you." He leaned back in his chair. Searching memories, he came up empty. No name. Then her yellow eyes locked with his. *Nefi Jenkins.* "Oh, man." He slapped his free hand on his face.

Stupid. Stupid. Stupid.

Nefi snorted just like the fourteen-year-old he remembered. "Did they teach you those *keen* observations skills at Quantico?"

Grateful that Nefi forgave him, he relaxed a little in his shame. "I could never forget you. I just didn't recognize you." He set down his drink and hugged her.

Senator and Mrs. Jenkins returned to the table. The Senator's glare led Blake to release Nefi and stand up.

Blake stepped around the table then he pulled out Mrs. Jenkins' chair. "Good to see you, Senator and Mrs. Jenkins."

"Uncle, Aunt, you remember Blake Clayton," Nefi said.

The Senator's expression softened as he shook Blake's hand. "Great to see you again!"

Mrs. Jenkins greeted him with a gentle hug. "You look so handsome in a tuxedo. Doesn't he?" she asked Nefi.

"Of course he does." Nefi closed her eyes as if to hide an eye roll. "Every man looks better in a tux."

Blake fidgeted as he stood between Nefi and her aunt. He sensed Mrs. Jenkins was granting tacit approval of him. He traded a look with Mrs. Jenkins to remind her to forget trying to redirect Nefi's heart from her obsession with Vincent. Before he could prevent humiliating himself further, the DJ announced the arrival of the wedding party.

The DJ announced the attendants, "...followed by Groomsman Vincent Gunnerson and his date Rose Moreno."

Rose's red shiny dress looked like the seams were being tested. It was a wonder she could walk in it.

Nefi had let out a strangled sound and high-tailed it out the nearest door. After glancing at Nefi's aunt, Blake had followed.

So here he was, outside the ladies room, waiting for Nefi to recover. The mystery accomplice he'd recruited to flush Nefi out of the bathroom was still in there. Was she as kind as she was smoking hot or would she tell Nefi that all men were worthless liars, cheats, and low-lifes? She didn't have that angry, hairy feminist man-hater look, but who knows what women think?

What a mess. Nefi's torch still burned for his best friend. And then there was the Rose factor. Blake believed Vincent was better off single than with a high-maintenance woman like Rose.

Poor Nefi.

Blake leaned against the wall, waiting. He braced one hand on his hip and combed his fingers on his other hand through his short reddish hair.

When Terri strode from the restroom, she thought Blake the Charmer looked like a *Gentleman's Quarterly* cover model the way he leaned against the wall across the hallway in a casual, sexy pose. The tuxedo-cowboy boot combo helped. Her heart skipped ahead of her like an eager child.

Blake gave them a double-take and a grin.

Nefi smiled, all dry-eyed and composed. "Terri Pinehurst, I'd like to introduce you to Blake Clayton, a man who didn't shoot me when he probably should have."

Air rushed from Blake's lungs creating an explosive sound between a cough and a laugh. His hand hesitated a few inches away from Terri's hand, but he recovered with a chuckle.

"Now there's an endorsement you don't get every day."

"Is she being melodramatic?" Terri shook Blake's hand.

"Perhaps you'd like to join us for drinks and an explanation?"

"I'm here for a convention." Terri remained rooted in place.

"Seriously, why does she believe you should have shot her?"

"I would love to tell you that story if you have the time." He held out his elbow.

Very smooth. Terri glanced at Nefi for her reaction.

Nefi added, "If you come to the reception I can point out Vincent, and you can tell me if I'm wasting my time."

Terri had spent so much of her life saying no to things outside of duty and work, what harm would it do to take a brief detour? "I can't stay long, but I'll take that dare." She slipped her hand into the crook of Blake's large, firm forearm.

Blake offered Nefi his other elbow, then he led the way into the crowded ballroom to a table, triangulated by the dance floor, the buffet, and the bar. After pulling out two chairs, he took their drink orders then headed to the bar.

The instant after he left, Terri placed her hand on Nefi's shoulder. "Is this awkward? Just say the word and I'll leave."

"Stay. Blake is eager to tell you how he rescued me."

Wait. What? "But you said he was going to shoot you."

"He tells it better than I do." Nefi's attention swung toward Blake at the bar. She took deep breaths and squeezed a tissue as if alarmed.

Terri followed Nefi's gaze.

Blake stepped in line behind a taller dark-haired man in a tuxedo as the bartender placed a flute of champagne and a beer on the counter. After the man dropped a bill in the tip bowl, he picked up his drinks and pivoted. He smiled broadly at Blake and spoke.

Nefi leaned close to Terri and whispered, "That's Vincent talking to Blake."

Whoa. Okay then. Terri immediately understood Nefi's attraction to Vincent.

A third man slid up beside Blake and Vincent at the bar.

"The shorter man is the groom, Ruis." Nefi smiled wistfully. "The three of them rescued me."

"I can't wait to hear this story." Fantasies of being rescued by them tickled her consciousness. *Maybe Justin was right about getting more life in my life.*

The bartender plunked a bottle of water and a glass on the counter. The groom twisted off the bottle top. With a sheen of perspiration on his face, he looked like an advertisement for a Spanish men's cologne.

The men laughed at something the groom said.

Blake glanced over his shoulder and waved at Terri and Nefi.

Vincent squinted in their direction, causing Nefi to gasp.

"Keep breathing." Terri placed a hand on Nefi's shoulder. She was grateful the dim lights concealed her own open-mouthed gape at the oh-so-handsome trio of testosterone.

Nefi leaned forward, her spine stiff. "What's he saying?"

Blake watched Vincent drop a ten-dollar bill into the tip bowl, pick up his champagne and beer, and wheeled around. The ballrooms lights dimmed to near darkness and the music began.

Normally a gentleman, Blake refused to pretend he liked Vincent's girlfriend Rose. Being a loyal friend meant speaking the truth, whether or not the listener wanted to hear it. He had hinted once he didn't believe Rose was in the relationship for the long haul by calling her a social climber.

"Getting her drunk won't help."

"I could get drunk." Vincent grunted.

Ruis slid up beside them at the bar. "Water, please."

The bartender plunked a chilled bottle and glass on the counter. Ruis twisted off the cap and downed a swig.

"I think it's simply poor form," Blake said, "when the groom is prettier than the bride."

"Are you saying my wife isn't pretty?"

Blake's hands and feet tingled from a surge of adrenalin. It wasn't smart to insult a SEAL. "No."

"What?" Ruis said.

Vincent muttered to Blake, "Digging your own grave, man."

"Your wife is pretty. Very pretty. I mean she's beautiful—"

Ruis laughed. "Go have fun with anyone but my sisters." He left with his water.

Blake exhaled. His heart rate slowed back to normal.

Vincent laughed.

The DJ announced the first dance for the bride and groom.

Blake glanced over his shoulder and waved at Nefi and Terri. "Hey, got a minute? You have to meet the ladies at my table."

"Rose will think you're trying to introduce me to other women."

"Better women," Blake said.

Vincent squinted at the ladies. "How did you find two?"

"Open bar. The more they drink, the better I look."

"Or it could be the tux." Vincent released his pointer finger from his grip on the champagne glass and aimed it at Blake. "Makes you look housebroken."

Blake told the bartender, "Rum and coke, and a ginger ale, please."

Vincent raised his eyebrows. "Mother and daughter?"

The young bartender snickered.

Blake stuffed a one-dollar bill in the tip jar as he glowered at the bartender. "What are you laughing at?" He said to Vincent, "The women are unrelated, thank you very much. You really *need* to meet them."

"Another time." Vincent waded into the crowd gathering at the edge of the dance floor.

"I wish I could read lips," Terri sighed. She wanted a warning if they were planning to come to the table. This might be too soon for Nefi to recover from the disappointment of a seven-year wait. Of course, now she had a clearer understanding of Nefi's infatuation. Vincent was manly handsome, the kind who drew second and third glances, and he appeared closer to Nefi's age than Blake. It also made sense that the towering young woman would seek out a tall man.

"So what do you think of Vincent?"

"I wouldn't throw him out of bed for eating crackers."

The men glanced back at Nefi and Terri. The bride and groom stepped to the center of the dance floor and Vincent headed away. Crisis averted.

"What does that mean?" Nefi asked.

Before Terri could answer, Blake placed their drinks on the table and sat between Terri and Nefi. He grinned and draped his arms over the backs of their chairs. "Let the rumors begin." He cupped Terri's shoulder, and gave Nefi's a quick squeeze.

"What does it mean," Nefi asked, "when someone says 'I wouldn't throw him out of bed for eating crackers'?"

Terri leaned forward to see across Blake's chest at Nefi. "It's just an expression." She downed a gulp of rum and coke. Heavy on the rum, it chilled and burned at the same time. *Let it go. Let it go.*

Blake laughed, raising an eyebrow at Terri before turning to Nefi. Terri looked away toward the dance floor. Blood rushed to her face. *Of course he thinks I was talking about him.* She suddenly envied all burrowing animals. *Oh, to tunnel out of here right now.*

"It means," Blake said, "a woman would forgive a man for some behaviors to keep him around." He patted Terri's shoulder, leaving his arm draped across the back of her chair.

"Oh." Nefi sipped her ginger ale.

The music swelled as the bride and groom danced.

"Speaking of forgiveness, Nefi, dear," Blake said just loudly enough to be heard over the music, "remember Matthew eighteen, verse twenty-two?" He pulled his arms away from the back of Terri's chair and faced Nefi.

Nefi whispered, "Yeah, yeah. We should forgive others, not just once or twice, but seventy times seven times." She stood and pointed into the crowd. "He's got four hundred and eighty-nine to go!"

Terri chuckled. Blake bowed his head and shook it.

Nefi dropped back into her chair. "I suppose he's forgiven me a time or two." To Terri she said, "Once I knocked Vincent down and threatened him with knives."

Who are these people? Terri leaned forward in her chair. "Why did you do that?"

Blake planted a hand on Nefi's forearm. "Technically, it was a machete and a hunting knife."

Nefi shrugged before taking another sip of her ginger ale.

"It was a simple misunderstanding." Blake leaned back in his chair and said to Terri. "She was distraught. Vincent had something of her father's so she logically suspected we might have been involved in killing her parents in Brazil."

Jenkins. Recognition slapped Terri in the back of the head. She gasped. "Nefi Jenkins. Are you Senator Jenkins' niece?"

Nefi nodded.

"I remember it on the news. Your parents were missionaries. Oh, I'm so sorry."

"And Vincent, Ruis," he pointed to the groom, "and I went down to Brazil to find her and bring her to the states. Our sweet girl was dehydrated, malnourished, covered in leeches, and wearing scary looking war paint when we found her." He patted Nefi's forearm like a protective big brother.

"And none of them spoke Portuguese," Nefi added, "so there we were, with me on top of Vincent, holding a machete to his neck and a knife at his ribs. Blake drew his gun on me while Ruis was trying to look up words in a *Spanish-Portuguese dictionary*."

Groups of men in Navy dress uniform assembled near the dance floor. Terri could imagine the groom blithely flipping pages in a book while a life-and-death drama unfolded in front of him. These men, who probably served together, were all military and all deadly handsome.

Blake rested his hand on the back of Nefi's chair. "Good times."

Terri and Nefi laughed. Their dance over, the groom tugged on the bride's arm and they strolled toward Terri, Blake, and Nefi.

"Happy Brazilian Independence Day," Ruis said, pulling Nefi out of her chair for a hug.

Nefi smiled. "Thank you." Then Nefi hugged the petite bride who looked like a precious doll adorned in crinoline and lace.

Ruis glanced at Terri. His expression was neutral.

"This is Terri Pinehurst," Blake said. "She's here for a conference, but I corralled her from the hallway."

A sudden tingly warmth spread through Terri when Blake said her name.

"Well done," Ruis said. "You're a chemical engineer?"

"I'm with the other convention, next ballroom down." Standing, Terri glanced at her watch. *Yipes. How time flies when you're having rum.* "Congratulations on your wedding. I'm sorry, but I really have to leave." She retrieved her name badge and a business card from her jacket pocket and clipped the ID to her lapel.

Ruis smiled. "It's a pleasure to meet you, Doctor Pinehurst."

Blake placed his hands on Terri's shoulders and spun her around to read her name tag. His touch warmed her down to her toes.

"You're a doctor?"

"Veterinarian." She braced for the look of disappointment that often followed when she clarified what kind of doctorate she had earned.

Blake's pupils widened and a smile lit up his face. His

aftershave wafted over her. He released her shoulders with a pat. "And you're the keynote speaker?"

Nefi and Ruis laughed, but Terri didn't know why. "That's why I need to be on time." She hugged Nefi. "Call me. I would love to know how this works out for you." She palmed Nefi her business card.

Blake tapped Nefi on the shoulder. "I'll be right back. Save a dance for me."

"Wait!" Nefi picked up her camera from the table and aimed it at them.

Terri reached her hand into the crook of his arm and leaned against him. A flicker of hope and friendship sparked within her toward Blake and his friends. She suddenly longed for more time with these unusual strangers.

Nefi took a photo of them and then one of Ruis and his bride.

Terri reluctantly released Blake.

"May I walk you to your meeting?" Blake asked.

Terri sought Nefi's reaction to the offer. Nefi nodded, her emotions apparently under control.

"Thank you, Blake. I'd like that very much."

They strolled in silence down the thickly carpeted hallway. Being escorted by a gorgeous man in a tuxedo and cowboy boots attracted the subtle attention of strangers. She lived in the moment, savoring his presence, his cologne, and his attention. There are people who are so uncomfortable with silence they fill every gap with small talk. Blake seemed at ease, and Terri found the silence companionable. At the open double-doors a poster on a tripod announced her as a Specialist in Large Animals.

"Thank you." Blake lifted her hand and gently kissed it. "You made my evening memorable, and you rescued a young lady from needless depression."

"And thanks to you, I've gone from being a respected professional to wedding crasher."

Long dormant sensations bubbled up inside her when his

warm lips touched her hand. She imagined peeling off his tuxedo to caress his muscled chest and arms, to touch his bare skin. Looking up, she expected to see an amused expression, but his face seemed relaxed.

His direct stare keened her attention. She stared back into his green eyes and sensed hunger there.

Conference attendees eased around them, gawking. Blake seemed unwilling to move away from her. When a fidgety man appeared beside them, clearing his throat, Blake slowly released her hand.

"Doctor Pinehurst?" the man squeaked. "I have your microphone."

Terri took the small device and hooked it over her ear then she adjusted the thin-wire microphone to the outer edge of her mouth. The technician then held up the transmitter. She clipped it to the back of her waistband with practiced movements.

"And back to the respected professional." Blake smiled and then gazed at her as if trying to anchor her image in his memory.

She brushed aside her professionalism about avoiding public displays of affection because she had to signal her interest as quickly as possible. If Blake served in the Navy like the other men in uniform at the wedding reception, he would understand her need to seize the day. If she never saw him again, she did not want to regret a missed opportunity. She pushed the mouthpiece away from her lips then planted her hands on his chest, rose on her tiptoes, and kissed him soundly on the mouth. For a moment during the kiss—gravity, time, and place lost their hold on her—nothing mattered beyond his full, warm lips that lightly tethered her to earth.

He tasted as wonderful as he looked.

The sound technician cleared his throat.

Terri reluctantly pulled away. She pivoted on her sensible heels then entered the grand ballroom. She floated across the ballroom and up the stairs. There she stood, waiting beside the podium, while the chairman of the conference, a fellow alumnus, introduced her. She pulled her note cards from her jacket pocket and tugged the mouthpiece back down.

At the back of the room, Blake stood in the center aisle with a trouble-making grin.

Blake danced with Nefi, and then the bridesmaids urged him to join them in the "Macarena," a song he remembered from high school. Some of the bridesmaids were Ruis's sisters, but despite Ruis's warning, he decided to risk it since they were under the watch of Ruis's father and Navy SEAL pals. Besides, as Vincent often pointed out, "Blake and dignity were rarely in the same place at the same time."

He waited until Nefi left with Senator and Mrs. Jenkins before he retired to his room and sat on the queen-size bed. The highlight of the evening had been meeting Terri Pinehurst, a genuine beauty with thick, wavy reddish brown hair, pale blue eyes, and fair, freckled skin. She glowed with health and the outdoors. And a veterinarian to boot.

He sighed. When he dug his cell phone out of his jacket pocket, a business card fluttered to his lap, the same card Terri handed to Nefi. *Sneaky*. Nefi had somehow tucked the card in his pocket without his knowledge.

"Thank you, Nefi."

So...Doctor Pinehurst's practice was in Poughkeepsie, New York. *Nice*.

He held Terri's business card to his heart for a moment, then he opened his phone and pressed the number seven for speed dial.

A woman's voice answered.

"Sorry to call so late."

"Blake, honey, are you calling from a hospital?"

"No."

"Jail?"

"Just called to say you were right." He fell back on the bed. His feet throbbed in protest of the very long day. He pried off his shoes, letting them fall. *Thump. Thump.*

"And what am I right about this time?"

"You said I would thank you one day. Today's the day I officially thank you and praise your infinite wisdom for dragging me to ballroom dancing classes." Tonight was just practice. He intended to impress a Doctor Terri Pinehurst with his dancing skills as soon as possible.

"You're welcome, son."

After taming five sons, his mama was used to being told she was right. It had simply taken him longer to admit it. Surely Mama would forgive his thick-headedness, being the youngest of the litter and all.

. 2 .

Terri pulled into Poughkeepsie's Victor C. Waryas Park to find Blake leaning on the bumper of a silver Toyota 4Runner. He was watching the construction of the one-and-one-quarter mile walkway bridge over the Hudson River. Noise from the jackhammers covered her approach as she climbed out of her car and eased up behind him. From boyhood on up it seemed that men longed to operate cranes, fire trucks, bulldozers, and other heavy equipment. He looked so calm. Calm wouldn't do at all. She needed to prepare him mentally for meeting her father. After pushing her sunglasses higher on her nose, she inhaled deeply to catch the scent of his subtly-seductive woodsy aftershave.

"Scary tall, isn't it?"

"Sure is." He swung one arm free and pointed. "It's odd. The bottom part of the bridge looks ancient, but the top—"

"It used to be a railroad bridge. They're making it into a pedestrian walkway. When it's done this fall, it's supposed to be the longest walkway bridge in the world." For the first time in ages she wanted someone to admire her hometown because she loved it so.

"So you wanted to meet here to brag about your bridge making it into the *Guinness Book of World Records*?"

"We're here to prepare you to meet my father. Dad's all riled up about GM and Chrysler filing for bankruptcy. He says the country's headed for another depression. I certainly can't let you drive up in a Toyota."

Blake dropped his arm off her shoulder and gently grabbed her hands in his. "I've met fathers before. I know how to behave. Will I meet your mother, too?"

"Mom will love you." Terri smiled at him. "Grab your gear. I'll brief you on the way."

Blake popped open the hatchback and handed Terri two wrapped packages. Peace offerings. He grabbed an overnight bag, then closed and locked his Japanese-made sports utility vehicle.

"How did the other fathers treat you?" She led him to her red Ford F-150 pickup truck.

"I'd like to say they treated me with the same respect I showed them, but that'd be a total lie. I never dated anyone my brothers dated, but somehow I got judged for all their breakups." His grin told her he did not fully appreciate his situation. He eyed her truck with a look akin to lust. "When did you get this ride?"

"I've had it a while. When I go to the city I rent a car. Easier to get around." She set the gifts on the floor behind the driver's seat of her truck.

Blake set his suitcase on the backseat. They closed the back doors with a simultaneous muffled *thud*. He wedged into the passenger's seat. She eased into the driver's seat. Blake's hands caressed the leather dashboard, and a twinge of jealousy passed through her. She kept her truck washed and detailed, so it looked almost new despite sixty-thousand miles.

Shaking off the distraction, she asked, "Did any of those fathers greet you by tossing a bullet at you?"

"Um, no." His knees pressed against the dash.

"Prom night, junior year. My father tossed a bullet at Alan and told him if he slept with me he wouldn't see the next bullet coming."

Blake chuckled. "Did Alan behave?"

"That's not the point."

Blake powered his seat back. "I get it. Your father's protective."

"In college I brought home a guy I was serious about. Trent." She sighed. "Dad took him out for a plane ride. I wasn't with them, but later—on his way out of town—he told me that Dad told him he'd be better off jumping out at eight-thousand feet than ever hurting me."

"You're an only child so he focused all his energy on you," he said buckling in.

"Prepare for resistance."

"I'd be disappointed if he didn't give me a hard time." He grinned.

She started the V-6 202-horsepower engine. "I'll remind you of that later."

The homes on Kingwood Park, Poughkeepsie, New York, sat at least a half-acre apart, separated by lush flowering summer gardens and trees. With gifts in hand, Blake put on his game face before he stepped through the threshold of the Pinehurst's brick mansion. As anxious as Terri seemed about introducing him to her parents, he was doubly nervous. First, he needed to win over her father and then he'd have a private chat with him.

"Dad, Mom, this is Blake Clayton."

Blake stuck out his hand to Grace Pinehurst first. "Pleased to meet you, ma'am." Then he reached out to shake hands with Terri's somber-faced father, George.

"My friends call me Skip," he said, shaking Blake's hand. "You can call me Doctor Pinehurst."

And here we go. "Yes, sir."

"My mother's name is Grace," Terri said.

"You aren't afraid of dogs are you?" George asked Blake.

"No, sir."

George said to Terri, "We're watching Tiny for the week."

"Oh, Dad. Really?" Terri's shoulders slumped.

How bad could the dog be? Blake wasn't fond of small yappy dogs. They tended toward skittishness and biting.

"I'll bring him out so you can get acquainted." George appeared a little too eager to open the door that led from the dining room.

The beast that emerged from the basement easily weighed one hundred forty pounds. He had a black face like a giant Labrador and the rest of him had reddish, shaggy fur like a Golden Retriever. The instant he spotted Terri he bounded toward her. Blake was about to throw himself in front of her to take the brunt of the animal's momentum when Terri spoke.

"Tiny, stop!"

The huge dog stopped so fast his back legs slid under him into a well-mannered sit.

Terri patted him on the head. Tiny responded by nosing her wrist and banging his tail on the Oriental rug. The glare she gave her father would have wilted a plant. Then she said to Blake, "Tiny is a Leonberger. German breed. Good temperament. However, this one thinks he's a lap dog."

"I'm glad I'm standing," Blake said.

George picked up Blake's suitcase and said, "I'll show you to your room."

Blake followed George into the basement where George deposited the suitcase in a makeshift guest room. "Terri's room is on the second floor. Our room is next to hers. I'm a light sleeper."

"Yes, sir." Blake had no intention of sneaking around. He wanted to say so, but instead he decided to show how much he respected Terri and her family.

Later, after a filling meat-and-potatoes dinner and dessert, George crossed his arms and addressed Terri, "I was expecting you to bring home your new business partner, the one who was your study partner at school. What's his name?"

"Justin Brooks. You can meet Justin and his wife Marlene at the office Christmas party. They moved here to take care of her father who has dementia. You remember Carleton, the man who ran the hardware store? He's Marlene's father. I believe he's your age."

George cleared his throat. "Sounds like Justin's a good man. So, dear, how well do you know your...boyfriend?"

Terri blushed. "We've been dating since October."

Blake assumed his poker face.

"You've been dating nine months. *Huh.* And why is it we are just now meeting him?" George asked.

Blake raised his eyebrows at Terri. He too was interested in her answer to that question. Was she ashamed of him? Perhaps her father had higher expectations, like the kind of expectations Justin met.

"Blake lives in New York City and most of the time I drive there because there's more to do in the City," Terri said.

George's half-lidded stare said he wasn't buying her excuse. It sounded lame to Blake, too. Grace chuckled.

Terri pursed her lips. "Okay, I'll tell you why I didn't bring Blake home to meet you until now. Remember my prom date?"

"That tall skinny kid?"

Grace cleared her throat.

"Yes," George said.

Terri and her mother stared down George. The situation had the feel of an old argument that everyone tried to avoid. Blake leaned back in his chair as if to remove himself from the line of fire.

"I might have been a little rough on him."

"And Trent?" Terri prompted.

"He was too old for you," George said waving Trent off with a flick of the wrist. "Just because a boy likes you it doesn't mean he's right for you."

Terri threw up her hands. Grace exchanged a look with George that Blake couldn't read.

"So why did you introduce him as Blake?" George asked.

"That's his name."

Uh oh. Blake took a deep breath.

"His legal name?" George eyed Blake.

"I prefer Blake," he said. "My full name is Elijah Blake Clayton."

"Elijah?" Terri repeated.

Apparently satisfied, George uncrossed his arms and sat back.

Terri and her mother exchanged a quick glance. Terri glared at her father.

Blake pulled papers from his pocket and unfolded them. He chose to face potential conflict head on rather than fall into a defensive position. "In the interest of full disclosure, I hired a fellow FBI agent to prepare a background check."

George bristled. "On whom?"

"Me," Blake handed the papers to Terri's father. In doing so, he handed over the appearance of being in control to Terri's father.

George's eyebrows gave him away like a beginning poker player. He took the papers.

"Look on through it and ask me anything you want to know." Blake longed to win over Terri's parents. If it took humiliating himself, so be it.

Mr. and Mrs. Pinehurst huddled over the papers.

"Are you serious?" Terri asked Blake.

"I thought it would save time."

She scrambled out of her chair to read over their shoulders. Was she afraid they would find something or was she driven by simple curiosity?

Without memorizing it, Blake knew what was in the report. The first page of a police report charged "the Clayton boys" with misdemeanor mischief for moving the principal's 1990 MG convertible onto the school roof. George flipped to page two, a police report from Blake's senior year that featured a sternly-worded warning about public nudity.

Terri chuckled. "You streaked?"

Blake shrugged. "The whole football team did, except our black running back, Pete. I was the slowest runner, so I got caught. Brought down by mace."

"That stuff really works." Terri's smile put Blake at ease. "Why didn't Pete streak?"

"Aside from being the only black guy on the team, he was afraid of his mama."

George cleared his throat and kept reading. They flipped through the other five pages quickly.

Terri returned to her seat at the table. "For pity's sake, Dad, it's not like he's a felon or secretly married with children. He served a tour in the Marines, earned his Masters from Columbia, and joined the FBI."

"You don't have any problem with his previous lawless behavior?" George asked.

Terri stared down her father. "He was in high school. I've done things, too. Things I wouldn't tell you about."

George blinked. Blake had to hand it to Terri, she knew how to deliver a genuine conversation stopper.

The monster dog plopped his head on the table.

George stood. After taking the long dog leash near the door, he called, "Come on, Tiny. Time for a walk."

Tiny galloped to the back door and sat, knocking over a metal container of umbrellas and walking sticks. The dog lowered his massive head in shame.

"May I go with you, Doctor Pinehurst?" Blake asked.

George nodded. He clipped the leash to Tiny's collar and led the way into the back yard. Lush lawn narrowed into a hard-packed dirt pathway through a copse of Black Walnut trees. Tiny loped along beside George without pulling against the leash or getting tangled in it. They continued downhill in silence between spruce trees and maples until they reached a stunning vista overlooking the Hudson River and the soon-to-be walkway bridge, both framed by high bluffs. Dusk painted oranges and reds across thin clouds. Standing on a bluff, Blake weighed whether or not to seize the moment to discuss Terri.

A rustling in the underbrush attracted Tiny's attention. He sniffed then barked. A squirrel dashed from the tall grass and ran up a spruce, which enticed Tiny to give chase, jerking George off his feet. Airborne, George yelped and crashed.

"Tiny, stop!" Blake ordered. He dove onto the leash to stop Tiny from dragging the old man over grass and rocks.

Tiny inched toward the treed squirrel before he twisted back to face Blake. He sat. George pried the leash off his wrist.

"Stay!" Blake rolled up onto his knees.

Tiny whimpered and laid down.

Groaning, George rolled to his back and grabbed his right ankle. It hung at an odd angle.

"Hold still, sir. I need to find out how bad it is." Blake knee-walked to George's side for a closer look. The foot pointed in the wrong direction. "Oooo. That can't be good."

Between deep breaths, George spoke through clenched teeth. "I suppose this would be an opportune time to apologize."

Blake suppressed a number of comebacks to stay on task. He'd come out here for a reason, and it wasn't to walk the stupid dog or to apply first aid. "I have something more important to discuss."

"I'm a captive audience." George held his hands out.

"Doctor Pinehurst, I'd like to marry your daughter."

George leaned back on his elbows. "Thank the Lord."

"You approve?"

"I was beginning to fear my daughter was gay."

Blake chuffed and stood. "Why?"

"The only time she ever had fun was when she was with her girl pals from school. I can understand being too busy in vet school, but she graduated eight years ago! One by one all her friends got married. Even the meanest, ugliest girl from her high school class is married by now."

"Terri was just more selective." Blake reached down and grabbed George's forearms. "Put your weight on your good leg. Ready?"

George nodded.

Blake hoisted him to a stand, then he bent over and draped George around his neck, with George's right hip and shoulder down, his injured leg hung loose in front. With sure footing and momentum, Blake could carry him uphill as long as the dog stayed out of the way. He couldn't bend down to reach the leash, and he didn't want the dog to run off. His top priority was getting George home safely and quickly. He trusted no one would own a beast that size without training it. Like Terri, he mustered a voice of authority.

"Tiny, heel!"

The giant dog picked up his leash in his mouth and followed Blake. After reaching the crest of the hill, Tiny paused to water a spruce, so Blake stopped to wait for him. George was getting heavy. Halfway to the house, Blake picked up the pace to stay ahead of the dog and the encroaching darkness.

"Do I have your consent to propose to Terri?"

"You do."

Even though they'd be spending the night at the nearest emergency room, Blake considered the evening a huge success. He had won over Terri's father.

"While we're getting to know each other, I'd like to confide something man-to-man."

"Sir?"

"Call me George."

Blake smiled. *Now we're getting somewhere.* He balanced the weight of his future father-in-law on his shoulders in a fireman's carry.

George cleared his throat. "I have to give up flying because of glaucoma. I'll tell Teresa eventually. For now all she needs to know is that I'm putting my plane up for sale."

Huh. Her real name is Teresa? Interesting. "Well, George, you won't need the plane anymore to scare off suitors."

George chuckled and winced. "I'm just the first trial in your quest for the princess. You still have to be approved by the STAR girls. They are closer than sisters."

"Who are they?"

"They've been best friends since first grade. In high school, they became known as the STAR girls because they were competing to be valedictorian and their names formed an acronym. Suki, Teresa, Arlene, and Reva."

"Thanks for the warning."

. 3 .

October 2, 2009

"A Jap, a Jew, A Polack, and an Irishwoman walk into a bar," Suki announced in the entranceway of Pat O'Brien's in the French Quarter of New Orleans.

Men swiveled in their barstools toward Suki. Terri sighed. *Let the bachelorette party begin.*

"Sounds like a joke, doesn't it?" Suki then did her famous hair flip, flinging her straight, waist-length, jet black hair off her shoulder. Taller than most women of Japanese ancestry, she had the look and bearing of a cover model with a porcelain complexion. If they had not been friends since Suki was a chubby first-grader, Terri would have been jealous of her.

The men at the bar gave a collective sigh. One of them tightened his abdomen, barely minimizing his beer gut.

"Why didn't you call Terri a Mick?" Arlene said. She bristled at being called a Pollack and by reflex used to remind people she was half German. She was easily as tall as Suki and outweighed her by twenty pounds of muscle.

Terri nudged Arlene through the entranceway bar toward the large open courtyard. It was a Friday night, and they had to be at the wedding in North Carolina on Sunday night. *Let's not waste time bickering.*

"I didn't use that pejorative for two reasons," Suki said striding toward a table on the far side of the courtyard's central fountain that had flames in the middle and water overflowing a giant bowl. "One, out of respect for the bride-to-be, and two because we're in an *Irish* bar in case you hadn't noticed."

With her back to the fountain, Reva planted herself in one of three metal chairs at the table. Her thick mass of dark curls fell into her face and onto her shoulders. "Quit arguing, you two. This is my first night out in months." She flagged down a waiter.

Terri sat on the second chair. Arlene nudged Suki out of the way to claim the third chair. Just like musical chairs in grade school, Suki was left standing, acting shocked that the world didn't cater to her the way her parents did. Suki plopped her glittery designer clutch bag on the table.

Reva's cell phone trilled from her purse. Her entire countenance sagged. She then pressed the screen of her smartphone. "What is it dear?" She rolled her eyes. "Eight o'clock is his bedtime, because if he stays up late he'll have a meltdown by noon tomorrow. And don't let either one drink anything this late."

Suki dragged a wrought-iron chair across the paver bricks as if to drown out Reva's conversation then she sat across the table from her. "That's why I don't want children. They take over your whole life."

Reva's pre-school age son and daughter were as energetic as they were beautiful. It marveled Terri that Reva could manage them so effortlessly.

The waiter arrived at the table and flipped open his order pad to a fresh page. Pen poised, he stood beside Reva.

"If you want to risk it, go for it, because you'll have to handle it all weekend." Reva put her hand over her phone and addressed the waiter. "I'll take a hurricane in a souvenir glass."

"Same here," Terri said.

"Look, honey, you know I'm out with my closest friends in the world, so no more calls. Remember you are the adult. Take charge. I'll see you Sunday night." With that, Reva tossed her state-of-the-art cell phone into the fountain.

Suki squealed. "Atta girl, Reva."

Unfazed, the waiter spoke to Suki. "And what would you like to drink, ma'am?"

"Don't call me that again. I'll take a hurricane in the souvenir glass, too."

Fidgeting with the plastic-covered drink list, Arlene, the teetotaler of the foursome, asked what was in the drink.

"Rum, fruit juice, and tradition," Suki answered. "It's their signature drink and I'm sure your church-deacon husband would not approve."

Arlene nodded at the waiter. Setting the drink list on the center of the table, she leaned in and said, "Don't anyone post me drinking on social media."

"Now you tell me," Reva said, eyeing her phone at the bottom of the fountain.

Over the first tall, red drink, her friends launched into what Terri thought of as bragging complaints. Suki whined about the cost of the cruises she had taken. She ranked the cruise lines from best to worst based on how they catered to her dietary demands. Arlene and Reva talked about their house payments, and that their husbands snored and didn't help enough with the children. Terri envied them their cruises, homes, husbands, and children. She sipped her drink and let her friends vent.

Terri did not envy her friends for their weddings. She had worn a Bohemian-style bridesmaid dress at Arlene's wedding. To Reva's wedding, she had donned a massive puffy yellow crinoline nightmare. Though yellow made her look jaundiced, she had braved the dress to please her friend.

Suki then tried to convince everyone her boyfriend's controlling parents were the sole reason she was still single.

"Oh, like you're not controlling?" Reva said to Suki.

"I'm driven," Suki said. As a prosecutor, Suki specialized in murder cases. As if her beauty and brains were not intimidating enough to scare off most men, she faced down killers weekly.

"Okay, enough complaining." Terri said setting down her drink. "Let me remind you I am about to get married to the man I love. I want Blake to be like Reva's husband who would walk through fire for her. And I'd be thrilled if Blake could move his business, like Arlene's husband did to be near her family. Suki, it seems like you have life exactly as you want it—on your terms."

Three sets of eyes focused on her.

Terri eyed them back. "So be grateful for your children, your sex lives, your homes, and your wonderful lives. Now celebrate the future with me."

All raised their glasses and drank.

Halfway through her drink, Arlene giggled. It didn't take much alcohol to send her into the land of tipsy. "I remember at my wedding," she broke into laughter, clapped her hands together, then pointed to Reva, "your bridesmaid dress." Nearly choking on the humor of a memory, she could not continue. Arlene's infectious laugh filled the courtyard.

Then Terri remembered Reva's dress and laughed along with Arlene and Suki. As the story went, Reva's daughter, then two, had eaten purple candy and then hugged Reva goodbye before Reva came down from her hotel room to the ballroom. Terri had first noticed the stains on the back of Reva's bridesmaid dress when she followed her down the aisle *after* the ceremony. Two small dark hand prints adorned Reva's dress, one print on each half of her rear end.

Reva shook her head. "What can I tell you? Small children are animals, they mark their territory. Don't they, Arlene?" She stabbed at the cherry in her drink with her straw.

Arlene nodded. "Mine leaves a trail of toys and the smell of diapers everywhere. Do I smell like a daycare center?"

Suki and Reva leaned into Arlene and sniffed. They shook their heads.

Suki shut off her cell phone and tucked it into her glittery evening purse. "I read that fifty percent of the women who earn a medical degree never practice medicine. They get married and *poof*. I suppose the same applies to other professional degrees."

"Oh, please, it's not like she went into veterinary practice to meet men." Arlene stared into her hurricane glass like it was a crystal ball.

Suki grabbed Arlene's forearm in feigned shock. "What? Reaching up cow butts doesn't impress men?"

Having finally speared the cherry in her glass with her straw, Reva bit the cherry and pulled out the stem. Chewing, she said, "That's why she took up flying, right?"

Terri said, "I didn't—"

"FBI agents get paid pretty well. But Terri's not high-maintenance, like me," Suki spoke over Terri then at her. "Be sure to get insurance on him, FBI agents have a—"

"Shut up, Suki!" Reva pointed at her. "You have a greater chance of…making dangerous enemies."

Sobering slightly, Suki tucked her hair behind her ear and muttered, "I'm just looking out for her."

"I don't plan to give up my practice or flying, thank you very much." Terri finished off the last gulps of her hurricane.

Three sets of raised eyebrows challenged her.

"Are you planning to move to the city to take care of police horses and carriage horses in Central Park?" Suki asked while waving a manicured hand in the air. Her black fingernails contrasted beautifully with her pale skin in a stylish, un-Gothic way.

"No."

Arlene jumped in. "Can Blake work from Poughkeepsie?"

"Not really." A nagging foreboding settled on Terri's shoulders. She and Blake would be living a two-hour drive apart as long as she kept her practice and he worked for the FBI in New York City. She hoped that absence really did make the heart grow fonder like the saying said.

Reva slurped the dregs of her drink from a long red straw then used it to poke ice cubes in the bottom of the glass. "She'll figure it out. Let her enjoy this stage of her relationship. Especially the sex. You don't get as much sex after kids. Everyone's too tired. And then there's the *supernatural* lack of privacy. I can't go to the bathroom without someone banging on the door demanding to talk or come in."

While Reva told about her firstborn wandering into the master bedroom at the worst possible moment, Terri thought of Blake and the promise of their future. How long before she complained about him to her friends? Would their marriage fall into a dull routine, allowing small resentments to grind their lives to dust?

Suki bragged of having an ongoing courtship without real commitment, without having to place the needs and wants of another person above her own. She refused to subjugate her personality or her career to suit her boyfriend. Aside from her boyfriend's parents, she spoke well of him. Was the source of her happiness the fact she could walk away at any time from the relationship without financial or emotional fallout? Or was she putting up a tough front?

Arlene, who taught business accounting in college, declined to chair her department when asked because it would have prevented her from spending more time with her child. She always claimed it was her choice and not her husband's to value her child's time over her career advancement. Had she been rationalizing her decision?

Reva had surrendered her journalism position with a Philadelphia television station to move with her husband to Nebraska. Her husband was an upper executive at Warren's Buffett's Berkshire Hathaway, possibly the fifth-largest public company in the world. *But still. Nebraska*? Reva claimed she chose to stop working because her husband made more than enough money for the whole family, but she had been a news junkie since high school. In college, she headed their newspaper and started up a television station. Was Reva a bird in a gilded cage in Nebraska?

Since high school, the STAR girls had spun off into separate orbits, drifting apart. Each year they had less in common, their paths crossing only for weddings, new babies, and family funerals. Terri loved Suki, Arlene, and Reva like sisters. She refused to let time and distance diminish their bond.

A second round of drinks arrived courtesy of a group of men seated in the garden courtyard near an outer brick wall covered in climbing ivy. A representative from the men's table approached the ladies. He was tall with a thick shock of wavy brown hair and incandescent white teeth.

"Ladies, I'm Nathan. My friends and I are Tulane medical students with no time for social lives. Once a month, however, we set aside a night to enjoy the town. There's a new dance club. Would you care to join us?"

Suki, Reva, and Arlene faced Terri and waited for her approval. It felt odd that her closest friends would so quickly abandon their time together. These well-groomed, tailored men had to be in their mid-twenties.

Terri eyed the second hurricane. "We're here for my bachelorette party."

The grinning young man rocked on his heels. A gold and silver Breitling watch gleamed on his wrist. Eyebrows raised, he said, "Sounds like serendipity. No commitment. Our lives are not our own until we finish school. We just want to socialize."

She remembered the loneliness of evenings and weekends spent studying in veterinary school. Her friends seemed to need a night of freedom and celebration.

Terri wasn't drunk yet. Her tell-tale sign was when her face went numb. She took a deep breath. The purpose of a bachelorette party was to celebrate her last few days as a single woman with her friends. In a city famous for *Mardi Gras*, the night beckoned "Celebrate. Dance. Let go." Four med students didn't pose much of a threat. Besides, if things got out of control, she had fresh mace in her purse.

With the weekend left to spend with her friends, Terri decided to put the student's offer to her friends for a vote. "Do we have time for drinking and dancing?"

Suki nodded. She could dance in three-inch heels on a tabletop if the mood suited her. Terri had witnessed it in New York City at Arlene's bachelorette party. Reva smiled.

Arlene sighed. "I hope I can remember how."

The young man signaled his friends who immediately carried their table over and parked it beside the ladies' table without spilling a drink. After quick introductions and shuffling of chairs, the group finished their hurricanes before the long, loud night of dancing with doctors-to-be.

. 4 .

Sunday, October 4, 2009

Newlywed Terri Pinehurst-Clayton eyed the handguns, knife, and taser on the table. *Who brings weapons to a wedding?* Overheating in her full-length lacy gown, Terri watched a groomsman and his new girlfriend kiss as if sharing the last air on the planet. Of the three hundred guests at the outdoor reception on the Clayton Ranch, in Western North Carolina, this kiss upstaged all others. The couple was silhouetted by a sunset of flaming reds and oranges, like the cover of a romance novel. She sighed. Vincent and Nefi had finally settled their misunderstanding without violence.

She felt partly responsible for bringing them together. Her eyes welled. "How romantic."

"Weddings tend to be." Blake tugged a linen monogrammed handkerchief from his tuxedo pocket and handed it to her. His broad shoulders tested the seams of his jacket. Pulling at his collar, he smirked.

"Call me old-fashioned," Terri dabbed her eyes with his handkerchief, "but it would have been more romantic if they hadn't…disarmed first."

Blake raised his eyebrows. "Aw, come on. That's what made it romantic."

So, this is life for an FBI Agent's wife. A spark of jealousy struck her. She understood that Blake admired his friend Vincent since Marine training camp. Blake also admired Vincent's girlfriend, Nefi, who was about to join the FBI. Blake's friends were now her friends, so she would have to adjust to the weirdness of being the unarmed, non-warrior civilian among them.

She was accustomed to being the odd one. Her classmates had been happily starting families while she'd been immersed in veterinary school. Long days of class and longer nights of study left her unfamiliar with fun. She often reminded herself when loneliness struck that it was tougher to get into vet school than medical school. After four years of college, four years of vet school, and eight years of practice—totaling sixteen years of delayed gratification in her personal life in favor of her career— she found love. Now, at thirty-five, she considered herself blessed to finally experience love and marriage.

Blake had been worth the wait, and she still had time for children. If her choices made her an oddball, so be it.

Around the table, more of Blake's law-enforcement friends watched Vincent and Nefi. One couple in their thirties held hands like newlyweds. Married only a year, they still glowed with happiness. Blake's retired FBI boss Quinn Flanagan and his wife Kate shared the like-mindedness of long-term lovers as they stared at the kissing couple with wistful expressions. Terri wanted to share the newlywed glow and the like-mindedness of long-term lovers with Blake. She also wanted the warrior intensity Vincent and Nefi shared in a kiss like heat lightning on a summer's night, silent and brilliant with a hint of danger.

Quinn Flanagan picked up his spoon and lightly clinked it against his champagne flute. Soon others joined in the *plinking*.

"To love!" Flanagan raised his glass.

Blake and Terri kissed.

All raised their glasses and drank. Blake's smoldering lips ignited Terri from the inside out. Afterward, she cooled herself by downing a glass of water. Just a few more hours remained before she could let her fire burn out of control.

Though she wanted to spend time with Blake's friends, she had many guests to greet and thank. Her husband's whole town, it seemed, showed up for the wedding. Her friends and family totaled a third of the crowd.

"I have to say your mother has done a heroic thing in planning this wedding in four months," Terri said.

"Whup," Blake said, glancing behind Terri. "Mama's ears must have been burning."

Maeve Clayton, the family matriarch, marched toward the group at the table. Her dark copper curls did not dare bounce out of place. Her pale green chiffon dress rustled as she approached, the seams snug at the waist. The men stood as Maeve neared. A five-year-old boy appeared from behind Maeve. Terri struggled to come up with the boy's name. He belonged to the oldest of Blake's four brothers.

Maeve said, "Micah, what do you have to say?"

Eclipsed in his grandmother's shadow, Micah sniffled and spoke toward his feet. "I'm sorry Uncle Blake and Aunt Terri." He then peered up at his grandmother Maeve as if awaiting judgment.

Terri quickly slipped her sore feet back into her shoes. *Oh, dear. What did he do?* She took his chubby hands in hers. They were sticky. She flipped his hands palm up and saw traces of white and pink goo. Terri grabbed a cloth napkin from the table and dipped it in a water glass. As she wiped his soft hands, she suppressed a grin. "What happened, Micah?"

His words squeaked out between quivering lips. "I tried the cake."

Blake chuckled.

"Don't you dare encourage him!" Maeve whispered. "The caterer is patching it up now with icing."

Micah trembled.

Terri wrapped her arm around his shoulders. She leaned close to his ear and said, "Why?"

He whispered, "Noah dared me."

Leaning back, she looked into his large eyes. "I see. So Noah didn't dare do it himself?"

As if illuminated with a sudden insight, Micah blinked rapidly and looked up. His mouth fell open into a perfect O. He slowly closed his mouth into a pudgy scowl.

"So, how was it?" Terri asked.

After a few quick blinks, the boy said, "It's as good as Grandma's."

Chuckling broke out behind Terri. The corners of Micah's mouth twitched as if he knew he was out of danger.

Terri made it official. "I forgive you. Just so you know, it's tradition to let the bride and groom try it first, okay?"

Micah nodded, spun around, and buried his face in his grandmother's green skirt. Patting his head, Maeve smiled down at the boy.

Papa Clayton grabbed Maeve's free hand. "My dear, meet Nefi Jenkins, the senator's niece."

"How do you do, Miss Jenkins?" Maeve Clayton said, tugging her hand free. She shook hands with Nefi. To Terri she said, "The cake should be presentable by now."

This was Maeve's way of saying it was time to cut the cake. Maeve had prepared a schedule to keep events flowing smoothly. Terri, trusting the planning ability of a woman who raised five sons, stood.

Micah darted off into the crowd, shouting, "They're gonna cut the cake now!"

Maeve's glance summoned Blake instantly to his feet. She addressed Terri's father with, "If you'd like, I'll bring you back a slice. It'll melt in your mouth."

All eyes turned to Terri's father and his crutches. Finally out of the cast, he was in a walking boot. The crutches were necessary because his vision was deteriorating. He smiled brightly at Maeve and gave her a nod.

Terri's mother, Grace, rose from the table to follow with her new digital camera, a gift from Dad. Bless Mom, she was doing her best to get involved, but big society gatherings intimidated her. Terri strode alongside her mother toward the cake. "Are you having fun?"

"I feel guilty for all the work Mrs. Clayton's done, but she said the first five weddings she helped to plan ran smoothly."

"Five?"

"Four previous sons and her own."

So this makes six. Terri hugged her mother and stepped up to the cake beside Blake.

The cake extended over half of the cloth-covered picnic table and ascended three tiers above the lace tablecloth on a series of plastic Corinthian support columns. So this cake could feed three hundred. *Ha!* The five Clayton brothers could wipe it out in half an hour easy. She couldn't tell where the cake had been violated, but the tiny bride and groom on the top tier had been rotated forty-five degrees according to indentations in the frosting.

The photographer positioned Blake and Terri so they both held the crystal and silver cake cutter over the outside edge of the bottom tier. The photographer's assistant held a filtered floodlight, inside a large white umbrella, high overhead on the other side of the table.

"And chins up, up, up. There," the photographer prompted. Flashes followed.

Temporarily blinded, Terri froze in place. White spots flooded her vision. "If we had eloped," she whispered, "we'd be naked by now."

For that, Blake sighed.

"Go ahead and cut," the photographer said.

"I can't see it," Terri said, blinking.

Blake's warm hand on hers guided the blade neatly

through the cake. White frosting stuck to Blake's knuckle. *Ooops.*

He licked it off his hand, prompting more flashes. The stout female caterer stepped forward. She cut two photo-perfect slices of cake and handed them to Blake and Terri. The caterer scurried out of camera range seconds before more flashes captured the moment. More white spots appeared.

Ernie, editor and reporter for the local newspaper, lurked behind the wedding photographer to capture the event for the society column. Even without a camera hanging from his neck, he stood out in the crowd thanks to his plaid jacket, comb-over hairstyle, and rumpled tie. It was rumored someone from *Southern Living* magazine was also taking photos. Seems Mrs. Clayton knew everyone who was anyone in the southeast.

Two ornate silver forks nestled beside the pieces of cake on real china plates. Terri carved a small chunk of cake and frosting onto her fork and fed it to Blake. Cameras flashed. She opened her mouth to be fed by Blake, when a cell phone sounded off in song.

"Bad boys, bad boys, whatcha gonna do, whatcha gonna do when they come for you?" People stared down the best man, a tall black gentleman better known as Sheriff Pete Ketchum, who grabbed at his pockets until he found the offending device and answered. "Ketchum here." With the phone to his ear, he ducked away from the crowd.

Terri smiled. What an easy campaign to run for sheriff with a name like Ketchum.

Blake steered his fork toward Terri's mouth slowly. His hands hesitated inches from her face. She opened her mouth and closed her eyes, remembering the mantra—*marriage is built on trust.* She didn't enjoy seeing brides and grooms smearing cake on each other's faces and laughing like hyenas. It seemed a hostile way to start a marriage. She trusted Blake's sense of humor did not stoop that low. The fork touched her tongue, so she closed her mouth around the buttery sweet, spongy mass. Micah was right. Camera flashes popped in quick succession.

Blake licked frosting from the corner of his mouth. He glanced down and his pupils widened in response. "Very nice."

"Are you referring to cake or cleavage?" She smirked.

He answered with a low growl.

The catering staff gathered to cut and distribute the cake.

Blake followed Ketchum. So did Terri, too. They broke through the herd to the outside ring of tables where Ketchum held a cell phone over one ear and a hand over the other. He raised his voice as the band launched into a lively dance tune.

"This sounds like a bad joke." Ketchum faced Blake. "Call me back after Ward sees them."

"Whup. Pete's got his game face on," Blake quipped.

Ketchum's caramel-colored skin and brown eyes set him off from the rest of the wedding party. Blake and Ketchum had been friends since kindergarten. Blake gave the impression that Ketchum refused to streak back in high school because of his mother, but Terri sensed he probably refused because of his religious upbringing. His toast to the bride and groom asked for God's blessings on the union.

A plump female server carried a tray of cake servings up to the sheriff. He scooped up a small plate and fork. Pocketing his cell phone, he headed to an unoccupied table and Terri and Blake followed, leaving the din of the celebration to a place where it fell to a dull background roar. The three of them settled into chairs.

Blake unraveled his bow tie and left the ends dangling from his collar. "Somebody called to tell you a bad joke?"

Sheriff Ketchum also freed his neck from his bowtie and collar. He shook his head. "Two drunk fishermen were waving bones around and telling ghost stories, so the bartender called my deputy."

Terri had assumed everyone in town was at the reception. It was comforting to know someone remained on duty. She indulged in another forkful of frosting and cake. It tasted even better than it looked.

Ketchum's pocket blared again. He cut it off with, "Ketchum here." He covered the receiver with his hand and said, "Listen to what I have to put up with." He activated the speaker phone.

"Sir, I found Ward here in the pool room," said the night deputy. "He said the bones are definitely human."

"Oh, man." Ketchum sighed. "Ask him how old they are."

"Old like an adult?" the voice on the phone asked.

"Old like Civil War."

"Who's Ward?" Terri asked in a whisper.

Blake's expression became somber. "Local coroner."

So it was not a joke after all, but a real case. While they waited for the deputy to get more information from the coroner, the local newspaper editor eased up behind the sheriff. Terri cleared her throat to get the sheriff's attention then she nodded at the man in the ugly plaid sports coat.

Sheriff Ketchum twisted around and grimaced. "Hello, Ernie."

As if invited to join them, Ernie stepped closer and plucked a pen and notepad from inside his sports coat. "What's up?"

The deputy's voice blared from the cell phone. "Ward says the femur is from an adult. And he said something else about evidence of a modern medical procedure."

"Carl, tell me you detained the fishermen." Ketchum closed his eyes as if in prayer.

"You bet I did. And they sobered up when they saw Ward. They even volunteered to take me to where they found the bones, five miles south of Suicide Bridge along the east side of Little Jordan river."

Ketchum cringed and switched the speakerphone feature off. He held the device to his ear. "When you get there, tape off the area. I'll call the crime scene techs." He glanced at Ernie, jotting in his notepad. "And don't say anything to reporters. Keep everyone away from the fishermen and the crime scene. I'll meet you at the river." He pocketed his phone and then stuffed a last, large bite of cake in his mouth.

Ernie sprinted down the lawn toward the parked cars.

Terri nudged Blake. "So much for our police escort."

Blake's attention focused on the sheriff as if he hadn't heard her. Color drained from Blake's face.

Ketchum swallowed his cake. He then patted Terri's bare shoulder. "I'll be back. A promise is a promise." He rose and strode down the lawn toward his cruiser.

Terri turned toward Blake, who appeared mesmerized. "Are you okay?" She waved a hand in front of his face to break the spell. For a man who had served in the Marines and worked as an FBI Agent, his reaction to death surprised Terri.

"Maybe I should go help him," Blake mumbled. He stood with his gaze locked on the sheriff's back.

Now? Terri stood. "Only if you want to become a gelding."

That snapped his attention back to her. "What?"

"You heard me." She leaned against him. "I'm proud of your mad crime-fighting skills, but for the next two weeks you are mine, all mine. Besides, that body has nothing to do with you. Mine does." She longed to unwrap him like a present and explore his wonderful body inch by inch, but that would have to wait. She knew how to keep a secret and she had a surprise of her own for him.

Blake hugged her and held her tight for a long time. "'Til death, honey."

That was the part of the vows that stuck with him? Why, oh, why did the specter of the grim reaper have to intrude tonight? And why on earth is my big, strong husband shaking?

Determined to steer Blake back to their happily-ever-aftering, Terri nudged him back uphill like a horse to harness toward the celebration.

Blake trudged up the lawn at Terri's command. He could not explain to Terri his need to go with Ketchum. Fifteen-year-old memories roiled in him.

It was a cool, breezy night in October 1994, back in high school when he was scared spitless.

Back then, his inner circle called him Boomer.

On the high bridge over the River Jordan at night, about a thirty-minute drive west from Asheville, he and his four brothers wrapped a blubbery body in chains. As the youngest, Boomer fought the urge to puke because he did not want Carrie Ann to think he was a sissy. No one was supposed to die, but somehow, some way, the whole plan went sideways. Who screwed up?

It would have been easy to blame the girl, but no one dared. If only they had not stopped to let her pee, maybe things would have gone as planned. There was enough blame to go around if they got caught.

Carrie Ann, who stood barefoot and shaking in the bed of a black Ford F150 pickup, finally stopped crying. Not that he blamed her. He was sniffling to hide his own urge to cry. A cold breeze ruffled Carrie Ann's stringy brown hair and coaxed crisp fallen leaves to skitter across the bridge into the shadows. Thunder roared in the distance, threatening rain.

Using chains was Moose's idea. He said it would prevent floating. Boomer struggled to keep his work gloves from catching in the bloody, slippery chains. Wet chains and blood smelled the same, strong and metallic. Once the chains were secured, the group paused to stare down at their effort. This was not death wearing a suit in a casket. This was messy, horrible, brutal death.

"Like roping a pig," said Gator.

Bubba's voice rumbled, "Shut up."

"You shut up," Butch said in Gator's defense.

"Lift on three," Moose ordered.

The boys crouched and dug their hands under the bulky body.

Boomer's throat tightened in a warning he might vomit. He shook it off.

"One, two, three...e." Moose's last syllable became a long deep groan.

Grunting, they heaved the body onto the bridge railing and rolled it over the edge. It disappeared into the darkness and, after a breath-holding silence, splashed into the river. Rain drops plopped on the pavement. Hoping it would wash the blood off the truck and the bridge, Boomer considered rain a good sign.

Moose climbed into the driver's seat while Carrie Ann plopped down in the truck bed and rested her head against the back window. Claiming claustrophobia, she refused to sit in either of the truck's two rows of seats. The others scrambled into the truck, leaving Boomer, a high school freshman like Carrie Ann, to climb in the back with her. His stomach clenched, forcing acid up. He swallowed. Cold rain fell on his left hand, so he glanced down. *Where's my glove?* He searched the truck bed and peered over the side, but the glove wasn't on the bridge. Nothing was going according to the plan. They couldn't afford to stay on the bridge because someone might spot them, so he decided against asking the others to search for it. Boomer vowed to look for it in daylight.

A crack of lightning split the sky. Rain clapped against the pavement like cautious applause.

Moose started the big, grumbling engine and called out over the noise of it as he drove down the road and off the bridge. "Where are we taking her?"

"I can't go home," Carrie Ann said to no one in particular.

The way she said it struck Boomer as the saddest words he had ever heard. "Why don't you want to go home?"

Her face scrunched up and she twisted away.

Oh, man. "Your parents don't have to know about...anything. Don't think I'm telling mine." He had never been able to lie convincingly, but his brothers swore that girls were naturally better at it.

Boomer hoped Carrie Ann could keep a secret.

After fifteen years of deliberately putting that night out of his mind, Blake tucked his fears back into the forgetting place. He shivered and once again fought back the urge to puke.

Terri led him by the hand toward the reception crowd. This was supposed to be the happiest day of his life. He swallowed bile. He wasn't good at lying, but he kept secrets secret. And he kept his promises.

Terri tugged on Blake's hand, pulling him up the hill. That he would even consider leaving their reception to help the sheriff investigate a call about bones infuriated her. Maybe he missed spending time with his high school pal and wanted to offer his FBI training to help, but this was not the time to impress an old friend.

She took a deep breath. *Perhaps I'm overreacting, too self-focused.* Confused by his reaction to the sheriff's call, she decided Blake might be dehydrated. How much alcohol had he consumed last night at the bachelor's party? Just under his chin he'd missed a spot shaving.

"Are you feeling ill?"

Blake's eyes widened, and he looked away. "A little, yeah."

"Let's get water and more food in you."

"Yes, doctor." He lightly squeezed her hand.

Blake's four brothers approached. *What now?* As the giants drew nearer, she assessed them. The Clayton brothers had their mother's fair skin and sorrel chestnut hair. It reminded her of a lesson she learned in vet school—foals favor the dam. While the combination of mischievous Irish and North Carolina charm made Blake an irresistible Southern gentleman, in his brothers, the combination shouted redneck brawlers. Their sheer size and southern drawls intimidated her in a way she could not quite pin down. And what was it with the macho nicknames—Moose, Bubba, Butch, Gator, and Boomer? Though she knew her husband as Blake, she double-checked at the registrar of deeds office that his real name didn't include Boomer.

When she read through the application for the marriage certificate, she learned a few disturbing facts. In North Carolina, for a mere sixty dollars cash, marriage applicants didn't have to prove mental competence, and they could be first cousins. Nonetheless, being of sound mind and body, she and Elijah Blake Clayton had bought a marriage certificate. Now it was official on paper and in the eyes of the church, family, and friends.

She was still going to call him Blake, not Elijah, and certainly not Boomer. Wasn't Boomer what they called men who worked on bridges? Though they had dated a year, it shocked her how few facts she really knew about him. Had he ever worked on bridges? Long-distance romance had serious disadvantages. There was much she didn't know about him.

Moose, the oldest of the five Clayton brothers, said, "The band is waiting."

"If baby brother doesn't want the first dance, you can choose one of us." Butch opened his arms to Terri. He was the fourth son, barely older than Blake.

Blake stood. "Ignore the teaser stallions." He held out his elbow to Terri.

She stood and slipped her hand into the crook of his arm while trying to shake off the image of herself as a broodmare.

The brothers stepped aside. Butch swatted Blake on the shoulder and said, "Show 'em how it's done, Boomer."

"How *did* you get that nickname?" Terri whispered as they headed toward the dance floor.

Blake sighed. "I was born when Mount Saint Helen's exploded." He was pale.

"Are you feeling dizzy?"

"I'm okay." His quick smile did not convince her.

They strolled to the center of the makeshift dance floor, a cement patio that sprawled from the back of the large farmhouse to the lawn. The band played "Breathe" by Faith Hill. Body heat vaporized Blake's cologne like a cloud of pheromones. She breathed in temptation while people gathered around the dance floor with cameras.

Terri didn't need to fear for her feet while dancing with Blake. He led with confidence, gently guiding his intentions through his warm, strong hands. Her friends told her dancing, if done right, was like making love with your clothes on. In love at last, she believed them. For a big man, Blake had athletic grace, that perfect combination of power and gentleness.

"I love dancing with you." She surrendered to his lead.

"Thank Mama." His giant hand pressed gently on the small of her back, drawing her against his body.

Heat radiated off him, warming her. "I'll add it to the list."

"List?"

"I have a list of things to thank her for."

Blake's green eyes focused on her. One corner of his mouth tugged upward. "Such as?"

"For setting up a wedding on three months' notice, for teaching you grooming, manners, patience, and other civilized behaviors."

He smiled. "She'll appreciate knowing her decades of hard work paid off."

"What did your father teach you?"

At that, Blake cast a glance over Terri into the distance. "Responsibility."

When the band wound up the last stanza of the song, Blake twirled her out and back with a flourish.

The leader of the band stepped up to the microphone and announced, "And now for the father-daughter dance. Considering Doctor Pinehurst's condition, the gentlemen have agreed that Papa Clayton will do the honors."

A waltz started at the same time Blake's father cut in.

"Your father was afraid of falling," said Ian Clayton, known locally as Papa Clayton. His bristle-cut, silver hair set off his steel gray eyes, and a lifetime of managing a horse-breeding ranch showed in his weathered complexion. When his face relaxed, the creases around his eyes transformed to white streaks.

Terri's father, at the edge of the dance floor, nodded. His broken ankle had long since healed, but he used it as an excuse so he didn't have to explain his vision problems. Poor Dad. With his vision failing, he was becoming more accident prone. Terri waved to him and blew him a kiss. He blew back a kiss. Her mother took photos.

"Doc, I'm honored to have you in the family," Papa Clayton said. He held out his arms in a dancing stance.

Glancing at Papa Clayton's calloused hands, Terri noticed clean fingernails. She stepped into position and took his hand. *Was he even wearing cologne?*

Her mother always said to judge a man's character watch how he treats his mother. To judge how a man will age look at his father. Blake was two for two. Papa Clayton led her in a gentle waltz as the music played.

"Would you be as glad to have me in the family if I were a small animal vet?" Terri teased.

After a sigh, he said, "Maeve calls our family a testosterone storm. We tried five times for a girl."

Outnumbered all those years, the dear lady must have felt isolated. "You know it's not up to her."

"We make plans and God laughs."

Of course, as a horse breeder, Papa knew gender was determined by the male. *Let it go.* If Papa Clayton wanted to blame God, that was his business. She decided to steer the conversation toward a positive topic. She spoke from her heart. Being an only child was at times a life burdened by expectations. In the back of her mind, she sensed her parents harbored an unspoken disappointment she wasn't a son. "I've always wanted to be part of a large family."

"So you aren't embarrassed?"

"About what?"

Papa Clayton whispered, "Our family being in the sex trade and all."

Breeder humor.

Terri whispered back, "On the contrary, I have high expectations about tonight."

Papa Clayton's robust belly laugh drew Blake's attention from the edge of the dance floor.

Worried that Papa's telling your secrets, Boomer? Terri grinned at him. Blake shook condensation off a water bottle and took a big gulp.

Papa Clayton's hand squeezed Terri's as he guided her.

Soon the next song started up. The dance floor filled with cowboy-boot clad men in tuxedos and ladies with hairspray-stiffened updos. Jostling and quick apologies became the norm.

"Thank you for the dance," she said. Terri suspected it would get wilder on the dance floor after another round of drinks. She feared for her lace hem.

Papa Clayton took the hint and escorted her to her parent's table. She hugged her father and kissed him on the cheek. After hugging her mother, she took an empty seat at the table. Papa Clayton sat across from her, quietly watching the crowd. There, under the cover of the long linen tablecloth, Terri slipped off her shoes wishing she'd broken them in. *I should have listened to my friends.*

So she'd misjudged her shoes. Fine. It wasn't as if she had experience getting married. Her pals would tease her about the shoes just as they had about marrying a younger man, as if being five years older made her some kind of mother figure. *Ha!*

Biologically speaking, the age difference gave them the same life expectancy. Logic aside, she suspected her friends were flat-out jealous. A group of them wanly waved at her from a table near the dance floor where they nursed hangovers and sore feet from the bachelorette weekend in New Orleans. Except for the power of industrial-strength hairspray, they would have appeared as spent as they felt. Terri, running on adrenaline and a B2 vitamin, waved back.

Her mother's words rang in her head. "You decided to marry him after only a year of dating? It took you longer than that to choose a college." Why weren't they happy about the wedding? Had they heard about Blake's wilder days in high school? Did they think she married him for his looks?

Sure, Blake resembled a Marine recruiting poster, but looks faded. What kept Terri's engines running was the way he embodied the Marine values of honor, courage, and commitment. Of course, the fact Blake was built like a football tackle stirred up happily-ever-after tingling she couldn't ignore.

Vincent, the best man, pulled back a chair at the table beside Papa Clayton. Vincent's tuxedo jacket bulged slightly over his Glock. No doubt his spare pistol was once again strapped to his ankle. "So, the son of a horse breeder marries a veterinarian. Makes perfect sense to me."

Emerging from her reverie, Terri believed Vincent had addressed his statement to her. Nefi eased into the chair beside Papa Clayton, making it clear Vincent was speaking to Nefi. Since Vincent and Nefi's passionate public kiss, they were apparently keeping within reach of each other. So romantic.

"They married for love and you know it." In her designer gown, Nefi appeared glamorously grown up. "Where are you going on your honeymoon?" Nefi leaned toward the table. Golden combs encrusted with stones held her hair away from her face and reminded Terri how young twenty-one was.

"Shhh."

Warm lips landed on Terri's bare shoulder, followed by a hand on her arm. Goosebumps erupted on her shoulders. "I haven't told my brothers anything about the honeymoon," Blake said. "I'm still recovering from the bachelor party."

"Was it fun?" Nefi asked.

Blake grinned. "The parts I remember. But this morning I woke up in my underwear tied to a post in the stables."

Terri's mother gasped. *Poor Mom.* She probably didn't know what to think of this raucous family.

Vincent raised his hands to shoulder level. "Just for the record, I had no part of shaving your legs and chest."

At this news, Terri's mouth fell open. *Shaved?*

She imagined his chest bare and hairless under his tuxedo shirt. She wanted to peel off his shirt to see for herself. Instead, she placed a hand on his lapel. Hairless, he would look even younger. Then visions of him, lightly oiled, posing for a calendar in his bare chest flashed in her mind.

Papa Clayton shook his head. "That wild streak comes from your mama's side."

Vincent, Nefi, and Terri laughed. Papa put his hand over his heart as if feigning a wound.

"Oh, don't be fooled by Mama's charm," Blake said as if taking his father's side.

"That sweet lady?" Terri asked. She would blame such behavior on the Clayton brothers in a New York second. "I think you're both teasing me."

Poor Mom. She smiled at her mother who seemed to be holding her breath.

"Mama wouldn't do anything to you. At least, not this soon." Blake patted Terri's forearm.

Terri's mother spoke, "Joining this family sounds like joining a fraternity."

"Stay away from hazing," Terri's father said. "People get killed doing that nonsense."

Terri sighed. Her parents weren't helping. She had to turn Blake's attention from death to celebrating their marriage.

How soon could they leave for their honeymoon? She checked her watch. They didn't *have to* wait for Sheriff Ketchum to provide a police escort to the airport. Who knew how long it would take him to handle that call about the bones?

. 5 .

Sheriff Ketchum's headlights illuminated a patrol car and a dented 2000 year model Toyota Camry along the roadway, five miles south of the Little Jordan River Bridge, known to locals as Suicide Bridge. He parked his cruiser and grabbed his flashlight. In the light of a full moon, he popped open the trunk, swapped his tuxedo jacket for his sheriff's jacket, and shut the trunk. He had one arm in the sleeve of his jacket when a shotgun blast sounded.

He sprinted toward the sound with his flashlight in one hand and his jacket flapping from his arm. Halfway to the riverbank, he realized he'd left his gun in the trunk. In a pinch, he could wield his metal flashlight like a baton. While he neared the riverbank, he took in the situation.

Carl, his burly, twenty-eight-year-old deputy, held a twenty-gauge shotgun by the wooden forearm. Pauletta Woods, a seventy-year-old, hundred-pound widow, was sprawled on the ground in her fluffy slippers and a long flowered robe.

Carl and Pauletta were yelling at each other.

Ketchum skidded to a stop between them. His arrival shocked them both into silence. He shone his flashlight on them. Neither of them was bleeding, thank the Lord. He faced his deputy, prompting him for an explanation by his tone. "Carl?"

"I told her to quit swinging her gun at me," Carl shouted.

Ketchum spoke in a near whisper. "I can hear you just fine. Who fired the shotgun?"

Carl gazed down to his left, barely shy of Mrs. Woods' slippers.

Ketchum glanced at Mrs. Woods.

"I did it on accident," she said. Pursing her lips, she squinted up at Carl as if daring him to contradict her.

Ketchum set down his flashlight and put on his coat before he gently pulled Mrs. Woods to her feet. Either the recoil of the blast or wrestling with his deputy had knocked her down. Either way, the situation demanded damage control. He didn't dare brush the leaves and dirt off her backside, but he cupped one of her hands in his hands. "I'm so very sorry about this, Mrs. Woods. And I'm so glad your shot missed him."

"This is my property, and I want everybody off it." With her free hand she swatted thin, white bangs off her forehead then she straightened her robe. A baby powder scent rose from her when she moved.

"I understand." A flash of artificial light reminded him that Ernie, the newspaper editor and owner of the Camry, had left the wedding reception ahead of him. He addressed the source of the flash. "Ernie? Did you see what happened?"

Ernie stepped from the shadows of a large oak into the moonlight. "That I did, Sheriff, and I have pictures of the whole assault."

Ketchum cringed. Leave it to a newsman to make news bigger than it should be. He eyed Ernie. "Oh, now I don't believe my deputy is likely to charge Mrs. Woods for assaulting him with a deadly weapon."

Mrs. Woods gasped.

Deputy Carl handed the shotgun to Ketchum.

"The way I see it," Ketchum said, "Mrs. Woods got surprised by the commotion on her property and came out to chase off trespassers."

"That's right!" she said.

The sheriff asked, "Are you wearing your glasses, ma'am?"

"No." She squinted in Ernie's direction. "Who all's here?"

"I'm Sheriff Pete Ketchum—"

"I know who you are. Who's the rest of them?"

"My deputy Carl and Ernie, the editor of *The Herald*."

"Why's everybody sneaking around in the middle of the night?" She peered up at Ketchum.

"I'm sorry to tell you, but the riverbed is a crime scene." He broke open her shotgun at the hinge, pried out the shells, and handed it to her. "Please take a safety class on this firearm."

Mrs. Woods tucked the gun under her arm with the barrel facing down. Concern lined her face. She nodded.

"I'd like your permission for my deputies and crime scene technicians to investigate on your property."

Carl's voice sounded behind Ketchum. "Sheriff, you don't need that old lady's—"

"Carl! Mind your manners."

"You don't need to bow and scrape to her just 'cause you're black," Carl muttered.

Mrs. Woods raised her eyebrows at Carl.

Ketchum took a deep calming breath. Carl's parents had been raging bigots. Carl, God bless him, had come a long way toward shedding their prejudices. Though he meant well, he was completely out of line.

"I'm showing Mrs. Woods respect because she's my elder and because she's a lady." He stared down Carl until the deputy retreated a step. He then addressed Mrs. Woods again. "May we have your permission?"

Mrs. Woods straightened to her full four-foot height. "What if I say no?"

Ketchum sighed dramatically. "Then we'd have to go to the other side of the river and stand in that very cold water." *Or get a warrant.* He really didn't want to generate paperwork.

Carl groaned. Both officers knew who would be standing in the water if it came to that.

One corner of Mrs. Woods' mouth tugged into a half-grin, then relaxed. "What kind of crime was it?"

"Two fishermen found human bones down there."

"Those old coots!" She shook her head. "I told them to quit stealing my fish. Can you arrest them for trespassing?"

"They're in custody," Ketchum said. He let her draw her own conclusion.

"Good. Don't block my driveway." She trudged back up the embankment to her house.

Carl muttered, "You got her vote for the next election."

Ketchum sighed. "Do you have the situation under control?"

"Yes, sir." Carl hitched his thumbs in his gun belt. "Ernie, get yourself back up on the embankment. You're trampling my crime scene."

Ernie grunted and then he headed uphill.

After Ernie was out of earshot, Carl spoke again. "Boss, are you gonna make me apologize to Missus Woods?"

"If somebody treated your mama like that, would you demand an apology?"

Carl's pained expression was answer enough.

Ketchum left Carl in charge. Back at his car, Ketchum flagged down the approaching crime scene van. "I don't want to hear any complaints from Mrs. Woods. She wants her driveway kept clear."

The driver stuck his head out the window. "Nice pants."

Ketchum glanced down and snorted at his mud-splattered tuxedo pants. What a night. *Why do the crazies come out on a full moon?* The thought about crazies reminded him of his promise to escort Blake to the airport.

Terri changed into her getaway outfit—navy blue chinos, deck shoes, a white silk top and blue windbreaker—in the downstairs bathroom of the massive Clayton farmhouse. She was hanging her wedding dress on a hanger hooked on the back of the door when another woman's voice came from the corridor.

"Martina, he kissed me!"

Terri opened the bathroom door in time to witness twenty-one-year-old Nefi Jenkins twirling in her lavender tea-length dress. Holding an iPhone in front of her on speakerphone mode, Nefi smiled at Terri.

"Where?" asked a female voice from the phone.

"In front of everyone." Nefi sighed.

Terri smiled. Young love was beautiful to witness. She considered stepping outside to give Nefi privacy, but apparently Nefi didn't care, so Terri stepped into the den, crossed the room to a leather sofa under a mounted bear's head, and zipped up her suitcase. Years of Nefi's hopes and prayers for Vincent had finally come to fruition. Nefi's best friend, Martina Ramos, was the sister of one of Blake's military friends. According to Blake, Martina and Nefi had been friends since Nefi first came to the States seven years ago to live with her uncle, Senator Jenkins.

"I mean," Martina said, "where on *you*?"

Nefi dismissed the lewd question with a puffing sound. "And he asked me out for a date on Friday."

At this news, Martina squealed. Terri nodded. *About time.*

"It was so romantic. He disarmed first." She sat on a stool at the bar in the den.

"He what?"

"He gave his guns to Blake, so I surrendered my knife and Taser—"

"Oh, you did *not* take weapons to a wedding!" Martina's voice hissed.

"The world is a dangerous place. A girl has to be prepared."

Terri rolled her suitcase behind her and parked it by the door. Nefi acknowledged her with a smile.

"Maybe now Vincent will give you jewelry instead of pink Tasers."

"Do you know how difficult it is to find a pink one?"

Martina groaned. "So is this date going to be a trip to the firing range or a real date like dinner and a movie?"

Nefi had a dreamy expression. "I don't care."

"You wouldn't." Martina sighed. "Aside from the fact that the best man was armed, how was the wedding?"

"It was like a fairy tale." She plucked fancy beaded combs from her hair, freeing her long brown tresses. She set the combs on the bar where light sparkled off them.

Terri was content for the moment to listen to Nefi and Martina while she waited for Blake.

Nefi had a dreamy, far-away expression. "After the kiss, I don't know what else happened."

"Were you drunk? Did he take advantage of you?" Martina's voice seemed to ring with scandalous hope.

"No and no." Nefi rolled her eyes. "I don't know what other people were doing once Vincent and I connected."

"You make it sound like you two are on your own radio frequency."

"It's more than that. He's like me."

"Hold on. You mean psychic?"

At that, Nefi glanced at Terri and blushed as if it were a secret revealed.

Psychic was the shorthand term for Nefi's abilities. Blake had explained to Terri that Nefi wasn't psychic. She had a rare, natural, innate gift for interpreting micro-expressions and body language like a trained MOSSAD interrogator. The effect of having one's true, hidden feelings accurately interpreted from body language and facial expressions was as unnerving as mind-reading. Blake said it was a laughable waste of energy to hide thoughts and feelings from someone like Nefi. He called Nefi a living lie-detector.

"He's not as good at it as I am, but he can sense other people's emotions. And he has an intuition for danger."

"And yet he asked you out."

"Ha. Ha. Ha." Nefi looked down.

Terri noticed Nefi's feet in lovely open-toed heels. The iridescent polish on Nefi's toes cast a pale lavender shine to match her dress. The nail polish gave her size nines a touch of daintiness.

Terri checked the weather for her trip on her own cell phone by typing in the departure and arrival locations.

"When's your first day at work?" Martina asked.

"I start the academy in two weeks."

Oh, dear. Terri felt sorry for them. The distance between Washington, DC, and New York City would separate her from Vincent once again. So many obstacles! But then again, she and Blake would be living in separate cities as well.

"So Vincent has two weeks to date you before you go for—what? Two months of training?"

"Five."

"Hey, what about Christmas?"

Nefi said, "We get the holiday off. What about you?"

"I'll be home for two weeks." Martina sighed. "You better call me after your date."

"Or what?"

"Or I'll call Vincent myself."

"Brat!"

"Freak!"

Nefi disconnected her call then she hugged Terri.

Nefi grew up in the Amazon rainforest. From the little Terri knew about the rainforest, she suspected growing up in such a hazardous environment had shaped Nefi into a survivor. Nefi's innocence about worldly social matters was another issue entirely.

Terri sat at the counter under a mounted bear head and folded her hands. A few moments of peace felt like a luxury. "You look so beautiful."

"Martina taught me how to shave and wear makeup," Nefi said, glancing up at the bear head. "This makeup is vastly different from tribal face paint. Different in purpose too, though I did see a few frightening examples of makeup at the reception."

Terri laughed. "And toxic levels of hairspray."

Nefi placed her hands over Terri's hands. "Thank you for inviting me."

"Consider it payback."

"And I didn't even have to crash the party." Nefi grinned.

Terri's mouth dropped open.

"So what's going on with Blake and his brothers?" Nefi toyed with her hairclips.

"What did they do this time?"

Nefi's perfect eyebrows flinched. She pursed her lips and then said, "Something upset them. Blake drew them away from the guests, and they huddled around him."

"They're probably planning a prank."

"They seemed very…somber." Nefi's concern was touching.

"Oh, then it's probably about the sheriff. Ketchum was called away to investigate bones found by the river."

Nefi pointed west. "The Little Jordan River that runs through the farm?"

"How do you know the name of the river here?"

"I asked. I grew up where rivers are the only roads."

Right. Where her parents died. Terri nodded. Death and thoughts of death kept intruding the wedding reception. It was time to get into a honeymoon state of mind. Terri checked her watch. She would wait another fifteen minutes and no more for the sheriff.

"I heard that people used to bury their dead on their own property." Nefi tucked her cell phone in a small beaded clutch purse.

"Wouldn't that be gruesome to have a long-dead relative show up today?"

Nefi nodded. She stood, purse in hand. "Do you want me to find Blake?"

"Would you, please? I have to make a phone call."

Nefi hugged Terri, then she bolted out the back door.

Terri plucked a paper from the zippered pocket of her suitcase. She unfolded it onto the counter and then pressed a speed-dial number on her cell phone. Enough talk of death. It was time for Blake's surprise.

Squeezing his sweaty palms on the steering wheel, Blake followed the sheriff's cruiser to the regional airport. Pete punched a code on the keypad that opened the airport's front gate. Of course, as sheriff he had middle-of-the-night access to the airport. After the cruiser pulled through the gate to the deserted tarmac, Blake followed. Serving in the Marines had taught him how to stay cool even when others panicked, however, at the moment, while everyone else was cool, calm, and collected, his emotions roared like jet engines. He struggled to maintain a calm demeanor. Even if he could get Ketchum aside to ask about the bones, he doubted he should. One thing at a time. He would call his brothers for news later. He needed to focus, to be in the here and now. Panic wouldn't help.

Be in the moment. Be in the moment.

The lights in the terminal building were off. *Where's our charter plane? And the pilot?* He glanced at Terri in the passenger seat of the truck. "Honey, I thought you arranged a flight."

"Please, pull up beside the sheriff," Terri said.

Blake obliged and rolled down his window. The gate squeaked shut behind them.

SOUTH OF JUSTICE

Ketchum shouted through his passenger side window, "Where to?"

Terri called out, "N-7-6-1 x-ray delta, the blue and white Cessna at the east end of the flight line."

"I see it." Ketchum put on his high-beam headlights and led the way to the plane.

Defying the laws of physics, the blue and white plane at the end of the flight line seemed to get smaller the closer they got to it. Blake parked to the side of the plane to keep the truck's roof clear of the wing. *Oh, no.* A prop plane. A glorified tin can with wings. He suspected his head would probably hit the ceiling in the dang thing. He and Terri climbed out of Papa's truck. Terri, dressed in casual clothes and a windbreaker, marched toward the plane.

Ketchum parked his cruiser at a forty-five-degree angle in front of the plane and redirected the floodlight mounted by his side mirror to illuminate the area. The sheriff's teenage brother hopped out of the cruiser and circled the plane. He was an exact, younger, version of Pete. Though the boy's name was Robert, Blake called him Re-Pete. Robert had come along to drive Papa's truck back to the ranch. Ketchum eased out of his cruiser and stomped mud off his dress shoes.

The plane was a high-wing, single-engine white Cessna with a dark blue belly and bronze stripes that began at the prop and swept up the tail. Twelve-inch white letters and numbers stood out against the deep blue side—N761XD—confirming that this scrawny private plane was their transportation to Atlanta.

"Too bad your pilot's late," Re-Pete said, circling the plane.

Blake stared at Terri for an answer.

She reached into her windbreaker jacket and pulled out a set of keys. A chill chased up Blake's back to his neck. Terri unlocked a small cargo door on the left side of the plane between the door and the tail. After a breath, Blake returned to the truck where he lifted out his-and-her matching wheeled duffle bags.

Ketchum grinned. He seemed to enjoy Blake's discomfort of flying. Back in high school he used to help Blake up off the ground after a tackle and laugh the whole time.

Blake wished he had mentioned his attitude toward flying to Terri during their courtship. He had not told her for two reasons: first, he doubted Terri had any phobias, and second, he didn't imagine his fear of flying would matter so soon. While he carried their bags to the side of the plane, he regretted withholding information from her. He steeled his nerves and hoped his bladder would outlast the flight.

Re-Pete ducked under the wing and announced his teenage-assessment of the plane. "Sweet. Six-seater."

Blake stuffed the duffle bags into the cramped cargo hold and stepped back to get a better look at the plane as if to determine its worthiness visually, the way he judged a horse. No duct tape. No visible rust. Nice paint job. Still, such a small plane. He handed Papa's truck keys to Re-Pete.

Terri unlocked the left door. The pilot's side.

Blake's pulse quickened. "We should probably wait."

Terri and Ketchum exchanged a glance.

"What exactly," Ketchum said, "are you going to wait for?"

"And you're a graduate of the Crimson Tide?" Blake snorted. "I think we should wait for the *pilot*."

At this, Ketchum grunted. He told Terri, "I get that kind of thing all the time."

Terri sighed and smiled back at Ketchum.

Blake had the vague notion he'd been insulted, but he couldn't quite figure out how.

Terri tugged a Velcro strap, freeing a red flag from the underside of the left wing that read "Remove Before Flight." She pushed a small clear cup against the bottom of the wing, filling it partway with fuel. Holding it up to the light, she examined it. A gasoline smell drifted to Blake.

"What are you doing?" Blake asked his bride.

"Pre-flighting the airplane."

Blake was so proud she had taken such initiative. He interpreted her behavior as a sign of two things. One, she had ridden in planes often enough to be familiar with them and, two, she was *extremely* eager to get to Atlanta, the first night's stop on the honeymoon. Would the pilot be upset that Terri did this? He glanced toward the gate in the hope of seeing another car arriving. "Did your father show you how to do that?"

Terri tossed the fuel sample on the tarmac. She kissed Blake on the ear. "My instructor did."

Blake sucked air in small gulps. His mouth dried to dust. A tiny spot in his chest tightened into a knot.

Ketchum struggled for composure and failed, bursting into laughter. Re-Pete hissed through his teeth, making a dismissive sort of sound. Terri scowled. She untied the rope that tethered the left wing to the ground, then untied another rope under the tail, and disappeared in the shadows on the far side of the plane. Blake and Re-Pete exchanged a raised eyebrow glance.

Re-Pete stopped Terri at the front of the plane. "Really? Are you a pilot?"

"Try to contain your disbelief." Terri reached into a panel near the nose of the plane and pulled out a metal dipstick. She examined it, stuck it back, and closed the panel. She retrieved a folding three-step ladder from the cargo hold, carried it to the front edge of the left wing, and unfolded it.

Blake ducked under the wing and held Terri's hips while she climbed the three-step ladder. "Why didn't you tell me earlier?"

"Your brothers," she said, poking a long clear tube into the top of the wing, "said you love surprises."

Payback. "Did you tell them you like surprises?" Blake asked.

"No." She examined the clear tube she lifted out of the wing.

"Who do you think short-sheeted your bed and painted Karo syrup on the toilet seat in the guest bathroom?"

Terri twisted around. "You."

Blake slowly shook his head. "Welcome to the family."

She backed down the step ladder and hugged him. "Oh, come on, who doesn't love to fly?" Her enthusiasm suggested only freaks would not.

Blake grimaced at Ketchum, who grinned back. *What else should I know about my wife?* That whirlwind romance thing suddenly felt like a tornado.

Ketchum elbowed his brother's shoulder, "Let's move these vehicles out of the way." To Terri he said, "If you don't mind, I'd like to watch the takeoff."

Terri smiled at him. "You'll get the best view from the edge of the lot," she said, pointing to the north. She practically skipped to the other wing with the ladder.

Ketchum whispered to Blake, "Don't worry. I'll be a reliable eye witness for the National Transportation Safety Board."

The mention of the agency in charge of investigating crashes amped up Blake's general distress. "Between my friends and my brothers I'm so—"

"Blessed." Ketchum climbed into his cruiser. He remained there, illuminating the plane with his headlights until Terri pulled the chocks out from around the left front wheel of the plane.

After she had loaded the ladder and chocks in the cargo hold, she secured the cargo door with a loud click. Blake resigned himself to go along with his surprise while he tried to ease his cramping stomach. He broke into a sweat over the fear he wouldn't survive to enjoy his honeymoon. Headlines of a small plane crash flashed across his consciousness like an old black-and-white movie.

Re-Pete started the truck's engine.

"So how long have you been flying?" Blake raised his voice to be heard over the truck motor.

"I got my private pilot's license the day after my seventeenth birthday."

Blake suddenly considered himself a slacker. *What did I*

accomplish at seventeen? Oh, yeah, I learned how to back up a horse trailer.

The truck rolled away and parked beside the sheriff's cruiser along the edge of the paved lot. Oh, swell. An audience. He imagined the newspaper story. *The last two people who saw them alive....*

"Then," she added, "I got my driver's license." She climbed into the left seat.

"And you're telling me this now?"

After a shrug Terri said, "A girl has to have a few secrets. Keeps life interesting."

Biding his time, Blake ambled around the back of the plane to the other side door that popped open as he reached it. Terri's confidence had a mild calming effect.

"I'm saving up to buy this plane from my father." Her excitement gave him a chill.

"Did he tell you why he's selling it?" He had to stoop under the wing to stand near the thin metal door on the passenger's side. It didn't seem strong enough to protect him in a crash.

"Glaucoma. His eyesight is failing so he'll lose his medical certificate." She drew a deep breath and her eyes welled.

"Sorry." He felt relieved he didn't need to keep that secret from her any longer. He prayed the man's vision would last to see his first grandchild. Grateful for his own eyesight, he viewed the safe, solid land. The runways were barely illuminated by the full moon. An orange windsock fluttered slightly, tethered to a twenty-foot pole impaled in the dead grass between the runways. He stalled for time to wind up his courage. "So do you have a license to fly at night?"

"I'm night current if that's what you mean. I have an instrument rating, so I don't even have to see the airport until we're two-hundred feet above the ground." Terri fastened her lap belt, and then she stretched back for her shoulder harness. She snapped that into the buckle of the lap belt.

Blake judged the space between the dashboard and the seat to be too small for his legs to fit.

"I'm a careful pilot," Terri said. "I won't do any stunts, just straight-and-level flying—on my honor. Marriage is built on trust. You trust me don't you?"

The mention of stunt flying stirred up fresh panic. He had not even considered the possibility of making a flight even more terrifying on purpose. *Did I marry a dare-devil?* He forced himself to breathe in through his nose and out through his mouth.

He trusted her. But airplanes? Not so much. Ducking, he crawled into the passenger seat and banged his knee on the H-shaped steering wheel. Having controls on his side of the plane was useless to the point of mockery. As if. "I trust you with my life."

He buckled his lap belt and reached way back for the shoulder strap. He grabbed the metal end of it and tugged. It extended a few inches then caught. He eased it back into the spool casing behind the door. Great, just great. *She can navigate an airplane and I can't even manage the stinking seatbelt.* Humiliated, he tried to reel it out and again it caught after a few inches.

Without warning, Terri's chest pressed under his chin. *Oh, hello.* This was the most fun he'd had in a plane, ever. He planted a kiss on her neck. She laughed and grabbed his shoulder belt. She jerked and released the belt a few times before it uncoiled to her arm's length. As she slid off him, his cell phone chimed in his shirt pocket.

Terri secured his shoulder belt to the lap belt. "There."

"Thanks." Disappointed and aroused, he dug out his cell phone and answered it one-handed. "Hello."

"I noticed the plane was rocking," Ketchum said. "Don't make me cite you for making out in a parked vehicle."

"We had a little trouble with the seatbelt."

"Shouldn't that be an issue a mile up? You know when you join the—"

Blake shut off his cell phone and stuffed it in his pocket. He'd never join the mile-high club in this cramped space.

Terri refastened her own seatbelt and shoulder harness, and then she flicked on a small red-filtered flashlight, aiming it at a laminated list of instructions in her lap.

Is she checking the directions on how to fly this thing? Oh, heaven, be with us.

Blake fumbled in the dark to tighten his seat belt. Soon the plane sputtered to life and the panel of instruments lit up. He gave his seat belt strap a serious tug. She handed him a headset, so he put it on, jamming something spongy up his nose. He grabbed the spongy thing and pulled it away from his face. It was attached to the headset. *Oh, the microphone.* They taxied past the sheriff's cruiser and Papa's truck.

No one would have dared deface Papa's truck with lipstick, sassy sayings in wax or streamers just because it served as a newlywed's getaway vehicle. Leave it to his brothers to find something worse to mark the occasion. Illuminated by the plane's taxi light, elephant-size rubber testicles swung ever so gently under the trailer hitch. Blake's face burned. Terri must have thought she married into hicks from the sticks. He glanced at her while she stared forward. Maybe she didn't see that.

A low-grade anxiety chewed him from the inside while the plane taxied in the dark. His thoughts drifted to his brothers and a night fifteen years ago. He had not thought about that night for so many years. He dreaded remembering.

Terri revved the engine, apparently testing it before moving onto the runway. The deep vibrations thrummed in his bones. His heart rate quickened at the fear of a long-buried secret. He vowed to find an attorney right after the honeymoon.

The plane rolled to the end of the runway. Blake's breathing came in gulps as he prayed on the way down the runway, rolling faster and faster, finally lifting off into the vast darkness. *Oh, Lord, do you forgive me?*

. 6 .

After they finally arrived at the Atlanta Marriott Marquis, Blake stuffed a generous tip in the bellman's hand and locked the door behind him. The flight had been, to his relief, an uneventful ride. He had not puked.

He checked his watch. Nearly midnight. Nearly Sunday. They would stay overnight before flying to Paris in the afternoon. Though exhausted, Blake longed to enjoy his honeymoon.

As his father often said, it wasn't how you felt that mattered; it was what you did. By the time he dimmed the lights in the honeymoon suite to set the mood, he was alert and eager to thrill Terri.

Terri rushed right by the bouquet of roses and the chilled bottle of champagne he had ordered when he had reserved the room. She simply peeled off her shoes and windbreaker on her way to the king-size bed. Following her lead, Blake pried off his shoes, shed his jacket and sweat-stained shirt, and dropped them on his way. He tugged off the puffy white bedspread and flung it, so it billowed to the floor at the foot of the bed. Terri pulled back the pale taupe top sheet. Blake peeled off his socks while Terri, wearing chinos, a sheer skin tone lace bra, and an expression of eagerness, crawled on her hands and knees over the bed toward him. Somehow he'd missed seeing her remove her top and regretted it.

"What are you thinking about now?" she asked.

"Field-stripping my rifle."

"Are you kidding me?"

"I am practicing delayed gratification by distraction."

She laughed. "Okay. Then walk me through the process."

"Really?"

"Sure. Talk me through field-stripping your rifle."

The way she said it sounded so suggestive he shook it off as his state of mind. He marveled at the strength of the sheer fabric of her bra. Like her, it was beautiful by design.

Terri rose to her knees and placed her hands on his chest. "Why did your brothers shave your chest?" Terri asked while her hands caressed his bare skin.

Like the faint smell of smoke, her grey-blue eyes keened his attention on a subconscious, primal level. Her touch ignited a fire in him that shot sparks throughout his nervous system.

He said, "Probably to remind me I'm the baby of the family."

"Oh, baby."

He burned from the inside out while his pulse quickened. An intoxicating spicy perfume rose off her skin. Cupping her head in his hands, he kissed her soft, warm mouth. Her hands slid down his ribs and stomach to his waist. His skin erupted in gooseflesh.

Remembering advice from long ago—ladies first—Blake mentally recited the steps in field stripping his M-16 rifle. He had to distract himself to contain his reaction to Terri's warm hands, alluring appearance, soft skin, and wafting perfume. This was the time to man up, to demonstrate the ultimate self-control. This time sex was for keeps, approved by family, friends, and God. Shameless, joyful, no holds barred, seal-the-promise sex.

Terri unbuckled his belt.

"Eject the magazine."

She smirked.

Blake stepped out of his pants and reached around Terri's back for the fasteners of her bra, but the back of the bra was smooth. Terri kissed his mouth again. She tasted like candy. He eased out of the kiss to peek down Terri's cleavage to discover the bra connected in the front. *Whup there it is.* He deftly tucked two fingers under the bra at the front and center, freeing her breasts. He dragged his fingers up between her breasts to the shoulder straps and slid the straps off her smooth, toned shoulders. He kissed her collarbone from the nape of her neck to her shoulder then up to just under her ear. She rolled her head back and sighed.

"Pull the charging handle back. Push the bottom portion of the bolt catch. Oh, man. Push the rear disassembly pin above the pistol grip."

He unzipped and tugged off her pants to reveal a tiny black lacy thong.

"Yeah. I mean, pull apart the upper and lower receivers and remove the upper and lower hand grips by pulling down on the—"

Terri tugged down on his boxers. Her grin challenged him to remember the next step as the room grew as hot as a grill in summer.

"O-boy—O-ring in the front of the magazine." He focused on Terri's eyes. As happy blankness cleared from his mind, the next step emerged from deep memory. "Pull the hand grips from the barrel."

Blake leaned over her and kissed her on the mouth, then down her neck and shoulder to her ribs. She was warm all over, soft here, firm there, and her skin felt soft as silk. He helped her out of panties that reminded him of a strand of ribbon from a present. And what a gift she was. He tossed the scrap of fabric over his shoulder and climbed into bed beside her.

"You look your best wearing only a ring and a smile."

Terri drew in a deep breath that caused her chest to rise. "Thanks for both."

Blake concentrated as well as he could on the next step in field stripping his rifle, but he felt so alive his whole body hummed. "Next, I'm supposed to do something with the bolt carrier group and the charging handle."

Terri laughed.

She was toying with him, so he dedicated himself to consummating his vows so thoroughly she would forget all other men. His body ached, but he needed for Terri to peak first. Using his lips and hands, he explored his bride, listening for moans and sighs and sudden intakes of breath to guide him. He had field stripped his rifle hundreds of times, even in the dark, step by step, by feel. He struggled to visualize his rifle while Terri's body filled his view. One day, he would be as familiar with her body as he was with his weapon. When he recognized his turn had finally arrived, he abandoned thoughts of his rifle.

Later that Sunday morning outside the Mecklenburg County Medical Examiner's lab in Charlotte, Sheriff Ketchum snapped paper booties over his dress shoes. He administered a precautionary drop of oil of Wintergreen to his paper mask. The last time he visited the lab was for the autopsy of a floater. The combination of chemicals and decomposition in the room created an unforgettable stench of decomposing flesh. This time, he wanted to be prepared in case Ward had more than bones in the lab.

He arrived with low expectations because there was so little evidence to work with. He pitied the coroner for having no teeth to compare to dental records and no tissue to get fingerprints or even skin tone. *Ah, well. They can't all be easy cases.* Leaning close to the intercom, he pressed the call button.

The small speaker hummed as Ward spoke. "This is the great and mighty Oz. Who dares approach?"

Ketchum pressed the intercom speaker button. "I guess that makes me the Sheriff of Munchkin Land."

"Enter."

The security latch on the double doors buzzed, and Ketchum pushed through. The open, brightly-lit room was tiled from floor to ceiling and had six square stainless steel doors lined across one wall. In the center of the room stood two metal examination troughs on either side of a floor drain. The room's design suggested it could be cleaned with a pressure washer, sending yuck down the central floor drain. The unmistakable smell of formaldehyde struck Ketchum despite the oil the Wintergreen.

Ward smiled from his spot on the far side of the first trough. His salt and pepper hair was neatly parted on the side and trimmed above his ears. Fit, lively, and hearty in his early forties, he contrasted with his surroundings. Wearing a white Tyvek jumpsuit, rubber boots, and elbow-length rubber gloves, he angled a plate-size magnifier so that it quadrupled the image of his mouth.

"Sheriff Ketchum," Ward said. "Thanks for calling ahead."

"Thanks for seeing me." Ketchum stepped around a draped form laid out in a deep stainless steel trough. By the shape and positions of the lumps under the drape, it was a large person.

"Two bones is not much to work with," the giant mouth said, flashing straight white teeth. He was seated on a stool behind a steel counter.

Ketchum stepped up to the counter and recognized a femur and a fibula. "I have a team of divers and dredgers coming tomorrow to find more."

"More would help." Ward raised the magnifier out of his way. The metal support arm of the magnifier creaked. "However, we have enough to identify the victim."

Ketchum raised his eyebrows. He peered at the bones again. "I think the chemicals you breathe all day have pickled your brain."

With a gloved hand, Ward picked up the femur and aimed the end of it toward Ketchum. "See this metal attached to the bone?"

He nodded.

Waving his free hand over the metal implant, Ward said, "From this, the great and mighty Oz knows that this adult victim had surgery to repair an intertrochanteric fracture of the hip. On closer inspection," he said, as he pulled the magnifier over the metal, "one can read a serial number of the implant."

The numbers were legible. Ketchum raised his head away from the magnifier. Hundreds, maybe thousands of people had hip surgery. "Can you match that with the manufacturer?"

"It's made by Synthes. The serial number is unique for each implant." Ward smiled as if waiting for applause.

Made by Synthes. That narrowed the list a bit to hundreds or thousands. "Do you mean like a model number?"

Ward slowly shook his head. "The serial number is unique for *every single* piece they make. It's more like a vehicle identification number. The manufacturer can tell us which hospital or surgery center bought it. The surgery records will identify the patient by name."

Ketchum inhaled. "You *are* the great and mighty Oz."

Ward bowed his head. "Still can't give you the cause of death, but I'm working on determining the approximate date."

Backing from the counter, Ketchum said, "I get it. You need more to work with. Can you give me a rough estimate of when death occurred in weeks, months, or years?"

"Over ten years."

"Thanks," Ketchum said. Outside the door, he dropped the paper booties and mask in the trash can and left the lab for his mother's house. Sunday after church meant a late lunch of real home cooking, followed by shooting baskets with his little brother. Once Ward identified the body, Ketchum could search for next of kin. Surely, someone had been looking for this person who had a hip surgery. On Monday, he would check records of missing persons. Maybe the poor soul had Alzheimer's and wandered into the river.

He considered himself blessed to have family who loved him and would miss him. This case might be solved easier than expected once Ward traced back the serial number. He hoped the dive team would find the rest of the bones so the departed would get a decent burial and the family could find closure.

. 7 .

On Monday afternoon, October 6, 2009, Sheriff Ketchum stopped across from a convoy of trucks and boats on trailers parked near the entrance to the Clayton Ranch. Young men had gathered around the hood of the first truck with their backs to the fancy gate where they argued and pointed to places on a county map. Ketchum climbed out of his patrol car and crossed the road toward the huddled men. They were right on time.

Behind the huddled men, Papa Clayton rode a stallion under the iron archway at the entrance. When Ketchum approached the men, he heard them bickering about the exact location of the Little Jordan River.

So far, none of them had noticed the man on horseback behind them.

Ketchum put on his hat. "Gentlemen."

"Sheriff," said one of the men. "We're looking for access to the river."

Papa Clayton chuckled.

The men gaped up at him.

"Fishing is terrible on the Little Jordan this time of year," Papa said.

The oldest stranger, who appeared to be in his early thirties, folded the map in half then stepped alongside the stallion. White lettering on his blue windbreaker read Harnett County

Underwater Search & Recovery Dive Team. "Good afternoon, sir. Did you hear about the bones found in the river?"

"Sure did." Papa Clayton's horse, Thunderfoot Junior, lowered his mouth to the dead grass, tugging the reins through Papa's hands. Papa gathered the reins and gently tugged the horse's head back up until the horse shook it in mild protest. "Heard it was south of here on Mrs. Woods' property."

"Yes, sir," the stranger said. He unfolded the map. "Sheriff Ketchum called us. We're looking for access upstream to search for the rest of the remains. Could you direct us to this bridge?" He pointed to a spot on the map.

Papa Clayton nodded at Ketchum, who nodded back.

The stallion lowered his great head toward the stranger as if to check the map. He pawed a front hoof on the dry ground, pulverizing leaves and twigs. The others backed away, but the man with the map held his ground and pointed again to the bridge on the map.

Papa indicated a place circled in red on the map. The label read Little Jordan Bridge. "The ground is too steep to put a boat in there."

"The nearest decent boat launch with public access is ten miles away in an old fish camp," Ketchum said. "It's closed this time of year and probably has the gate locked with chains."

"How far up river do you need to go?" Papa Clayton asked.

"As close as we can get to that bridge."

Ketchum counted five vehicles, three boats. The team was larger than he'd expected. "Gentlemen, allow me to introduce Mr. Ian Clayton. He owns this ranch."

"How do you do, sir." The leader handed business cards to Papa Clayton and Ketchum. Ketchum gave the leader one of his sheriff's cards.

"Is this your whole team?" Papa asked.

"Besides us, we have a search dog in the last truck."

A large dog face appeared behind the windshield of the last

truck. Since it wasn't caged, Ketchum figured the dog would be safe around horses. He watched Papa's expressions.

"Gentlemen," Papa said, "Welcome to Clayton Ranch. Follow me."

The men and Ketchum scrambled into their vehicles. Papa led the convoy over twelve acres to a large open area of gently sloping land along the river. It put them halfway between the bridge and Mrs. Woods' place. There, Papa dismounted, took off his brown cowboy hat and work gloves, and shook hands with the team. They introduced themselves and looked him in the eye like gentlemen. So young and fit and full of energy, they reminded Ketchum of years gone by.

Papa granted them permission to camp if they needed to, and he marked their map with a blue circle to show their location and another smaller circle to mark where the bones had been found.

"This is perfect!" the leader, Neal, said. "We appreciate your help, sir."

Papa pointed to the stables in the distance. "There's a shower and a bathroom at the front of that red building. You're welcome to use it. All I ask is that you don't smoke around the barn or the hay bales."

They thanked him, hauled out their gear and freed a chocolate Labrador that bounded to the nearest tree.

Papa led his horse twenty feet away from the search team, and Ketchum followed, keeping Papa between him and the horse.

"Thank you for giving them access, sir," Ketchum said. "They have a lot of riverbed to search, so they could be here a while."

Papa shook hands with Ketchum. "No problem. I figure the kinds of folks who scour an icy, muddy river on behalf of a dead stranger have to be good people."

"Yes, sir." Ketchum returned to his car. There wasn't much he could do to help the search team or the coroner, so he decided to turn his attention to other cases until new information or evidence showed up. Law enforcement investigations often came down to hurry up and wait that he'd resigned himself to it.

Papa climbed back in the saddle and rode back to the barn. It chilled him to imagine getting in the water in October, and he wondered how the bones ended up there. Who was that poor dead person?

His cell phone rang, so he fished it out of his shirt pocket. His sister's face filled the little screen. "Hey, Dottie." He wanted to tell her she missed the wedding of the year, but he suspected she hadn't come because it wasn't worth putting up with the relatives who snubbed her. Like the rest of the family, he didn't understand her choice to stay single, but he loved his big sister unconditionally.

"Sorry, I couldn't go to the wedding. I hope Boomer wasn't too disappointed."

"I suppose he'll get over it. Did you hear his wife Terri's a large animal vet?" He wished Dottie had stayed in school. She would have been a great veterinarian.

"Good for her!" She sighed. "Will you tell them to come visit me?"

"Of course, I will." He patted Thunderfoot Junior's soft brown neck.

"I saw something on the Internet today I wanted to ask you about."

"I don't know much about the Internet." His sons obsessed over their computers, always sending messages to their friends when they could just as well call them on the phone and have a real conversation. The way he saw it, his boys lived one electrical failure away from complete isolation. It was getting worse with each generation. A couple of the grandkids would spend their days hunched over little electronic gizmos if he didn't pry the wretched devices out of their hands. If his sons weren't already married, he would have been worried about their social lives.

"I read a story about bones showing up in the Little Jordan."

Papa told her what little he knew about the bones and about the search team he let on the property. Still holding the cell phone, he swung his right leg over the back of the saddle and slid off his horse. He headed into the barn. Like a giant dog, the stallion heeled, stopping by the stall when Papa did. Impatient, the horse nuzzled him, so Papa scratched behind Junior's ear.

"Do they know who it was?" she asked. Dottie always loved a good mystery.

"I heard all they found were two bones. I suppose they could do that carbon dating stuff to see how old they are." The word 'dating' triggered an idea. Papa couldn't resist teasing his sister. "Come to think of it, whatever happened to that boy who took you to prom?"

Her laughter had begun like a snorting sound, later breaking into her familiar unrestrained hilarity that alternated between a high shriek and a howl. When she caught her breath, she said, "All I killed was his ego."

"And since then," Papa said, "I filed my matchmaking efforts for you under lost causes." He slid the reins over the horse's head and let them fall at his feet. He missed her. "You know I miss you."

"Will I get the boys next summer?" Dottie asked every year for the grandsons to spend time at her farm, and so far every year their mothers told her the boys were too young. The oldest was seven; the youngest, three.

"Come for Christmas. Let them get to know you better." It was understood his reference to 'them' meant the boys' mothers. Good church-going women, Papa's daughters-in-law had more fear than knowledge about Dottie. She wasn't militant about being single. She just took her work so seriously she didn't take vacations."

"I might."

"Come at Christmas."

Dottie sighed. "I'll think about it. Love you."

"Love you, too." He hung up and his thoughts returned to the bones in the river.

. 8 .

On Monday, October 13th, partway through their honeymoon, Terri awakened to insistent knocking. Their otherwise quiet, 700-square-foot suite at the Shangri-La Hotel Paris had a seventh-floor view of the Eiffel Tower. The room was larger than her apartment in vet school. She reached across the king-size bed for Blake, but his half of the bed contained only cool, ruffled bedding. The room felt luxurious for two; massive for one.

"Blake?"

Untangling her feet from the sheets, she flung her legs over the edge of the bed.

"Blake?" She called louder this time in case he was in the sitting room of the suite. The open bathroom door revealed it unoccupied. Where was he? Her watch reported ten a.m., a scandalous time of day to be in bed. She reasoned that she wasn't getting out of bed in the late morning, but six hours ahead of her business partners—in New York.

A polite rapping sounded on the door. "Room service!"

"Just a minute!" She picked up her robe from the floor and covered herself, tying the sash tight. Blake's cell phone was missing from the nightstand on the far side of the bed. She reached the door of the suite and hesitated. How far would Blake's brothers travel to pull a prank? Would Blake test her sense of humor? *Hmmm.*

"Could you slide the receipt under the door so I know you are who you say you are?" Of course, this made her sound paranoid, but experience gave her reason to be cautious.

A paper slipped under the door. The form listed the selections she and Blake had ordered. She opened the door and stepped aside. A gray-haired waiter rolled the cart into the room wafting aromas of bacon and coffee in its wake. The waiter set the small table by the window with two place settings, followed by two covered plates, followed by a basket of wheat toast. He then set out a carafe of coffee and lastly a two-tiered server filled with various small condiments, tiny jars of honey and jellies, and genuine butter.

Terri signed the receipt and added a fifty-Euro tip before she handed it back to the waiter. "*Merci, monsieur.*"

He glanced at the receipt and nodded. A faint smile broke through his bored-efficient manner. "*Je vous en prie, Madame.*" On his way out, his head ever so slightly angled toward Terri's red silk nightgown draped on the lamp.

After the waiter had left, Terri plucked the gown from the lamp and stuffed it in the pocket of the thick terrycloth hotel robe. She located her cell phone on the dresser and thumbed out a text message to Blake—*breakfast here, u r not*—ending the message with a frowning face icon. A picture message chimed on Terri's cell phone. Blake's smiling face.

On her way to the bathroom, her reflection froze her in her tracks. Her hair stood out like furry road kill. She gasped and immediately discovered her breath would knock a fly out of the air. She dashed to the bathroom in hopes of restoring herself to sexy bride status before Blake returned. She would find out what was on his mind and why he was so moody, but she had to find a way to help him talk about his feelings. How does a woman do this without harping or prying? Could she charm him into talking? It was worth a try.

At ten on a Monday morning in Paris, Blake had the indoor pool area to himself. After texting a photo to Terri, he returned to his call. "Terri just woke up. No, I'm by the pool, but I need to get back upstairs. So what did the divers find?"

"All I have is rumors, and rumors say they found more bones and chains," Samuel "Moose" Clayton, the oldest brother, said.

Dread constricted Blake's chest. If he were home, he could talk with Ketchum. His brothers knew Pete, but not well enough to get information from him without being obvious.

"Come back, will ya?" Moose pleaded.

"I can't cut a week off my honeymoon." Blake knew Terri would neuter him if he even suggested it. He couldn't make up a reason important enough to justify leaving Paris early, and he certainly couldn't tell her the truth. His brothers had to handle things for another week.

"So you're coming back home in a week?"

"I'll be back in New York City in a week. I have a job."

Moose groaned. "We are so screwed."

"Did you get a lawyer yet?"

"I have an appointment later this week." Moose's weary tone carried across the ocean.

Blake rubbed his face with his free hand. Besides Ketchum, they had one more local contact with information on the case. "You're still friends with the coroner Ward, right?"

"Yeah, but it's tough when you have kids and your friends don't."

"Take him deer hunting," Blake said. His voice echoed off the tiled walls.

"I think the season just started in Franklin County."

"Crossbow or gun?" With a crossbow in his hands, Moose was a greater danger to himself than to deer. He broke his thumb once trying to load a crossbow. The other brothers referred to the incident as premature ejection.

"Gun."

"Good." Blake strolled along the pool toward the door to the hallway.

Three small boys rocketed through the door and ran screeching toward the water. Blake stood still as they raced by him. Their high voices echoed in the tiled room.

"Guess Terri's glad to see you."

Blake snorted.

An older man entered the pool area. He carried thick, rolled towels to a lounge chair. He barked something in French to the boys that slowed them down. He threw up his hands and said to Blake, "*Garcons.*"

Boys will be boys. Blake nodded and smiled at the gentleman who appeared old enough to be their grandfather. Once outside the pool area, he said, "I have to go. Happy hunting, Moose." Blake tucked his phone into his pants pocket. He had an elevator ride to shake off dreadful images of skeletal hands dragging him to the bottom of the river.

By the time he reached the honeymoon suite, he decided to prepare for the worst. He needed a lawyer.

9.

It was October 22, 2009, Blake's first day back at work from his two-week honeymoon. Not bad to start the work week on a Thursday. At precisely eight a.m. the elevator doors opened. Whistling and suit-clad Blake strolled to his work station. His cramped cubicle, beside Vincent's, was the farthest one from any window in the Jacob Javits Building, the FBI's New York City field office. It was a reminder of his lowly status as the newest agent on the floor.

"So that's what happily married looks like," Vincent said.

When he sat at his desk he stopped whistling. "What no flowers? I thought you'd miss me."

Heads popped up from cubicles. "He-e-e's ba-a-ck," someone said.

Blake sat in his desk chair, opened a drawer, and chuckled. He lifted a handful of brightly colored condoms over his head. "Thank you for the balloons, whoever you are." He peeled open a packet and pressed a red condom to his lips.

He had it partly inflated when Vincent signaled him with a fake cough. Blake spun his chair around toward Chief Watson, who was standing in the corridor. Blake released the red condom, and as he stood to attention, it sputtered and circled until it landed on Watson's shoe.

Poker-faced, Watson said, "Welcome back, Clayton."

"Thank you, sir." Torn between the need to ignore the condom and the urge to pluck it off his boss's polished shoe, Blake held his ground.

Chief Watson turned his back on Blake to hand a paper to Vincent. "I don't see any conflict."

Blushing as only a redhead can, Blake swept condom packets off his desktop into a drawer.

"Thank you, sir," Vincent said, taking the paper.

The paper, Blake spied, was a form that acknowledged a personal relationship between employees, in this case, a relationship between Vincent and Nefi Jenkins, an FBI candidate in training at Quantico. Vincent nodded at the paper as he read it. After her training, Nefi was expected to work in the Washington Bureau's behavioral sciences unit. As a field agent, Vincent would not be expected to have any overlap of company responsibilities, financial or otherwise, with her. With Nefi in Washington D.C. and Vincent in New York City, they would probably spend a lot of time on the road.

Like Terri and I will.

Vincent slid the form into his desk drawer.

Chief Watson, with the deflated red condom on his shoe, said to Blake, "Special Agent Albritton asked for you by name to work on a case. You and Gunnerson, follow me. Bring your gear."

Blake gladly abandoned the paperwork piled on his desk. Eager for a field assignment, he shouldered his duffel bag and followed Chief Watson toward his office. Vincent closed his laptop, jammed it into his duffle bag, and Blake took up the rear of the line.

In the corridor, Chief Watson started their briefing. "Albritton is waiting in my office. Give her your complete cooperation."

Blake and Vincent kept pace behind their boss. Blake prayed the condom would fall off before they reached Watson's office.

"The Bureau has been asked to lead the investigation as an objective outside authority," Watson said. He glanced over his shoulder.

Calling in the FBI typically meant nobody wanted the case because of jurisdictional conflicts among local law enforcement authorities or politics.

They entered Chief Watson's office, where a stocky fiftyish woman stood in a no-nonsense slate gray pants suit, a white button-down Oxford shirt, gold stud earrings and shoes a nun might wear. He estimated her height at five-feet-five tops, but her confident demeanor filled the room.

"Special Agent Albritton," Chief Watson said, "meet Agents Blake Clayton and Vincent Gunnerson."

Vincent shifted his duffle bag to his back before shaking her hand.

Blake's curiosity compelled him to glance down. The condom defiantly remained on the Chief's shoe like a prank gone bad. He then stepped toward Albritton and discovered she had a firm handshake.

She squinted at Blake. "How long has it been since you worked with horses?"

"A month, just before my wedding."

Albritton pinned him down with her stare. "What would cause a horse to attack someone?"

"I'd have to know more about the circumstances moments before the attack," Blake said.

At this, Albritton blinked. "Inside a stall."

"Was the horse a thoroughbred? Was it well taken care of? Was it in pain?"

Albritton nodded at Chief Watson. "Good questions." Her gaze fell on Watson's shoe. She blinked.

Chief Watson peered down. He then raised his shoe, peeled the rubber blob from his shoe, and dropped it into his wastebasket. "Be safe out there, too."

Too mortified to laugh, Blake felt his face radiating heat. *And we're off to a fine start.*

"Gunnerson, Clayton, follow me." Albritton led the way to the elevators. "We're going to Wallkill Correctional Facility to investigate a non-inmate death. The body was found in the stall of a racehorse."

Numerous questions flooded Blake's head. What was a racehorse doing at a prison? Where was Wallkill?

They exited the front of the FBI building. Albritton strode to a black Suburban parked at the curb and took the driver's seat. Vincent climbed into the front passenger seat leaving the back seat for Blake.

On the hour and forty-minute drive to Wallkill, New York, Albritton briefed them.

"The victim has been tentatively identified as head of the Thoroughbred Retirement Foundation. They rescue retired racehorses," Albritton said. "The Foundation delivered two horses to the prison yesterday as part of their public-relations campaign."

"Did the guards miss their headcount?" Vincent asked.

"It's a prison without walls." Albritton handed a thin folder to him. "Here's the background on it."

"Ma'am," Blake's voice from the back seat said, "Why did you ask for me?"

"When my daughter turned thirteen, my husband and I bought her a Missouri Fox trotter from Clayton Ranch. I need someone on this case who knows horses. Everyone wants the horse to take the blame. I haven't had a suspect like this before."

What a small world. "Do you want me to investigate the horse?" Blake asked.

"The crime scene technicians are scared to process the horse. When we get there, help them."

"Yes, ma'am."

During the last half of the ride, Blake took his turn reading the file on Wallkill Prison. A series of deadly prison riots in the 1930s forced states to reevaluate the whole system of incarceration. Wallkill, one of the first prisons in the United States designed to rehabilitate inmates through education, offered training in twenty-four trades so the men would not return to crime as a source of income. Prison officials brought in horses in 1984. The first horse was aptly named Promised Road. An all-male facility, it had extremely few escape attempts over seven decades of operation. When they arrived at Wallkill, Blake understood why.

The entrance road to Wallkill ended near a cluster of Gothic-style, gray stone buildings nestled in 950-acres of rolling hills. Nothing about the place had the look of a prison. Wallkill Prison resembled an English resort village. Two chapels graced the grounds. Cows grazed in open fields near the buildings. The Shawangunk Mountain range filled the western horizon. Trees, in their autumn nakedness, lined the fields. He assumed the grounds greened up as lush as any resort in the summer.

A dozen men in dusty clothes huddled around the breezeway of the stables. Four sheriff's cruisers, an ambulance, a coroner's van, and an evidence van parked haphazardly inside the line of yellow crime scene tape. A cluster of deputies lingered inside the taped perimeter.

Before he climbed out of the Suburban, Blake strung his FBI identification badge chain over his head. This was his first field investigation thanks to his expertise with horses. *Wish Papa could see me now.* Blake, Vincent, and Albritton strode toward the stables.

Vincent elbowed Blake. "This is a prison?"

Blake said, "Appearances can be deceiving." This was the prison he wanted to go to if he ever had to be incarcerated. He couldn't name another prison with horses.

Beyond the crime scene tape, reporters jostled and shouted. A bald, heavyset, grey-bearded man in a black suit lifted the crime scene tape to let Albritton and her team through to the stables. He introduced himself as the warden. The pungent odor of horse dung surrounded the investigators the moment they stepped into the breezeway of the stables. A broad-shouldered sheriff stood in the shadows alongside two men in white jumpsuits marked with large letters on the back that read, Crime Scene Technician. Two equipment cases lined the outside wall of the stall.

The warden led Albritton to the open stall marked Polka Dancer. After introductions, the warden handed the briefing over to the sheriff.

"The body hasn't been moved," the sheriff said. "Two inmates found it when they came to check on the horses at six this morning. One moved the horse to that stall." He pointed across the breezeway at a closed stall labeled with a memorial plaque to Promised Road, the first racehorse brought to Wallkill.

"Have you processed these inmates?" Albritton asked the sheriff.

"Yes, ma'am," the sheriff said. "Bagged and tagged their clothes and shoes. Isolated them in separate cruisers."

Albritton said, "Excellent."

"The crime scene technicians," the warden said, "need help with the horse."

From inside the stall came huffing, braying, and whimpering, followed by sharp kicks against the door. Everyone flinched.

"Clayton, you handle the horse. Gunnerson, stay with the body," Albritton said. "Warden, I need the paperwork on the horse and files on everyone who had access to the stables in the last three days. Sheriff, can your people help with the interviews?" She headed out of the stables as she talked.

On their way outside, the sheriff and the warden discussed the logistics of interviewing the inmates at the sheriff's station. Their voices faded into the distance.

Blake and Vincent peered into the open stall. Crumpled in the far corner was a bloody mass, roughly human-shaped, with limbs bent where they should not bend, creating a gruesome zig-zag of body parts.

"FBI Agent Gunnerson." Vincent identified himself. "How can I help?"

In unison the technicians said, "Don't touch anything." One technician wore wire-framed glasses. The one with the camera had a sagging belly.

Blake stared at the broken body in the stall as if in a trance. *So much blood.* Vincent nudged his shoulder, breaking the spell. Blake turned away from the carnage and stepped to the far side of the passageway where he rubbed his hands over his face. His pulse thudded in his ears. *Pull yourself together. Investigate the suspect.* If the horse became violent, then what triggered the violence? Pain? Fear? Reading human behavior and expressions were tougher than reading a horse's. Sure horses had personalities, and a few were unpredictable, but horses didn't know how to mask their reactions. Whatever they felt showed in them from their ears to their hooves if one knew how to read them.

Blake knew how.

Horses didn't keep secrets. Horses, God bless them, lacked that uniquely human talent for lying.

The crime scene technician opened his toolkit and took out a small vial. To Blake, he said. "You're welcome to use what you need. It'll take ten ccs of this, slow push in the rump. At least that's what the vet told me." He held up the vial.

The horse brayed as if he knew he was being discussed.

"Why isn't the vet here?"

"He's an inmate."

And therefore, a possible suspect.

"You'll need a jumpsuit and booties," said the heavyset technician.

Blake set the vial on top of one of the technician's kits. "Think big and tall size."

The technician in glasses nodded. "I'll check the van."

Meanwhile, the heavier technician knelt with a grunt before opening his kit. He wrote on the labels of two empty tubes and stuck them in his chest pocket. He then pulled a cellophane-wrapped syringe from the kit and tucked it beside the tubes.

The other technician returned with a giant white jumpsuit. Blake climbed into it and tugged on rubber gloves and paper booties. Next, he took the tubes and syringe into the stall. The horse brayed and snorted. Blake closed the stall door.

After five minutes, he emerged triumphantly from the stall and handed blood vials to the technician in glasses. The horse calmly rested on his side, looking back at the men.

Blake said, "Fools rush in where technicians fear to tread."

The technician in glasses placed the vials in a cooler. "Whatever you gave that horse must be strong stuff."

"I'm not qualified to administer medicine to a horse," Blake said, "but I know how to draw blood."

The sedative vial sat on the technician's kit. The techs exchanged a glance.

"How did you do that?" asked the technician.

"Horses pick up on the emotions of people around them," Blake said. "I went in calm and treated him like he was innocent. I suggest you do the same."

"Innocent until proven guilty, eh?" said the chubby technician. "All right then, let's process his hooves first."

"I'll keep him calm." Blake stepped to the open doorway of the stall. "Move nice and easy and talk slowly and softly like you would around a sleeping baby. You might want to avoid using the flash on your camera."

The technician smiled. "Who knew we had a real cowboy in the agency?"

Blake didn't mind having his experience with horses heralded as something exotic. He had taken his experience for granted, but it was clear that city-raised folks feared horses like they were animals in the wild. Why not play up the role of a super-agent cowboy? A little fame could advance his career. "I'm even better handling mares."

At the mention of mares, Blake thought of home. He also realized he had not yet spoken to Moose. What had Moose learned from the coroner?

Back in Poughkeepsie, Terri methodically sorted through the stack of charts on her mahogany desk, signing dictation, writing prescriptions, ordering supplies and drinking coffee. She treasured working at her father's carved wooden desk. She remembered it from her childhood as sturdy enough to climb on yet handsomely ornate with acanthus leaves curving around the corners. After she had worked with her father for three years, her father retired. His eyesight failing, he sold his share of the practice evenly to Dr. Anders, Dr. Everly, and Terri. He sold the building to Terri with the expectation that the business would lease the building, thereby providing Terri with the income to pay off the note.

Their building was huge by Poughkeepsie standards. Big enough for her to convince her partners to take Justin in as a potential partner. Though they didn't need another large animal vet in their practice, some older clients preferred to work with a man. He had been with them for a year, so it was time to either offer him partnership or let him set up his own practice.

During the honeymoon, her business partners Dr. Anders and Dr. Everly—small animal vets, or pet vets as she thought of them—referred her urgent client calls to Justin. The new secretary had pulled files to match up with the call message slips, for which Terri was grateful. The previous secretary had barely kept up with delivering messages.

Terri's phone chirped, indicating lunch time. She knew full well that if she didn't take precautions like the timer, she'd work until her legs went numb. It was one of her workaholic habits. She stood, stretched, and then grabbed her purse on the way to the front desk. Since the new secretary was hired during Terri's honeymoon, she decided to spend lunch getting to know her. The twenty-something secretary greeted her with a warm smile. At first glance, Terri didn't have to guess why her male business partners hired this one. Cleavage, lots of visible cleavage was probably also the reason the partners didn't enforce the uniform dress code, leaving this young woman to her own fashion choices. Perhaps in her previous job she had modeled for Goth fantasy comics.

"May I take you to lunch?"

The young woman glanced behind herself as if to see who Terri might have been speaking to. She grinned. "Me?"

After reading the woman's nametag, Terri said, "Yes, Melanie. I thought we could get to know each other."

"Sure!" Melanie picked up the phone and forwarded calls to the service. She opened a desk drawer and plucked out a messenger bag on a long strap. After she had slung the strap over her head, she stood. Melanie towered over Terri by half a foot.

They climbed into Terri's red Ford F-150.

Melanie buckled up then ran her hand over the dashboard. "I figured you for a Lexus instead of *Motor Trend's* Truck of the Year."

"I'm the large animal vet. My clients live in remote rural areas."

"This is a sweet ride. Is this the Triton V-8 five point four liter powertrain?"

"Yes. I'm sorry I haven't read your file yet. When did you start working with us?" Terri drove toward her favorite restaurant on the Hudson.

"Monday, October sixth, the same day your partners interviewed me." Her blue eyes practically glowed through a thick black frame of eyeliner. The sunlight caught a streak of deep burgundy in her black hair.

October sixth was the first workday after the wedding. The partners didn't waste a day in their search for a new secretary. The last one had been pleasant, but inept.

"Thank you for pulling the files with the messages," Terri said.

Melanie nodded. "I was nervous about meeting you. The last woman boss I worked for in the city had jealousy issues."

Because Poughkeepsie was an hour north along the Hudson River from New York City, it was understood that references to the *city* meant that city.

Terri noticed Melanie's bare left hand. "I can understand why some women would feel that way. Are you single?"

"You aren't allowed to ask that," Melanie teased.

"Not in an interview." Terri mused that the young woman had reasonable working knowledge of her rights. She planned to inform Melanie of the dress code and her allowance for uniform scrubs over lunch.

"Oh, yeah."

"You don't have to answer. I just want you to know my partners and Justin are married. One of them has an insecure wife."

"How insecure?" Melanie raised one eyebrow.

"She tends to drop in during the monthly evening business meeting."

Melanie grinned. "Mrs. Everly, right?"

Terri nodded.

"Yeah, she seems a little…insecure."

Dr. Everly had one photo in his office. It was taken on their honeymoon on a barefoot sailing cruise in the Bahamas, ten years and forty pounds ago. Both the doctor and his wife gained twenty pounds since the photo, but the weight gain mattered to Mrs. Everly.

Terri pulled into the parking lot of the red brick, green roofed Shadows on the Hudson. Aside from an impeccable menu, the restaurant had a spectacular view of the Hudson River and the newly renovated Walkway on the Hudson. "So you've met Mrs. Everly?"

"I wouldn't have recognized her, but Doctor Everly greeted her with a hug." Melanie shook her head. "You never really get to know someone until you're married."

"So you were married." Terri climbed out of the truck and stepped toward the back.

Melanie met her there. "Three months and then it all fell apart."

"I'm sorry."

Melanie took a deep breath when she pivoted toward the Hudson River. "Wow. I've heard this place is *the* place to eat with the best view of the walkway. Have you been on the walkway?"

"It opened while I was in North Carolina. Then the honeymoon." Terri admired the tall span. Once a plain railway bridge, the city had transformed the structure into a pedestrian walkway over a mile long. She smiled at the city's new pride and joy. The late October chill blew across the parking lot. Terri stuffed her hands into her jacket pockets. "Have you been on it?"

Melanie nodded. She flipped up her collar against the brisk wind and opened the door to the restaurant. "I hope your marriage works. In my case, the man I dated wasn't the man I married."

How much could a man change in three months to lead to divorce? A shudder ran through her. It took the Everlys ten years to deteriorate from the adventurous couple on the beach to the frumpy couple they had become. Terri silently prayed she wouldn't let herself go, then she prayed Blake was exactly the man she fell in love with. She had promised to love him through sickness, health, for richer, for poorer, until death. Being an overachiever, she wanted more than duty to bind her to Blake. She wanted her marriage to include all the best things the happiest couples enjoyed. She would make her marriage one to envy.

Melanie and Terri stood by the hostess' stand. Most of the tables were occupied. The hostess was on the phone taking notes on a reservation.

"What kind of food do you like?" Terri asked Melanie.

After disconnecting from her call, the hostess plucked two lunch menus from under her stand.

Melanie tugged her shirt sleeve. "I suppose it's awful to admit to a vet that I'm a carnivore."

Terri smiled. "Give me anything but dog, cat, monkey, or any form of roadkill."

The hostess's head snapped up from her seating chart. "I think we can manage that."

Terri and Melanie laughed like school girls.

By late evening, Blake was conducting interviews alongside a flirtatious bosomy female deputy at the sheriff's station in an interrogation room. Between interviews, he stepped into the corridor with his cell phone to call Moose, but Moose didn't answer. He then called Terri and left a message stating he was out of town on a case and would call again later tonight. A shadow, cast from the break room, fell across the corridor.

Special Agent Albritton appeared, coffee in hand. "Newlywed?"

"It shows, huh?"

"Looks good on you." Her gold wedding band glinted while she took a sip.

"How long have you been married?" Blake asked.

"Thirty years."

"Any advice?"

Albritton gave a wan smile. "Never take each other for granted. You may one day be each other's only comfort."

Torn between curiosity and fear of offending her, Blake wanted her to elaborate. It sounded like hard-earned knowledge. He kept his questions to himself. If Albritton wanted to tell him more, she would. If not, he could research her.

The female deputy led another inmate into the interview room, so Blake followed her in and shut the door. Blake settled in his chair then jotted a few questions on his notepad to allow time for his witness, the one who found the body, to remember details. The witness chewed the cuticle of his thumb. Learning how to apply silence was an art. The more uncomfortable the witness was, the more likely it was he would reveal valuable information.

Blake sighed. He had many more inmates to question. It was going to be a long, tedious night, and he was doomed to spend this first night since his wedding with a strange woman by his side discussing death.

Preparing to discuss death with strangers caused a growing awareness of his own mortality to grip him. The future wasn't in his hands any more than it was in the hands of the man who died in the stable. Control was an illusion; nonetheless, Blake wanted to pretend he could guide his future. Maybe he couldn't control how or when he died, but he could focus his heart, mind and soul on protecting his life.

. 10 .

At nine the following morning, Doctor Terri Pinehurst-Clayton had one gloved arm elbow-deep in the back end of a mare. She was thinking how proud Suki would be of her when her cell phone rang in her pocket.

Mr. Cooper, the owner and breeder of Cooper Racing Farms, drawled, "They never do ring when you want them to."

"That's the truth." She had waited up the night before for a call from Blake that never came. Focusing on her work, she felt the foals. "There's a second one."

Cooper swatted his hat in his hand, causing a small dust cloud. He had already gambled on breeding the mare three months later than most thoroughbreds to get a lower price on the stud fee. Perhaps he wanted to breed instead of race this foal.

Terri gently held the hind legs of the female foal. She had already told him that bearing two foals would produce two weaker, smaller offspring than bearing one. As a breeder he paid top dollar for a thoroughbred race horse, so he probably wanted just the male. The decision was his alone.

Her heart sank. Racing males earned more money than racing females. An animal represented a multi-million-dollar investment in the thoroughbred racing business. Her duty was to provide the best result for her clients, the breeders, and the investors. She could not afford to think of the horses as her clients. She likened her duties to a pediatrician's. If the parents were satisfied, they called the doctor a hero. If the parents were dissatisfied, they called the doctor a plaintiff.

It was what it was. The client wanted the healthiest, fastest racer from the chosen sire and the dam. If Terri had to remove the female foal the dam would not realize the loss. Her hormones and her swelling would tell her she was still carrying. *But still.*

Cooper patted the mare's neck. "I'm gonna miss the season anyway. Might as well get two for the price of one."

Relieved, Terri released the legs of the female foal and tucked them snug against the foal's belly. She withdrew her forearm and peeled off the long-sleeve glove into a trash bag. She scrubbed her hands and arms up to the elbows in the stables' sink and dried them off.

Cooper scheduled regular checkups to monitor the mare's progress.

Outside the barn, after saying good-bye to the breeder, she returned to her truck and started it up. On her cell phone, Terri logged the invoice. The Bluetooth connection message flashed on the navigation screen on her dashboard. She checked her phone to see whose call she missed.

While she drove up the long gravel driveway of the ranch, she talked to the dashboard.

"Call Prince Charming."

"Calling Prince Charming cell phone," the dashboard device answered.

"Hello, Blake here." His voice lifted her mood.

"Miss me?"

"Desperately. How's your day?"

"Checking on mares."

"Tell me again how thoroughly you wash your hands afterward."

Terri smiled. "When are you coming home?"

"No telling yet. This investigation will take a while."

"Are we talking in terms of hours, days, or weeks?" She stopped at the end of the drive and checked the crossroad for traffic. Stirred up dirt plumed behind her truck. She had a twenty-minute drive to the office.

"I hope to come home for part of the weekend."

Home meant his apartment in New York City. Though she had kept her condo in Poughkeepsie, they had agreed it was too small and too far from his job to be their permanent home. She had planned to work four days a week in Poughkeepsie and commute to New York City for long weekends. They were searching for a place north of Manhattan. Blake's only requirement was for a "nicer" place. Nicer to him meant larger and newer. To her it meant a place that did not reek of beer, dust, pizza, and gym socks.

"Where are you?"

"Wallkill prison."

Wallkill was near Poughkeepsie. Terri calculated she would need one hour round trip for her next appointment. "Forget going to the city, you can come to Poughkeepsie. It's only half an hour from my office." Terri slowed for a tractor-trailer rig taking up a lane and a half of the road.

"I'm working sixteen-hour days."

"I could drive there. I'd be willing to share a room with you and Vincent."

"Hey, hey. There will be no sharing." He cleared his throat. "I have my own room."

"Fine. Call me if you have any energy and free time this weekend."

"You bet. Oh, in the interest of full disclosure, there's a deputy here on the prowl. I have no idea why she hasn't latched onto Vincent, but I've done nothing to encourage her."

"What have you done to discourage her?" The tractor ahead slowed, causing Terri to brake.

"I'm ignoring her. I think she's just caught up in being worldly."

It pleased her that he described the woman's character instead of her appearance. "You're the new stallion in town. The one she hasn't ridden."

"I'm so glad you're not the jealous type." His laugh warmed her heart.

"Just for the record, if she touches you I'll neuter her and leave her for dead."

"Better if I come to Poughkeepsie then."

"Good idea."

The tractor-trailer headed off at an intersection, clearing the highway ahead.

"Do me a favor and stay away from the vending machines. Eat real food, okay?"

"If I get fat there will be more of me to love," Blake said. He sounded as if he was smiling.

Perhaps weight was still a sensitive issue with him. In the family photos, he had been a fat kid until high school. "If you get heart disease," she said, "you won't be around to love."

"So you're being selfish when you tell me to eat well."

"I want to grow old with you."

"I love you, too." With that, he ended the call.

She shrugged off the idea of a deputy chasing Blake. He was handsome so he attracted the attention of women. But, she trusted he loved her and meant his vows. She rubbed her wedding ring on her lips. *He is a good man.* It was Friday night, and she was heading home for dinner and a rental movie. Blake was probably eating candy bars and processing evidence in a homicide investigation. She was beginning to resent death for keeping them apart.

Mid-morning on October 23rd, 2009, Ketchum sat in his

cruiser outside the Western Regional Crime Lab in Asheville to review the latest news from Ward, the coroner. The coroner's preliminary report, based on the skeletal remains found in the river, estimated the date of death between 1990 and 1995. Ketchum needed to narrow the date range. He had hoped the death was accidental, but Ward's summation obliterated that hope. The nearly-complete skeleton revealed multiple fractures of the femur, ribs, neck, and shoulder; the fatal blow being the one that fractured the skull. Ketchum would have to change the case book to a murder book.

He had been hounded by families of missing people for weeks since they found the first bones. Everyone wanted answers. The callers claimed they read about the discovery online. He blamed Ernie and his newspaper for spreading the news before the facts were all in, and he dreaded talking to the families.

The coroner's search to identify the bones by tracing the medical implant had taken far longer than expected. Ward explained the delays were part of the new medical privacy laws. After he contacted Synthes for information on the implant, he was given the name of the hospital that received it.

From there, Ketchum had to beg for a court order to get the hospital surgical records. He dug out his cell phone and dialed Ward.

"Hello, Pete. Miss me already?" Ward asked.

"What state was that hospital in? The one where the implant you were asking about was sent?"

A rustling of papers preceded Ward's answer. "Ohio."

"Thanks."

He pocketed his phone and climbed from his cruiser. Trudging to the crime lab, he sent up a silent prayer for answers.

After he signed in, the secretary led him back into a long corridor. The scent of powerful antiseptics wafted through the hallway. In the last room on the right, the secretary pressed a buzzer.

"Sheriff's here," she said into the small intercom.

The door buzzed and popped open. Ketchum entered and stood near the wall. The room contained examining equipment and test tubes. A few feet away, two hooded technicians peered over a stainless steel table laden with chains, muddy cloth, and plant material. The room smelled like the river in spring when it runs fast and stirs up sediment, all wormy and muddy with a trace of mossy. Since the bones had been removed from the chains and cloth the day before and were in the coroner's office in Charlotte, Ketchum wanted news of the evidence that had been dredged up with the bones.

"The news isn't pretty," said one of the technicians. He stepped from the examination table and stood by the sheriff. Pointing to photos clipped to the wall, he said, "The divers brought the whole knot of chains and bones and junk up intact. The clothes and the bones were found inside the chains, see?"

In the photos, a rib cage and spinal column showed through tattered cloth and chains. Bony fingers reached out between lines of chain. Ketchum nodded. His stomach clenched. He stepped closer to examine the photos. The hand was large. Large enough to be an adult's?

"The bones also showed signs of extensive trauma," the technician pointed to gouges and cracks in the photos of the bones. "But it's up to the coroner to determine if the trauma happened before or after death."

Every large bone in the photographs showed damage.

"What can you tell me about this mess?" Ketchum asked.

The technician described in mind-numbing detail about an emerging science that studied river levels and currents. Late summer flooding had eroded the riverbanks, freeing the chains and bones from the mud. Ketchum hoped the technician was coming to a salient point and not just talking to impress. At last, the man explained that the application of this riverbed erosion science helped pinpoint the most likely place where the body entered the river—at the Little Jordan River Bridge. The technician calculated the probable date of death between September and mid-December of 1994 before the river froze solid.

Deeply impressed, Ketchum jotted this information in his notebook. "That's amazing and helpful. Is there anything else I should know?"

"Like how we've been begging for a larger lab with better equipment?"

"I'm not the one to ask about that," Ketchum said.

"This section of the chains was preserved in muddy clay. We found a work glove caught in the chains." The technician took a few steps to a side table and snatched a Tyvek envelope and long tweezers from the table. He opened the envelope and used the tweezers to lift out a man's once-yellow leather glove. "Normally, leather would decay much more over the years than this. Fortunately for us, this one was saturated with chemical preservatives."

"Construction workers, farm hands, landscapers, everyone uses those," Ketchum said.

"But look here." The technician rotated the glove palm down.

Stamped in the leather were two letters, one-inch high, in the center of the back of the glove. C.R.

Recognition accelerated his heart rate. *Oh, no.* "Could this have gotten caught in the chains after the bones and chains went into the river?"

"It was found between the chains and the victim's pants. In all likelihood, this glove is either the victim's or the killer's."

Ketchum rubbed his face with his free hand. He bit back the urge to curse. This was going to be awkward. In a town this small, how could someone go missing without being noticed? Were there any ranch hands missing from that time period? If so, why hadn't it been reported?

"Wow, Sheriff, you're turning, uh, pale." The technician's eyebrows scrunched together. "Do you know what or who CR is?"

"Clayton Ranch." Remembering the workers had to earn embossed gloves, Ketchum gently clasped the technician's gloved hand and twisted it to see the wrist side of the work glove. Despite discoloration from mold, three smaller embossed letters showed through that personalized the glove to the owner.

Ketchum's throat tightened and the room suddenly felt cold. Few people knew the glove owner by his legal name, but Ketchum had gone to grade school with him before he started going by his middle name instead of his full legal name. The small embossed letters EBC stood for Elijah Blake Clayton.

Meanwhile at the sheriff's office near Wallkill Prison, Blake longed for coffee and donuts while he, Vincent, the sheriff, and his deputies listened to Special Agent Albritton's morning briefing on the investigation. The aroma of fresh donuts beckoned him.

Albritton announced the arrival of surveillance recordings gathered from the prison. She waved her hand over a banker's box packed with digital recording discs.

"Each tape is marked with the camera's location so please refer to the location in your reports. The time stamp appears in the lower right corner of the recordings. Did everyone get a copy of the prison layout?"

Heads nodded in the crowded conference room.

"The numbers correspond to the names of inmates, guards, and visitors. Visitors are required to present a photo ID. We also have photos of the guards and inmates. If you need to refer to a photo, come see the wall." Albritton pointed to a whiteboard papered with photos grouped under headings: inmates, staff, and visitors.

The photos, arranged alphabetically by last name, listed a name, a job title, and a number under each face. Blake was daunted by the sheer number of faces on the wall. Every one of them had to be tracked. Every one of them had been interviewed. Soon, the daily activities of every face on the wall would be tracked for the days leading up to the death. Woe to anyone who lied.

"Ladies and gentlemen," Albritton said. "Time of death is between two and four a.m."

Murmuring and whispers circled the table.

Albritton waited for the noise to die down before she resumed. "Cause of death is blunt force trauma to the head. Because of the many crushing injuries to the skull, it is unclear which fracture or fractures killed Mr. Chilton. The FBI has sent over two forensic specialists to piece the skull back together. Until they finish the process, I can't give more specific information about the fatal injury or what may have caused it. Questions?"

Queasy officers stared into their coffee cups to avoid eye contact. Blake shared a general uneasiness about the process of examining a body as evidence. He was grateful for the iron stomachs of coroners and forensic technicians. He glanced at Albritton, who happened to be watching him, but he didn't have any questions. His mind was on coffee. He should have poured himself a cup before the briefing, but he had rushed out of the break room after Deputy Trent invaded his personal space. She cooed that she preferred being called Debbie, so Blake insisted on addressing by her as Deputy Trent.

Chilton's bloody death hit Blake like a delayed echo, a memory he wanted to keep buried in the past. He shook it off. Why would someone want to kill a man who made a living rescuing race horses?

A nudge from Vincent roused Blake from his mental detour. Officers, deputies, and FBI agents lined up to view security camera recordings. Vincent trudged to the back of the line. Blake followed.

Special Agent Albritton tapped his back. "Clayton, where's your laptop?"

"I left it on...." He was about to point to the empty desk where he'd left it, but it was gone. "It was on this desk." *Silly me. Why would I assume it would be safe to turn my back on my laptop at a sheriff's station?*

Deputy Trent waved at him from her desk back in a corner of the bullpen. "I saved you a desk over here, Blake."

The others snickered. Blake clenched his jaw so tight his teeth squeaked. Vincent raised his eyebrows. Albritton turned her back to Deputy Trent and sighed before walking away. When it came to Blake's turn to sign out a surveillance disc, his face had heated up so much he knew he was blushing. *Oh, great. Let the teasing begin.*

The male deputy who logged the disc out to him pointed to the clipboard for a signature and muttered, "*Illigitemae non corburundom.*"

"Is that Latin?" Blake signed the clipboard.

"It means 'Don't let the bastards get you down.'"

"You must have had an interesting Latin teacher." Blake carried his recording disc to the desk beside Trent's to set up his laptop. He plugged the power cord into his laptop then he knelt at the desk to search for an outlet.

A hand with red nails held up a multi-plug outlet. "You can plug in my outlet."

Blake followed the hand up the arm to the ample bosom beside it. Deputy Trent's uniform blouse was a size too small for modesty. She was a sneeze away from popping the already stressed buttons. He handed her the end of the power cord rather than shove it in her outlet. She would undoubtedly find bragging rights in it that he never intended. Ignoring her, he took his seat.

"Aren't you even going to thank me?" she asked, pouting.

"No." *And oh hell no.*

Deputy Trent huffed and left the desk area.

"Not your type?" asked a heavyset deputy at the desk to Blake's left. He paused his recording.

Blake held up his left hand to show his gold wedding band.

"It'll take more than that," the deputy whispered. "If you're polite to her, she takes it as a green light. Be rude to her and you're a challenge."

"Bucket of cold water?"

The deputy shrugged and resumed work on his laptop.

Blake loaded the disc labeled East Parking Lot into his laptop. The date stamp at the beginning showed it began two days before the discovery of the body. Blake matched drivers to cars and noted the time when each car arrived and departed.

Hours later, his butt numb, he hit the pause button and headed to the break room. First, he poured a large Styrofoam cup of coffee for himself then, fishing quarters from his pocket, he stood in front of side-by-side vending machines. *Sugar or salt? Salt or sugar?* He fed quarters into the machine until he overpaid then he pressed his selection by letter and number for a bag of corn chips. A Hershey's chocolate bar dropped to the bottom instead. He sighed and fished it from the bin. When he spun around to leave, Vincent was at the doorway.

"I'm going cross-eyed. I wanted a bag of corn chips." Blake held up the candy bar. "It kept my change, too."

"They call it the Vegas vending machine." Vincent stepped up to a three-gallon coffee server parked on the counter where a smaller version sat yesterday and plucked a large Styrofoam cup from the stack beside it.

"What's on your recording?" Blake asked.

"A view of the stables. Counting horses is too much like counting sheep. I need caffeine."

"I get to watch the parking lot tapes."

Vincent poured himself a coffee from the tall dispenser. "Looks like we're stuck here for the weekend."

"I'd rather spend it with Terri," Blake said.

"I was supposed to go out with Nefi tonight."

Blake raised his eyebrows. "I wouldn't want Nefi mad at me. Oh, no." He recalled how Nefi used a machete to hack off the hand of the man who killed her parents when she was only fourteen.

Vincent chuckled. "I called her this morning. She understands."

"Hope so. She's been more than patient waiting for you."

"I waited seven years, too, you know."

"No, you didn't." Blake leaned against the wall and lowered his voice to a whisper, "Not like she did. You waited to see if she remembered you. You waited to see if she turned out okay after the tragedy in her life. You waited until she wasn't jailbait."

"So how did Nefi wait differently?"

Blake shook his head. This was the second dumbest thing he had ever heard Vincent say. The first had been years ago when he offered Vincent grits and Vincent said he'd try just one, thank you. This was the difference between stupid and ignorant. Vincent couldn't help his ignorance, or lack of knowledge, about Nefi because he had not seen her in her high school years.

"What?" Vincent spread his arms.

Blake answered, "At Nefi's high school graduation party, her aunt said she felt guilty for allowing Nefi to idolize you."

"Then why did she allow it?"

"Loving from afar, she said, was the best form of birth control." Blake patted Vincent on the shoulder.

"Are you suggesting she didn't date in high school?"

Blake nodded.

"She must have dated in college," Vincent said.

"Why would she date when she has her heart set on you?"

"That's not funny."

"Did Nefi ever tell you what happened at Ruis's wedding when she spotted you with Rose?"

Vincent shook his head.

Blake told him in humbling detail so Vincent could judge the depth of Nefi's devotion for himself.

Nefi settled into the sofa in her tiny apartment in suburban Washington, D.C., with chopsticks, a ginger ale, and two boxes of Chinese takeout on the coffee table. Friday night was supposed to be spent with Vincent on their second date. His job intervened, so Nefi plunged into studying to avoid feeling sorry for herself. Her cell phone played "Anchors Away," her best friend's ringtone. She immediately answered it.

"So where's he taking you to dinner?" Martina asked. She rarely remembered the time difference between Oxford England and Washington DC.

"He got called upstate to cover death-by-horse."

"What?" She groaned. "Gotta give him points for originality. I haven't heard that excuse before."

"Don't expect normal in my life."

"Oh, Nef, I'm so sorry." Martina sighed. "When will you get to see him again?"

"Who knows? I'm supposed to report at oh six hundred on Monday. And I have a pile of books to read for months of training at Quantico."

"Poor, poor, thing," Martina said, "You find your soul mate and he stands you up for a dead guy."

"Keep teasing. Wait until you see the maid of honor dress I choose for you."

"Such faith. Not even on a second date and you're planning the wedding."

"I'm not letting go of a man who can kiss like that." Having idolized Vincent for seven years, Nefi imagined sharing her body with him. She dreamed of sharing her life with him.

"Yeah, yeah. Blake texted me about it. He said he broke a sweat just watching you two lock lips. So what are you going to do if Vincent wants to go farther?"

"He can't take me home to meet his parents. His father was killed on the job. His mother passed away last year from cancer. The only family he has left is his younger brother Oscar."

"That's not what I mean."

Nefi smiled, savoring the moment. "Oh, did you mean *further*?"

"Stinker. Remember who helped you learn English. Yes, I mean further as in getting naked."

Nefi cupped her hands around the box of fried rice to check the temperature. *Still hot.* She snapped apart her wooden chopsticks and set them on the coffee table, before picking up her drink. "At this rate, I'll never get to test the pill."

Martina let out a high-pitched wail. A thump sounded. A moment later, more thumping followed. "Sorry, I dropped the phone." She gasped for air between guffaws. "You're like my fat cousin Ricardo, carrying a condom in his wallet just in case."

Nefi held her soda aloft. "That maid of honor dress is getting uglier by the minute."

"Seriously, don't wait until your honeymoon. Vincent was a Marine, he'll understand *carpe diem*."

"The Marine motto is *Semper Fidelis*, as in ever faithful."

"That works too. You know what I mean."

Nefi sucked ginger ale through a straw. It fizzed in her throat. "I'm not having sex until my honeymoon."

"Why not?"

"I promised my dad." Nefi placed her cup on the table.

"Oh, Nef. He was trying to protect you from dating the natives."

Nefi shook her head. Being raised in the Brazilian jungle, she had known even as a child she would wait until she reached the United States to date. "Papa said the most precious gift I can give my husband is my virginity."

Martina groaned. "I can't argue with the dead."

Nefi plucked sauce packets from the takeout bag. *Sweet and sour. Mustard. Where's the soy sauce?* "We must be the last virgins in Washington, D.C. and London."

Martina said, "If you tell a soul, I'll hurt you."

Nefi snorted. "What does it say about our society that we're ashamed of virtue?" She opened a paper napkin and two packets of soy sauce fell into her lap.

"Preacher's kid!"

"Navy brat!" The line fell silent.

Nefi smiled and popped open the orange beef and the fried rice containers to let their scents mingle. She then lifted a thick textbook on federal law and opened it to the bookmark.

Her cell phone rang again. The display showed an unfamiliar number. She did not give out her number easily. *Who could it be?* Using her finger to hold her place in the textbook, she took the call.

"Hello, is this Nefi Jenkins?"

"Yes." *Who else would answer my phone?*

"Hi. We met at the Clayton wedding last month."

The voice sounded oddly familiar. She set her book face down on the coffee table.

"I'm a friend of Blake's. Well, sort of."

"Uh huh." She could not place a name to the voice though it sounded somewhat familiar. What was a sort-of friend?

"I noticed you didn't have on a wedding ring, so I was wondering if you would like to go out."

"I'm dating someone." *In theory.* Her curiosity trumped her hunger, so she remained on the line.

"Is it serious?"

Nefi laughed at his persistence. "I'm serious about him, but I suppose you could ask him if he feels the same way."

"Who is he?"

Persistent and impertinent. "How did you get this number?"

"I bribed a bridesmaid for it."

"Okay, stalker."

"So who are you dating?" the caller asked.

Whether he was a friend of Blake or Terri, she decided to put fear in his heart. "FBI agent Vincent Gunnerson."

The man laughed. "No, really. Who?"

Why was that funny? "He was the best man at the wedding."

"I know Vincent. I doubt he's dated since he broke up with Rose."

Nefi was impressed he knew so much about Vincent, annoyed that he thought so much of Rose. Was he one of Blake's cousins? "I give up. Who are you?"

"I'm Oscar. Vincent's brother."

Remembering a tall, nice-looking man, Nefi winced at the idea of being asked out by Vincent's brother. *How awkward.* "You didn't tell me your name at the wedding."

"I didn't get the chance because Blake pulled you away. Vincent told me a little about you, but he failed to mention you two were dating."

"We were supposed to go out tonight, but he was called out of town on a case. But, hey, if not for your brother, I would have given you my number."

"That's a nice letdown."

"Why are *you* single?" She cringed. *Too blunt.* She had meant it as a compliment.

"School was demanding, and then I had to hunt down a job. I haven't really had much time to date."

Nefi detected sincerity and regret in his voice. He probably had not taken the time to notice women noticing him. "Uh, huh."

"I don't mean to sound desperate," Oscar said, "but do you have any single friends looking for a lonely engineer?"

Nefi closed her eyes. *How sweet.* She liked him all the more for showing such vulnerability. "What are your plans for Christmas?"

"Uh, I don't have any." His voice took on a wary edge.

"My aunt and uncle host a party every year on Christmas Eve. I plan to invite Vincent and if you can be there, I'll introduce you to my friend Martina. You two might like each other."

"Tell me about her."

"She's my best friend and Ruis's little sister. Has Vincent told you about Ruis?"

"The Navy SEAL?"

"He's a US Marshall now," Nefi said. That sounded much more intimidating than the Ruis she knew.

"Great. Her big brother could kill me and not leave a trace of evidence."

"Oh, don't worry. Ruis probably hasn't killed anyone in weeks." The silence on the phone disappointed Nefi. "Sorry. I don't tell jokes well. Even if Ruis was scary, Martina's worth the risk. She's smart, fun, and loyal."

"That's how I would describe a good dog."

Nefi added, "Did I mention she's beautiful?"

"How beautiful?" His voice perked up.

"Can you receive photos on this number?"

"I'm an engineer. I live for gadgets. My phone can link to the internet, translate text messages into twelve languages, and download movies via satellites," he said.

"Okay." Nefi set her cell phone on speaker mode while she switched to search her photo folders. *Wedding...school...those.* Vacation photos from Rio last December.

"If Martina's so terrific then why does she need you to find her a date?"

"She has high standards." Nefi scrolled through her collection of whimsical, posed, and natural shots of Martina. Finding one that flattered and showed personality, Nefi sent it.

"Such as?"

Nefi quoted Martina's mother without going so far as imitating her voice. "Candidate must have a job, at least a bachelor's degree, live independently, and have a clean criminal record. Speaking Spanish or having military experience is a plus."

"Those don't seem like high standards to me."

"I suppose men have different standards," Nefi said, "like breathing and walking upright."

"Ouch."

She toyed with her textbook. "I think one of your biggest advantages is that your family's Catholic."

"Is Martina devout?"

"She doesn't carry around rosary beads or a *Bible* if that's what you mean."

"Actually, I was fantasizing about a Catholic school uniform. Oh, got the photo. Wow."

"She's in London, but she graduates in May." Nefi glanced at the ominous must-read stack of papers and books on her end table.

"So if she and I connect at your party," he said, "I have to wait another five months until she comes back to the states?"

"And when was your last date?"

A chuffing sound came through the phone. "Five months is a long time."

Nefi rolled her eyes. *Try waiting years.* "I guess that depends on how well you two connect."

Oscar cleared his throat. "You know Vincent is seven years older than you. In fact, you're younger than me."

"What did Vincent say about me?" *Beautiful? Brilliant?*

"He said you tracked down the man who killed your parents."

How did that come up in the conversation? "Anything else?" She shook her head at the fact she was seeking a compliment.

"He didn't date you when you were fourteen, did he?"

"Of course not." She supposed that the age difference between the brothers created a little social distance. How could Oscar misjudge Vincent's basic decency?

After a moment had passed, his warm voice returned. "I really enjoyed meeting you at the wedding. I don't know why, but you're easy to talk to. And this call has been a strangely pleasant and awkward experience."

"Mark your calendar for Christmas Eve. I'll send you an invitation through Vincent. Don't tell him about it. I haven't asked him yet and that would be weird."

"I'll feign ignorance until I get an invitation. Good-night, Nefi."

"Good-night, Oscar."

Nefi disconnected the call and nodded at the photo of Martina she had sent, one taken on the famous Ipanema Beach in Brazil. Martina in a bikini impressed the Brazilian boys, a fact made more notable because she was one of two college girls on the beach wearing clothing. *So there. Hot virgins and proud of it.* She smiled at the idea of Oscar and Martina together.

. 11 .

Two days shy of Christmas, Sheriff Ketchum was catching up on paperwork when Carl stepped into his office. His deputies had been decorating a fake Christmas tree all morning between calls. By appearances, they had not dug too deeply into petty cash for the bulbs, tinsel, and ornaments.

Carl plucked a candy cane from his mouth. "Excuse me, Sheriff."

"What is it?"

"There's a coroner named Ward here to see you."

To Ketchum's knowledge, Ward had never visited the sheriff's office before. When the coroner wasn't in his lab, he was off on a physical challenge, like mountain biking, a triathlon, rock climbing, or hang gliding. In his late teens, Ward had been arrested for BASE jumping. Ketchum thought it insane to parachute off a building, antennae, span, or earth-like a cliff. Fined and released, Ward finally switched to more legally dangerous activities. On a beautiful December day like today, it meant something that Ward showed up in person. Had the FBI lab sent the DNA results to Ward by mistake? As the county medical examiner, Ward was the usual source of DNA requests, but Ketchum had clearly marked that the report should come to the sheriff's office.

Ketchum followed Carl from his office through the bullpen of desks to the reception desk. He found Ward clutching a few papers in one hand while he prodded the limp potted ivy on the counter with his other hand.

"You might as well put it out of its misery," Ward said with a nod at the dying plant.

Ketchum lifted a cold coffee from the counter and poured it on the ivy. "Come on back to my office."

When they passed the Christmas tree, a deputy swore under his breath at a tangled string of lights. Ketchum led Ward to his office and shut the door. Compared to the sterile neatness of the coroner's lab, Ketchum's office had the appearance of a room dusted with a high-powered leaf blower.

Ward picked up a handful of files from the seat of a leather chair in front of the desk and sat. Holding them in his lap, he fidgeted as if he didn't know where to start. Ward's athletic build showed in his civilian clothes. Ketchum reminded himself to work out more often. Too many sheriffs grew the dreaded donut gut.

"I thought you'd be skiing out west." Ketchum dragged his chair from behind the desk and sat facing him.

"March has the best skiing," Ward said.

"The most co-eds?"

Ward nodded. He held the files from the chair on his lap. "I traced the implant to a hospital in Ohio. Thanks to privacy laws of medical records, it took a small paper war to get them to identify their patient, but they finally did after they got the death certificate. The dead man was Curtis Frank, no middle name. The records show he was only thirty-five when he supposedly fell down a flight of stairs in prison and fractured his hip." He handed the papers he brought to Ketchum.

Ketchum shoved them in Frank's file to read later. "What was he in for?"

"Mister Frank was known as the King of Kiddie Porn in Ohio."

Ketchum leaned back against his chair. *Scum of the earth.* "No wonder somebody wrapped him in chains and left him in the river." The good news was that finally the newspapers would get a name to go with the body. Curiosity was ramping up interest in the case. He was getting calls from the big city television stations daily fishing for news.

Ward nodded. "So what was he doing here?"

"Frank. *Huh.* That's not a common last name around here," Ketchum typed the name into a search field. The department records system produced a list of reports matching the last name. "Here we go. Yeah. We used to get regular complaints about old man Frank's property. Kids used to party out there in the abandoned barn. We had to board up the windows to keep them out of the house."

"Do you think the porn king was related to the old man?"

"I can check with the county clerk. See if he had a will on file."

"And one more thing." Ward stood and restacked the files on the chair. "For your timeline on this creep, you should know that Frank had his surgery in nineteen ninety-three and he was released from prison in February of ninety-four."

Ketchum said, "So he died in nineteen ninety-four between February and the middle of December."

Ward tilted his head slightly. "How'd you pick December?"

"The crime lab consulted with the water management folks," Ketchum said. "They did some fancy calculations about the water levels and how the river banks shift. I won't pretend to understand it, but they say they can prove the body was dumped near the Little Jordan Bridge before the river froze in mid-December."

"So what are you going to do next?" Ward leaned on the edge of the desk.

The question surprised Ketchum. *What does he mean?* "I'm going to keep investigating."

"Why?"

Because that's what a sheriff does. Ketchum eyed him. Had

working with the dead numbed him to real life? "Because someone killed him."

After a sigh, Ward said, "And if you find out who did it, I suppose you're going to be obligated to arrest somebody. Between you and me, I suspect Curtis Frank's death was more like a public service than a murder." He shook his head and departed.

Ketchum stared at the door long after Ward left.

That afternoon, warrant in hand, Sheriff Ketchum, one of his deputies, and a couple of crime lab technicians arrived at the abandoned home of the late Wilber Ernest Frank. Even though it was two days from Christmas and a blustery cold, overcast day, no one complained. Research at the county clerk's office showed that Old Wilber Frank had willed his property to his only known relative, his nephew Curtis, the *King of Kiddie Porn*, Frank. The old man died a few months before Curtis got out of prison.

Ketchum mused that Curtis must have been mighty disappointed when he showed up to claim this dump. Hip-high weeds had overtaken the narrow cement walkway from the driveway to the front door. A massive dead oak in the front yard had large branches hanging half-broken from the trunk with their tips dragging on the ground. The house showed fifteen years of neglect. The roof sagged, the gutters had rotted, Spanish moss grew up the north wall, and only the suggestion of blue paint remained in patches on the wood frame structure.

Ketchum plucked latex gloves from a box and insisted his deputy, Carl, wear them. He snapped on his own pair and grabbed the crowbar from his trunk. The crime techs photographed the front door to capture the rusted hinges and nails before they gave Ketchum the nod to break in. In their cherry red Tyvek suits, they reminded Ketchum of the two creatures from his favorite childhood book, *The Cat In the Hat*. Unless he got up close, he couldn't tell Thing One or Thing Two apart.

"Don't you usually wear white jumpsuits?" Carl asked.

Thing One sighed heavily. "The county got a bargain on these."

Ketchum handed the crowbar to Carl, who smirked at the red suits.

Carl appeared to shake off the temptation to tease the techs when he turned toward the farmhouse. Carl pried out the first squeaking nail. "I always wondered what was in here."

Ketchum set up a digital camera tripod on the porch. The equipment had come in a month earlier, and he was eager to try it. He set the camera to record.

It took ten minutes to remove the boards from the front door.

When Ketchum picked the lock, both the doorknob and the lock shed layered flecks of rust. Despite mild winters, North Carolina received enough rain to achieve rainforest designation, so the rusted lock refused to move. He gave up trying to finesse the lock. *Time for brute force.* No sooner had he shouldered door open and stepped in, his boot crushed through a crumbling floorboard up to his knee. Planting his gloved hands on the floor, he was grateful he hadn't fallen into the basement.

"A little help, please," he hollered. His leg stung. *That stunt's going to leave bruises.*

The others lifted him out. Wood rot, dust, and mold rose from the floor like fog, proving the place had not been disturbed in years. He sneezed. From the safety of the porch, he shone his pocket flashlight into the room, illuminating a thick carpet of dust.

"Hope you're up to date on your tetanus shots," Carl said.

Ketchum lifted his pants leg to check for scrapes and cuts. Carl shone his flashlight on the bare leg. No blood.

The crime techs hauled scaffolding platforms from their van and eased them over the floor like a bridge into the room. Thing

One hauled a pole with camera and lights mounted on top. After hefting them to the ceiling of the center of the room, he secured the pole to the scaffold and backed from the room.

"What're you doing?" Carl asked. He held the crowbar down by his leg.

"I'm photographing the room before you stomp through it and destroy evidence," said Thing One.

Carl sneered. Ketchum sat on the front steps waiting for his turn to enter. Carl wandered around the perimeter of the house before he, too, planted himself on the steps. It took hours for the technicians to set up walkways through the house. They hauled in special floodlights, cameras, and equipment for each room. Later on, the wind kicked up, shooting crisp brown leaves, twigs, and grit at the front of the house. Ketchum shielded his face from the flying debris with his arm.

He glanced at his camera which continued to record the entire boring event. He considered turning it off, but let it go. It wasn't in the way.

"This isn't like the TV shows." Carl held his arm over his face until the wind died down. "Don't you want to just kick the doors in and poke around?"

Ketchum nodded. He suspected even the crime technicians dreaded the tedium of processing the potential crime scene. They had been on the site for three hours. A dark line of clouds menaced the western horizon. Would he and Carl be able to move indoors before the downpour? Carl stood to stretch and then headed off around the house again. Ketchum stood and ambled to the front door. He leaned in the doorway to listen and heard voices. They were shouting. *Were they bickering?* Oh, for pity's sake, get on with it.

"Out!"

Ketchum stepped over the threshold. Was he going to have to go downstairs to break them up?

"Grab the cameras," said a higher voice.

Ketchum's breath caught in his throat. The techs sounded frantic.

"Watch the wire, the wire!"

Stepping back onto the porch, Ketchum searched for Carl. If this old structure gave way, they'd have to dig the techs out.

Suddenly, laden with equipment, Thing One and Thing Two waddled and clanked onto the front porch, past the sheriff, and far out on the barren lawn. Panting, they gently lowered their gear.

"What did you find?" Ketchum asked.

They answered in unison, "A bomb!"

It did not make sense, but the techs seemed convinced. Ketchum leaped from the porch and ran to the east side of the house. "Carl! Carl!" *Where did he go?* "Deputy Carl!"

Moments later, Carl appeared from the west side of the house, zipping his pants. "What?"

"Get over here," Ketchum hollered. Leading Deputy Carl to the techs, he turned to Thing One. "Tell me what you saw."

Carl jogged over to Ketchum's side.

Thing One pulled back his hood.

Thing Two staggered to a dead oak tree and pulled back the white hood to reveal a long blond ponytail. *Thing Two was a woman!* She steadied herself using one hand on the tree trunk while she panted.

Thing One fixed his gaze on Ketchum. He appeared to be in his early thirties with sandy blond hair and brown eyes. "We found about twenty sticks of dynamite tied to the basement ceiling." His eyes widened while he gestured. "There was a wire from the dynamite that ran up the stairway to a button just inside the front door."

Carl inhaled sharply.

Tingling shot up Ketchum's back and neck. If he had gone into the room he might have groped around for a light switch out of habit and blown them to kingdom come. A surge of adrenaline burned through him, like the rush at kickoff when he played running back in high school. *That low life Frank played for keeps.* "Did it look like a meth lab in there?"

"The basement has one big open area and a closet in the back. Looks like hundreds of videotapes," said the technician. He glanced at his partner. He squeezed his eyes shut and covered his mouth with his hand.

"You're safe out here," Ketchum said. "The power was shut off years ago. Even if the bomb had a battery, that's probably dead by now."

"I'm not betting my life on that," the technician said.

Ketchum retrieved his cell phone from his chest pocket and searched his directory for the number of the FBI field office in Charlotte. *Time to call in the bomb squad.*

A clap of thunder sounded. All of them jumped.

Deputy Carl patted his chest and laughed.

The male technician tugged a large bulging white Tyvek envelope from his tool kit. His eyes brimmed. "We found a bed down there, with chains on it," his voice quavered as he held out the bulging envelope, "and these."

Ketchum peered into the bag at two dusty, size five, flat pink sandals.

Terri and Blake rode on horseback along the roadway north of the Clayton Ranch. They had crossed over fields and through a forest for the best view of the Clayton Ranch in the last few hours of daylight. Warm vapor from the horses clouded up in the brisk winter air. Brittle leaves and twigs crunched under hooves. December in North Carolina was far more pleasant than in New York. It was perfect weather for gathering around a fireplace or a bonfire.

"Are we there yet?" Terri asked. She sniffled and tugged off a glove with her teeth to search her pockets for a handkerchief.

"Relax. We'll be back in plenty of time."

"I should have brought hot chocolate." She pulled a hankie from her coat pocket. She would have preferred to stay indoors to help prepare Christmas Eve dinner, but both Blake and his mother had practically ordered her out for a ride. How was she going to improve her cooking skills if she couldn't watch better cooks? Then a second thought struck her. Perhaps they had wanted her out of the kitchen because of her weak cooking skills. Though insulted, she understood. She had once baked a turkey with the plastic bag of gizzards inside. Had her father told them about the turkey incident when they were swapping stories at the wedding reception?

"We're almost there." He ducked under a low-hanging branch.

She blew her nose. She didn't have time for a cold or the flu. There were too many relatives to meet and precious little time to spend with Blake before he had to fly back to New York. He had not talked about his case at all. What she had learned about it came from the television news. According to one news service, an unnamed source confirmed the death had not been caused by the racehorse at Wallkill. Speculation grew that the death was staged to focus blame on the inmates and a feisty retired racehorse. She found it a stretch of the imagination to believe a horse would stomp a man to death in a stall. Had he threatened or spooked the horse? Only an idiot would terrify a thousand-pound animal in close quarters.

The trail opened to the bald area of a low mountain. Blake climbed off and tied off his horse to a tree branch at the base of a steep rise to a ridge. Terri eased herself to the ground. Her feet felt the frozen ground through her boots. Easing the reins over her horse's head, she tied off her horse and followed Blake uphill on foot.

She used the gouges left from Blake's boots to hike up the ridge without slipping. There she overlooked the vast Clayton Ranch valley spread out before her.

Blake pointed out the boundary markers, such as the Little Jordan River Bridge to the north, partially hidden by hundreds of bare trees. Far beyond the farmhouse, stables, and the river, mountains marked the western edge of the vast property. To the south sat Mrs. Woods' house and barn, with the Little Jordan River bisecting part of her land. The ridge they stood upon marked the eastern boundary of the ranch.

Blake then faced eastward, toward the other side of the ridge. "If you look down to the county road—" He gasped.

Terri moved next to him to see through trees down the other side of the ridge. A half a mile below, on the far side of a country road, a dozen vehicles with flashing lights surrounded a small dilapidated farm house. Two men in grey padded suits and black helmets headed into the house. Others in flak jackets stood behind the vehicles. On the back of a jacket, large yellow letters stood out. FBI.

"Looks like your neighbor's in deep trouble," she said.

Blake's cell phone chimed. He tugged off a glove, dug into his jacket pockets, and answered, "Blake here."

At arm's distance, she could not discern the content of what the caller said, but the tone came through loud and clear. Someone sounded frantic.

"Yeah. I'm looking at it now. Seven black trucks and a bomb team. The FBI is all over the old Frank place. Ketchum's there, too." Blake's voice sounded oddly emotionless. "Okay. Okay. We're heading back right away." He pocketed his phone and tugged his glove on.

"Did you say a bomb team?" Terri waited for an answer. What she got was a view of his back while he hiked down the incline toward the horses. She glanced at the crime scene and wondered what the heck would bring a bomb team, the FBI, and the sheriff to a crumbling old farmhouse on Christmas Eve. She spotted Ketchum by his dark skin and sheriff's jacket. He was facing her, but she suppressed the urge to wave. He was working on something big.

By the time Terri reached her horse, Blake and his horse had disappeared into the thicket. As soon as she and her horse reached a flat open field, she urged her mare to catch up. She caught only glimpses of Blake in full gallop a quarter of a mile ahead of her.

Thirty minutes later she handed her horse off to a stable hand. The cold no longer bothered her thanks to her fury at being abandoned. She stormed into the house in search of Blake. Five grandsons played a video game in the front room near a sixteen-foot-tall real pine tree buried under ornaments, ribbons, and lights.

"Hey, Aunt Terri! Wanna play?" asked a chubby seven-year-old whose name Terri struggled to place. *Colt? Remington? Walker? Noah or Micah?* He was Moose's oldest. In a video game, he guided a red race car through the streets of Monaco.

Maeve entered the room and passed out drinks to the boys in the room. She gave sippy cups to three-year-old Walker, and five-year-old Micah, and Moose's oldest. It seemed a mistake that the oldest boy would get a sippy cup, but the way he glared at it and then at Maeve caught Terri's attention.

The other boys pointed and laughed.

Maeve's soft voice shut down the teasing, "We do not delight in the misfortune of others. Tell Noah you're sorry."

"Sorry, Noah," the boys intoned.

Maeve carried the empty tray from the room.

Terri bent down to talk to Noah. "Have you seen Uncle Blake?"

"He's in the den with Dad and the uncles."

The man cave. Replete with shelves of books and a shocking variety of animal heads on the walls, the den practically oozed testosterone.

Noah returned his game in time to watch his car slam into a wall. "Dang it."

"And which way is the den?" Terri asked. The house had two floors and a basement, amassing five-thousand square feet of living area, excluding the full wrap-around porch. She did not want to barge into a room where other family members were bunking.

The boy smirked and set down his game controller. "I'll show you." He grabbed her by the hand and led her to the basement door. "It's down there. The second door on this side," he said gesturing with his right hand.

Terri hesitated at the top of the stairs. "What's with the sippy cup?"

Noah heaved a great sigh. "House rule. I broke a glass, so I have to use a baby cup the rest of the day."

"Good to know." Consequences lead to changes in behavior. She intended to clarify that concept to Blake. His odd behavior needed to be discussed as soon as possible.

"Are you scared?"

Noah's voice reminded her that she was still standing at the top of the stairs. "Of what?"

"The dead heads."

She pictured the moose head, the deer heads, and the bear head mounted on the walls of the man cave. She patted Noah on the shoulders. "A little, but I'll be okay. Thanks, Noah."

He blushed and then dashed back to his game.

Still in her coat, she tromped down the stairs. In her mind, she prepared what she wanted to say to Blake about ditching her. She grabbed the doorknob of door number two on the right and tried to turn the knob. It was locked. She balled up a fist and pounded on the door.

The door swung open.

Moose's glare changed to surprise. "Sorry, thought you were one of the boys. Can I help you?"

"Send Boomer out, would you?"

Moose turned his back on her. "It's Terri." He angled sideways in the doorway which provided enough room for Blake to see out.

"I'll be up for dinner later," Blake said. "Why don't you help Ma in the kitchen?"

Dumbstruck, Terri stared at him. He knew full well she couldn't boil an egg.

Moose shut the door. An unmistakable click followed.

Her pulse roared in her ears and her skin burned. They had locked her out like she was an annoying child. Terri judged the quality of the thick solid wood door that separated her from Blake. At first, she considered how much force she'd have to use to kick it open, then she closed her eyes and silently began counting to fifty. By thirty, she decided breaking the beautiful door would label her a drama queen. By the count of forty, she considered whatever caused Blake to hurry back was an emergency. With patience and self-control, she would eventually learn why he abandoned her and why the Clayton brothers decided to lock themselves away from the rest of the family on Christmas Eve. At the count of fifty, she vowed if this was a prank, then they would discover payback wore high-heels.

. 12 .

Terri hoped that Blake had a reasonable explanation and an apology for his peculiar behavior. He had come to bed long after she fell asleep and was up before she woke, so she was still waiting for a chance to talk to him through the day. He was clearly avoiding her under the pretense of helping his father with the horses. While the other women cooked and the children played, a simmering anger grew in Terri so she isolated herself in her room for most of the day.

After Christmas Eve dinner, Terri and the other Clayton wives chatted in the living room while the men cleaned up the dishes and entertained the children. Terri found herself banished from the kitchen a second time, and all her offers to help clean were denied. For the major holidays the family held fast to a "women cook, men clean" policy.

She raised her wine glass to Maeve Clayton. "I like this family tradition."

The others raised their glasses. Maeve acknowledged her own wisdom with a nod.

The doorbell chimed. Maeve smiled at Marilyn-Anne. The other wives burst into laughter.

"Oh, no. He couldn't be that stupid," Marilyn-Anne said.

"Who?" Terri asked.

Marilyn-Anne set down her wine glass. She told Terri, "Last

year, my boy Noah sneaked out to watch for Santa and locked himself out of the house."

Marilyn-Anne was married to Samuel, better known as Moose. Terri struggled to avoid thinking of her as Mrs. Moose, so she would never accidentally call her that. It had taken no small effort to learn Marilyn-Anne's real name, because the way everyone said it, the name sounded like Merlenan. Finally, Terri had asked her to write out her full name and then it became clear.

Marilyn-Anne hefted herself from the deep-cushioned sofa and headed off to the foyer. She was not a small woman. She was, as Terri once heard middle-brother Gator say, short for her weight. Terri adored Marilyn-Anne for welcoming her into the family with a hug.

Muted voices carried from the foyer to the ladies.

The lone female voice rang loud and clear. "Hate to break it to you, but this is not April Fool's Day."

That brought the women to their feet. Marilyn-Anne appeared in the doorway to the living room. Her penciled eyebrows rose to their limit and held there while she hurried to Maeve.

"Some men here are asking for Mr. Ian Clayton," she said.

"Only strangers and peddlers call him that," Maeve said on her way toward the voices.

The women found solemn-faced men and women crowded inside the double front doors. Sheriff Pete Ketchum stepped from the group, hat in hand.

"Sorry to interrupt your holiday, Mrs. Clayton," Ketchum said. "This is Special Agent Theron of the FBI. They have a warrant to search the property." He handed a paper to Mrs. Clayton.

Ketchum burned with shame. He had been the one who called

the FBI about the bomb. Seems the Feds had been looking for Curtis Frank, so they muscled into the investigation of his death. Ketchum had briefed the FBI team and when he handed over the evidence, he had to mention the glove found in the chains bore the brand mark of Clayton Ranch. He was horrified they had moved on that evidence in time to ruin Christmas Eve for the Claytons.

Maeve Clayton, the family matriarch, did not open the paper. Instead she grabbed Ketchum's forearm. She directed her words to Special Agent Theron. "My grandchildren are here. This has to be done now?"

"Yes, ma'am." Theron nodded to his team. A stout, bald man, Theron exuded authority in his bearing.

Ketchum's stomach tightened into a knot. The FBI team swarmed into the house. Mrs. Clayton was not the kind to faint or scream or create drama. Ketchum was not holding her back so much as he was holding her up. She shook while she gripped his forearm with one hand.

"I don't understand," she said, waving the warrant in the direction of the FBI officers who passed by her.

Ketchum planted his hand over Mrs. Clayton's hand. "We need to have everyone out of the house during the search."

"If they'd say what they're looking for I could help them find it," Maeve Clayton said. Speaking through her teeth, she raised the warrant and added, "Does it say in here what they want?"

"Not specifically, ma'am."

Moments later, Papa Clayton strode in from the kitchen holding his wife's coat. "The FBI wants us to wait outside. The boys are rounding up the kids. Can we bring apples?"

Apples? "Sir?" Ketchum felt a step behind Papa Clayton's plan.

Maeve Clayton addressed Ketchum. "We could tell the children we're going to give the horses a treat." She donned her coat and buttoned it up.

Ketchum followed her into the kitchen, picked up a large

basket of apples, and carried it to the front door, where he handed it to Papa Clayton.

A parade of squealing children, quiet women, and stone-faced men exited through the double front doors. Of the brothers, only Blake looked Ketchum in the eye as he passed. Ketchum sighed.

Papa Clayton held out an elbow for his wife.

"I'm glad you're here, Sheriff," said Mrs. Clayton. "We'll be in the stables."

"Thank you." Ketchum's heart sank at her kindness. He watched two FBI agents herd the family to the stables.

Theron emerged from the family room with a framed photo in his latex-gloved hand. He held it up. "Are you in this picture?"

It was a football team photo from Ketchum's freshman year. In it, Ketchum stood between Blake and Blake's brother Jeremiah. Looking up from the picture, he nodded.

Special Agent Theron lowered the picture to his side. "I'm going to lean on the side of caution and say that as a potential friend of the family, you should wait outside to secure the scene. I wouldn't want to be accused of overlooking a possible conflict of interest."

Ketchum took a slow, even breath before he spoke, "Have I done anything to suggest a conflict of interest?"

"I've already noted in my report that you and your deputies performed a thorough, professional job of investigating Curtis Frank's death." Theron tapped the picture frame against his leg. His expression softened. "If our roles were reversed, what would you do?"

His honor intact, Ketchum pivoted smartly on his heel and gently closed the double front doors behind him.

After a few moments, Theron stepped out to the porch. "Is there anything I should know about those embossed work gloves?"

Ketchum said, "Among the family and the field hands and stable hands, I'd say about five people a year earn a pair of

Clayton Ranch gloves. You might say they're a local status symbol. Most folks in town consider it an *honor* to work here."

"Did you ever work here?"

"No." Ketchum shoved his hands in his coat pockets. "I read *The Legend of Sleepy Hollow* when I was a kid. That horse scared me stupid."

Theron smirked. "We all have our monsters to deal with."

Ketchum nodded. Theron had to deal with monsters like Curtis Frank, the King of Kiddie Porn. *May Frank burn in the hottest part of hell.*

Later Christmas Eve, at the Jenkins' new home in McLean, Virginia, amid the noise of seventy people clustered in conversations, Nefi leaned into Vincent. His arm swept behind her and wrapped her shoulders. Joy bubbled up within her. It was the kind of natural gesture long-time married couples shared.

Others standing nearby acknowledged it with fleeting glances while they listened to Martina's father, Admiral Ramos, tell the story of the Christmas Truce of 1914. Though Nefi had heard him recite the story before, she enjoyed the way he told it in his rich, smooth voice. Few people studied military history with his intensity and passion.

Nefi's cell phone vibrated through the thin satin fabric of her purse against her hip. She refused to interrupt her best friend's father by answering the call. Besides, her relatives, her best friend, and her boyfriend were in the house. She decided to let the caller leave a message.

The Admiral's voice softened when he told everyone that according to soldiers' letters from both sides of the battlefield, the men joined to sing carols and trade food. If caught sharing food they could have been charged with treason.

A vibration tickled Nefi's arm. It came from inside Vincent's tuxedo jacket. Vincent traded a glance with Nefi that meant he was letting his call go to voicemail. She adored him all the more for trying to ignore the call. When the vibrations stopped, Nefi and Vincent exhaled.

Admiral Ramos wrapped up his story by saying that the war lasted until June 1919 when the Treaty of Versailles was signed. Discussion ensued about the causes of the war, so Nefi and Vincent eased away from the group. They traveled to the kitchen and then they pulled out their phones. Nefi checked hers. The last call had come from Terri, Blake's wife.

Vincent paced the kitchen while he held his phone to his ear. After a minute, he scowled at his phone and hung up. "Blake's not answering."

"Terri called me."

"Did she leave a message?"

"No."

"Maybe they wanted to wish us a Merry Christmas," Vincent said. He did not sound as if he believed it.

"Why would they call separately?" Nefi asked Vincent, who stared at his phone as if willing it to ring.

He raised his head.

Weren't they together on Christmas Eve?

Nefi and Vincent spoke simultaneously. "Something's wrong."

Nefi sent a text message to Terri. "R U OK?" She showed her phone to Vincent so he could read Terri's reply: "FBI SEARCHING HOUSE."

Vincent placed another call.

Nefi keyed in, "Y?"

Terri's reply was, "?!"

Vincent spoke into his phone. "Merry Christmas, Pete. This is Vincent Gunnerson." After a pause, he continued, "Hey, I've been trying to reach Blake, but he's not answering. Is he okay?" He scowled and squinted while Pete's muted voice sounded from his phone.

Nefi's passionate longing surged to the surface whenever she saw Vincent, which prevented her from reading his expressions clearly. She closed her eyes, but then his presence washed over her like a warm tide. When she opened her eyes, he was watching her.

Nefi's phone vibrated, indicating an incoming message that read: "GOTTA GO THEY R SEARCHING STABLES." What were they searching for? What kinds of crimes would involve horse breeders?

"I see. Uh, huh. Yeah. Yeah," Vincent said. "Sure, they have to follow the evidence...No, they don't strike me as the kind of people who hold a grudge. I got it, thanks." Vincent tucked his phone into the inner pocket of his jacket. "That was Sheriff Pete Ketchum. He said the FBI is investigating the death of a man named Curtis Frank who inherited a house near the Clayton's ranch. His bones were found on Blake's wedding day."

"Of course," Nefi said, "remember when they were cutting the cake and the sheriff's phone rang?"

Vincent shook his head and grinned. His pupils were wider than expected in the bright lights of the room. "What I remember from that day is a kiss."

Nefi fell into his embrace to refresh his memory. His full, warm lips pressed on hers and they shared a mutual awakening like inner laughter. *The happiest place in the world is in his arms.* She yearned to stay there, nourishing each other's souls.

"No way," announced a male voice from the direction of the doorway. It was Oscar, Vincent's younger brother.

Martina stood beside him, smiling. "How much do you want to bet?"

"Twenty says you're wrong," Oscar said.

Laughing, Vincent and Nefi broke away from their embrace to face the voices. Oscar in his custom-tailored tuxedo had apparently impressed Martina because she showed an easy rapport with him. She propped a hand on her hip. Her fiery red nails matched her dress and her temperament.

"I bet that right now, both of them are carrying weapons." Martina held her other hand, palm up, in front of Oscar.

"My brother's off duty, and you said yourself that Nefi's in training." Oscar put his hand on his hip. The visual effect was that of asymmetrical bookends, one tall, one short.

Because they would not leave without settling their bet, Nefi rolled her eyes and bent forward. She gathered her deep green silk dress up to her knee and reached under it to the Velcro strap on her thigh. She tore the strap loose and pulled out her taser, letting her hem fall.

Oscar's mouth fell open.

Vincent pulled up his pant leg to reveal a Beretta in his ankle holster. "I'd rather you didn't tell the world about it."

Martina eased her open hand to Oscar's chin and gently nudged upward to close his mouth. Then she tapped her open hand against his chest, prompting him to dig his wallet from the inner pocket of his tuxedo jacket.

"Is it legal to carry a taser in this state?" Oscar opened his wallet while he stared at Nefi.

Martina peeked into Oscar's hands and smiled.

"In Virginia, it's a class six felony for a felon to carry one," Nefi said, "but anyone else can. Please, don't tell Aunt Louise I have it."

"Nef, where's your hunting knife?" Martina asked.

"I left it at home," she said. To goad Oscar she added, "It didn't go with my shoes."

Oscar shook his head, plucked a twenty-dollar bill from his wallet, and placed it in Martina's open hand. Nefi turned her back on them to hike up her skirt to secure the taser back in place. Vincent's shadow fell over her.

"Need any help?" he asked. His husky baritone stirred up Nefi's fantasies.

She longed for him to touch her, but this was not the time or place for it. She slowly stood up. In her heels, she was tall enough to peer straight into his smooth-shaven chin. Her fantasies tended to begin face to face with a kiss. Vincent's full lips, the kind that Hollywood actresses got injections to achieve, beckoned her.

Oscar cleared his throat. "Let's go back to the party." He reached down, took Martina by the hand, and led her with a gentle tug into the hallway.

Nefi marveled that Martina let him lead her. Maybe Oscar was softening Martina's contrary nature. Or maybe Martina decided Nefi wanted time alone with Vincent.

Vincent lifted her hand to his lips and lightly kissed the back of her hand. "We should rejoin the crowd."

The heat from his lips told her that he, too, fought temptation. She ached for him.

"Let's not mention the search to anyone," Vincent said.

Nefi nodded. What an awful thing to happen on Christmas Eve. The ranch employed many workers. Maybe one of them had a criminal background and it would be just like the Claytons to give someone a fresh start or second chance.

An FBI raid was not the traditional visit to mark Christmas Eve, but that was how Terri would remember her first Christmas at Clayton Ranch.

The FBI team had left with computers, work gloves, and employee files after their three-hour search.

She pried off her boots then dropped them at the end of the bed. Blake had stripped down to his t-shirt and jockeys on the other side of the bed. Though still upset about being abandoned on their afternoon horseback ride, Terri fumed over more urgent events. She needed to confront Blake to get answers. He knew more than he had shared with her. What was in the warrant and why the blazes had the FBI searched the ranch?

At midnight, sleigh bells sounded on the roof of the Clayton mansion.

"Papa rigged the bells for the grandkids," Blake said. He pulled back the thick down duvet and sheet on his side of the bed.

Hungry, cold, and tired, she had endured a lousy evening with no explanation. Blaming the FBI did not resolve her feelings. "You know why the FBI was here, don't you?"

"Yes." He slumped down on the bed, sitting with his back to her.

"Are you going to tell me, or do I need to resort to Ketamine?" As a veterinarian, she kept the drug on hand for anesthetizing animals. On humans it had the same effect as a truth serum with the added benefit of short-term amnesia. She could get her answers, and he would not remember the interrogation.

He twisted around to face her. He repeatedly blinked as if his brain tried to assess the threat. She hoped he would not call her bluff. Her request for the truth was reasonable, because if the family was in trouble it would affect her life, too. A marriage had to be built on trust. This was a moment of testing.

"The FBI is investigating bones found down river. They belong to a criminal who was involved in prostitution."

Terri sucked air. "Did he live in that abandoned house on the other side of the ridge?"

Blake nodded.

Terri dreaded asking her next question as much as she dreaded receiving an answer. This was more than morbid curiosity. She had to know. He and his brothers had been wild in their high school years, but how wild? Should she get tested for sexually transmitted diseases? "Did you ever use his...services?"

"I'm insulted you think I would."

Relief washed over her. "Well, somehow the FBI found a connection between your family and that—"

"It's not like they're going to tell me about their investigation."

If the FBI suspected an employee, they would have searched the stables first. They were focused on the house. Maeve and Papa were the salt of the earth, Christians to the core. Terri couldn't imagine them breaking any commandments. The Clayton sons however were younger and wilder a decade ago. How wild?

Moose, the oldest brother, was the responsible one, the one being groomed to take over the family business. Bubba was the family accountant and, in Terri's opinion, the least handsome of the brothers. Gator was the best looking and full of charisma. Butch, the second youngest, was a minister.

"Did one of your brothers use his services?"

"No." Blake climbed into bed and pulled the sheet and cover up to his waist. "I don't know what the FBI has or what they're looking for. I read the warrant, but it was vague." His voice was tinged with anger.

Terri nodded and brought her nightgown into the bathroom. Behind the closed door, she changed into her gown. To obtain a warrant, the FBI had to prove to a judge that they had a valid reason to search. Whatever led them to search the Clayton home put the whole family under suspicion. Anger crept in to replace her frustration. Something connected the dead man to the Claytons. She ran water in the sink to cover the sound as she wept.

She gasped for air. Did she see only what she wanted to see in the Claytons because she loved Blake? The Claytons were not perfect people simply because she wanted them to be. *Everyone makes mistakes. Everyone has a dark side to either subdue or hide.*

She understood her own dark side. It showed up in full force the day she found a farm where four horses had been beaten and starved so badly she had to put three of them down. She did not earn her veterinarian license to shoot horses. As she reloaded her shotgun, she told herself she was only going to wound the owner, but he had probably read the intention in her eyes because he ran out toward the sheriff to turn himself in.

She couldn't imagine the Claytons involved with a criminal. Papa Clayton's offhand joke at the wedding about the family being in the sex trade meant horse breeding.

She washed her face with cool water and toweled off. Maybe the family had an explanation. For all she knew, the FBI might have searched all the surrounding homes.

Fifty-two-year-old, "Sweet" Sally Marie Henson idled in Florida's Polk County lockup awaiting her second hearing on fraud and drug charges when she saw the news of an old lover's death on the news. She immediately told the guard she needed to make a phone call. The guard checked the schedule and found Sally was eligible for a call. Escorted from guard to guard, Sally soon arrived in the phone room.

With the state footing the bill, she placed her call. She had served time in Florida long ago on assault. Combined with another stint in Ohio for fraud, she faced trial this time as a repeat offender. Her attorney, a public defender, had told her he would do his best, but he had not sounded convincing.

"Who's this?" her attorney asked.

"Your client. Sally Henson."

"Oh."

"Have you heard about the murder in North Carolina? A man named Curtis Frank?"

"Yes."

"I have information about that murder. If I talk to the police up there, will they help me out with my charges?"

"What kind of information do you have?"

"I know who killed him."

"Is this a confession?"

"No!"

"And what do you want me to do?"

"Call the police in North Carolina. Bargain with them."

"I suppose your information might be worth something. If they ask for proof, what can I tell them?"

Sally hesitated to trust him because there might be a reward. She gave him enough information to show she knew more than the news said. "He was kidnapped by five guys around Halloween in nineteen ninety-four."

"Is this something you heard about?" He sounded like he doubted her. He'd probably been played before.

"I was there."

"Why didn't you come forward sooner?"

"I didn't know they was gonna kill him. Hell, they looked like high school boys."

"All right. I'll call the sheriff up there."

She would tell the sheriff what's what. *Ha! Curtis finally got me a Christmas present—a chance to beat the system.*

. 13 .

Dawn struck the field in front of the Clayton house transforming dew into a sparkling sea of diamonds. Blake paused over his coffee to admire the view from the front porch. He had put his sleeplessness to work by feeding the horses before the rest of the family woke up on the last day of the year. The mares were happier to see him than Terri was.

His phone buzzed in his pocket. The small screen showed the caller's phone number. Blake did not recognize it. He set his coffee on the porch railing. "Blake here."

"Hey, Boomer. Are you at the house?" Ketchum said, his voice rough.

"Yeah, come on by, Pete." Blake leaned on the thick wooden handrail. "Moose has his usual stash of fireworks for tonight."

"I'm calling from a payphone." Ketchum cleared his throat.

"I didn't know the town still had one."

"Did you kill Curtis Frank?"

Though it stung, it was a fair question. "No."

"That's all I need to know." The line went dead.

Blake's knees shook so hard he had to settle into a big rocker to keep from falling. His heart hammered while he sucked cool morning air. Pete's call sounded like a goodbye. Pete knew something he couldn't say without compromising his own integrity and he called from a payphone. It was a warning.

He fumbled his cell phone and dialed a friend in town.

"Casey's, how can I help you?"

"Hey, is the FBI group there by any chance?"

"Yup. Heavy on the caffeine like we used to get before a big game."

"Thanks, man. Don't mention my call." Blake disconnected the call. The nearest FBI field office was in Charlotte an hour away. They were back for a bad reason.

He stood and reached for the last of his coffee, but his hand trembled and the cup fell off the railing, bounced off an azalea bush and struck the concrete walkway.

"Sorry, momma."

The time had come to set his doomsday plan in motion.

He called Moose's cell phone. "Get dressed. I believe we're about to get another visit from the FBI." He forced himself to take deep breaths to tamp down panic. After his heart rate slowed slightly he called his boss, Chief Watson.

"Hello?"

"Chief, this is Blake Clayton." His throat constricted.

"This is the second call this morning about you."

"I'm so sorry, sir." He coughed to clear his throat. "I'm in trouble and I don't want to bring any dishonor to the FBI, so please accept this call as my resignation."

"I can put you on suspension until this—"

"Please, sir, accept my resignation." The silence that followed made Blake wonder if the call had been dropped or disconnected.

"If that's what you want."

"Thank you, sir. It's been an honor to work with you." Blake hung up. He would call his attorney when the time came. He did not have enough time to say goodbye to Terri, so he quickly texted a message. The moment after he sent it, he deleted it from his phone and cleared the phone log and the folders of his messages. If anyone wanted to read his messages they were going to have to work at it harder than merely reading them off his phone. *Any delay might help.*

He brushed straw off his khakis and his green polo shirt. At least he was presentable if today was the day he and his brothers would be arrested.

One by one his brothers stepped through the front door. Bubba sat on the steps to put on his cowboy boots. Moose handed Blake a thick shearling duster coat. Gator ran his fingers through his hair, but it did little to improve his appearance. His beard stubble showed. Just like a minister, Butch had taken the time to shave and put on a dress shirt and slacks. Together they descended the front porch steps toward the front gate to distance themselves from the house, from their wives, and from their children. They were almost to the front gate when flashing lights and a dust cloud down the road signaled it was time to face the past.

Blake gazed back at the house. The field that had sparkled with beauty and promise earlier now appeared as wet dead grass. The scent of manure carried uphill, reminding him he was deep in it.

Butch muttered under his breath, "Who's got a phone?"

Blake handed over his.

Butch pressed the keys rapidly. Moments later he said, "Hey, sorry for the early call. You're now the head pastor. Yes, as of this minute, you understand? I resign. This is not up for discussion. Believe me, you'll understand by the end of the day. I'm sorry to drop this on you, but whatever happens, don't let this change your faith in God." He disconnected the call while flashing lights raced silently toward the front gate. He handed the phone back to Blake.

Blake pocketed it. He counted three vehicles. The first was a sheriff's cruiser and the others were black SUVs. Blake considered it classy Ketchum did not wake the countryside with sirens. *Very classy.* He sighed. Three vehicles would do just fine. Packing the five of them in a cruiser would resemble a clown act because they were not five average-sized guys. When the convoy stopped, Special Agent Theron climbed out of the first of two large black Escalades. Men in dark suits rushed from the trucks toward the Clayton brothers. Blake mourned the fact his first arrest since joining the FBI would not be as an agent, but as a suspect. Shame burned deep.

Ketchum hopped out of his cruiser and held his hands up to block the FBI agents. "I appreciate the assistance, but I don't expect trouble. Please, let me handle this."

Theron said, "It's your collar." He nodded to the other agents. They solemnly formed a line behind Ketchum.

Ketchum tugged his handcuffs from his back pocket and held them between his hands in front. He cleared his throat, but still his voice broke. "Elijah Blake Clayton, you are under arrest and being charged with the kidnapping of Curtis Frank."

The words 'under arrest' echoed in his head like the starting bell of a prize fight. With no way to un-ring that bell, Blake felt his friend's declaration in his chest like a punch even though he had expected to be arrested. Was it better or worse to be arrested by a friend than by strangers? Ketchum appeared stoic. He had to perform his duty whether or not he liked it or agreed with it. *Why a kidnapping charge?* Blake put his hands on the back of his head.

The other brothers stepped forward.

"Don't make this worse," FBI Special Agent Theron warned. He held up an open hand at Moose, who was closest to him.

Moose raised his hands and placed them on the top of his head. Bubba, Gator, and Butch copied him. Moose and Theron glared at each other. Moose had a notable height and size advantage over Theron, but Theron and his men didn't back down.

Ketchum said, "Please, step back."

Moose took one step back. The brothers turned toward Blake. They had all expected to be arrested. *What's going on?*

"I'm not resisting," Moose said softly.

"You are obstructing," Theron said.

Ketchum stepped to face Theron. "Please, step back."

Moose gave Blake his *huh?* expression. These FBI agents did not know Blake or the family. They might see belligerence instead of honor.

Theron raised his eyebrows and clamped his jaw. He took a step backward.

Ketchum eased Blake around to face his brothers while he handcuffed Blake's hands behind his back. Ketchum then guided Blake to the back of the cruiser where he thoroughly patted him down. After plucking Blake's phone from a pocket, he nudged him toward the open back door.

The FBI agents walked backwards to their vehicles as if they expected to get jumped. At that moment, Blake realized he was the only one being arrested.

From the back seat, Blake called out to Moose, "Tell Pa I'm sorry."

Ketchum's hands shook while he secured Blake's seatbelt. He whispered, "I'm taking you to Asheville."

The brothers lowered their hands and stared open-mouthed. They appeared as confused as Blake felt. Was this a divide-and-conquer strategy by the District Attorney? Sweat trickled down his back. Weeks ago, Blake and his brothers had arranged for lawyers. Blake had warned them repeatedly not to speak without a lawyer present. Sometimes a skilled interrogation starts out like an idle conversation.

Theron stood behind Ketchum to address Blake through the open car door. "Looks like you were expecting us."

Ketchum grimaced and then backed out of the doorway, causing Theron to step aside.

Blake refused to allow Theron to question his friend's professionalism. "No one's invisible in a small town." Just to prove his point he decided to recite the Tuesday special. "I'll bet you had three scrambled eggs, cheesy hash brown casserole, wheat toast and hickory smoked bacon this morning at Casey's Diner."

Theron's eyes widened then narrowed. Blake guessed Theron was a city kid, born and bred, so he probably reasoned like one. He worked in Atlanta, where more than one restaurant served breakfast. Blake considered this a lesson to Theron on small town life. The Special Agent grunted and headed back to his sleek, black big-city Escalade.

Ketchum closed the door. After he had buckled himself in, he said, "It was their idea to come along to protect me."

"They don't know us."

"No, they don't."

No one spoke for the rest of the ride to Asheville. The only sound that disturbed the mournful quiet of the ride was the incessant ringing of Blake's phone.

Terri paced the front room until her third call to Blake went to voicemail. Maybe he was mucking stalls or couldn't hear his phone. Something had happened while she was in the shower. Blake had left a peculiar text message, and his parents were in their bedroom talking with Moose. It sounded like Maeve was crying. Had there been a death in the family?

She entered the massive kitchen where Marilyn-Anne was banging pots and pans on the stove. Bacon sputtered and coffee percolated, filling the room with aromas. Noah and Micah carried their dishes across the kitchen and quietly set them on the counter by the double sink.

Noah stepped up beside his mother. "Why is grandma crying?"

Marilyn-Anne rested her hand on his shoulder, then she

regarded Terri. "Go on upstairs and play. Daddy and I will tell you later."

"Is grandma hurt?" His stricken expression jabbed Terri's heart.

"She's just upset. Now take your brother upstairs."

He buried his face in her hip and wrapped his arms as far as he could reach around her. His muffled "Okay" sounded weary. He released his mother and took his brother by the hand from the room. On his way from the room he glanced up. "Morning, Aunt Terri."

"Good morning, Noah and Micah." Terri trod across the tile floor toward Marilyn-Anne.

Marilyn-Anne turned off the burners, moved pots and pans, and wiped her hands on a kitchen towel. Tears welled in her eyes.

Blake's brothers—Bubba, Gator, and Butch—entered the kitchen and stopped short as if surprised. Maeve was usually preparing breakfast, but was it such a shock to see Marilyn-Anne near the stove? The atmosphere in the room was as taut as a violin string. What was going on?

Marilyn-Anne gripped Terri's elbow and steered her toward the breakfast table. "Come sit with me."

"Has someone died?" She searched Marilyn-Anne's face for answers.

Marilyn-Anne's brown eyes brimmed over. She shook her head. "There's no gentle way to say this. The FBI and the sheriff came again this morning."

The coffee pot stopped percolating. Terri gulped air. She had not heard any disruption in the house. Even the children were quiet all morning. Terri had assumed they were sleeping in.

"They arrested Blake for kidnapping." Marilyn-Anne was too distraught to be faking it. This wasn't a prank.

"What? Why?" Terri sank into the nearest chair. This had to be a monstrous mistake. Blake worked for the FBI. Kidnapping? *No.*

Large hands warmed her back. The brothers had gathered

behind her to comfort her. Marilyn-Anne stared at her apron. Tears plopped into her lap.

There are times in life when breathing doesn't come naturally, such as at high altitudes or when running, and one must breathe by force of will. This was one of those times. The air felt thin and insubstantial as if even deep breaths didn't draw in enough oxygen. After a few deep inhalations and exhalations, a thought formed into sound from Terri's mouth.

"I need to hire an attorney."

"He already has one," said Butch, better known to his congregation as Jeremiah Clayton. He knelt beside her. "Would you like us to pray with you?"

She spoke through clenched teeth, "I'd like you to tell me what's going on."

Butch pursed his lips and bowed his head. "I'm so sorry. On the advice of my attorney I can't discuss anything about it."

"None of us can." Gator, also known as Gideon, sank into a chair across the table from Terri. His eyes were bloodshot. "I wish we could."

"The fact that you all have attorneys tells me enough." With that she rose and left the kitchen on wobbly legs and climbed the stairs to her room. She shut the door, and then tossed her suitcase on the bed. There was no point in staying if no one would speak to her about the only thing she wanted to discuss.

Blake stared at his fingers. The FBI used glass-topped devices to read fingerprints instead of the old-school ink and paper method. The thin bare mattress did little to soften the underlying metal grate bed bolted to the wall. As the shock of being processed as a criminal wore off, he noticed his cell did not have a sink. Alone in a two-man cell, he wore a large loose orange jumpsuit, slip-on shoes, no wedding ring, no socks, and no underwear. He understood the reasoning behind placing him in a cell alone. It was disruptive and hazardous to mix hardened criminals with law enforcement officers. Even ex-law enforcement.

If he wasn't going to stay long enough to need sheets or a blanket, fine, but the county should have given him underwear and socks.

A burly correctional officer paced the hall and stopped at the barred doorway wall of Blake's cell. "We'll be bringing your meals to you."

"I understand."

The man stepped closer to the bars. "Do you understand that you won't be given silverware and that someone will stand by to watch you eat?"

"Someone's gonna watch me eat without silverware? Sounds entertaining. What's the matter, no cable television in here?"

The officer grunted. "Something like that." A commotion down the hall attracted his attention for a moment. "Do you have friends and family outside?"

"I do."

"Behave and you might be out by tomorrow, maybe the day after."

Blake combed his fingers through his hair. Just being in the cell made him feel grimy and guilty. "That's a happy thought."

"Hold onto it." The correctional officer then headed in the direction of the commotion.

Blake had another question to ask. *So much for my keen observations skills, I didn't read his name tag.* "Hey, Officer Sunshine."

The officer stepped back into view. His attention remained down the corridor toward rising voices.

"Is the state too broke to offer underwear, or socks, or sheets?" Blake asked.

"No." The officer moved toward scuffling sounds.

"Then why single me out?"

The officer's voice carried down the corridor. "Your attorney demanded you be put on suicide watch."

Blake slouched to his mattress.

Laden with an overnight bag and crushing desperation, Terri Pinehurst-Clayton had caught the last commercial flight of the year from Charlotte, North Carolina, to LaGuardia. The cab ride into Manhattan featured a mix of rain and snow, turning everything shades of dirty gray. The city resembled her situation—bleak.

She could not pretend she was simply dropping in, but she was afraid to call ahead. Maybe Blake's friend would not want to be seen with the wife of a man charged with a felony. Maybe he would turn her away. She had to risk it. She had to do something more useful than crying like a girl. The only help her parents offered was consolations. She had to do something to fight this nightmare. Crying did not change the situation.

Crying reminded her of Nefi, the young woman she met in the bathroom at the Plaza. Her advice then to the tearful Nefi was— you can hide from the world or you can master your feelings and deal with it. *Time to take my own advice.*

After the cab slid into the curb at a row of brownstones, the cabbie gallantly slogged through the cold to retrieve an overnight suitcase from the trunk and to open the cab's back door. Freed from the cab's stench of wet dog, Terri climbed out into the freezing rain and handed a fifty-dollar bill to the driver.

He pulled off a glove with his teeth and dug into his coat pocket.

"Keep it."

"Happy New Year, lady."

Maybe next year. At the moment, happy existed in another dimension. Terri sighed while she wheeled her suitcase up the steps to the door. The cab departed, spraying water onto the sidewalk and parked cars. She prepared to beg.

Odors of wet garbage rose from black plastic bags piled three deep on the sidewalk. The doorbell glowed below a sign declaring in one-inch letters 'No Soliciting.'

Undeterred, Terri pressed the button. Moments later the door flung open, revealing Quinn Flanagan in black jeans and a green Fighting Irish sweatshirt. Retirement suited him.

"You probably have plans for New Year's Eve, so I won't be long, but I need to talk to someone who can give me useful advice. Blake's been arrested for kidnapping." Terri choked back the urge to cry. With the cabbie gone, she had no alternate plan if Quinn Flanagan refused to see her.

"Come in out of the cold," Quinn said.

She stepped through the doorway and hugged him hard. He patted her back. Awash with hope, she rolled her carry-on suitcase behind while she followed him to the warm, dry, cozy living room. "I came straight from LaGuardia."

Inside she was greeted with hugs from Quinn's wife Kate. Her heart swelled at their kindness.

"Take off your coat," Kate said. Petite, red-headed and rosy-cheeked, Kate was as Irish as a leprechaun.

Vincent, Blake's best friend and former FBI partner, stepped out of the shadows of the kitchen. Why was Vincent here? Had she interrupted a party?

After Terri handed her coat to Kate, she noticed a whiteboard and papers in the living room with Blake's name on them. Her throat tightened up, wringing tears from her. *Such loyal friends.* They had known him longer, so their actions filled her with hope.

"You believe Blake's innocent?"

Quinn said, "Well, now proving innocence is like proving virginity."

"Quinn!" Kate scolded.

"The point is, we aim to help him." Quinn hung Terri's coat on a peg in the hall.

"Let me get you something warm," Kate offered, "Cocoa, tea or coffee?"

Terri rubbed away tears. They had not asked if Blake was guilty. Even if they had, Terri didn't know the answer. She had been unable to speak to Blake since his arrest. She didn't even know his attorney's name. For the first time since his arrest, she glimpsed hope. His friends were taking action. "Do you have something stronger?"

"A hot toddy it is." Kate disappeared through a doorway.

"Where's Blake now?" Vincent asked.

"He's in jail pending a bond hearing. He refuses to talk to anyone but his lawyer." Terri's throat tightened at the thought of being shut out.

Quinn nudged Terri into a roomy recliner. "Tell us everything you know."

Between sips of the hot toddy she relayed all the information she had on the bones found in the river, Curtis Frank's house, Blake's statement about Frank running a prostitution business from the house, Blake's secrecy, and the FBI raid on the Clayton Ranch. Vincent took notes. Quinn nodded. Kate handed her an embroidered linen handkerchief that seemed far too lovely to use. Terri was more comfortable talking to Blake's friends than his family because his friends approached the discussion with experience instead of emotion. Vincent jotted the time of the raid on the Frank house on the whiteboard under the heading *Timeline*.

"Oh, and the morning he was arrested he sent me a text message." Terri recited it from memory. "Ask Aunt Dottie about Carrie Ann."

Three faces aimed at her as if they were waiting for the rest of the message.

"That's it. I don't know what it means," Terri said. "I checked the guest list twice. No Carrie Ann. The closest thing to Dottie is Dorothy Clayton, but she was a no-show at the wedding."

"Where does Dorothy live?" Quinn asked.

Terri wrestled the guest list from her suitcase and found Dottie on page two. She read the address in Ocala, Florida aloud.

"Must be Ian's sister," Vincent said. "I heard the brothers asking about her. Moose's wife—Marion? Maryanne?—she called her a black sheep."

"Who would name a child Moose?" Kate asked.

Terri smirked. "His Christian name is Samuel. He's the oldest brother. He manages the ranch under Papa's supervision." She toyed with the warm mug. Was Samuel the natural leader among the brothers, too? Perhaps he had led Blake into a terrible crime. Surely Blake would not have done anything without his brothers at that age.

Vincent added Dorothy Clayton's information to the whiteboard. On it was a timeline that began on 2-12-1994.

"What happened on February twelfth?" Terri asked.

Vincent said, "Curtis Frank was released from prison in Ohio."

"Honestly, this is so absurd. Blake was a freshman in high school in nineteen ninety-four." Terri rubbed her fingertips against the grooved surface of the ceramic mug. "Blake was too young to kidnap someone. Besides, why would he?"

"That's a good question," Vincent said.

"I doubt Blake acted alone," Quinn said. "Frank stood five seven and weighed two-fifty when he left prison."

"Then why didn't they arrest anyone else?" Terri asked.

Quinn said, "They follow the evidence. Apparently the evidence connects to Blake."

Terri set her empty mug on the doily covered end table beside her recliner. *But Blake is one of the good guys.* Hope remained just beyond reach, slipping off the edge of her fingertips.

She asked, "Isn't there a statute of limitations on kidnapping?"

"Not in North Carolina," Vincent said, "And not when death is involved."

Terri had vowed to love Blake through better or worse. Clearly, having her lawman husband arrested for kidnapping represented the 'worse' part. It could get much worse. What if he was convicted? *No. No. Think positive.* How long could his sentence be? "Well, thank God they didn't arrest him for murder."

Vincent and Flanagan exchanged a solemn look.

Gnawing dread held Terri's heart in its teeth. "Do you think they might add that charge?"

Flanagan placed his hands on his knees. "I believe they charged him with kidnapping because they have evidence to support that charge in court."

Flanagan and Vincent exchanged glances as if in a silent debate. Were they trying to decide whether or not to trust her with something? Did they suspect he was guilty?

Vincent said, "She needs to know."

Flanagan nodded. "Don't suppose you've heard of the Felony Murder Rule?"

Murder. There it was roaring back into the room where no one wanted it. Terri's heart galloped. "No." And she did not want to hear about it. *Not at all.*

"Most states, like North Carolina, have this rule."

"What is it?" Terri asked. She would have preferred having a root canal over having to associate the word murder with her husband, but the situation did not allow a choice.

"Let's say Vincent and I hold up a liquor store in Charlotte," Flanagan supposed.

"Okay." She could handle a hypothetical case. But what did this have to do with Blake?

"The store owner shoots me dead, and Vincent gets arrested for the robbery. Because Vincent committed a felony and someone died, my death is charged to him as a murder."

What? She replayed his words in her head, yet they still did not make sense. Her throat tightened with panic, constricting her voice into a childish whine. "But the store owner killed you."

Flanagan and Vincent nodded. They watched her as the truth sank in.

Like Alice down the rabbit hole, Terri felt herself freefalling in darkness. Her life had become surreal. Nothing made sense in this alternate reality where her beloved husband faced going to prison. He could also be held responsible for murder whether he did it or not? How was that possible? She took a deep breath and voiced her deepest fear. "What kind of sentence could he get if...if convicted?"

Flanagan's low voice rolled across the room. "The death penalty."

. 14 .

Blake was released on bail at noon January 2nd to find his oldest brother pacing on the curb outside the jail. Moose met him with a quick backslapping hug.

"Let's get out of here," Moose said.

He led the way through the sad-faced crowd of strangers waiting for their wayward children and friends to be processed out of jail. Smoke clouded above the ill-dressed, barely sober mob of regulars. Blake wanted to bathe in industrial cleaner to scrub off the stench of jail. Even back in his own clothes, he felt filthy as if his stained reputation was freshly tattooed on his skin for all to see.

"You a lawyer?" a gap-toothed woman asked. She leered at Blake.

"No, ma'am." His khakis and polo shirt were formal wear in this crowd.

She elbowed the older woman beside her. "Wonder what he done to get arrested."

An unkempt, scrawny, fidgeting man pointed to his newspaper. "Kidnapping says here." He waved the paper that featured a large photo of Blake under the heading ACCUSED KIDNAPPER FORMER FBI AGENT.

As the group of strangers gathered around the front page, Moose grabbed Blake by the elbow and pulled him toward the parking lot. Blake's whole body burned with shame on the long walk to a dull brown SUV.

"It's a rental." Moose unlocked the doors with a key fob and climbed into the driver's side. "Didn't want to bring anything with the ranch logo on it."

Moose's comment stung as much as the front page story. They had reached the halfway point on the ride home before either of them spoke again.

"I know we agreed not to talk to anyone but our lawyers, but I need to tell Terri," Blake said.

Moose did not reply. Had Moose already told Terri the whole story? Or was he going to explain how blood was thicker than water? Terri was family now. After giving Moose five minutes to brood, an odd tingling crept up Blake's spine. *What now?*

Moose adjusted his grip on the steering wheel while he stared ahead as if the traffic veering around a semi-truck fascinated him.

"What now?" Blake focused on staying calm.

"She packed up and left right after your arrest."

Moose's comment felt like ice water poured on his heart. Blake checked his cell phone. The battery was dead. "Give me your phone."

Moose pulled a small cell phone from his chest pocket and held it out for Blake. "She hasn't answered my calls, or Mama's. She got spooky quiet after we told her we couldn't talk to her because our attorneys said so."

Blake's body sagged. He took the phone from Moose's hand. He called and after six agonizing rings, he left a message on Terri's phone to please call him back. He couldn't blame her for going home to be with family. It was what he wanted to do. The SUV raced down a steep hill. The highway hugged the curve of a foothill with semi-trucks on the inner lane and cars on the outside two lanes. Next, he dialed the number to Terri's parents. A male voice answered on the first ring.

"Hello?"

"It's me, Blake. I'm looking for Terri."

"What?" Doctor Pinehurst, retired veterinarian and Army veteran shouted. His voice lowered to a dangerous whisper, "You've been arrested for kidnapping and now you say my daughter has disappeared?"

"My brother said she left a couple of days ago."

"Well, she's not here."

Did she go to a friend's house? Reva, Arlene, or Suki? "Please tell her I called."

After a few moments of silence, Blake glanced at the phone. The call had been disconnected. Had he lost service in the mountains, or had Terri's father hung up? He didn't have the nerve or a reason to call back.

Where did she go?

On Monday, January 4th, 2010, Sheriff Ketchum arrived at his office at eight and headed straight to the conference room the FBI team had commandeered for their investigation. He nodded at Carl, the deputy on night duty, on his way through the office. The room reeked of coffee and stale pizza. Five tables, set up like workstations to process evidence, filled the room. Boxes of evidence sat unattended at each station. Ketchum's heart rate accelerated. *Who left the room unlocked?* A headset dangled from its cord off the table in front of a laptop. An overturned chair sat on its backrest nearby.

Ketchum righted the chair.

The door to the conference room swung open and Special Agent Theron, in charge of the FBI team, entered carrying a trash can.

What if I had been so careless with evidence? "The evidence was left in an unlocked room." Ketchum put his hands in his pants pockets.

"I was gone two minutes tops," Theron said. He ran his hand over his beard stubble. "Besides, your night officer was here."

"What's this stuff?" Ketchum pointed to a stack of DVDs.

"The DC lab converted the brittle video tapes to DVDs. They came in last night by courier."

"Were you here all night?" Ketchum pulled up a chair.

Theron nodded, stepped into the room, and dropped into the nearest chair. His head bobbed. "I'm glad I never had kids." He appeared wrung out, pale and tired. "The others gave me the hardcore stuff because they couldn't bear to watch them." He planted the empty trash can on the floor by his chair.

Ketchum glanced down at the trash can. He didn't want to ask if the recordings had sickened Theron to the point of puking though he understood the reaction.

Theron nudged the can back under the desk with his shoe. "I took the pizza boxes to the dumpster. Last year we were staked out in Florida and the leftovers attracted roaches. Mutant roaches big enough to set off mousetraps."

Though Theron did not talk about his private life at work, Ketchum had done a little research and learned that Theron had come from a Midwestern family, the youngest of seven children. Now in his forties, he probably had nieces and nephews.

Ketchum crossed his arms. *Kiddie porn is the worst.* "Did you identify any of the subjects?"

Theron hauled himself up and plodded to his workstation. He shuffled through a stack of papers, plucking a few pages as he went. He carried them back to Ketchum.

Twelve children's faces, some smiling, stared up at him from missing person's file sheets. Ketchum scanned them. *Ohio. Wisconsin. Kentucky. A five-year-old from Kansas.* Ketchum's breakfast threatened to rise. If Theron identified these missing children, then they had been in the hardcore films.

Ketchum shuddered. "Those poor kids."

"One is out of her misery." Theron's words echoed in his haunted eyes.

A chill raced through Ketchum. Though he preferred to imagine that filming murders was a matter of urban legend, he acknowledged that evil knew no boundaries. *But children?* "Are you saying you found a snuff film?"

Theron closed his eyes and nodded. "One. Might have been accidental...hard to tell. I labeled each DVD with a copy of the kid's printout. I matched the recordings with the ID photos using the facial recognition program. The murdered girl's DVD and papers are on the top."

Ketchum clenched his teeth. His heart sank at the concept of a child being tortured and killed for entertainment. He prayed he never became numb to such evil. *Curtis Frank and his kind were monsters. Monsters!* Good people doubted the climbing number of sociopaths in modern society, but these vile creatures moved around in human form. In Ketchum's experience, the evidence from the Frank House struck a horrifying low in the depths of human depravity.

Theron smoothed down the front of his shirt. "I didn't use to believe in the death penalty. Now? I think torture would be justice for the animals who made these recordings." His hands clenched into fists and his eyes narrowed. "And those who watch them."

Ketchum understood the temptation to be judge and executioner. He had to pull Theron back over the line. "You watched them."

Theron snorted. His eyes had dark circles. "I would welcome a head injury to get those images out of my brain."

"For what it's worth, this work matters. Even ugly evidence matters," Ketchum said.

Theron selected the recordings wrapped in missing children's info sheets and handed them to Ketchum, "I made these copies for notification processing."

"Do you want me to do the notifications?" Ketchum sorted through them with a growing sense of dread.

Theron shook his head.

On top of the stack, a young girl's face stared back at Ketchum. Brown hair and freckles, Samantha represented the wholesomeness of the girl next door. She disappeared at age fourteen from a town in Ohio Ketchum had never heard of. He pitied the person who had to decide how to notify the next of kin. Was a videotape record enough to warrant notification? What if the families wanted proof of death? He shook off a chill. *No. No. No way.* He handed the papers and DVDs back to Theron.

Other agents arrived, so Theron briefed them on his findings. When he explained that the FBI would hand off the information on the missing children to another task force, Ketchum nodded. Theron would pass those DVDs back to the FBI chain of command for others to agonize over. The FBI had the national reach to handle the further investigation.

The flimsy recordings weighed heavily on Ketchum. Each one represented a childhood destroyed, a family's tragedy, and a dreadful, pre-meditated crime. When Theron announced that he would personally notify the family of the dead girl, Ketchum silently thanked God. No one wanted to deliver such news, to cut the final thread of hope to parents, but Theron's compassion could soften the horror. Ketchum prayed that the family would find peace in closure.

Ketchum learned in his research that Theron had worked for twenty years on the human trafficking task force. The FBI had lost track of Frank two weeks after he left prison in Ohio. "If we had found Curtis Frank in time," Theron once said, "the bastard probably would have named his contacts rather than return to prison."

But no. Frank ended up in chains in a river. *What had happened in that farmhouse?* Ketchum wanted to wash the taste of bile away with a coffee.

As the other FBI agents conversed over coffee, Theron asked no one in particular, "How did high school boys get the jump on a hardened felon like Frank?"

They all knew Blake could not have acted on his own, but the evidence tied Blake and Blake alone to the body in chains. Ketchum shrugged.

Parking himself in his chair, Theron shook his head. "The only suspect tied to Frank by evidence is a fresh-from-training FBI agent, and he isn't talking. The only theory I can come up with is that the boys turned vigilante. But why didn't they just call the police?"

Ketchum felt less and less convinced that *anyone* should go to prison over the death of that monster, but he had to follow the law and leave judgment up to God. The coroner's comments about Frank's death being a public service felt truer with each new piece of evidence from the house and Frank's life.

***

Later on January 4th, Terri drove her rented Ford Escape while Quinn Flanagan wrestled with a Florida state map. Determined to learn everything she could get from Dorothy Clayton about the mysterious Carrie Ann, Terri was a woman on a mission. Since Carrie Ann was the only tidbit of information Blake had given her, she knew it had to be important. The trip from Orlando airport, to the Florida Turnpike, to North I-75, to Ocala had taken an hour and a half. It took another half an hour to navigate the unmarked rural dirt roads to find Dottie Clayton's property. The GPS had been useless since Ocala. Terri eventually identified the address by a tall ironwork arched gateway because it resembled the gateway at Clayton Ranch. This one read *Dottie's Place*.

Terri drove up to the locked, motor-driven gate and pressed a button on the keypad. It seemed a bit odd to have such security for a horse ranch, but perhaps Dottie lived alone. They had passed a prison on their way to town.

A woman's voice blared from the keypad's speaker. "I shoot salesman and trespassers."

"This is Terri Pinehurst-Clayton. I'm sorry, but I don't have your phone number."

After a gasp, a voice said, "Are you Blake's wife?"

"Yes."

"My number's unlisted. Follow the drive to the house. I'll be right there."

The gate lurched and rolled open, so Terri drove under the archway and over the cattle grate down the quarter-mile-long driveway. They passed an oblong training track and a field of grazing thoroughbreds to a Mediterranean-style cement block house with a clay barrel tile roof, Doric columns, and large windows. Ocala was the winter training ground for race horses. The odors from the stables confirmed they were well used.

Terri had barely climbed from the SUV when a tall, heavyset woman with cropped gray hair rushed from the stables, held Terri at arm's length, and exclaimed, "You're just as pretty as your wedding photos. You poor thing. Barely out of your honeymoon and then this nonsense falls on you."

Terri nodded. "You must be Dorothy." She considered whether to offer her hand or hug her. The family had mentioned Aunt Dottie was different, but they had not specified what they meant by different.

"Call me Dottie, please. We're family." She hugged Terri. After releasing her, Dottie gasped.

Terri followed the direction of Dottie's stare. "Oh, and this is my friend Quinn Flanagan."

Dottie nodded stiffly at him. "I suppose I should have warned you not to bring a man."

"What's wrong?" Terri asked.

Dottie kept her attention on Flanagan. "You wouldn't be divorced would you?"

Flanagan chuckled. "Happily married and only death will separate me from my Kate."

Dottie sighed heavily. "The last time I heard that kind of declaration of love, it ended violently."

Terri added, "Quinn Flanagan was the New York City FBI Bureau Chief and Blake's boss."

Dottie squinted at him. "Best we go inside."

Terri had heard bits and pieces of conversation about the black sheep of the family who lived in Florida. Had the family kept their distance because she was crazy? Dottie practically shoved them into the house and shut the door. Pressing her back against the front door, Dottie shook her head and spread her fingers across her mouth and chin. Moving her fingers out of the way, she asked Flanagan, "May I see some sort of identification?"

Flanagan handed over his wallet. Dottie opened it up to the New York driver's license.

"Have a seat while I check this," she said. "I'll explain in a minute." With that, she left the room with the wallet in one hand and a cell phone in the other.

Flanagan and Terri stood in the granite tiled entranceway. Flanagan didn't seem as insulted about the way Dottie treated him as Terri would have been. Perhaps Dottie distrusted everyone. Perhaps she distrusted law enforcement. Perhaps she distrusted men in particular. Whatever Dottie's problem, Terri had to overcome it because Blake needed information about Carrie Ann.

Flanagan smiled at Terri.

She whispered, "Do you know what's going on?"

Flanagan's eyes aimed at the ceiling for a moment to indicate someone was upstairs. Terri listened for footfalls. Perhaps someone was upstairs in the mansion. *Are we being watched?* Dottie's half of a conversation sounded from the other room, her words loudly indistinct like the public address system at the airport. Moments later she rushed back to the entranceway where she handed Flanagan his wallet.

"All clear," she shouted. "He's retired FBI and he's with my niece-in-law."

Six women emerged from doorways to greet them. Their voices low and their manners guarded, they appeared, then disappeared again. Was Dottie harboring illegal aliens? Terri snuck a glance at Flanagan. His face tense, he shrugged. Dottie led Terri and Flanagan through a corridor to the back of the house onto a vast stone deck overlooking a lush flower and vegetable garden. Two picnic-size ornate metal tables and a dozen matching chairs adorned the shaded area of the deck. Dottie took a seat at the end of the far table and directed them to sit with her.

"I operate a horse training facility, but this is also a women's shelter," Dottie said to Flanagan. "Most of the women come here angry and scared."

"I'd never hurt a woman," Flanagan said.

Dottie said, "I was concerned for *your* safety."

That explained the extreme caution. Flanagan sat with his back to the wall. Terri took the seat across from him, beside Dottie.

Dottie took Terri's nearest hand in hers. "I'm so glad to meet you. I wish this could have been under better circumstances. How can I help?"

"Blake sent me a text message before he was arrested. It said *Ask Aunt Dottie about Carrie Ann.*"

Dottie had a puzzled expression while she slumped back in her chair. "Oh."

The door to the porch opened to let women through with loads of bowls, plates, platters of fruit and brownies, a giant stockpot, and a tray of drinks. The women served themselves and their guests. A thin, pregnant black girl, who appeared to be in her late teens, switched on overhead fans, stirring up the scent of chili. Terri's stomach growled. She had not been hungry for days. Grief and worry consumed her. Observing the women, Terri wondered what they had suffered to make them flee their husbands and boyfriends. Were their men criminals?

"Why don't we eat now and talk about that later?" Dottie asked.

Flanagan waited until Dottie took a bite before he dug into his bowl of chili. Terri followed suit. Comfort food. Warm, packed with beans, hamburger, tomatoes, and spices, the thick chili quickly filled her.

"After my friend Lucy's husband died, she asked me to take over the care of the farm and the horses. She let the fields go to pasture land, and we repurposed the place to be a horse rescue and rehabilitation service. We ran that business for five years." Dottie stared out at the pasture.

The other women gradually carried off their dishes to the house, leaving Flanagan, Terri, and Dottie alone on the spacious deck. Terri leaned forward to indicate she was ready to get back to the reason for her visit.

Dottie took a long drink of tea. "Carrie Ann is the reason I started this shelter. Used to be my whole world this horse business. I know people thought ugly things about Lucy and me, but people will think whatever they want."

Terri detected a level of rebellion in Dottie's voice that hinted at the cruelty of misplaced judgment.

"Horses have been better company to me than any man." Dottie shrugged with a glance at Flanagan. "They don't expect me to lose weight and walk in high heels."

Flanagan pulled a pen and pad of paper from his jacket. He jotted the day's date and the names Dottie and Lucy at the top. Beneath that he wrote Carrie Ann.

"Carrie Ann showed up in nineteen ninety-four, the weekend after Halloween."

"Why do you remember the date?" Flanagan asked.

"It was the same weekend Lucy got her diagnosis. Stage four breast cancer. At first, I suspected Carrie Ann was pregnant, that the boys sent her to stay with me to spare her family and theirs. I expected her to ask about abortion or adoption."

Baby? Terri held her breath.

"But," Dottie said, "Carrie's story wasn't the usual one. She showed up broke and terrified and wouldn't talk to me about what happened to her for months. I've worked with abused horses, so I figured it would take a while for her to trust me. I kept expecting her to run away, but she had nowhere to go. She offered to work for her room and board, so I kept her on. She gave me time to help Lucy in her final months." Dottie used her napkin to wipe her eyes.

Terri took shallow breaths. "What usual story?"

"Carrie Ann wasn't pregnant, and she was the only girl the boys ever sent to me."

Terri bit her bottom lip. "Was she abused at home? Why did she run away?"

"She said she was kidnapped in the Midwest," Dottie said. "She never told me her hometown because she knew I'd call her parents. The man who took her drugged her and pimped her out at truck stops from Ohio to North Carolina."

Terri inhaled sharply. She had read about such things but never imagined she would cross paths with a victim of human trafficking. Flanagan took notes. Certainly a career in law enforcement toughened up a person to handle stories like Carrie Ann's. The only sign that Dottie's words bothered Flanagan was an occasional bulge at his jaw, an indication he was clenching and unclenching his teeth.

"She ended up at a farm house near Clayton Ranch, and that's when one of the boys came to the house." Dottie raised an eyebrow at Terri. "She called him the best-looking one."

Terry understood which brother she meant. *Gator.* Christened Gideon, he was the oh-so-handsome middle-born of the five

Clayton boys. Terri nodded to confirm she understood the boy in question was not Blake.

"Frank sent him to the basement to sleep with Carrie Ann, but the boy couldn't do it. When he saw how young she was, he asked her for her name and why she was there. He promised to come back for her. She told me she was as scared as she was surprised when he unlocked her ankle chain the next night."

"Chain?" Flanagan's face flushed.

"She showed me scars on her ankle." Dottie glanced down at her hands. "She said five boys freed her from a man she called Curtis Frank. Ian told me they identified the remains from the river as Frank's." Dottie was the only person Terri heard calling Papa Clayton by his real name.

"We need to find her," said Flanagan. "Your testimony is second-hand."

Dottie rubbed her fingers over her mouth as if lost in thought then changed the subject. "How illegal is it to take on the name of a dead person?"

Flanagan puffed air from his lips. "It's a felony called identity theft."

"How can it harm the dead?"

"It can't harm the dead, but it leads to other forms of fraud and theft. People have been known to cash Social Security and welfare checks of the dead," Flanagan said. "Steal inheritance, take out loans—"

"What if no fraud is involved?"

"It *is* fraud to take someone else's name." Flanagan set down his pen and paper. "Let me speak plainly. The FBI is going to get Blake's phone records, including his text messages. Soon, they'll be knocking on your door to ask these same questions. With a head start, we will find Carrie Ann first and see if her testimony will help or hurt Blake's case."

"She doesn't want to be found. I know that." Dottie rested her forehead in the palm of her hand, propping her elbow on the table. "Carrie Ann took on the name of a runaway she met."

"Maybe the girl gave a false name," Terri said.

"In situations like that," Dottie said, "I believe two young, frightened girls would trust each other."

"What name did she take on?" Flanagan asked.

"Samantha Adams. We ordered a copy of Samantha's school records." Dottie lowered her gaze to her bare, weathered hands. A distinct tan line separated her palms from the back of her hands.

"Where is the real Samantha Adams?" Terri asked.

"I don't know," Dottie said. "Carrie Ann didn't talk to her childhood friends while she lived here. She left after high school graduation. I haven't seen her or heard from her since the summer of nineteen ninety-eight."

Twelve years. Terri groaned. "She could be anywhere. She could be dead. What if she changed names again?"

Dottie scooted her chair close to Terri. Draping an arm around Terri's shoulders, she said, "She loved her new name. It's not likely she'd let go of it. Besides, she would need her high school diploma to get a job or go to college."

"Or to get a driver's license," Flanagan added. "Did either of you apply for a Social Security card for Samantha?"

Dottie's posture straightened. "Yes. She needed it to graduate. We found the number in copies of her school records from Ohio. That and a copy of her birth certificate. How much trouble am I in for helping Carrie Ann start fresh with a new name?"

Flanagan tucked his paper and pen in his jacket. "I suggest you hire a lawyer and keep his number handy. Don't talk to the FBI without your lawyer in the room and do exactly what the lawyer says."

Dottie eyed Flanagan while they both stood. "What about what I told you?"

"I'm retired. If anybody asks if we've met, be honest. Tell them we talked about Blake and that we're worried about him."

"That's the God's honest truth," Dottie said, hugging

Flanagan. She then embraced Terri. "Don't let this situation break you, darling. Let me give you a photo of Carrie Ann from graduation. Maybe it will help you recognize her if you find her." Dottie led them back into the house.

"One more question," Flanagan said. "If you had to guess what kind of career Carrie Ann would go into, what would it be?"

Dottie paused at a mahogany bookcase to pull a framed photo off a high shelf. Carrie Ann in her cap and gown radiated a girl-next-door wholesomeness that belied her tortured loss of innocence. She had graduated with high honors.

Dottie rubbed the glass clean with her sleeve then she handed the precious framed photo to Terri. "She was truly gifted at nurturing abused horses."

Back in the car, Terri secured her seatbelt. "So how do we find Samantha Adams?"

For the next three months, Terri devoted herself to her work and her search for Carrie Ann, also known as Samantha Adams, through various online resources while Flanagan used his own methods. She told Blake she was working to pay the attorney's fees. In truth, she was hurt that he had not confided in her about what happened to Curtis Frank. She got more information from the evening news than from him, so she kept her investigation to herself. Flanagan might have talked to Blake, but it didn't matter. Terri decided to avoid sleeping with Blake again until he was willing to share more than his body with her. Secrecy and intimacy were mutually exclusive. She nursed that belief like it was a sick puppy, rocking it to sleep at night with tears.

As Blake's April trial date drew near, Terri cleared her work schedule to attend. She dreaded watching the evening news because the media fed on the case—emphasizing and perhaps exaggerating the wealth of the Claytons—while portraying Blake as a rogue FBI agent, whose dangerous behavior might have begun in high school.

In late March, Terri's business partners pleaded with her to stay away from it so clients would not see her on the news. After silently counting to ten, she told them, "So are you suggesting our clients would think better of me if I abandoned my husband during the trial than if I stood by him?"

They did not answer.

The morning of the trial, April 1, 2010, Terri arrived before dawn to preflight her plane at Duchess County Airport near Poughkeepsie, New York. She had her flight plan filed and bags packed to head for Asheville. She planned to leave early to beat a weather system moving east across Maryland.

. 15 .

On Thursday, April 1st, the State of North Carolina versus Elijah Blake Clayton launched its first day of trial in Asheville. Blake's parents and his brothers' wives, sat directly behind him in the Buncombe County Courthouse. Terri was conspicuously absent. According to the defense attorney, Blake's brothers were prohibited from attending the trial because they might be called to testify. Blake did not have the stomach to ask which side had asked them to testify.

While the attorneys presented their opening arguments, Blake worried about Terri. For months she had stayed in New York to work. Conditions of his bail did not permit him to leave the state. He had called her every day, and every day she had asked if he was ready to tell her about the death of Curtis Frank. Every day he declined on the advice of his attorney. He would not have blamed her for staying away from the trial.

He missed her desperately. Was she really catching up on work? Or was she staying away because she was angry he hadn't told her everything? His attorney warned him not to discuss the case with anyone, because his life was on the line. Maybe she was shopping for a divorce attorney. It crushed him to imagine losing her. Last night's text message from Terri was a reservation number for a suite in the Vanderbilt wing of the historic Grove Park Inn and Resort near the courthouse. Had she reserved the suite for two or for one?

The District Attorney's deep voice rolled across the quiet, packed courtroom. "And we intend to prove, based on forensic evidence and eye-witness testimony, that on the night of October twenty-ninth, nineteen-ninety-four, the defendant Elijah Blake Clayton kidnapped Mr. Curtis Frank from his residence." The prosecutor mentioned the volume of evidence and witnesses marshaled to prove his case.

Blake cringed. His attorney had warned him about Sweet Sally Henson's statement to the FBI as part of a plea deal. Blake tried to remember Sweet Sally, but that night he had not been paying much attention to that old hag. She had a plea deal with the DA related to charges in Florida. After sixteen years, what did she remember? What would a desperate hooker say to save herself?

A protest group outside carried signs denouncing the Felony Murder Rule. Blake's attorney called them the April Fools and warned him not to speak with them, look at them, or even think about them. He explained that they had their own agenda and attracting media attention would not help Blake in any way.

His mind swirled with thoughts of fear and doubt. At night, when the world quieted and his fears filled the room, he choked up in panic. In the daytime, he feared losing his freedom, his wife, and his mind. He doubted his attorney could refute both forensic evidence and an eye-witness. He doubted the jury's sympathy for him. They probably considered him a pampered rich kid who never had to work for anything. Even back in high school, the other kids envied the horses and the large farmhouse and the acres of land, calling the Claytons royalty. They never saw the work it took at all hours to keep the horses healthy, alive, clean, and fed. The other kids, except a few close ones like Pete, never saw the Clayton boys covered in muck, mud, sweat, and blood during the birthing season. Strangers saw the wealth, not the work it took to earn every dollar of it.

Then there was the Ernie factor. Ernie, the local newspaper editor, despised the Claytons. Papa called him a closet socialist.

Papa said socialists believed it was inherently wicked to keep what you earned, and somehow noble to give it away to those too stupid or lazy to earn it for themselves. Blake did not know Ernie's political beliefs, but he did not expect any mercy from Ernie regarding the trial. Ernie treated journalism as a calling.

So while others argued his future in open court, Blake silently prayed for the hand of God to sweep this nightmare away. He glanced at his attorney's notes. In neatly handwritten block letters, the top of the first page read: April 1: Opening arguments.

April Fool's Day? *Of course. Not funny, God. Not funny at all.*

Meanwhile, in Florida, retired FBI Field Office Director, Quinn Flanagan raised his binoculars to watch a young woman in colorful scrubs stride through the parking garage of Jacksonville Memorial Hospital to the employee entrance. She matched the photo of Carrie Ann from Dottie Clayton. He jotted down the code she keyed into the pad by the door. He climbed from his car and slowly strolled by the young woman's parking spot, where he observed her tag number, make, model and color of the car, as well as a car seat in the back. Doubling back, he entered his car and wrote another log entry. Flanagan judged this the most promising lead in three months.

He drove to a florist shop for an arrangement of bright red tulips.

To confirm the nurse's identity, he headed into the hospital through the main entrance with the vase of tulips. He set the vase on the welcome desk.

"Who are they for?" the volunteer asked. Her white hair puffed like a cloud around her scalp. Her spotted hands gently caressed the flowers.

Flanagan had forgotten to attach the card from the florist's shop, so he recited what he had intended to write. "To nurse Samantha from a grateful patient." Was she still living under the name Samantha?

The lady jotted it down then raised her head. "Do you know which floor she works on?"

"No, ma'am. I'm sending these on behalf of a friend. He said she was pretty, maybe close to thirty years old."

"Oh, yes. She's on the orthopedic floor. I'll send this up to her."

Flanagan wandered to the cafeteria to read a book. There he overheard mention of Samantha working an extra shift. When he was leading the New York City office of the FBI he could have effortlessly collected pages of information on Samantha from the license plate on her car, but as a civilian, he used old-school methods of observation. At three that afternoon, Flanagan waited in his car while he watched Samantha's car. *No show.* He lingered in various waiting rooms until ten thirty, then he returned to his car. At the end of the three-to-eleven shift, Carrie Ann, known as Samantha, carried a vase of tulips to her car. Following her home had been easy.

Thunderstorms on her route of flight delayed Terri from reaching the Asheville airport until eleven thirty p.m. It then took her thirty minutes to reach the beautiful stone-walled Grove Park Inn and Resort. By midnight, she was tiptoeing in to surprise Blake when her cell phone blared. Flinging her duffle bag onto the sofa, she freed a hand to answer.

"I'd like to update you in person." Flanagan's voice rang like music through the tiny speaker.

Terri's insides fluttered like a bird freed from a cage. She spoke softly so she wouldn't wake Blake. "Say where and when."

"Asheville airport, noon tomorrow."

"I'll be there." Terri disconnected the call.

When she turned toward the bedroom, Blake filled the doorway. "And here the D.A. suggested I was a flight risk." He disappeared in the shadows.

Terri caught him from behind and wrapped her arms around him. "That was Quinn Flanagan," she whispered into his warm back. "He wants to meet me tomorrow."

He raised one arm, twisted toward her and hugged her. He grinned for the first time in weeks. "Hmm. Never suspected you'd leave me for an older married man."

She smiled and pressed her face against his soft cotton tank top. "Ha! I'm not reckless enough to challenge Kate." His embrace warmed her inside and out.

"So you're skipping court again?"

Terri peered up at him. Certainly Flanagan would tell her if Carrie Ann was in fact dead and save her the trip. The fact that he wanted to meet at the airport had to signal good news. It just had to. "I might be gone longer if Quinn has good news."

Blake nodded. He did not appear even slightly cheered by the possibility that Flanagan might have good news. Was Blake succumbing to depression? He had lost weight since the last time she saw him. He probably wasn't sleeping well either.

"Talk to me."

Blake broke off his embrace. "Before I'm convicted, I want you to file for divorce."

Her heart clunked to the bottom of her chest. "Don't say that." Terri's lungs labored as if the air had grown thicker. She refused to imagine failure. She fell against him and, pressing her ear to his chest, listened to the *tha thump, tha thump, tha thump* of his great heart. "Don't give up."

She wanted to get him to talk, but he needed sleep. Despite her previous pleas for him to tell her what happened with Curtis Frank in 1994, he steadfastly declined. He simply explained he could not talk about the case on his attorney's orders. Terri did not fully understand the law, but she realized justice did not always prevail. Attorneys sometimes blundered. Juries could be swayed by emotions, or confused over facts, and even judges made mistakes. She appealed to the highest judge. She prayed for divine mercy to protect Blake from conviction. While she struggled to shore up her faith, nagging questions ebbed back into her consciousness.

What happened that night with Carrie Ann? Who killed Curtis Frank?

. 16 .

The next morning on Friday, April 2nd, in the Asheville courtroom, the prosecutor presented a discolored, torn, yellowish-leather work glove into evidence. Blake had cherished his gloves. Clayton Ranch gloves had to be earned. Employees and family alike had to meet the criteria of a year's work of adhering to safety rules and embodying company policies. Also, even family members had to get a recommendation from the ranch foreman to be granted a pair of gloves stamped with the fancy CR brand on the back. The wrist side of the gloves bore smaller stamped initials of their owner. Family members had their gloves stamped with first and middle initials only. The prosecutor placed a giant photo of the front and back of Blake's glove.

Pointing to the smaller letters in the photo, the prosecutor said, "The only Clayton Ranch gloves issued with the personal initials E-B-C were given to Elijah Blake Clayton, the defendant." He had already introduced the company's glove records into court as an exhibit.

Blake had earned his gloves on Valentine's Day of eighth grade. He remembered the date because by the end of that day he got them dirty. His mind wandered back to that proud day. Immediately after school his mother had called him downstairs to help the vet.

"An injury?" he shouted. He did not want blood on his new gloves.

"Collection."

It was understood what was to be collected. In his whole life, Blake never heard his mama say the word *sperm*. Standardbred horses were bred by artificial insemination. Everyone expected him to handle the teaser mare. He had become adept at it after a year of training and practice. The Clayton's best stallion, Thunderfoot, a descendant of the Thoroughbred Storm Cat, was a reliable sperm machine though it took a team of people to help the process.

Blake called back down the stairs. "I'll get my overalls on." He put on his yellow work gloves and proudly stretched the stiff leather by making fists. He was the youngest on the ranch in gloves. Motivated by pride, he had oiled them and sprayed them inside and out with a preservative until water beaded off them. His brothers had teased him that they would last forever. He just wanted them to repel blood, and sweat, and pee, and all other kinds of horse excretions.

Though his other four brothers had more experience, everyone acknowledged Blake was the family horse whisperer. He had a natural skill at calming horses, mares especially, which bordered on the supernatural. He didn't even have to touch the horse or speak to calm it. His father claimed horses just had to lay eyes on Blake or catch a whiff of him and they'd calm down.

Blake changed into an old flannel shirt and overalls. His work boots had been peed and bled on so many times they had an odd brownish color and a smell that helped him find them in the dark. He clomped down the stairs, through the back of the house, toward the breeding barn.

He had learned about the family business that year when he was promoted from mucking stalls to handling the horses. The large barn was mostly a laboratory for testing, dividing, and documenting sperm and mare urine. In the winter, the mare urine was collected, filtered, and used to make hormone replacement medicine for women in their change of life. The first of these drugs was known under the brand name Premarin which told of its source ingredient—pregnant mare urine.

In the spring, the laboratory was dedicated to sperm handling. The layout of the building suggested the collection area was the least important because it was barely larger than a horse stall, whereas the majority of the building was the laboratory. Freshly collected sperm was shipped cooled, never frozen, by courier to the buyer if the mare was not staying on the premises. His father had explained it without even blushing, making it seem all so lofty and scientific.

Papa had taught him about famous breeders in history like Aga Khan, Federico Tesio, the 17th Earl of Derby for whom the Stanley Cup Race was named, and Thomas Darley who smuggled an Arabian out of Turkey. Papa made it sound like the Claytons held a proud place in horse breeding history. Blake was never proud enough to admit to his classmates that he helped collect sperm from horses. He had endured enough cruelty for being a fat kid in grade school.

Leaves crunched underfoot while he marched on the well-worn path to the collection building. Pacing outside on a short rein was the stallion, Thunderfoot. Blake shook his head at the grave injustice of the stallion's life. Despite years of breeding, the poor thing was technically a virgin. No one would risk allowing Thunderfoot go at it the old-fashioned natural way. He might hurt himself or the mare. Blake, himself a virgin, deeply pitied the horse.

Blake's job consisted of staying with the mare on the safe side of a stall, separated from the stallion's area by a tail-high wooden barrier. Blake backed the mare into the stall then stayed put while the stallion sniffed and paced from his side of the barrier until he was ready to engage a cloth-covered pommel-like mound. The vet stood in an observation window, overlooking the stalls. Blake's brothers handled the stallion, the mount and, underneath the mount, the collector. Gloved and serious, they waited while Samuel led the stallion into the stall.

The entire collection process took about fifteen minutes.

Blake owned his gloves from Valentine's Day until October 29th, 1994, two days shy of Halloween. The first day using his gloves involved starting life; the last, involved death.

Terri drove south on Interstate 26 to the Asheville Regional Airport, near Henderson. She was missing the second day of trial, but Blake said he understood why. With her overnight duffle and her flight bag in the rental car, all she needed from Flanagan was an address. The distance between Asheville and Carrie Ann would determine whether Terri would drive, fly her plane, or fly commercial.

Flanagan met her in the spacious lobby of the commercial terminal building. She settled into a plastic chair beside him.

"Our friend is a registered nurse at Baptist Medical Center downtown in Jacksonville, Florida. She regularly works the three-to-eleven shift Mondays, Wednesdays, Fridays and one weekend a month on the orthopedic ward. I was lucky to spot her after she worked a double shift last night. She's married to a wounded sailor, named Mike Young, and they have a three-year-old son."

Hope swelled in Terri's heart. She could fly from Asheville to Jacksonville in two hours tops.

Flanagan handed her three eight-by-ten glossy photos. One showed a lovely young woman in scrubs walking on a paved path between two buildings. Samantha Young had been captured in black and white. The second showed a brawny, bearded man with a cane in one hand and a bag of groceries in the other. The third photo featured a round-faced toddler bounding mid-step toward a pair of legs. The boy's open mouth nearly squealed from the paper. He bore the unabashed joyful expression of a child seeing his mother.

Terri's pulse quickened at the news. Carrie Ann, now Samantha Young, had seized her chance at a new life. Their little family appeared so happy, so normal. With a husband and a child, would she risk dredging up the past to save Blake? Terri doubted Samantha had told her husband about her teen years. Women tended to hide emotional scars more diligently than physical scars.

"What's the boy's name?"

"Here's their home address in Atlantic Beach." Flanagan flipped the photo of Carrie Ann over to show a map of the Jacksonville suburb marked with a red dot. He was all business, ignoring her question about the boy. Perhaps he didn't know the answer. The boy's name did not matter anyway.

The Young family lived on the ocean. Terri imagined a small house with a beach view and the roar of the surf where they watched seagulls riding on the breeze. "Have you spoken to her?"

Flanagan shook his head. "I'm on the next flight home."

"I thought you'd go with me."

"I suspect you stand a better chance of gaining her confidence without me around. Besides, how do you think she'd react to a strange older man asking about her past?"

Terri sighed. He was right. "She'd probably spray you with mace."

"Or worse. We still don't know who killed Frank. So be careful." Flanagan checked his watch. "How's Blake?"

The public address system warbled and echoed. Terri picked out the few clear words "to New York's LaGuardia" so she stood to hug Flanagan. "He's facing the fight of his life."

"Remind him who's in his corner," Flanagan said. "Oh, and I suggest you approach Carrie Ann alone. Her husband and son go to the park on Saturday mornings."

"Thank you, Quinn. I don't know how I can repay you."

"Always glad to help friends." He picked up a carry-on suitcase and headed to the security checkpoint.

Terri drove back to the general aviation terminal to prepare a flight plan for Jacksonville. She dreaded turning Carrie Ann's world upside down, but it had to be done. If her testimony—no matter how disturbing or painful it was—could save Blake, then so be it. Who would weigh the discomfort of revealing past horrors against a man's life? Unless Carrie Ann had more to lose by testifying.

What if she killed Frank and the boys covered it up?

After landing in Jacksonville, Terri directed the lineman to top off her tanks. Thanks to her three-axis autopilot, she had spent most of the flight reading Flanagan's notes on Carrie Ann.

She switched on her cell phone and marched across the steamy tarmac to the terminal. The part of her call log not obscured by glare showed she had missed a call from a New York City area code, so she called the number.

"Terri, hey, I'm coming down this weekend," Vincent said. "And I'm taking next week off. How's the trial going?"

Why didn't he call Blake? "The prosecutor has an eyewitness and forensic evidence against Blake. The eye-witness is supposed to appear next week. I'm sure Blake will be glad to see you."

"Would you tell him we wrapped up the prison case?"

Hmmm. Maybe Blake isn't answering calls from anyone. Maybe I'm not the only one he's shut out. "I'm not in Asheville right now." The second day of the trial and she was a no-show. What would the jury think about her missing the trial so far?

Silence weighed between them.

"I guess you've taken a lot of time off work," Vincent said.

Though she longed to explain where she was and why, she feared her cell phone was tapped. Even hinting about Carrie Ann involved risk. "Let's just say my business partners aren't happy."

Shifting him from the topic of her whereabouts, she said, "How did the case resolve?"

"We arrested his fiancée. She found out Chilton had given his secretary a large sum of cash the day before the secretary disappeared. The fiancée confronted him and he said it was none of her business, so the fiancée leaped to the wrong conclusion. She took revenge by staging it to look like the inmates or the horse beat him to death. We found her fingerprints and Chilton's blood on a baseball bat. Turns out the secretary needed money to flee her abusive husband."

Terri shook her head. "Are you saying he was murdered over a misunderstanding?" *What a waste of life.*

"Jealousy is the oldest reason to kill."

"The oldest?"

"Cain and Abel," Vincent said.

"Brothers." Since Genesis, brothers continued to cause trouble for one another. Terri shouldered her duffel bag to open the door to the air-conditioned terminal. "I have to go. I should be back by Monday. Say hello to Nefi for me."

"Will do."

Terri obtained a rental car and map in record time. She logged the address Flanagan had given her into the GPS and drove as the device directed. After a construction detour through downtown Jacksonville, she followed directions to the coastal suburb of Atlantic Beach. Her unease increased when she parked across the street from a charming one-story, stucco-covered house with a clay barrel tile roof. A white picket fence lined the side and back yard. Two giant bougainvillea bushes framed the house with mountains of brilliant hot pink flowers. Carrie Ann's fresh start as Samantha, married, mother of a toddler, had a middle-class fairy tale appearance.

Terri dreaded having to drag Carrie Ann's nightmarish past into her present life, but Terri wanted her own happily-ever-after married life. She had worked to get top grades, to compete for a place in the best veterinary school, to build her practice, to create her ideal life. All those long years of delayed gratification had paid off with respect and income.

Blake, a loving husband, was supposed to complete the plan. In the months since their wedding, they had not even had enough time to *discuss* becoming parents. In the shadow of the trial, their future was less and less destined for marital bliss and more destined for weekly conjugal visits.

Easing her grip on the steering wheel, Terri took deep breaths and wiped away tears. She did not want Samantha's first impression of her to be that of a weepy, desperate nutcase. She checked her face in the mirror and performed a few quick repairs of mascara and lipstick. To the mirror she said, "Hi, I'm Terri. I need you to come with me to Asheville to save my husband's life." She sighed. *Yeah, that'll work.*

She flipped the visor up and stuffed her makeup into her purse. Taking only her car keys and her cell phone, she climbed out and approached the front door of the picturesque home of Carrie Ann, alias Samantha Young. She squared her shoulders and pressed the doorbell. Muted chimes rang. A breeze carried salty sea air along with humidity. Sweat trickled down her back while she waited for someone to answer the door. She checked her watch. Three thirty. *Oh, crap. What day is it?*

Friday. According to Flanagan's notes, Samantha worked the three-to-eleven shift on Mondays, Wednesdays, and Fridays. Muttering, Terri retraced her steps to her car to drive back to downtown Jacksonville, to Baptist Hospital. She debated with herself on whether or not to wait until Saturday to introduce herself to Samantha, but the closer she got to the hospital, the stronger the argument grew for pleading with her immediately. Samantha would need time to notify her boss that she had to go out of town to save a life. She would need time to tell her husband. Talking to Samantha immediately would give her the weekend to prepare for travel.

Terri also hoped the element of surprise would work in her favor. Samantha might be less likely to run off or cause a scene at her place of work.

At the hospital, Terri asked for directions to the orthopedic floor. From the elevators to the nurse's station on the orthopedic floor, she took deep breaths. Feeling composed, she addressed a lady in a white uniform who sat behind the long counter with her face lit by a computer screen.

"Hello, I'm looking for a nurse named Samantha Young."

"She's not in. How may I help you?" the fortyish woman behind the counter stood. With her hair pulled back into a tight bun, she exuded experience and professionalism.

"I was told she worked on Fridays. I really need to see her," Terri said. "Is she working a different shift?"

"What is it you need?"

Terri sighed. "It's a personal matter."

"Oh. You can leave your phone number with me and I'll be sure to—"

"It's urgent. I need to speak with her as soon as possible."

Another younger nurse approached the counter. "Who are you looking for?"

"Samantha Young." Terri put her hands on the counter,

"I'm so sorry she's not here. She called in this morning and said there was a death in the family. We don't expect her back until next week at least."

"I just flew in to see her." Terri rested her face on the back of her hands. Not another delay! *Should I drive back to the house and wait? Has this trial changed me from veterinarian to stalker?*

A hand settled on Terri's back.

Terri raised her face. "Please, can you reach her? Could you give her my phone number?"

"We can do that, can't we?" asked the younger nurse.

The older nurse nodded.

Terri dug through her purse and handed over an older

business card. It had her maiden name on it, but it was the only card with her.

The younger nurse read the veterinary business card. "Samantha doesn't own a pet."

"I'm here on behalf of a friend who desperately needs to talk to her."

The older nurse's eyes narrowed. "Is this friend of yours male or female?"

The younger nurse inhaled sharply and dropped the card on the counter. "Samantha warned us her sneaky, no-account ex-boyfriend might try to track her down."

So, Samantha had built a wall of protection around her new life. Did she have a crazy ex or had she fabricated one as a plausible reason to keep her past to herself? Friends and neighbors would naturally want to help guard a young married woman from an ex-boyfriend.

Terri shook her head. She needed the nurses' cooperation, but whatever she told them would be repeated to Samantha. How could she win Samantha's trust? *Ah. Yes.* Terri picked up her business card and flipped it to the blank side. She dug a pen from her purse and scribbled a message on the card. She then handed the card to the older nurse.

"Please, call Samantha. Tell her it's life-and-death urgent." Terri fought back tears while she jammed her pen in her purse. She marched to the elevators and followed a man on crutches into the middle elevator. If weather permitted, she might reach Asheville before nightfall. Though empty-handed, she would be near Blake. Before the doors closed, she overheard the older nurse's voice.

"It says, 'I'm a friend of Dottie Clayton.'"

A downpour drenched Terri on the short dash from the hospital door to her rental car in the parking lot. With shaking hands she checked the weather through her smartphone. She needed clear weather to fly back in her single-engine Cessna. A solid line of thunderstorms from the Gulf of Mexico up through the North Carolina coast was moving east. The radar image glowed red and orange, indicating lightning and heavy rain. Turbulence was a given under such conditions.

She swatted the steering wheel. A crushing weariness landed on her. Long ago she had promised her father she would never "die to get somewhere." The squall line was too great a risk to cross. *A person can only do so much.* She considered driving the rental car to Asheville, but then she would have to come back for the plane. But when? *Better get a hotel room for the night.*

She drove to the nearest hotel and dragged her overnight bag up to the room.

By the time she tossed her bag on the bed, she felt a burning need to cry. *I failed. Flanagan found her, and I lost her.* That admission opened the floodgates, releasing pent-up emotions. Failure. It had been decades since she'd failed at anything.

She had forgotten how painful failure felt.

It wounded her, slowly grinding her to dust from the inside out.

She stretched out on the bed and cried. Tears rolled down her cheeks her ears and neck. Maybe Carrie Ann *was* away at a family funeral on her husband's side. It was possible. The timing was beyond suspicious, but sometimes life was strange like that.

No. Carrie Ann ran. Maybe she killed that man who lived in the old farmhouse. She's gonna run to save herself and let Blake go to the chair.

God, that's not right. You can't let this happen. Make her come forward, make the FBI or the sheriff find her. If I call them, will you guide them to her?

She stared at the ceiling.

I'm sorry, Blake. I failed. I'll call Flanagan again and admit it. This is beyond my skill set. I'd be better at finding a lost, injured animal than a human on the run.

Why did I even think I could do this? Because I had to. I had to prove to Blake I could help. I've always had to prove my love, to earn a place of respect from the men in my life.

She thought of her father, and though she couldn't remember he ever spoke the words, she believed he was disappointed she was not a boy. She had achieved everything in life she thought her father expected from a son—to follow in his professional footsteps, to take up his hobby of aviation, and to succeed academically. Everything.

What would ever be enough? Giving birth to a grandson? Is that why getting married was so important?

She sat up in bed. After finding her phone in her flight bag, she called her father. A son would ask for advice, right?

"Dad, tell me the truth. What does it take to earn a man's love?"

"Where is this coming from?"

Bracing for whatever ugly truth might emerge from the phone, she voiced her feelings. She had to know. "Blake won't confide in me what's going on, what happened that led to his arrest. He says it's because his attorney told him not to talk to anyone, but I feel shut out. No matter what I do, I've always felt it wasn't enough. That I'm not enough. Even with you. I've just always had the feeling you wanted a son instead—"

"Oh, my dear child. I never meant for you to know."

Air rushed from Terri's lungs. She covered her mouth with her hand and pulled the phone away so her father wouldn't hear her pained moan.

"Terri? Are you there? Please listen."

Her world shifted on its axis. She regained balance by grabbing her suitcase with her free hand. "I'm here, Dad."

"Mother and I didn't want to tell you, but you were not our first child."

"What?"

"We had a son. He would have been two years older than you." His voice cracked.

Weeping came through the phone. Her mother's voice sounded in the background.

"Who are you talking to?"

"Tell her. It's time."

There was rustling of the phone, then came her voice, "Terri?"

"I had a brother?"

"He died just before you were born."

"When the hell were you planning to tell me?"

"We weren't." Her mother sighed heavily. "The loss of a child leaves a hole that nothing can fill. We were just trying to cope."

"All my life I've been trying to be the son I thought you two wanted." The unspoken void in their lives was not her failure to be a boy, but the loss of one. The secret had haunted her all her life, hanging between them like a ghost. Terri felt suddenly empowered by enlightenment. "So that's why I always felt like I wasn't enough."

"Oh, Terri, you were more than we ever hoped for. We love you. You healed us from the pain of losing…Brian." A small gasp sounded, followed by sobbing. "You are the best child we could have ever hoped for."

Terri had rarely heard her mother cry. "Don't cry, Mom."

"I have to go." With that, the line went dead.

Reeling from the revelation, Terri flopped back on the bed. Her identity as an only child drifted apart, like leaves from a tree in autumn leaving the trunk bare. *I am, and yet I wasn't an only child. I am the one who lived.*

She remembered aborting an unwanted female colt. She remembered whispering to the mare's belly, where the male colt remained, "Live for two."

I have lived for two.

Terri's phone chimed. She answered.

"Why haven't you answered your text messages? Suki and Arlene and I have been trying to reach you," Reva said. "I figured you had your phone off during court, but then I didn't see you on the news with Blake and his attorney."

"I'll be there Monday."

"Uh huh. So why aren't you there now?"

"Bad weather."

"Suki explained the Felony Murder Rule to me. I want to come join the protesters outside the courtroom. Think it will help? I could get my in-laws to watch the kids."

"No, Reva. That won't help. Prayer might."

"You got it. How are you holding up?"

"I'm scared for him. His attorney told him not to talk about anything related to the case."

"Even to you?"

"Yes."

"A little ketamine might help."

Fearing the call might be recorded, Terri said, "I know he didn't do this. I just don't know how they can find proof to exonerate him. This…whatever. It all happened fifteen years ago. If he did, I don't want to know. Ignorance is bliss in this case."

"Excuse me a second." Reva groaned and came back on the line. "I have to go. One of my gifted genius children has a Lego stuck up his nose. Call me if you want me to come to Asheville. I'm just a flight away."

"You're a superstar."

Terri plugged her phone into the charger. The phone had only ten percent power. She was operating on emotional reserves. Her failure to find Carrie Ann crushed her spirit. Whether Carrie Ann was the real killer or a witness didn't matter anymore. Carrie Ann was gone.

I might be the worst detective on the planet, but I am still a great veterinarian, a great daughter, and I will be a great wife. I keep my promises.

Terri knew that her presence at the trial would show the world that she stood by Blake for better or worse. She would be there to comfort him even if he didn't talk to her. Win, lose, or appeal. For better or worse. Worse was the realization that even if Blake killed that man, she would still love him. 'Til death.

. 17 .

On Monday morning, April 5th, 2010, while Blake's trial resumed, Sheriff Ketchum carried a copy of the DNA report into the Asheville courthouse. The FBI already had the girl's shoes from Frank's basement, so Ketchum decided to hand over the report to the prosecutor. He had submitted the sample to Asheville's certified forensic crime lab, which in turn submitted a report to the FBI's National Missing Person DNA Database. Earlier that day, Ketchum had uploaded the report to his email and sent a notice to the medical examiners in North Carolina to check for a match to a Jane Doe. She was probably a teenager with size five feet, missing since 1994 or before. He was scheduled to testify, so he'd see the prosecutor anyway.

Wearing his freshly pressed uniform and polished shoes, Ketchum strode unarmed into the courthouse. *It isn't every day I testify against a friend.* He emptied his pockets, set his hat down, and placed the DNA report into a plastic bin in front of the security checkpoint. He did not expect to get waived through because he was a Haywood County sheriff in the Buncombe County Courthouse.

"Morning, Sheriff Ketchum," said the middle-aged courthouse security officer. "Come on through."

The scanner buzzed, so the security officer wanded Ketchum's belt, badge and watch with the hand-held metal detector. The device warbled at each item. A second security officer hunched over a small screen on the far side of the X-ray machine. He sent the plastic bin down the conveyor belt rollers past the walk-through metal detector, where Ketchum collected his belongings.

After riding the elevator, the sheriff sat on a bench facing the doors to the courtroom. The prosecutor had told him when to be there and to wait until called to come in the courtroom. Ketchum knew the drill. He had been idling for ten minutes when Papa Clayton bounded through the courtroom doors and parked himself on the bench.

"Sheriff," Papa said.

Ketchum nodded at him. "Mr. Clayton." He got up and moved to the far end of the corridor by a window overlooking the front of the courthouse where protestors gathered to wave signs denouncing the felony murder rule. From this vantage point, he estimated the crowd at close to two hundred.

Moments later a young man, perhaps thirty years old, stepped out of the courtroom. He glanced at Papa and halted in his tracks. After a pause, he approached and stopped in front of the bench. Even from twenty feet away, the man's voice carried to Ketchum's end of the corridor.

"I'm terribly sorry how this turned out, sir."

"I don't hold any ill will toward you," Papa Clayton said.

"Thank you, sir." The young man pivoted on the heel of his hiking boots and disappeared into the stairwell.

The voice sounded familiar. *Ah, yes.* He was the leader of the Harnett County diving team brought in to search the river for remains. The team had found the glove with the chains and the remains.

Ketchum dreaded having to testify. Whatever happened with Curtis Frank left its mark on Blake, who had been the happiest fat kid Pete Ketchum ever met through grade school and middle school. They had become friends in middle school when they started playing football. He recalled how Blake had changed halfway through freshman year, becoming withdrawn and sullen. He had assumed Blake had been rejected by a girl, but never really pressed him for a reason. He had been wrong not to ask. So wrong.

The elevator doors opened, taking in the dive team leader and letting out Terri. She could have passed as an attorney in her deep green pants suit and white top. She sat beside Papa and draped an arm over his shoulders.

Papa planted his meaty hands on his thighs. "I heard your partners are giving you grief."

"They're worried," Terri said. She patted his back then her arm slid down to her side.

Papa had aged a decade in six months. Even his posture hunched under the burden of worry.

Special Agent Theron stepped out of an elevator and strode to the far side of the corridor where Ketchum sat, away from Papa Clayton and Terri.

"The day we searched the Frank house, I requested DNA testing on the shoes we found in the basement," Ketchum whispered to Theron. "The next day your team took over the investigation. After that the report came in, so I uploaded the DNA to the National DNA Index System."

"Why did you test the shoes?" Theron asked.

"Looking for answers. I sent copies to our state's medical examiners. Maybe one of them has a Jane Doe that matches."

Every law enforcement agency agonized over unsolved cases. A closed case would be satisfying for someone. Had the attorneys mentioned anything about Curtis Frank's record or criminal activities in the trial? He couldn't recall any public statement by the FBI about the pornography found at the Frank house. Surely the prosecutor did not want the jury to despise Frank so he would not bring up Frank's reputation as Ohio's King of Kiddie Porn.

Theron eyed Ketchum. "What makes you suspect the girl who owned those shoes is dead?"

Ketchum spoke softly. "I don't know what happened to her. But the crime scene techs found a chain tied to the bed. That kind of thing raises ugly questions, especially considering the kind of recordings we found."

Papa Clayton inhaled sharply. Ketchum cringed. Had Papa heard the discussion from fifteen feet away? Ketchum glanced down the hall at Terri. She held a hand over her mouth. *Uh oh.*

Special Agent Theron faced the window. "Thank you for the test results."

Terri said something to Papa, but Ketchum couldn't tell what she said. Relieved, he decided she and Papa had not heard his discussion with Theron.

Papa leaned against the wall and grabbed his left arm halfway between the shoulder and elbow. He let out a low groan through clenched teeth. Terri's wide-eyed expression alarmed Ketchum. Red-faced, Papa reached for Terri and pitched forward. Terri grabbed Papa's right arm and lowered him to the floor on his side. Terri dropped to her knees and rolled him to his back. Gasping, Papa clutched at his chest.

Ketchum gasped then dashed toward the couple on the floor. Theron followed.

Terri pressed two fingers on his neck. "Get an ambulance." She whisked off Papa's tie and unbuttoned his shirt.

Ketchum groped his pockets for his cell phone, fumbling with it for a moment before dialing 9-1-1. The emergency services line answered with a recording, asking the caller to remain on the line to be served. At that moment, a deputy for the court came through the courtroom doors.

"Get a doctor or EMT," Ketchum told him. He too felt short of breath. "This man is having a heart attack."

The deputy pressed the button on the walkie-talkie on his shoulder and barked directions into it.

"Does anyone have an aspirin?" Terri asked.

Theron handed her a two-pill packet, the kind that came from dispensers at hotels and airports. Terri tore open the wrapper and pressed the pills into Papa's mouth. She ordered him to chew them, so he did between gasps. He coughed, spewing pieces of pill onto his chest. Terri gathered up the tiny white chips and poked them back into his mouth.

Her authoritative tone convinced Ketchum that the aspirin would help. He didn't understand how it would help, but it couldn't hurt.

Papa winced.

Was that his opinion of the taste of the aspirin or had his heart seized again? "Hold on, Mr. Clayton," Ketchum said, dropping to his knees at Papa's side.

Papa grabbed his hand and squeezed it. His grip was weak; his expression fierce. Ketchum had never before seen fear in Papa Clayton. *Oh, Lord, don't take him now.*

"Sheriff Peter Ketchum?" the deputy asked.

"That's me."

"Sir, I came out here to call you to the witness stand."

"I'm a little busy just now." This was an immediate matter of life and death. Sure, so was the trial, but that was a matter of delayed consequences. *If I help save Papa's life could it offset the harm of my testimony?*

Two uniformed women with medical kits rushed from the stairwell.

"Help is here, Papa." Terri stroked her hand over Mr. Clayton's sweaty forehead.

The emergency medical technicians nudged Terri and Ketchum aside to tend to Papa. One checked his heart with a stethoscope while the other flashed a tiny light in his eyes. Terri briefed them on the situation. Somehow, she had even kept track of the time since Papa fell. Ketchum wished he had thought to check his watch. He reluctantly labored to his feet.

Terri patted his knee. "Go ahead, Sheriff. He's in good hands."

Was she calling him by his title out of respect or to distance herself from him? At the rehearsal dinner, she had called him Pete. Ketchum straightened his uniform, picked his hat off the bench and tucked it under his arm. He followed the deputy bailiff through the double doors to the hushed courtroom. The dramatic event outside the doors of this room continued without notice of those gathered inside. He silently prayed Papa would survive. The family faced enough heartbreak already.

Ketchum's heartbeat pounded in his ears down the center aisle, past the rows of reporters, past the glares of the Clayton wives, past the attorney tables to the witness stand. He would take the oath to tell the truth, the whole truth, and nothing but the truth, so help him, God. Placing his hand on the Bible, he prayed Blake's attorney would ask the right questions to reveal the truth. *So help him, God.*

Blake does not deserve to die on account of Curtis Frank. Neither does Papa Clayton.

Surprise guests interrupted Dottie Clayton, who had to set down her newspaper in the middle of the news about her nephew's trial. She fretted over not being there, but her responsibilities held her in place on her ranch in Ocala, Florida. She ushered her shelter ladies off to the stables to take the little boy and his father to see the horses. She then targeted her full attention to her latest guest, who sat on the back porch blowing through a box of tissues. Pulling up a chair beside her, Dottie waited. Carrie Ann, rattled to the core about something, had been babbling and weeping and had begun to sputter down to a state of relative self-control.

"They found me," Carrie Ann choked out. Another round of air-gulping sobs followed.

"Who found you?" Chills raced up Dottie's back.

"The bastards who buy and sell girls." Her eyes narrowed. She balled up tissues in both fists.

"Why do you think that?" Dottie kept her voice low and controlled to calm Carrie Ann. Sometimes victims saw danger where none existed. Women who had never seen combat could suffer from Post-Traumatic Stress Disorder.

"Last week a man followed me home from work."

"What did he look like?"

"An old, old guy, maybe sixty."

It stung a bit that Carrie Ann emphasized how old sixty was because Dottie would turn sixty by summer. Nonetheless, the girl's instincts had come from hard experience. A man that age might have been part of that human trafficking network Carrie Ann feared. *But how on earth could he have found her under her new name after all these years?* "Did you recognize him from…before?"

"No." Carrie Ann hugged herself and rocked side to side.

A whisper of relief brushed Dottie. "Maybe he was just your garden-variety stalker or a patient who fell in love with you."

Carrie Ann chuffed. A smile tugged at half of her mouth. "Mike was a patient. That's how we met."

Dottie sighed. For Carrie Ann to trust a man, he had to be someone exceptional. "Mike is—?"

"My husband."

Was the boy his, hers, or theirs? "Go on."

"When we first met, I told Mike I had a crazy ex-boyfriend, so he never asked me to talk about my past. Mike assumed that stranger who followed me was my ex. He wanted to confront the guy, but I begged him to pack up and leave with me and the baby."

"Did you call the police?"

Carrie Ann stared at her. "And say what?"

"That you were being stalked."

"And the guy would drive off. Then the police would ask for my fictional ex-boyfriend's name. No. I knew he followed me from the hospital. I couldn't risk staying. They know where I live. What am I going to do?" Carrie Ann flung herself into Dottie's embrace. For a moment, Carrie Ann seemed fifteen again.

"Oh, dear. I think I know who it was," Dottie said. "Was this man clean-shaven with no glasses?"

Carrie Ann lifted her head and nodded.

"His name is Quinn Flanagan. He worked for the FBI with my nephew."

"The FBI? Oh, no. No. No." Carrie Ann seemed on the verge of withdrawing to that place where victims of violence hide, where the outside world cannot be heard or felt.

Dottie held Carrie Ann by the shoulders. "You aren't in trouble. My nephew Blake is. He sent his friend Flanagan to find you. Blake is on trial for kidnapping a man named Curtis Frank."

Fear flickered in Carrie Ann's eyes. She bit her lip.

"If Blake is convicted he could get the death penalty."

"For kidnapping?" Carrie Ann broke away from Dottie's hold and stood. "That's crazy."

Dottie explained how the Felony Murder Rule raised kidnapping to a capital crime.

"Which one is Blake?"

"The youngest."

Carrie Ann's shoulders slumped. "He didn't kill Curtis."

Relieved to hear it, Dottie sighed. *So who did?*

"I'm as guilty as he is," Carrie Ann said softly. "And the other guys, too."

Was she confessing? Dottie shook her head. How could they all kill him? There were things in this life Dottie didn't want to know. She needed to relay the facts to Carrie Ann to show her the gravity of the situation. "His brothers weren't charged."

"That doesn't make any sense." Carrie Ann circled the table and chairs before returning to her chair.

"Would your testimony help Blake?"

"I can't testify. Mike doesn't know. If he knew—"

Dottie wanted to shake Carrie Ann from her selfish perspective but she stopped at simply grabbing Carrie Ann's shoulders. "You were a victim and Blake's life is at stake."

The phone rang. Dottie left Carrie Ann to stew over the situation while she marched into the house. She interrupted the third ring. The voice from the phone pierced the air in tones only dogs could hear. *Another female in crisis.*

"Calm down and take a breath," Dottie said. "I can't understand you."

"Papa had a heart attack," Marilyn-Anne said. "He's at Mission Hospital in Asheville."

Dottie grabbed the kitchen counter. "Oh, no." Her body numbed and her thoughts came to a standstill. *Not my brother. Oh, Ian.*

"He's going into surgery. Terri's on her way to pick you up at the Ocala airport."

"What do you mean she'll pick me up?"

"She's a pilot. A real over-achiever and Lord knows how she found time to learn to fly aside from vet school, but she's gonna fly you to Asheville. It will shave hours off the long drive."

"I'll be there as soon as I can." Dottie's eyes welled as she tried to hang the phone on the blurry wall. On the third try, it fit into the cradle. *Out of all the relatives, why Ian? Maeve, Dear Maeve, would be lost without him.* Dottie gathered her wits and headed to the bedroom to pack a bag. She had not traveled anywhere for years because she carried the responsibilities of running the shelter and the farm alone.

Where is that suitcase? She flung open her closet door and searched the crammed shelves, stepping over work boots and shoes and boxes of photos, shoving aside coats and dresses and slacks. She spotted the suitcase handle buried under a blanket so she jerked the suitcase free. A pile of blankets billowed to the floor. She swung the musty-smelling suitcase around toward the doorway.

Carrie Ann stood in silhouette, framed by the doorway. "Where are you going?"

Startled, Dottie realized Carrie Ann had followed her. The other ladies in the shelter never entered her room. When Carrie Ann had lived with her years ago she had full run of the house and stables. "My brother had a heart attack. This trial is too stressful for him." Her voice did not sound like her own as it forced its way through her tight throat. Her eyes stung. Energy jolted through her. She had to go. She had to pack. She had to get to the airport.

Carrie Ann backed out of the way, so Dottie carried the dusty suitcase to the bed where she unzipped it and flipped the top open. She grabbed clothes from the dresser and toiletries from the bathroom, tossing them into the suitcase each time she passed by it. She threw in shoes and a hairbrush, a nightgown and a framed photo of her with her brother in their teens side by side on horseback.

"I've only seen you cry once before."

Dottie paused to touch the photo of innocent times. "I cry. I just don't cry in front of people. I have to be the strong one others lean on." A crushing weight descended on her. *What if I lost Ian? Who would I have to lean on?*

Carrie Ann clasped her hands under her chin. "I'm so sorry. This is my fault."

"Don't you say that." Facing Carrie Ann, Dottie held her by the wrists. "I owe you. Because of you, I set up this women's shelter. Thanks to you, I had time to tend to Lucy in her last days. Remember that."

Carrie Ann nodded and hugged her.

When Dottie finished packing, she and Carrie Ann dashed to the stables. Dottie announced where she was going and why, then she assigned duties to the ladies. She told Carrie Ann that she and Mike and the baby could have her room as long as they needed. She asked Mike to take charge of things and like a good soldier, he agreed to shoulder the responsibilities with a simple, "Yes, ma'am." She asked Carrie Ann to drive her to the airport. They were on the road minutes later with Carrie Ann driving.

"I don't understand how the police connected Blake to Curtis Frank." Carrie Ann grimaced as if the name tasted foul.

"The prosecutor found Blake's work glove in the chains that were around the body. Oh, and supposedly there's an eyewitness."

"No way." Carrie Ann's eyebrows bunched over her nose. "One of his brothers?"

"Someone called Sweet Sally."

Carrie Ann clutched the plastic steering wheel so tightly it squeaked. Her jaw bulged as she clenched her teeth.

"Do you know her?" Dottie asked.

Carrie Ann nodded in jerky movements.

"Who is she?"

"A whore. She was in love with Curtis Frank. She'd do *anything* he asked."

They rode in silence to the terminal and waited in the lobby. Dottie let Carrie Ann stew in her own thoughts.

After watching planes come and go, Dottie recognized Terri climbing out of a small plane. She had no problem trusting a woman to fly the plane. She did, however, have reservations about getting into a plane that small. Were they as safe as the big commercial jets? She decided to fly in this tiny plane for her brother's sake. It would be fine. She could do this for Ian. Terri appeared so purposeful and professional on her way to the terminal. She was a woman on a mission.

"That's Blake's wife." Dottie stood and picked up her suitcase." Do you want to meet her?"

Carrie Ann stood. "I can't."

"Carrie Ann—"

"Call me Samantha."

"I love you no matter what you decide to do. This is a life-and-death decision, so make sure you can live with it for the rest of your life."

Carrie Ann hugged her before bolting from the terminal.

Terri opened the door from the runway at the same time Carrie Ann fled out the other door to the parking lot. Dottie stood in the middle of the small terminal lobby holding tightly to her suitcase and her conflicting loyalties.

Blake couldn't remember a longer day. He'd gone from sitting in the courtroom waiting for strangers to decide his fate, to pacing in a waiting room at the hospital waiting for strangers to announce his father's fate. If he could have had a moment of privacy he would have cried out of sheer helplessness.

It's my fault. This trial stressed Papa beyond his limit. He's not young anymore.

The Clayton family and friends camped in the waiting room closest to the operating room while surgeons inserted stents in two arteries of Papa's heart. Terri had breezed in thirty minutes ago with Aunt Dottie. Bubba's son Walker snored in his mother's lap. Butch's wife rocked baby Jeremiah in a car seat on the floor with her foot. Gator and his wife had the twins Remington and Colt asleep in their laps. Across from him on a sofa, Aunt Dottie stroked the hair of Moose's youngest son Micah who had fallen asleep in her lap. Noah slept sprawled on the other side of the sofa. Blake remembered his aunt had comforting ways with animals and small children. Pity she never had children. She would have been a loving parent. *It was a mighty shame she lost track of Carrie Ann.*

In the corner, high on the wall, a flat-screen television blared. Pacing the room, Blake considered the television background noise until the game show ended and the late evening news began.

"At the courthouse today, a kidnapping trial brought drama inside and outside of the courtroom. Mid-way through the day's proceedings, the father of accused kidnapper, FBI Agent Blake Clayton, had an apparent heart attack and had to be taken by ambulance from—"

Blake reached up, jerked the television plug from the outlet, and left the power cord dangling from the shoulder-high stand. He lowered himself to a seat between Terri and Vincent.

Bounding into the waiting room, Marilyn-Anne hefted oversized bags labeled KFC. Marilyn-Anne had gained weight in the middle. She was a stress eater and a fine cook. Bad combination. Blake felt responsible for the stresses on her.

Moose jumped up from his chair and took the heavy bags of food from his wife. "I told you to call me from the parking lot."

Marilyn-Anne planted a kiss on Moose's lips. She then smiled at Dottie. Leaning over her sleeping son Micah, she hugged Dottie around the shoulders. "I'm so glad you're here."

While the women handed out food and drinks, Blake realized he had not eaten since breakfast. Thanks to a diet of stress, fast food, and legal discussions, he had lost forty pounds in four months. At this rate, he was on his way to resembling the bones they'd dredged from the river.

His mother thumped him on the scalp with her finger. He peered up at her scowling face.

"You're too thin." Mama tended to fall into mothering overdrive during a crisis. One raised eyebrow warned him to eat or be force fed. She handed him a drink and a dinner box of chicken, biscuit, mashed potatoes and macaroni with cheese.

He took his dinner to deflect discussion about his weight. When his mother stepped away, he noticed her clothing hung loosely on her. He blamed himself for Papa's heart attack, Marilyn-Anne's stress eating, and his mother's weight loss. "How much have you lost, Mama?" he dared ask.

She carried a dinner box to her seat near the door and sat facing him. From across the room, she shrugged. Her gaze settled on him as if she had more to say, as if she might say she was losing a son and feared losing a husband. Her silence carried weight. Blake added that burden to his own.

Marilyn-Ann handed a dinner box to Vincent, who thanked her. The family had taken Vincent in like a brother, except for Marilyn-Anne's single sister Lynette, who flirted shamelessly with him. Twice Terri started a conversation about Nefi with Vincent, but Lynette steered the conversation back to herself.

Blake's thoughts drifted back to the trial. Watching the trial was like watching someone build a brick wall. Each argument, each bit of evidence, each testimony plopped another brick in place. He had hoped that Carrie Ann might knock the whole structure down. Terri said Carrie Ann was at a family funeral, but Flanagan said she was probably on the run. Flanagan tracked Mike Young's family back to Indiana. He even called Mike's parents, pretending to be a pal from the Navy, but they told him Mike was in Jacksonville. They even gave Flanagan his phone number, but Mike was not answering. *Another dead end.*

The lawyer said the prosecutor would call Sweet Sally to testify soon. He told Blake he should not take the stand to refute her version of the events that night, because once on the stand, he would have to answer any questions posed to him. No doubt the prosecution would have to pressure wash Sweet Sally and disguise her in presentable attire for the jury. The jury would not see a prostitute, but a friend of the deceased ready to serve her duty as a citizen to report the crime as she saw it.

Blake crunched through the crispy coating of a drumstick. It tasted like salted dust, but Mama wanted him to eat.

The last time he saw Sweet Sally, she had driven off with another woman, Frank's cash, and his car. He never expected to see her again. How did it come to pass that Sweet Sally would be available to testify while Carrie Ann had vanished? It was worse than dumb luck. Dread wrapped cold fingers around Blake's heart. What if his attorney lost the case?

The door to the waiting room suddenly swung open to reveal an Oriental man dressed in green scrubs. His brown eyes scanned the room and stopped at Mama, who stood to meet him. Moose stepped up beside her and swung an arm around her. He was strong enough to hold her up if need be.

"Good evening, I'm Dr. Chang. Your husband is resting in the recovery area. In a little while he will be moved to the intensive care unit," he said. He then addressed the room. "Mr. Clayton must rest. The fewer visitors the better, and it is imperative that he have *stress-free* recovery time. Peace and quiet will help him heal. If he does well he could go home in a few days."

Mama said, "His sister and I will take turns staying with him."

Dr. Chang nodded at Mrs. Clayton. He glanced at the rest of the family. Blake took it as a warning to stay away from his patient. His gaze rested on Blake as if in recognition.

"Thank you, doctor," Mama said, embracing him. She sniffled and let him go.

He patted her back. "My nurse will come for you when he is moved." Dr. Chang flashed a smile as he ducked out of the waiting room.

A collective sigh sounded. Blake finished his meal and tossed the box in the trash. Moose and Marilyn-Anne gathered their sons.

Noah yawned and stretched. "Daddy? How come you aren't going to the courthouse every day?"

Moose glanced at Blake. "Uncle Blake's attorney said I should stay home in case he needs me to talk at the trial. And somebody has to keep the ranch running."

Moose led Noah to Mama for a hug on their way out. The other relatives broke camp by gathering their purses and toys. The relatives exchanged hugs. They mumbled their goodbyes softly and shuffled out. Lynette managed to hug Vincent as she passed him. Blake, Terri, and Vincent were the last to encourage Dottie and Mama to pass along their good wishes to Papa.

Blake kissed his aunt on the top of the head while he hugged her. "Papa will be very glad to see you. So am I. Thanks for coming."

Tears welled in Dottie's eyes. She hugged Terri then she wept into her handkerchief. Blake followed Terri and his best friend Vincent to the hallway. Despite the good news about his father, his mood sank. Aunt Dottie avoided eye contact, caught up perhaps in her own fears of loss; she gave every impression she blamed him for Papa's heart attack. Or maybe she expected the jury to convict. She had distanced herself from Blake, but not from the rest of the family.

Wearily, he followed Terri and Vincent. He dreaded leaving the hospital. Even at this hour, the ghoulish media wanted to add Papa's heart attack to Blake's trial. Blake imagined half a dozen reporters camped at the emergency room entrance, blocking the only way into the hospital after visiting hours.

Vincent redirected Blake and Terri through the hospital to the employee entrance and parking garage to his rental car. Vincent evaded the media horde by driving out to the main road and on to the Grove Park Inn and Resort.

It was ten o'clock by the time Terri and Blake were done showering, dressing, and falling into bed at the Grove Park Inn and Resort. When Blake rolled onto his side to face Terri, her heart rate picked up the pace. It had been too long since they had been in bed together. As exhausted as she was, she still ached for him.

"I appreciate you picking up Aunt Dottie today. Everyone was pretty amazed you offered after flying up from Jacksonville."

She didn't remember mentioning Jacksonville to anyone. How

did he know where she had been? *Flanagan.* "We couldn't have her trying to drive when she was so upset."

Blake nodded and sat up. His body seemed to be shrinking with each week. Fat, muscle, posture, all seemed to be collapsing in on him. He rubbed his face with his hands, then let them drop away. "I think you should skip the trial."

Terri sat up. "Why?"

"My career is ruined. I don't want to ruin yours as well."

"I've missed a little work, but—"

"Please, don't come to the trial." He spoke without making eye contact.

Stung, she bit her tongue. She didn't want to argue. Blake might be trying to justify sending her away out of shame. "I want to support you."

"Please, don't come to the trial."

Exhaustion and guilt bore down on her. "Did Flanagan tell you that I lost Carrie Ann?"

Blake nodded.

She wanted to argue she couldn't have scared off Carrie Ann because Carrie Ann was already gone. Excuses couldn't help Blake. Excuses were all she had to offer besides her presence and apparently he didn't want that. "I'm so sorry. I'll fly home tomorrow."

"I'm sorry too."

With that, Terri fell back on her pillow and rolled on her side with her back to Blake. *Oh, God, please don't let my failure kill Blake.*

. 18 .

On Tuesday, April 6th, Ernie had enough time for breakfast at Casey's Diner before driving to Asheville to cover the day's trial. He sat at the far end of the counter, away from the Christian Businessmen's Breakfast Meeting, hoping he would not be invited to join them. He scanned the menu and ordered the Tuesday special—three scrambled eggs, cheesy hash brown casserole, wheat toast, and hickory smoked bacon. He suspected the breakfast special was the reason the group met on Tuesdays.

He noticed Jeremiah Clayton's absence. *Guess Jeremiah was ashamed for dumping the responsibilities of the church on the associate pastor.* Ernie judged churchgoing a waste of good fishing time.

Mandy, a part-time waitress and full-time single mother, served Ernie his food. The scent of bacon rose to his eager nose. He anticipated the cheesy hash browns to be crispy on the outside and warm gooey inside. Mandy had topped off his coffee before she headed to the men's group. While Ernie salted his eggs, the bell that hung on the diner door clanked on the glass. Out of habit, he checked to see who entered.

Marilyn-Anne Clayton. She stood at the door as though she'd never been inside before. Suddenly, her whole body aimed at Ernie. Chins up, eyes narrowed, she had the look of someone determined to pick a fight.

"There you are," she shouted to the back of the room, the section Ernie had to himself.

Ernie flinched. He spun his stool to face her while she tromped toward him, all two hundred pounds of her. Conversations among the businessmen stopped. He braced for wrath. Last year, he had accidentally omitted her son's name from a T-ball team listing which brought on a blistering phone call.

"I am sick to death of your lazy, biased reporting," she said, stopping within arm's reach of him. "Why all you do is write a *Reader's Digest* condensed version of what happened at trial every day. Not a single kind word about Blake or the family. Why is that?"

"I don't expect you to understand."

"Huh. Oh, I don't understand. I don't understand why Maeve won't stop the half-page ad we run every week." Marilyn-Anne shook a copy of the paper at him. She held an armload of newspapers. Slapping his newspaper on the counter beside his food, she added, "This isn't fit to put under puppies."

Chuckles sounded from the far side of the diner. Ernie cringed.

"Maeve won't stop the ad because she says it would look *petty*," Marilyn-Anne said. "Well, I say, we look *stupid* to continue paying money to somebody who badmouths us."

"I have to report the trial. It's news." Ernie set down his fork.

"I know that. But you go out of your way to be mean about it. Every time you use his name you call Blake the alleged kidnapper. But here *The Charlotte Observer* calls him a Marine and former FBI agent." She smacked the paper on the counter and pointed to a paragraph circled in blood-red marker and planted a third paper on the stack. "And in the *Asheville Citizen-Times*, they ask, 'What would drive a fifteen-year-old high school boy to kidnap a convicted felon?'"

Ernie's face burned. He despised being lectured by a housewife. He pitied Samuel Clayton for marrying her. Though he longed to denounce her accusations, the clarity of her argument gave him pause to listen.

She propped a fist on her hip. "And what about Papa? He's a leader in our community," she said over her shoulder, "and you don't even mention he had a heart attack."

Chagrined, he realized he forgot to write up a piece on it. He had heard that Mr. Clayton came out of surgery after the paper's deadline, but he should have written about the man being rushed to the hospital. "Well, it happened in Asheville."

Marilyn-Anne arched an eyebrow and puckered her cherry red lips. "The mayor broke his arm last year in Florida, and he got a front page mention." She pivoted and addressed the men at the other end of the diner. "How many of you knew about Papa's heart attack?"

Half of them raised hands. Mandy raised hers, waving her pen. Ernie cringed. Southern women could devastate like a tornado when they got riled. All the more reason to enjoy being single. He feared anything he said would be sharpened into a weapon to stab him with, so he bit his tongue. His other advertisers sat within earshot.

"So, mister *newsman*, you aren't even keeping up with the grapevine. Why don't you get off your butt and do some real investigative reporting? And while you're at it, why don't you tell your readers who Curtis Frank was, what he did for a living, and what he was doing in that old farmhouse? I got news for you—he wasn't *farming*." With that, she grunted, spun on a sharp heel, and waddled out of the diner.

Her two sons, their faces pressed against the outside window, stepped back when the diner door swung open. The bell clanked, like the bell signaling the end of a fight in the ring. Dazed and wounded, Ernie had clearly lost this round against the formidable Marilyn-Anne Clayton. She had uttered the word 'butt' in public, which for a Southern lady, had the equivalent impact of a true swear word. She had delivered him a bruising verbal smack-down.

Ernie sighed at his cold breakfast. He sensed the eyes of the entire Christian Businessmen's group boring into his side. Mandy's distant voice prompted a man to order the special.

Casey, the diner's owner and cook, stepped from the passageway between the kitchen and the counter. "Want me to reheat your food?"

"Please." Ernie pushed the plate across the counter.

"I couldn't help but overhear," Casey said. "Have you ever asked yourself why the Clayton Ranch advertises in your paper?"

"I'm the only newspaper around." Ernie took a swig of warm coffee.

Casey planted his hands on the edge of the counter. "They don't breed horses for local folks. Their customers come from around the country."

The Clayton Ranch had run a half-page weekly ad since Ernie took over the newspaper. *Why advertise for twenty-three years if it didn't help their business?* "Are you sure about that?"

"Moose told me when we went deer hunting last year."

"Then why do they spend money on an ad? Do they just throw money around to impress people?"

Casey lowered his voice. "Could be they want to support the local newspaper. They buy their vehicles local. They get their feed from a local store. Just like the rest of the Christian Businessmen's group, they stick together to support the community."

Guilt, like the dawn, illuminated Ernie's mind, changing his perspective. He had assumed the Claytons needed to advertise in his paper. He had also assumed they bought a huge half-page ad to flaunt their wealth. What else had he been wrong about? "Say, Casey, do you think I've been biased?"

"I think Marilyn-Anne is asking the same questions I've been thinking." Casey carried the plate back to the kitchen.

Ernie stared into his coffee. The Clayton boys had a reputation for wild stunts. Ernie had assumed Frank's death was a stunt gone wrong, that the boys had disposed of the body to cover up the worst blunder of their lives. Perhaps they had, but he had no evidence to back up his assumption. Why would they involve Frank in a prank? As much as he loathed admitting it, Marilyn-Anne was right. Being editor and chief reporter meant he didn't have anyone to answer to, allowing him to get lazy. The situation reminded Ernie of something his hero, Lester Markel of the *New York Times* had once said, "What you see is news, what you know is background and what you feel is opinion."

Ernie recognized he had allowed his assumptions and opinions to guide him. If he had worked at a major metropolitan newspaper he would have been fired. Working nearly solo over the years, he had let his standards slide. The community depended on him. He had let them down.

He vowed to develop the bigger picture on the kidnapping trial. He would show everyone he had the skills to mine this story for all it was worth. He would redeem himself as a professional journalist by digging deeper for the truth. This should be his story for crying out loud; he had the home-field advantage. He could get the big story, the kind the Associated Press or UPI picked up for national exposure. He could win back respect from his advertisers and readers, and his self-respect.

If nothing else, I could get Marilyn-Anne Clayton off my back.

⁌─╂─⁌

That day, after flying from Asheville to Poughkeepsie, Terri convened a video conference call meeting with the STARs. She vented about the trial, about Blake, about losing perhaps the only witness who could exonerate Blake. She speculated that the witness ran because she was guilty of the murder. When she had exhausted every thought and afterthought about the situation, she asked her dearest friends in the world what she should do.

Suki weighed in with her legal assessment. "Jury trials are a gamble. Even if he didn't do it, he could be convicted through the circumstantial evidence. However, his attorney has a top-notch reputation and there's always the appeals process if things go south."

Arlene groaned. "Good pep talk, Suki."

"Hey, if she asked you about a tax problem," Suki said, "would you shine her on with talk of rainbows and butterflies or would you tell her the truth?"

Arlene gave a heavy sigh. Arlene taught accounting to college students, so Terri imagined she had more patience than most people, but Suki tended to exasperate her. "Do you think he's guilty?"

A heaviness settled on Terri. She'd followed the newspaper reports and the televised news broadcasts. The prosecutor's evidence pointed to guilt. That glove with Blake's initials on it was a one-of-a-kind. Blake was being evasive. His brothers all lawyered up. Should she believe the mounting evidence or her heart? She didn't like being wrong, but it was more than pride that led her to hope for his innocence. She believed in Blake. "No. I can't reconcile the Blake I know with someone who would kidnap his neighbor. Blake was only fourteen years old when this guy disappeared."

"You didn't know him back then." Suki crossed her arms.

"Can anyone change that much?" Terri glanced at the small section of the laptop that showed Reva's face. "Reva? What do you think?"

"I'm worried about you." Onscreen Reva tucked a handful of thick brown curls behind her ear. "You're used to achieving your goals by working harder, putting in more hours, and delaying gratification."

"So?"

"When was the last time you were happy?"

"At my wedding."

"Six months ago." Reva raised her eyebrows. "In all the years

I've known you, you always put off your own happiness. In high school you said you would be happy after you got into the right college. In college you said you'd be happy after you got into the *right* vet school. After vet school you told us how great life would be once you joined your dad's practice."

"I have goals. What's wrong with that?"

"You don't *achieve* happiness. Happiness isn't conditional. You can't store it up for retirement. Honestly, you act like you don't deserve it."

Terri had played by the rules and life wasn't paying off the way she had planned. Why couldn't her friends see this injustice crushing her? "Are you saying I should be *happy* my husband is on trial and facing the death penalty?"

Reva shook her head and closed her eyes. "I'm saying life is short. You made a vow to love Blake no matter what, for better or worse, until death. We don't know when our time will end. If Blake is convicted, then your marriage will have an expiration date. How you handle that and every other tragedy in your life shows what you really value."

"He told me to stay away from the trial," Terri said.

Suki snorted. "And you always do whatever a *man* tells you to do? Seriously? Who are you and what have you done with my friend Terri?"

After a fitful night, Terri awoke determined to fly to Asheville, however the Wednesday weather was equally determined to prevent her. She couldn't fly until Thursday, so she decided to put in a day's work and then tell her partners she was taking time off. She logged Wednesday, April 7th, 2010, in her smart phone and saw an appointment to visit to Cooper Racing Farms. The twin foals were due at the end of the month.

She chewed her last antacid tablet, tossed clothes into her suitcase, and then she drove to the office for supplies. Melanie was writing notes and listening to messages on the answering machine when Terri entered. The other partners' offices were dark.

The drive to the farm gave her time to think. Taking time off would cost her dearly. They'd need all her income and then some to pay off the attorney. If convicted, Blake would need years of the attorney's time to fund an appeal.

Arriving at Cooper Racing Farms, she drove directly to the stables. She climbed from her truck with her kit. Hay, feed, mud, and manure scents wafted downwind from the stables. In the distance a dog barked. She entered the stables in search of the pregnant mare's stall.

The owner of the stable, Mr. Kit Cooper, and his jockey stepped out of a stall. Cooper said something to the man, who ducked out the far side of the stables. Terri waved as she approached the owner of the stables.

"Hello, Doc." Cooper did not make eye contact.

Terri stepped up beside him and glanced at the open stall. The round mare chomped through the feed. "How's her appetite?"

Cooper closed the stall door. "I meant to call you."

"She's okay?"

"She's fine. I'll be hiring another vet to take care of her."

Rejection slapped Terri as painfully as if Cooper had used his hand. "Why?"

"I'm sorry. This business about your husband...I can't afford even a whiff of scandal if I want to race my horses." With his head bowed, he peered at her.

"If you knew the whole story," she said. But she understood Cooper had already made up his mind. He was an honest man in an industry pockmarked with criminals. She moved her medical kit to her left hand. "I understand your position. We recently added a new partner to our group. If you call the office and ask for Justin Cook, I'm sure he'll take great care of your horses. We were in the same graduating class."

Cooper nodded and cleared his throat. "Already called him. Doctor Cook told me you were the top of your class."

She nodded. *Thank you, Justin.* "Sir, just so you know, the grade point average between the top of the class and the bottom of the class is less than a tenth of one percent." She stuck out her hand.

Cooper shook her hand. "I am sorry. Hope things work out for you."

Terri reined in her urge to scream. Instead of raging at the injustice of the situation, she forced her body to behave, to obey her will. Her blood raced hot and cold with each step back to her vehicle. This was business, not personal, though it hurt at a personal level. Why did it seem twice the distance back to her truck?

On the way to her office she activated the Bluetooth on her truck. After Melanie had recited her standard greeting, Terri told her to transfer the Cooper account to Justin.

"Okay, I'll do that right away," Melanie said. "Will you be back for the four o'clock meeting?"

Since when did we meet on a Wednesday? Terri checked her watch. She had a two-hour drive. "I can be there. Who called the meeting?"

"The other partners," the secretary said. Her voice dropped to a whisper. "Just between us, girl to girl, it sounds like they're plotting to boost you out. They mentioned something about your husband being in the news."

Oh, dear. Terri fished for more information, girl to girl. "By any chance did they invite a lawyer to the meeting?"

Other voices sounded in the background. "Yes, ma'am," Melanie's voice grew louder and her tone more businesslike. "Is there anything else I can help you with?"

"Is Justin going along with this?"

Male voices sounded in the background.

"I'm not sure, ma'am. Will there be anything else?"

"See you at four." Terri disconnected the call. None of the partners had mentioned a meeting this morning when she stopped by to pick up supplies. So. They intended to meet behind her back. *Those cowardly jackals.* How sad that an employee watched out for her when her business partners did not. Her father had started the business. Too bad he was retired or he would have told them off. It was up to her now.

Blake's eyes glazed over while the prosecutor presented forensic specialists who detailed their calculations on the exact date of death of Curtis Frank. The current witness, a balding man in his seventies, rambled on about the Jordan River's tides, about the dates it froze and thawed over the previous twenty years. Even the charts and graphs threatened to put him to sleep, so he ventured to look for his few fans in the spectator area.

Mama's presence meant that Aunt Dottie was with Papa. His sisters-in-law flanked Mama, except for Marilyn-Anne. A few townsfolk had shown up, but he didn't know if they were here to show support or to watch the spectacle of the trial. The good news was that Ernie wasn't taking notes in the back row. In fact, he wasn't in the courtroom. Maybe he was late. Maybe a fire or a business bankruptcy displaced the trial as the biggest news story in town. Terri was back in New York. Even though he had sent her away, he missed her. It was purely selfish to ask her to hang around. He needed for her to seriously consider divorce. No need to drag her down just because she felt the need to do the right thing.

Vincent, who sat directly behind Blake, nodded at him. Blake nodded back and then he settled in to pretend to pay attention to the expert witness.

He could have mainlined coffee and still felt drowsy as the witness droned on in a monotone. Outside protesters chanted, their voices carrying into the courtroom whenever the prosecutor paused. He watched dust swirl in a shaft of light beaming down from the ceiling.

Terri climbed out of her truck as the dust settled in the parking lot from her arrival. Three fifty on the clock. She had decided during the drive to the office that she would pretend she had not been tipped off about the meeting. If her partners were cold enough to try to push her out, they would be ruthless enough to fire Melanie for warning her. During the drive, she had also consulted her attorney. He reminded her of the morals clause in the contract. Though they could kick *her* out for being arrested and charged with any of a long list of crimes; they were on tenuous legal standing to apply that clause to her husband's arrest. The attorney said a conviction would strengthen their position because it could cause harm by association.

Swinging open the back door to the office, she strode to her office without stopping at the front desk. Dog smells wafted down the hallway. Barking from the kennel across the hallway from her office filled the building with sound. Despite the vast numbers of dogs, cats and birds the other two partners treated, their combined earnings did not match hers.

She stashed her medical kit in her closet and parked herself in the soft leather desk chair behind her father's desk to watch the hallway traffic. Even though her name was on the door and the letterhead and the sign outside, she still felt at times like a child in her father's office. Her father's massive oak desk had been a pirate ship, a cave, the Great Wall of China, and other such places in the afternoons when her mother filled in for a sick employee. One corner of the desk bore indentations from the galloping tiny hooves of Terri's horse figurines.

She straightened the picture frames of her parents and Blake on the desk as if to claim the space as her own. Her licenses and diplomas hung on the walls. Her books and tools adorned the credenza. Her computer anchored one corner of the desk. A pile of charts sat in her inbox awaiting her signature on the transcribed dictation. She plucked a file from the inbox and pretended to read it while she waited.

Barking filled the hallway. This indicated someone passing through the pen area from the back door.

Moments later, her two senior business partners and a heavy-set man in a shiny black silk business suit passed her office door, toward the front office, without a glance in her direction.

The door to the conference room closed. Terri took a few deep, cleansing breaths. She then headed after them. One of the assistants led a collie toward the kennel. She stopped abruptly when she spotted Terri. She bit her lip as Terri passed. Being the last to know news about her own business infuriated Terri, but she needed to shut down her emotions for the time being. *This is a business.*

She headed to the conference room and opened the door. Her partners Anders and Everly gasped. She took a seat at the conference table. The attorney had the face of a veteran poker player. He was the first to regain composure.

"Doctor Pinehurst," he said.

"I go by Pinehurst-Clayton since my wedding."

Everly fidgeted. Anders cleared his throat. Justin was not in the room. *How interesting.*

The attorney said, "I've been invited today to explore the business contract."

Terri didn't care to mince words with this fat eel of a man. "Whose?" She eyed her partners. "Because if we're exploring Justin's contract he should be here now that he's a full partner."

And he might even the vote. Terri deplored obfuscation, the specialty of business lawyers who charged obscene amounts of money by the hour for it.

Anders pursed his lips as if fighting to hold back his bluntness. He was almost as old as Terri's father. She thought of him as an uncle. She had trusted him.

Everly spread open his hands at Terri. "We wanted to review your contract. We could lose clients because of your husband's trial."

Anders spoke gently, "That's not—"

"Have you lost any business?" she asked Everly, who managed the money part of the business while Terri and Anders managed the people.

"I'm not sure yet. People might not tell us when they decide to go elsewhere."

"Blake was arrested four months ago. I haven't seen our net earnings change," Terri said.

"But the trial is in the news now," Everly said. "People are becoming aware of it."

Terri sat back in her chair. "Do you really believe anyone would stop bringing their pets to you because of me?" She glared at Everly and Anders. "Somehow I've worked fewer days and still managed to pay my share of the overhead."

The attorney reentered the conversation. "And how long will you be able to sustain this level of work?"

Terri's lips parted. Her mind paused. She was emotionally and physically exhausted. By sheer determination, she kept tears back. "I was planning to take a leave of absence."

After a few moments of silence, the attorney said, "I've looked through your business contract and there is no clause for a leave of absence beyond medical reasons."

"So if I had a heart attack, we wouldn't be having this discussion."

"Terri," Anders said, "your father taught me how to manage a business. He also taught me to watch for signs of burnout."

Terri's eyes burned. Her father worked long after he should have retired to keep the business running until she could fill his place. His eye problems got in his way so that he became more and more dependent on assistants to double-check his work. When he retired, he sold the building to Terri.

Everly's voice rolled softly over the surface of the table. "We could buy you out. That would give you enough income to last two, maybe three—"

"We were going to meet today to hash out figures so we could make you an offer," Anders said, interrupting Everly, who was better at dealing with animals than with people.

Despite her immediate reaction to argue, she took a deep breath and tamped down her emotions. Anders had been a loyal friend to her father. He had allowed her father to set his own timeline to retire when a more money-driven partner would have boosted him out. Everly was a different kind of partner, not the kind she considered a friend. Were Everly and Anders being good business partners by trying to design a win-win situation? Or did they want to take over the business her father and Anders had built now that Justin could be their big earner?

Justin entered the room. He pulled up a chair beside Terri. "Hey, Terri. I thought you'd be in Asheville." Justin's calm, friendly demeanor seemed incongruous with a forced buy-out.

"Tell me, Justin," she asked evenly, "what's the purpose of this meeting?"

Justin's eyes softened. "We're worried about you. The trial doesn't look good for your husband. I suggested we find a way to help you support yourself and pay legal expenses."

"If you were me, would you give up your practice?"

"If you fight half as hard for your husband as you did to bring me into this practice, then he's a lucky, lucky man," Justin said. "I can't imagine what you're going through, but if he is convicted and you have to appeal his case, well, it could take years of appeals. I've never seen you give up on something you believe in. I don't think you know how."

Everly, for all his awkwardness in human interactions, nodded along as if to second what Justin said. Anders gave a half smile.

Warmth welled in her chest. Emotions roiled and mixed in a way that confused her. She couldn't identify the feelings warring inside her. Fearing an unbridled outburst, she stood. "All right. Make me an offer. I'll be in my office."

Anders nodded.

Terri trod to her office. After shutting her door, she settled into her father's old leather chair behind his great desk. She planted her hands on the smooth worn oak and took deep breaths to stop shaking. She had achieved her childhood goal of joining her father in the business, even though he retired. The stone cold reality— she estimated that packing the personal items that anchored her childhood goal to her current reality would take less than an hour and five boxes. Anders, Everly, and Justin could have the business. She could rent the building to them. Her mind tried to convince her body she could manage upheaval. This was, after all, just material stuff.

What do I value? I want my daddy's desk. Swirling emotions ebbed and in the quiet an unexpected sensation crept in. Relief.

. 19 .

On Thursday, April 8th, only days after Papa's Clayton's heart surgery, Blake endured another emotionally devastating day. Mama wasn't going to be in court today because she was supposed to bring Papa home from the hospital. She'd be far better off at home today fussing over Papa than listening to today's presentation of evidence and the witness.

Then a witness was sworn in under the name Sally Marie Henson. With her garish makeup, she gave the impression of being a drag queen. She had the look of a nag that had been ridden hard and put up wet.

She slapped her right hand on the Bible and in a deep smoky voice she promised to tell the truth. Dressed in a high-neck black dress, she could have passed for a normal seventy-year-old woman, except for her jet black hair. When she stated her full name and age, a few jurors raised their eyebrows at her. Sweet Sally said she was fifty-two. Judge Parker's glance swept from Sweet Sally to the prosecutor. The prosecutor nodded at the judge.

The prosecutor stood by his table. "What was your relationship to the deceased?"

"Me and Curtis was what you call common law married."

"And how long were you together?"

"I stayed with Curtis for ten years," Sally said. She tugged a white handkerchief from her sleeve and dabbed her eyes. "Curtis always called me his Sweet Sally."

The attorney had warned that eye-rolling would be interpreted as arrogance, so Blake closed his eyes to hide it. He tasted bile. Would she cry on cue while she told the heart-wrenching saga of a whore and her pimp? Blake twisted around in his chair toward his family. Again, only the wives were in court. Blake wished his brothers were there. If they had been, Butch would have been upset because he did not take it lightly when people used a Bible as a prop. Gator's wife gave a thumbs-down gesture meaning Sally was going to hell.

Until the defense's turn came, all Blake could do was listen and wait. His attorney had explained that court cases are played like chess, each move planned out and timed for maximum effect. Blake, more of a checkers player, itched to see a counter strategy in motion. They had to discredit Sweet Sally, to expose her untrustworthiness, to reveal to the jury that her testimony was her attempt to cash a get-out-of-jail-free card. Gator's wife was right. Sweet Sally aimed her life for hell. Too bad she wanted to drag someone down with her.

Blake recalled the night he heard Gator confess he was going to hell. At age seventeen, Gideon, better known as Gator, was unanimously the best looking of the Claytons. He could get beer from senior girls anytime he asked for it, so when Blake found him puking in the bathroom one night, he left him alone. When sobbing sounded from the bathroom, Blake decided to check on him.

"Gator?"

"I'm going straight to hell."

"You're going to bed." Blake hefted Gator to his feet then hauled him to bed.

Gator fell onto his back. He grabbed Blake's arm. "I went to old man Frank's house."

The old farm house on the edge of their property had been abandoned for months. "Did you break in?"

Gator pulled Blake down close enough to share his beer breath. "Noooooo. I heard a guy at the diner say there was a party there. I followed him."

That did not make sense. Girls called Gator for dates. Blake enjoyed the flirtations of older girls only to find out they wanted to use him to get to Gator. Girls went to extremes to accidentally run into Gator after school, at the mall, at the Casey's Diner, and after football games.

Gator grabbed Blake's shirt and whispered, "He has women in the bedrooms. And then he unlocked the door to the basement and took me downstairs. Said he had one my age."

"Is somebody living in old man Frank's house?"

Gator nodded.

Blake pulled away as far as Gator's grip allowed. "What women?"

Releasing Blake, he slapped his hands on his face and rocked side to side. With his face scrunched up like he was in pain, he said, "hookers."

Disgusted, Blake whispered, "Are you kidding me?"

Gator shook his head.

Why Gator would even consider paying for something half the senior class wanted to *give* him was a question with only one answer. "You're out of your damn mind."

"She was chained to the bed." Gator resumed rocking and patting his hands on his wet face.

"Who?"

"Carrie Ann Snow."

Had he taken something stronger than beer that made him hallucinate?

"I told her I'd call the police, and then she pointed to the ceiling." Gator imitated her. He stared upward in horror, then he wept and drew himself into a ball. "She's trapped. She's trapped. Trapped."

Blake hated that he'd been baited into his brother's drunken hallucination. "Why did she point up?"

Gator unraveled his arms and legs and solemnly stared at the ceiling. "There was a bomb in the ceiling. I saw it. That bastard pimp told her if the place gets raided, he's blowing up the house with her in it."

"You're full of it."

"Dynamite and two gas cans say I'm not lying."

Between the details and his brother's distraught behavior, Blake started to believe Gator. Cold fear crawled into his heart. Maybe Gator really did see a girl chained in the basement of the old Frank place. It was like a horror film. They had to save her. "Let's tell Pa."

Gator said, "He'd call the sheriff."

Of course he would. And the sheriff would raid the place and the pimp would blow up the evidence. Papa's faith in law enforcement and the American legal system ran deep, almost as deep as his faith in God. Blake couldn't live with himself if he didn't rescue Carrie Ann. Nobody should be treated like that. Even farm dogs ran free.

Gator snorted. It was a sound between a laugh and a cough. "Pa always says that if we put as much energy into something other than getting into trouble we could change the world."

Blake swatted Gator's shoulder. "That's it!" Blake dashed into the corridor and woke Moose. "Get up. Come to Gator's room. We got us a situation."

Moose threw off his covers. He glanced out the window toward the barn. "What kind of situation?"

A barn fire was the most urgent kind of situation on the ranch. Blake hissed, "Get Bubba while I get Butch. And don't wake Mom and Dad."

Moose headed to Bubba's room without another word.

Blake shook Butch awake. "Shhhh. I need your help."

Butch, the peacekeeper of the family, prayed like he meant it, so the brothers believed he had a hotline to God. Butch was the last one to lose his temper, but on the rare occasion he was pushed to the limit, he would fight until he was pulled out of the fight.

The five brothers gathered cross-legged on the floor of Gator's room. They listened closely while Blake briefed them on Carrie Ann's plight. To a man, they reacted with the same disgust and horror Blake had.

Moose was the first to emerge from shock. "Tomorrow's the parade. Everyone, even the sheriff and the town cops will be there. That's when we can rescue her."

"But how?"

"Did you see any locals at the house?" Moose asked Gator.

"Naw. Just truckers."

"What about the guy in charge?" Moose asked.

"Never saw him before. He acted like he owned the place," Gator said.

"Pa said no one but the pastor and the digger came to old man Frank's funeral," Bubba said.

Gator's voice came out raspy, "This wasn't a ghost. It was a fat guy."

"Hear me out and if my plan has any gaps, let's fix 'em," Moose declared, "Tomorrow, we rescue a soul from hell."

If only their plan had worked. Blake leaned back in his chair in the courtroom. Moose had been right about rescuing a soul from hell. He didn't know then that they would also deliver one.

Blake's attorney scooted his chair back. The action startled Blake from his memories. "So after you witnessed your beloved common-law husband of ten years being forcibly taken away by strangers," the attorney said with a voice of concern, "what did you do?"

Sally pursed her bright red lips and answered directly to the jury. "I took off in Curtis's car 'cause I feared for my life."

Blake snatched up his pen and jotted on his legal pad: *She was not alone with Frank. There was another woman there.* The attorney nodded at Blake. After tugging down the front of his jacket, he stood to cross-examine Sally Marie Henson.

"Was this car registered to Curtis Frank?"

"Yes, it was his car." Sally sounded a bit annoyed at being interrupted.

"And was anyone else in the house with you that evening?" the attorney asked.

Sally blinked rapidly. "No, sir. It was just me and Curtis. We was just having a quiet evening."

Blake reminded himself that his attorney was the finest criminal attorney in the southeast, so he tucked away the urge to call out the woman for lying. The attorney's favorite phrase, often repeated to Blake, was "all in good time."

"And when did you report to the police that your beloved had been kidnapped?"

"What do you mean?" Sally leaned back slightly, eyeing the attorney.

"And after you ran for your life in Curtis's car," the attorney said, "did you rush to the nearest police station or call the sheriff?"

"I...was too scared to think straight. I just kept going."

"And now, sixteen years later," he paused for emphasis, "have you calmed down enough to tell what happened that night?"

Spectators snickered and a few jurors smirked. Blake focused on Sally.

Sally scowled at the attorney, her eyelids narrowed to slits, and her jaw clenched tight. "I don't trust the police after what happened to Curtis in Ohio."

The attorney's voice dropped to an intimate tone, "And what happened in Ohio?"

"Objection!" The prosecutor bolted to his feet. "What is the relevance of the victim's past?"

Judge Parker sighed. Hope rose in Blake's chest like a helium balloon. His faith in his attorney bolstered, he silently blessed the man.

"Your honor," Blake's attorney said, "the witness's state of mind was influenced by something from *her* past. We have established she was Curtis's common law wife for ten years prior to his death."

"Objection sustained. Tread lightly."

Blake's attorney lowered his head as if examining his papers. A stillness settled in the room. Blake believed the jury was stewing over why Sally didn't report the kidnapping.

The attorney raised his attention back to the witness. "When you fled for your life, did you have time to take anything from the house?"

Sally's eyes tracked to Blake. She rolled her shoulders back and raised her chin. "I grabbed a little bit of money that me and Curtis had saved up."

"How much money?"

"Well, I don't recall exactly."

"Do you remember what it felt like? Was it a few bills? A wad of bills, perhaps?"

Sally shrugged. Judge Parker glanced down at the witness like a warning.

"You are under oath." The defense attorney tried again. "How much money would you estimate you and Curtis had saved up?"

Sally squirmed and primped her hair with her fingertips while avoiding eye contact with the attorney. "Maybe close to ten thousand."

A collective gasp sounded from the spectators. A few jurors dropped their jaws. Blake remembered seeing the roll of cash.

The attorney nodded. "Ten thousand dollars cash, I see. In your ten years with Curtis, did you file income taxes on your earnings?"

"I don't know. Curtis handled the money." Her right eyelid twitched.

"And how did he earn his money?"

"Objection as to relevance," the District Attorney said.

"Objection sustained." Judge Parker lifted one eyebrow at Blake's attorney.

After gently smoothing his tie, Blake's attorney resumed his cross-examination, "Did the boys tell you what they were going to do with Mr. Frank?"

"They said they was going to take him to the sheriff." Sally snorted. She rubbed her twitching eyelid.

"So why did you feel the need to flee for your life?"

"I told you. I don't trust the police."

"So it was the police and not the boys that you were running from."

"Objection!" the District Attorney said. "Is there a question in there?"

Judge Parker's voice rang sharply at Blake's attorney. "Counselor, you know better than that."

The defense attorney shuffled papers on his table.

Blake watched him. It seemed his attorney was counting silently to himself. Either he was tamping down anger or he wanted his accusation of cowardice to settle into the minds of the jury before he spoke again. The attorney let go of the papers to face the witness.

"When you drove away with Frank's money and his car, leaving your common law husband behind, did you double back to follow the boys?"

"No." Sally squirmed in her chair and brushed a stray curl from her forehead.

"Now the next question requires a simple 'yes' or 'no' answer. Did you witness Curtis Frank's death?"

Sally squinted at him then at Blake.

The attorney addressed the judge, "Your Honor, the witness has not answered the question."

Judge Parker glared down at Sally. "You will answer the question or be held in contempt."

"Yes or no. Did you witness Curtis Frank's death?"

"No." Sally added, "I didn't personally see what—"

Blake's attorney raised his voice over Sally's, "I have no

further questions at this time for the witness," the defense attorney said, "but I reserve the option to recall her."

Blake longed for the jury to learn how Curtis had earned the money. Bless him, the attorney tried to present Curtis's past. Would the guy be able to discredit Sally or her testimony when it was his turn to present the case? Reasonable doubt, that's all they needed and the more the better. The jury probably wasn't there yet.

Sheriff Pete Ketchum wrote his weekly report on the Frank case in his office on Friday, April 9th. Relieved that his testimony about the search of the Clayton Ranch showed his team had processed the evidence properly, he nonetheless despised himself. The prosecutor had tiptoed around the reason the FBI had been brought into the case. He never asked about it so Ketchum could not talk about the bomb squad or the bomb. The prosecutor had not asked about the extensive pornography either. Why didn't the defense attorney bring it up during cross-examination?

Of course Ketchum abhorred vigilantism, but if anyone deserved to die by beating it was Curtis Frank. So how did it come to pass that one out of five of the boys who killed him could get the chair? Blake had served in the Marines and became an FBI agent. He had always been a loyal friend and an honest person. Weary of the ethical dilemma raging inside him, Ketchum washed down extra-strength headache pills with coffee.

Deputy Carl stepped into Ketchum's office and closed the door. "Boss, we got a problem."

Ketchum had an open-door policy. The only times he closed his door involved reprimands. He managed his people by the adage: praise in public, reprimand in private.

Carl's face grew pale. He chewed his bottom lip. He exhaled

loudly and dropped his hands to his sides. "A lady is here looking for you. She calls herself Samantha Adams. She wants to talk to you about the Frank case."

"Bring her in." Ketchum closed the file on his desk.

"She's in the lobby, but that's not the problem."

"Spit it out, man."

"Samantha Adams was the name of the girl who died in the film."

Ketchum sucked air. *Oh no. Had the Bureau already notified the next of kin?* He had not personally reviewed the recordings. "Put her in an interview room and offer her soda or coffee."

Carl held his ground. "Sir?"

"I know. I know. I'll call Special Agent Theron if this isn't a crackpot. You run the recording equipment."

"You betcha, sir."

Ketchum called Theron and briefed him.

"I see," Theron said. "I'm in Asheville. Go ahead and interview her. I'm on my way. I have some questions for her. Record everything and send me a photo of her so my men can run facial recognition. We need to compare it to the aged images made from Samantha Adams' missing person images."

"So the death wasn't really—"

"Sheriff, that girl in the video died. I double checked the recordings and none of the action was doctored. The metadata—"

"I don't need the techno-speak explanation," Ketchum said. If asked the time of day, Special Agent Theron would describe how to build a watch. He didn't seem to be showing off his knowledge, but he insisted on explaining the precise how and why of things, which made him a great mentor to his team.

"I'll get a photo to you right away." He hung up the phone and stood.

Deputy Carl's head popped around the door frame. "She's ready, sir."

Ketchum grabbed a pad and pen and strode from his office.

Carl kept pace with him and asked, "Who do you think she is, then?"

"Don't know."

"So you think Samantha had a twin?"

"I suppose that's a possibility," Ketchum said dryly. "But this woman might not be who she claims to be."

Ketchum did not dare entertain the possibility the Bureau had mistakenly informed the family of Samantha Adams that she was dead. Without a body, the only proof of death was the recording. The moment their jubilation died down, they would sue this office and the FBI. It would be a public relations nightmare. What jury would deny her family a settlement for pain and suffering? He paused outside the interview room while his mind worked through a strategy for conducting his interview with the mystery woman.

What did she want? Did this woman really have anything to offer in the Frank case? Could she be a plant hired by the Claytons? The sudden appearance of a witness smacked of a desperation stunt. He had known criminals who made witnesses disappear. Was this a reverse strategy to create a witness?

Within five minutes, he entered an interview room where a pretty woman he guessed to be about thirty years old sat with her hands folded in her lap. She had shoulder-length light brown hair secured into a ponytail. She presented a wholesome contrast to Sweet Sally, who had been in that same chair not so long ago.

"I'm Sheriff Ketchum." He shook her hand then sat across the table from her, with his back to the one-way mirrored window. He set a pad of paper on the table and placed his pen on top.

"You're leading the investigation on Curtis Frank?" she asked.

"The investigation began with my office, but the FBI is now in charge of it. Before we go on, I need you to know that we are being recorded. I need you to state whether or not you are waiving your right to have an attorney present."

"Go ahead and record. I don't want an attorney. Please, stop the trial," the young woman said. Her voice strong and clear, she added, "There's been a horrible mistake."

Ketchum settled back in his chair. "That's not my call."

With a stiff back, Samantha leaned forward and planted her hands on the table. "Blake Clayton did not kill Curtis Frank."

After a moment of soul-stirring relief, he realized she did not refute the kidnapping charge. "Why don't we start at the beginning?"

"Okay."

"What's your real name?"

Grimacing, she said, "First, I'd like immunity from prosecution."

There it was. Ketchum hesitated then said, "I need to know what you would be prosecuted for, because if you killed Curtis Frank, then I can't make that deal."

"Oh, I wanted to kill him." Hatred flared in her eyes. Her hands had balled into fists for a moment before she pulled them down to her lap. "I took the name of Samantha Adams because she was my only friend for the worst six months of my life. When Curtis told me she died, I took her name to keep her alive. I don't suppose that makes sense to you."

Ketchum picked up his pen to jot a note. "And when was that?"

"Nineteen ninety-four. The last time I saw her was in early October. I remember the leaves were changing." The young woman wiped her eyes with the back of her hand.

"And where was this?" Ketchum wanted to keep her talking.

"Somewhere in North Carolina." She sighed and frowned.

He watched her. "Where in North Carolina?"

Her eyes welled up. "Curtis kept us drugged. I remember it was less than a days' travel from where she died to the farmhouse."

"What farmhouse?"

"Near where the Clayton brothers lived. The ones who rescued me."

Ketchum stared into her eyes. Her story was short on details, but the timeline matched. The kidnapping of a felon by five high school boys began to make sense. "Did you kill Curtis Frank?"

"No, sir." She wrung her hands.

"Did you ask anyone else to kill Curtis Frank?"

"No, sir."

"Would you be willing to take a lie detector test?"

"Yes, sir."

Guilty people rarely volunteered to take the lie detector test. Sociopaths sometimes did because they believed their own lies. The fact that she had more to lose than to gain led him to dismiss the sociopath angle. He read fear and shame in her, but not deception.

"I would like immunity for taking Samantha's name," she said. "I graduated from high school and college and got a nursing license under her name. I also got married as Adams and became Samantha Young."

"I see. When Special Agent Theron gets here we can ask him to petition for immunity for you. What's your real name?"

Her voice quavered as she said, "My real name is Carrie Ann Snow." She went on to name the small town in Ohio where she lived so long ago.

He wrote her name and hometown on his pad. He tapped his pen on his pad. It was his signal to Carl to chase down information. "Now what can you tell me about Curtis Frank's death that would make immunity worthwhile?"

"Everything. And I'll tell you about that whore, Sweet Sally, too."

That Friday night at dinner in Asheville, Sweet Sally cherished attention from the media especially when they took her to one of Asheville's finest restaurants. Previously called the Savoy, the restaurant reopened as Vinnie's Italian Restaurant. The journalist taking her to dinner explained the award-winning nature of the restaurant as they were seated. It had been a long time since men paid her that kind of attention. Most of all, she enjoyed being treated like a lady. They opened doors and pulled out chairs for her. Sure, the judge had told her not to talk to the jurors or the Claytons, or anyone connected to the trial until it was over, but he never said she couldn't talk about herself. She was no longer afraid to be recognized, no longer hiding from anyone. The cops in Florida could not touch her thanks to her plea deal.

She reveled in her new freedom and fame so much so she decided to stick around for the verdict before moving on. Her dinner companion for the evening, Ernie something-or-other from a newspaper, asked about Curtis.

Sally sipped her bourbon and water. Annoyed that the middle-aged male journalist seemed more interested in a dead man than a live woman within reach, she sighed. Her best years were behind her. "Poor Curtis. No one understood him like I did. He was just a man trying to make a living in tough times."

"So you were together for ten years?"

"Yes." She believed the reporter would be impressed by her loyalty.

"Does that time include the years he served in prison in Ohio for child pornography?"

"I would rather not talk about that." A twinge of anger warmed her.

The journalist flipped to the next page of his notebook. His stringy hair had been drawn across his bald spot. He looked like an Ernie. "What would you say to those who believe your relationship was more business-related than romantic?"

"What do you mean?"

"There was talk that he was...your pimp." He said it so matter-of-factly Sally wanted to slap him.

She noticed heads turn toward her and the sideways glance from a passing waiter. "Those people are just hateful and mean. It's easy to say ugly things about a dead man who can't defend himself. And I'm not *rich* like the defendant, so people think they can say anything they want about me."

The journalist wrote it down in his little notebook. Glancing up, he said, "Do you believe the defendant should get life in prison or the death penalty?"

"That's what you get for kidnapping in this state?" Sally shuddered.

"Haven't you noticed the protesters carrying signs outside the courthouse?"

"Yeah." Without her glasses, she couldn't read the signs, and she didn't want to be seen on television wearing glasses.

"The protesters want to use this case to repeal the felony murder rule."

"Murder? This is a kidnapping trial," Sally said. She didn't believe *one* high school boy could have murdered Curtis. He was too tough. He had survived prison.

The journalist explained the felony murder rule to Sally. If convicted of the kidnapping, he could hang for the murder.

"You heard me in court, right?"

"Yes."

"Why haven't the cops arrested them other boys?"

Ernie pushed his glasses up on his nose. "Eye-witness testimony is often the weakest part of a case."

"Weak? I was *there*. I told them what happened."

He shrugged. "Perhaps the police are waiting until the trial is over so they can gather more evidence against the others." He chugged his beer.

Sally nodded. Maybe that prosecutor was planning to put the other boys in the hot seat. She wanted to tell the reporter about a reality television show she'd been offered to be in, but the producer had insisted she couldn't tell anyone until the day the show came out. They were coming any day now to film her side of the story at the ranch house. Paying real good money, too. She couldn't queer that deal, so she kept her mouth shut about it.

―――

As first-year agent at the New York City field office, Vincent should have worked through the Easter holiday, but Chief Watson let him take vacation early to attend the trial. So here he was at six a.m. on a misty Saturday, April 10th, wearing Moose's cowboy boots and standing in the stables. Vincent thought he'd packed appropriately, but hiking boots had a deep tread that tended to collect whatever he stepped in and there was plenty to step in.

"Just think of her as a half-ton dog," Blake said. "You don't pull her. You lead her."

Yawning, Vincent took the reins of the mare and walked with his back to her, like Blake had instructed. When he headed out of the stall, the horse followed. Once clear of the stench of the stables, Vincent breathed deeper. The men led two mares to a gate that accessed the field between the front of the Clayton Ranch house and the road. Blake swung open the six-foot-wide metal pole gate.

Vincent yearned for coffee. He ached for Mama Clayton's daily breakfast feast. Nonetheless, he was game for new experiences and he wanted time to talk to Blake privately. Blake had been disturbingly quiet all week, so uncharacteristic of him. The mounting evidence proved to Vincent that Blake and his brothers had in fact kidnapped Curtis Frank. Guilt on the kidnapping charge meant guilt on the murder. The prosecutor did not offer a motive. Establishing a motive was not necessary to get a conviction, but juries tended to expect it.

Vincent was curious about how Curtis Frank died. He refused to believe the Clayton brothers murdered him. He would have to hear Blake confess before he would believe it.

Vincent's mind roiled while he walked. In contrast, Blake's calm familiarity with the animals seemed to put the beasts at ease. Vincent's experience with horses was limited. If pressed to identify what kind of horses they were, he would say black or brown. Of course, he could tell the difference between a male and a female horse, but the only reason he knew these were Quarter horses was because Blake had said so. He followed Blake through the gateway with his horse trailing him. Blake secured the gate.

"Remove the reins like this," Blake said, demonstrating. He gathered up the leather in one hand and rubbed the mare under her jaw with the other hand.

The mare nuzzled Blake's neck. Vincent unhooked the reins from the second mare and handed them to Blake. The horses were certainly as affectionate as dogs, at least toward Blake. Vincent reached under his mare's warm chin and rubbed her soft fur. She ducked her head and nudged her ear against his shoulder. Imagining a large dog, Vincent scratched her behind the ears. The mare gave a deep fluttering sigh.

"Watch this." Blake stepped over to a blue blanket-size tarp by the fence and flipped the tarp off a large exercise ball. He tossed the ball into the field.

The horses bolted after the ball, jumping and kicking at it. Vincent laughed.

"Typical two-year-olds," Blake said. He pressed his back to the fence while he watched the horses.

From a distance, they could have been mistaken for long-legged dogs playing.

"How's it going with Nefi?" Blake asked.

Vincent's heart soared at the thought of her. "She managed to get through FBI training without injuring anyone. She has two weeks off before she starts work in the Behavioral Sciences section in D.C."

"So where are you two going?" Blake eyed him. One side of his mouth tugged up into a half grin.

How could he ask that? Vincent propped an arm over the white fence board. "She's coming here."

Blake scowled at the ground.

"Your mother insisted she stay here." Vincent shifted his weight to his heels. "We have separate rooms."

Blake watched the horses playing. "I don't want to be the first criminal she studies."

"Nefi's not going to profile you. She wants to support you."

Blake's eyes welled then his jaw clenched and relaxed. He cleared his throat. "In that case, I appreciate it." He pulled his cell phone from his pocket.

Terri wasn't here. It seemed Blake checked his phone often as if he was expecting a text or email from her. Vincent's phone rang in his pocket. He retrieved it and read the small screen's caller identifier—Gator. Why would Blake's brother call? Maybe Blake stopped answering his phone. He stepped away from Blake. "Excuse me, I should answer this."

Blake nodded and let himself out through the gate.

"Vincent here."

"Is Blake taking a plea deal?"

"Not that I've heard." Vincent watched Blake head back to the stables.

"Then why would the attorneys and Special Agent Theron meet in Asheville today?" Gator asked.

"I don't know. How could they negotiate a deal without Blake?"

"What do you mean?"

"He's here at the ranch."

"*Hunh.* Then I don't know what's going on. Maybe it's about a different case. I have another call. Gotta go."

"Okay." Vincent stared at his phone. He assumed the only times the opposing attorneys met was to trade evidence or other trial information. The defense was supposed to begin arguments Monday. Vincent let himself out through the gate and ran to catch up with Blake.

Marilyn-Anne waved a newspaper from the front porch. "Boomer! Boomer! Come read today's paper."

Blake stopped in his tracks. "Which one?"

"*The Herald.*"

Blake waved it off and headed toward the stables.

Marilyn-Anne rushed down from the porch to block his path. Vincent caught up behind Blake. The front page of the local newspaper featured a large mug shot under the headline: *Curtis Frank, Convicted Child Pornographer*. Marilyn-Anne unfolded the paper. The entire front page described Frank's life, including a timeline and an extensive listing of his arrests and convictions. A blown-up quote from Special Agent Theron read: "Of the two hundred eighty-three pornographic recordings found in the basement of the Frank home, twelve involved minors. Curtis Frank was a person of interest in a sex-trafficking network up until his disappearance in 1994."

Vincent's stomach clenched. *Porno? Minors?* He watched Blake for his reaction.

Blake glanced at Marilyn-Anne. "This doesn't read like Ernie's usual fluff."

Marilyn-Anne straightened. "Looks to me like Ernie grew a spine." She handed the paper to Blake.

"Blaming the victim," Blake said, "won't get me acquitted. It's against the law to kidnap anyone, even a low-life felon." Blake handed the paper to Vincent.

As if wounded, Marilyn-Anne spun on a heel, marched back up the front porch into the house, and punctuated her departure with a door slam.

Blake sighed. He trudged toward the stables.

Vincent let him go while he quickly read the rest of the front page. While he read, he considered a motive for the kidnapping. Blake was right. Frank's criminal character would not affect the kidnapping charge. Wrapping the body in chains pretty much negated a self-defense plea. It had all the signs of a pre-meditated act.

The sound of tires on gravel caused Vincent to look up. Dust settled around a large black Ford Bronco. Terri climbed out of the driver's side. Nefi stepped out of the passenger's side. Nefi's long brown hair flowed like a horse's mane down her back. Vincent's pulse quickened. Seeing her made him feel sixteen again. He had not expected her until Sunday.

Nefi spotted him, squealed and ran, collided with his chest, and nearly knocked the breath out of him. Her embrace squeezed the rest of the air from his lungs. After she had released him, he took in a deep breath of her lavender perfume.

"I found an early flight," Nefi said. "Look who I ran into at the Asheville airport waiting in line for a rental car! She flew in her own plane."

Terri strode up to Vincent and gave him a quick hug. "Where's Blake?" Her eyes were puffy and bloodshot.

"In the stables," Vincent whispered, "He's been real quiet."

"I need to tell him the good news. Looks like I'll be able to stay for the rest of the trial." She gave a wan smile and headed toward the stables.

Nefi and Vincent traded a glance. Nefi's guarded expression warned Vincent not to celebrate Terri's news.

. 20 .

Monday, April 12, 2010, Blake slumped into his seat at the defense table in the eighth day of his kidnapping trial. The courtroom was packed with journalists and spectators like Romans at the Coliseum ready for blood. Already burdened by the specter of the death penalty looming over him, he mourned his wife's humiliation. Her partners kicked her out of the practice her father had started. Sure, they gave her the opportunity to resign and notify her clients, but she was being punished for her association with him.

Terri deserves a better life than this.

She insisted on coming to the trial, so he let her. She would soon regret the media circus and the slow-motion torture of the trial as the attorneys parsed words until every detail and fact was nailed down for the jury to understand. So far it had taken eight days of presenting evidence, and interviewing experts, and questioning witnesses to examine one night's tragedy. Only the attorneys knew how many more days, if ever, it would it take to reveal the horrifying truth.

Due to his actions years ago, he brought shame to his family name, caused his wife's career to disintegrate, and destroyed his own future. Despite it all, he could not summon genuine remorse for what he did that night. *Didn't Frank get what he deserved?*

The prosecutor rested his case. The spectator section was

packed to capacity. Vincent sat with the family right behind the defense table. Blake expected Nefi to sit beside Terri, but he didn't see Nefi in the room. With every seat filled, a few reporters stood in the back along the wall. Blake did not spot Sweet Sally, but that made sense because his attorney had reserved the right to recall her. What more damage could she do? She had probably moved on to ruin someone else's life. Blake's attorney stood and called Samuel Clayton to the stand. Blake flinched. He hated that his brother Moose had to testify, at all, let alone for the defense.

Blake's attorney leaned close to whisper, "He has immunity," while Moose strode to the witness box.

Relieved that Moose wouldn't have to join him on death row, Blake settled back into his hard wooden chair. But how would Moose's testimony help? If he told the truth, the jury would hear a second witness verify the kidnapping. Blake's heart rate increased and the room grew warmer.

Jurors kept their attention fixed on Moose, who towered over the bailiff by a foot. In his Sunday suit and tie and his best cowboy boots, Moose could have passed for a banker or a lawyer or a professional football player. After being sworn in, he unbuttoned his jacket and wedged himself into the witness chair, draping both elbows over the sides.

The chair creaked under him, causing him to grab the side rails of the booth. An expression of alarm flashed on his face.

Blake held his breath. He expected the chair to collapse under Moose. When Moose released his grip on the railings, Blake blew out a breath. Part of him regretted that the chair held, because he really needed a good laugh.

The defense attorney asked Moose to identify himself and his relationship to the accused.

"I'm Samuel Lee Clayton. I'm thirty-five years old, and Blake's my youngest brother." Moose announced it as a schoolyard challenge.

"According to your statement, you were with your brother Blake on the night of October twenty-ninth, nineteen ninety-four. Is that true?"

"Yes, sir."

"Would you tell the court what caused you to go to the Frank house?"

"We planned to rescue a girl who was chained up in the basement."

Blake bowed his head to listen. Moose took credit for planning the rescue, for loading tools in the truck, and for switching off the power to the house, to force Curtis Frank to come out. He was smart to accept immunity before testifying.

The attorney interrupted Moose. "Were you wearing masks or disguises when you approached the house?"

"No, sir."

"What did you intend to do to Mr. Frank?" the attorney asked.

"We were going to tie him up and take him to the sheriff for breaking the law. We were going to make a citizen's arrest."

"Then why didn't you simply call the sheriff?"

"We believed Mister Frank would kill Carrie Ann if he saw the police, so we wanted to get her safe first."

"Please go on."

"Mister Frank came out the front door with a flashlight. When he turned the corner to the side of the house where the power box was, we jumped him. He put up a fight, but we hogtied him."

"What did you use?" the attorney asked.

"Rope. We tied his hands behind his back and lifted him into the truck bed."

"Why did you put him in the truck?"

"We didn't want him to get back in the house to set off the bomb."

The jurors' mouths dropped open. Spectators murmured. Judge Parker tapped the gavel twice as a warning for quiet.

The defense attorney's gaze swung from the jury back to Moose. "What bomb?"

Blake had told his attorney about the bomb and about every ugly detail of that night. The crafty old attorney managed to act as if this was all news to him.

"Gator said he saw dynamite and gas cans fixed to the ceiling of the basement. Carrie Ann told him that Curtis would blow up the house if the cops raided it."

The prosecutor raised his voice over the conversations of the spectators. "I object on the basis of hearsay."

His honor glared down at the defense attorney. "Objection sustained."

"I'm sorry, Your Honor. We'll let Gator, also known as Gideon Clayton, tell that part. What happened next?"

"Two women came out of the house and started yelling at us. Gator—"

"Excuse me, please use his given name for the court," the defense attorney said.

"Gideon took the bolt cutters and ran into the house to get Carrie Ann from the basement. Bubba, I mean Caleb, and Blake corralled the other two women by the truck."

"I'm sorry to interrupt, but could you tell the court why Gideon had bolt cutters?"

Moose nodded.

The attorney raised his eyebrows and opened his hand. "Tell the court."

"Gideon said Carrie Ann was chained to the bed," Moose said.

"Objection," the prosecutor said.

"Sustained," Judge Parker replied.

"Mr. Clayton," the defense attorney said, "Please testify to the things you saw firsthand."

Moose sighed. He scowled at the defense attorney as if waiting for him to ask the right question.

The defense attorney said, "Your honor, I have sworn

testimony from Gideon Clayton taken before the trial. The prosecutor has a copy. I plan to call Gideon to the stand to address the matter of the chain and the bomb."

Judge Parker said, "I remind the witness to testify to what you personally saw and did."

"Yes, sir," Moose said. "I mean Your Honor, sir."

The defense attorney faced Moose. "Tell us what you did next."

Blake regarded Moose and his effect on the jurors. The entire panel stared at Moose in rapt attention.

"The women screamed at us."

"These women, who were they?"

"They called each other Sally and Evie. Sally had black hair and Evie was blonde."

"How old were these women?" the attorney asked.

"They were about mid-thirties, or early forties. Hard to tell cause they looked rough."

"I see. Go on."

"I told them we came to get Carrie Ann, and that we were going to take Curtis to the police. That's when Curtis Frank told us he was going to kill us. Evie said she wasn't going to jail, so she punched Frank and took his car keys. Sally said she was going back in the house to get money. Butch—sorry—Jeremiah went in with her. A little while later Gideon and Carrie Ann came out. Curtis was cursing up a storm, so I stuffed a handkerchief in his mouth to shut him up."

A spectator chuckled.

"Excuse me for interrupting, but you saw three women and one man at the Frank residence that night?"

"Yes, sir."

The attorney opened his hand toward Moose, signaling him to continue.

Moose continued. "Sally stormed out of the house with a purse stuffed with dollars. She handed a few bills to Carrie Ann and told her to get lost. She and the other woman got into a brown Cadillac and headed west."

The defense attorney pointed to an enlarged map the prosecutor had brought in to show the proximity of the Clayton Ranch to the Frank house and to the bridge, which was believed to be where the body entered the river. He pointed a pool stick at the Frank house on the map.

"The women headed in this direction?" the attorney asked. He dragged the tip of the pool stick westward on the map.

"Yes, sir."

"Where does that road lead?"

"It goes to the bridge over the Little Jordan toward the state highway." Moose's brief answer showed he had grown cautious as if waiting to answer specific questions rather than volunteering information.

The attorney slid the tip of the pool stick along the road to the bridge and stopped it at the highway. He did not ask the name of the highway. It was clear on the map that it led west toward the mountains. Like every highway in North Carolina, it had more than one identifier because the highways converged and overlapped when they funneled into mountain passes and bridges.

"And what time of day was it?"

"Just after dark around eight o'clock."

The attorney lowered the pool stick to his side. "What did you do next?"

"We got in the truck and headed west."

"West?" The defense attorney pointed toward the map. "But you said you were going to take Curtis to the sheriff. Isn't the sheriff's office in town to the east?"

Moose answered calmly, "The east end of town was blocked off for the Halloween parade. We couldn't drive through the parade with that fat guy tied up in the back."

Chuckles rose from the spectators.

The attorney asked Moose to describe the route he planned to take, so he did. On the ten-mile detour toward the north entrance to town, Moose explained they had to stop so Carrie Ann could pee.

"And where was that?"

Moose stared at the railing in front of him. "At Carson's farm."

Blake closed his eyes against memories that blasted into his consciousness, images of Frank rolling off the truck bed and staggering toward the barbed wire fence. Blake had vaulted over the side of the truck after him and shouted for his brothers.

Frank spit out the handkerchief moments before he dropped on his side. By the time Blake reached the fence, Frank had somehow rolled underneath the barbed wire. Blake dropped on the dead grass to roll under the wire, but hands pulled him back.

"Watch out!" Butch screamed so high his voice broke.

The ground vibrated and a giant shadow thundered along the fence. The five Clayton Brothers fell back into a shallow ditch. At eye level with Frank's prone body, they witnessed his death by hoof and by horn as Carson's bull repeatedly charged Frank—stomping and snorting, goring and kicking—until Frank's bloody, broken mound of flesh stopped moving.

Moose's words rang through Blake like the voice-over to a nightmare. Blake dropped his face into his hands on the table. After fifteen years of telling himself he had done the right thing, he realized intent did not matter compared to the result. It was over at last. The secret revealed to the world. *Curtis Frank died because I couldn't catch him.*

Blake couldn't catch a fat man running with his hands tied behind his back. Carson's bull was faster. If only Gator or Butch or Moose or Bubba had been in the back with Frank instead of being inside the truck, Frank would have lived. He would have gone to trial and maybe even died in prison. As it was, Blake carried the guilt for allowing a man to die unredeemed. Would Frank have found God in prison? Maybe not, but who was he to say? Papa always said it wasn't for anyone to judge any man's life but his own. Blake finally stopped justifying Frank's death. He accepted responsibility for it and silently begged for God's forgiveness.

Lost in his epiphany, Blake tuned out the prosecutor's cross-examination of Moose. By the time Blake raised his face from prayer, Moose was taking a seat in the back of the courtroom. Judge Parker called the attorneys to the bench. They conducted a whispered huddle. Blake tugged his cloth handkerchief from his back pocket and wiped his eyes.

Judge Parker adjourned for the day.

Blake's attorney gathered his papers then stuffed them into a black leather case secured by a three-digit lock. He thumbed the numbers on the lock and nodded at the other attorney who appeared to be waiting for him.

"Are you negotiating a plea?" Blake balled up his handkerchief.

"No." The attorney sat and leaned close. "The judge wants a break to review new testimony that came in over the weekend. Go spend time with your family."

A chill raced up Blake's back. "Who's testimony?"

"I can't discuss it here. All I can tell you is that someone approached the FBI with information on the case." The attorney grabbed his briefcase handle and smiled. "It isn't over yet. Remember, don't talk to the press. Don't even say 'No comment.'"

Blake nodded. He trod to the double doors that led to the corridor. Vincent and Terri joined him.

The new witness was probably the other hooker seeking a moment in the spotlight at his expense. Blake had to trust his fate to God.

His brothers were gathered at the courtroom doors by an officer stationed there. Moose opened a large plastic bag from which he handed out white Stetson cowboy hats and aviator-style sunglasses. A devoted fan of westerns, Moose had taught his brothers that the good guys always wore white hats.

"Let's go out the front doors today," Moose said. The sunglasses, it seemed, represented the celebrity part of the style.

Blake snorted at him. "This is your idea of cheering me up?"

Moose nodded. He pinched the front of a hat and dropped it on his head. At a glance, because of the suit and the dress cowboy boots, he resembled a country-western singer.

"You know," Blake said, "I expected your chair to collapse."

The brothers laughed and swatted at Moose.

Moose addressed the guard. "That chair wasn't made for big and tall size." He put on sunglasses. "It might not hold up for the next witness."

Blake paused at the door to say to Moose, "Tell me you didn't bring horses."

Moose grinned. "Couldn't."

"A team of Clydesdales would be our style," Gator said donning his hat and sunglasses.

"Pulling a wagon of beer," Bubba added.

Butch, still an ordained minister, peered over his sunglasses and shook his head.

Blake said to Vincent, "Might be better if you and Terri weren't part of Moose's departure plan."

Vincent nodded and escorted Terri to a side door.

Holding his white hat and sunglasses, Blake considered what impression wearing their props would make on the media. If he appeared solemn, they criticized him. If he appeared calm, they criticized him. The media from big cities, would call him a redneck. To the local media, he was the spoiled son of wealthy ranchers. He knew in his heart who he was. They didn't know his full story yet. *Maybe they never would.*

"Let's do this," Blake said.

The five brothers crowded into the elevator and rode it to the main floor. Blake put on the hat and sunglasses while the elevator doors opened. *Might as well look good.* His brothers flanked him.

With solemn expressions, they headed out of the courthouse, through the surging gauntlet of shouting reporters, past the crowd of sign-waving anti-felony rule protestors who cheered, and to the parking lot to Papa's beat up hay-bale hauling truck. It was the only vehicle Moose owned without the Clayton Ranch logo plastered on it.

While Moose was testifying in Asheville, Sweet Sally posed on the front porch of the Frank house for the cameraman and crew of the reality television show called "Prison Romance." The twenty-five-year-old director had hired Sweet Sally to tell the world her love story as a memorial to Curtis Frank. He had prompted her through describing how and where they met. Of course, she took out the embarrassing parts because the director said they wanted to concentrate on the romance, not on the criminal aspects of their life together. He had explained that the narrator would fill in the blanks with factual statements, like the date and exact charges against Frank that led to his serving time.

Sweet Sally said they had been to every state but Alaska and Hawaii, claiming Curtis had promised to take her to Hawaii once they had saved enough money. She told the camera, "Unfortunately, Curtis never got to take me on our dream vacation to Hawaii. The last time I saw him, he was being kidnapped right out of this front yard." She sighed and stared at the road in the late afternoon light.

"Fabulous, fabulous. That's just what I'm looking for," the director said. "Okay, pan to the road aaaaaaaand fade out. People, that's a wrap!"

Cheers rose from the workers. The crew scrambled to break down the equipment while the director waved to his assistant.

The assistant, a round-hipped college-age girl, approached

Sweet Sally. She withdrew a white envelope from her messenger bag and handed it to her. "This episode is scheduled to run in two weeks. We appreciate your taking the whole day to film."

Sally opened the envelope to reveal a satisfying, thick stack of twenties. "I could talk more tomorrow, too."

The smile fell off the girl's face. "I believe we have enough." She glanced over her shoulder at the sheriff's deputy who had checked earlier for a permit.

Sweet Sally interpreted the girl's nervousness to mean they had to clear off the property by a certain time or the deputy would arrest the whole bunch for trespassing. Sally didn't want any trouble. "I do need to get back to Asheville."

"We'll take you back. Please have a seat by the craft cart."

"The what?"

"By the food table."

"Oh." Sally headed over to graze off the table. Fried chicken wings, chips, cookies, and fruit adorned the table. What she wanted most was Bourbon on the rocks and aspirin. What the catering service offered to drink was bottled soda and water. Twelve hours of standing around while men moved equipment had taken its toll on her. *All this for a one-hour show? It was crazy.* Though she liked the way the hairdresser had fixed her up, and the money helped, she did not like working on her feet. After grabbing a plate, she loaded up on chicken wings and cookies. From the distance of more than a decade, she found it easy to shape the past into something better than it was. As the survivor, she had a right to control how she would be remembered.

⁕

Nefi read a text from Terri. Moose's testimony contradicted Sally's. A woman named Evie and a young girl named Carrie Ann were at the house with Frank and Sally. That was exactly the kind of information Nefi needed. She tucked her phone in her back pocket.

The crew folded and packed equipment into large metal crates lined up nearby. One of the women who'd been around all day wasn't helping the rest pack up. She had long brown hair and long legs, and she was reading her fancy telephone screen, the kind that could send thumb-typed messages. The tall young thing could have been a model. Sally watched her wander over toward the food table. She figured the girl to be the director's girlfriend because she was so pretty and no one talked to her.

The young-looking sheriff's deputy strolled over to Sally. "Did you hear what happened at the trial today?"

"I've been busy." She dabbed her mouth with a napkin.

"Seems your boy Curtis killed himself." Deputy Carl grinned.

Sally snorted. "Ain't no way Curtis took his own life."

"If you say so." He ambled to his patrol car and climbed in it.

She wanted to smack that smile right off his face. *Somebody lied in court today. Nothing on earth would cause Curtis to hurt hisself, no, sir.* He liked to take life in both hands and wring pleasure out of every day. That man loved his smokes and his liquor and his women. She itched to get back to her motel to watch the news about the trial. She silently vowed to sit in on the rest of the trial no matter what. *No one was going to make her look like a fool. No, siree.*

The tall model plucked fruit off the food table. When she got closer, Sally noticed the girl had yellow eyes.

"Do you wear contacts to make your eyes that color?" Sally asked.

The girl answered, "That's all me."

When the girl's eyes met hers, Sally sensed those eyes saw straight into her soul. "Are you the director's girlfriend?"

"No."

"Then why are you here?"

"I asked permission to watch."

"Why?"

"To see what I could learn." The girl popped a strawberry in her mouth. She eased into a folding chair.

Sally took a chair across the food table from her. Standing so long had swelled her feet. "So what did you learn?"

The girl chewed and swallowed before answering. "I don't think you were alone with Curtis in the house that night."

Sally gasped and checked that the director was out of earshot. "Says who?"

"It's something I picked up when you talked about what happened."

"I didn't say anything like that." Sally had been very careful.

"You didn't have to."

"Who are you?"

"Nefi Jenkins. People say I'm a psychic."

Sally snorted and squinted at her. "So how's the trial going to end?"

"I can't see the future."

"Then what kind of psychic are you?" Sally bit into a cheese cube. *Some people are just plain crazy.*

"Who's Evie?"

The name Sally had not heard in years startled her like she'd been backhanded across the face. "How do you know Evie?"

"Is she still living?" Nefi's matter-of-fact tone alarmed Sally.

Evie died in prison after killing a john who got rough with her. "No."

"Pity. She could have corroborated your story."

"Could have what?"

"She could have backed up your story in court. You know, as a second witness."

Sally had not mentioned Evie to anyone during the trial. It would have looked bad to have two women in the same house with Curtis. Would have made him like their pimp. *Evie was the whore. Curtis never declared his love for her.* How did this girl find out about Evie? Sally gasped. "Maybe you are psychic."

Nefi nodded. "So how many people were at the house the night Frank disappeared?"

"He didn't disappear. He was kidnapped." *What is this girl's angle?* "I gave my testimony in court just like I told it to the cameras. Are you going to write a book about the trial?" Sally asked.

"It is quite a story."

"You have to give me credit for my part."

"You bet I will." Nefi popped another strawberry in her mouth. She stood and hiked off the property, the wrong way from the road, uphill toward the woods.

Sally stared at her until she disappeared into the shadows of the trees. Where was she going? Did she live in the woods? Was she a witch? Was she a trial groupie? *Some people are just plain crazy.*

Moose's testimony on Monday was the talk of the town. Tuesday had showcased the attorney's tedious detail-building defense tactics. The defense attorney's strategy seemed to be designed to drive the jurors to boredom by examining the evidence and testimony in excruciating, mind-numbing detail. His approach had dampened the sensationalism of the trial as surely as if he had piped in elevator music.

Gator's testimony on Wednesday had filled in the blanks about what happened in the basement of the Frank house, specifically how he had used bolt cutters to free Carrie Ann's ankle from a chain that tied her to a bed. A forensic expert on Thursday confirmed that the marks found on the chains in the basement were made by a bolt cutter consistent with the kind Gator described.

On Friday morning, April 16th, Marilyn-Anne declined to go to the courthouse. She appeared pale and said she wasn't feeling up to it. When Terri asked about her, Maeve said Marilyn-Anne was going to the doctor. Was Marilyn-Anne's weight contributing to other health issues like diabetes? Terri suspected Marilyn-Anne was a stress eater and a great cook. In combination, those factors conspired to pack on the pounds. Terri felt her own waistband tightening more by the day since the trial began.

She settled into a bench three rows behind Blake with Aunt Dottie by her side. Dottie and Maeve took turns, one staying with Papa while the other attended the trial. Terri had declined Maeve's coffee so she could sit through the entire morning session of the trial without having to sneak out to the ladies room. She hoped she would not regret the lack of caffeine.

The defense attorney and another man carried in an armload of cloth draped poster boards. Terri's heart shrank in fear. More enlarged photos of the glove? Or of chains?

Moose leaned forward and addressed Terri over Dottie's lap. His gaze tracked a man who followed the defense attorney. "That's Ward, the coroner."

Ward sat behind in the spectator's bench directly behind the defense attorney and Blake. The man beside him on the bench turned his head. Special Agent Theron. Terri considered it odd he would take the time to watch the trial after he had testified. Perhaps another agent was scheduled to take the stand.

Terri whispered back to Moose, "How on earth can the coroner's testimony help Blake?"

Moose shrugged. When the prosecutor had unveiled giant X-ray images of Frank's bones and fragmented skull, the juror grimaced and shook their heads. Terri shuddered. Why would the defense attorney reinforce those images with the jury?

The bailiff called for all to rise. The assembly rose while Judge Parker adjusted his robe and eased into his throne. After the usual announcements and warning to the media and spectators to maintain decorum, the judge opened the day's proceedings.

The defense attorney stood. "Your honor, I call Medical Examiner Anthony Ward to the stand."

The bailiff returned with the coroner following.

Ward attracted stares especially from the ladies as he strode by in his dark gray Armani suit, steel gray tie, and shirt. Death never looked so fashionably sexy. His broad, athletic shoulders tapered to narrow hips. When he faced the Bible to swear in, his gray suit enhanced his light blue eyes.

So this is why people nicknamed him the angel of death.

Terri sneaked a sideways peek at Dottie.

"Well, now. Isn't he beautiful?" Dottie whispered.

Terri nodded.

"In your report," the attorney said, "you listed the probable cause of death as head trauma, is that correct?"

"Yes." Ward's shoulders tapered enough that he fit in the witness booth better than Moose.

The defense attorney picked up a tagged packet of paper from the evidence table. After he had leafed through it, he handed it to Ward. "And would you read paragraph five of the third page of your report aloud?"

Ward read, "Multiple fractures of the skull, ribs, spine, scapula, and left femur indicate severe trauma."

"What could cause such trauma?"

"I've seen injuries like this from fights, farm equipment, rodeo deaths, and car accidents."

The attorney asked Ward to identify each fracture on the prosecutor's blown-up X-rays. The attorney lifted an enlarged rendering of the skull fragments that he placed on the easel in front of the X-ray image. The skull appeared as a line drawing with the pieces shown as if blown out in all directions. He pointed to the fragments of the largest injury floating to the right of the skull.

"In your opinion, what could cause this particular fracture pattern?"

"A battering ram could. The central fragment is round, indicating a flat circular object struck the skull with intense force."

"Could a human hand, or knee or boot create that pattern?"

Terri recognized the fracture pattern.

"No. It had to be something shaped like a coffee can. A boot, for example, couldn't deliver a uniform level of force on impact. A knee or a hand would have created a shattering fracture, like spokes on a wheel, radiating from the center of impact."

"Would a large animal hoof meet the criteria for creating a similar injury?"

Terri nodded. She had seen what a horse could do to a stall wall with a well-placed kick.

Ward blinked a few times before he answered. "I suppose. I'd have to measure the hoof to compare it to the fractures."

Terri's faith in the defense attorney grew stronger. A few jurors took notes. The women jurors openly gaped at Ward, hanging on his words, lulled by his smooth baritone voice. The prosecutor's medical examiner had been a pale, gaunt older man with a greasy comb-over. He had slouched in the witness stand, creating an uncanny resemblance to a vulture. He was an academic ghoul compared to Ward the hunk.

Ward withstood cross-examination with calm professionalism. Terri pondered the purpose of trying to prove the fatal blow matched a bull's hoof. Though it reinforced the testimony of Moose and Gator, it also reinforced the connection between

Frank's kidnapping and his death. Wasn't the point of the defense to disprove the kidnapping? As long as Frank's death resulted from the kidnapping, Blake faced the death penalty.

Terri ached for Blake. This nightmare trial didn't portray the real Blake Clayton. She fell in love with a gentleman FBI agent, a charming giant. Blake won Terri's heart the night she watched him comfort Nefi. That night demonstrated the real Blake. Would she ever have *him* back again?

Ward kept his eyes on the door as he left the courtroom. Next, the attorney called up a legal scholar who explained, in great detail, the definition of kidnapping. After a few objections from the prosecutor, the defense attorney asked a rhetorical question about a situation in which a man escapes from the back of an open-bed truck and flees into a field. He asked if the fleeing man still fits the legal definition of being held captive against his will. The expert declared that according to the legal definition of kidnapping in North Carolina, it could be argued that the moment Curtis Frank left the truck and ran, he had freed himself from the control of others.

Terri grabbed Dottie's hand. Separating Frank's death from the kidnapping would leave Blake with only the kidnapping charge. Dottie squeezed Terri's hand. A tiny ray of hope pierced the oppressive darkness. If Frank was free and acting according to his own will, then his death was accidental and separate from the kidnapping.

Her heart fluttering, Terri took deep breaths and closed her eyes. She refused to cry in public. She silently prayed. For a moment, she wanted to hug the defense attorney.

The prosecutor objected. Judge Parker called both attorneys to the bench where he spoke in a harsh whisper. His face reddened and his eyes narrowed at the attorneys. Parker overruled the objection, allowing the defense attorney to continue.

A short while later, the judge announced a break for lunch. Blake's attorney hustled him off to a conference room while Terri and the rest of the Blake fan club piled into cars. For the first time in weeks, Terri had the appetite of a horse.

On their way to the courtroom for the Friday afternoon portion of Blake's trial, Terri's phone vibrated in the pocket of her suit jacket.

Dottie said, "I'll save you a seat in the back," before she entered the courtroom with Moose.

"Ask me why Sweet Sally wasn't at trial on Monday," Marilyn-Anne said.

"Because the attorney reserved the right to call her back?"

"Oh. Well, there's another reason. That vile heifer was filming some kind of reality *tee-vee* show at the Frank house. Can you imagine the gall?"

"Anything for money."

"Say, would you tell Sam to turn his phone back on?" While the rest of the family called him Moose, Marilyn-Anne's use of his given name seemed more intimate than formal.

"He went back into the courtroom. This judge hates cell phones, so we have to keep them off. How are you feeling?"

"Not so good. Please tell Sam I need him to call me right away," Marilyn-Anne said.

"I'll get him." Terri found Moose parked at the end of the back row beside Dottie. She switched off her cell phone and nudged Moose's shoulder. "Marilyn-Anne wants you to call her right now."

Moose stood and ducked out the courtroom doors. Terri took his seat beside Dottie. Terri hoped he would continue to tear apart the kidnapping charge until it disintegrated. With a clear view of the crowd, she counted fifteen reporters including Ernie, dozens of strangers, two rows of townsfolk, and a few people she recognized by name. It seemed as though spectators chose which side of the courtroom to sit in like guests at a wedding.

Special Agent Theron sat at the end of the row behind the prosecutor. He had already testified for the prosecution. Sweet Sally strolled in and sat beside Special Agent Theron, forcing the entire row to crowd in to make room.

Terri wanted to send Marilyn-Anne a text to let her know the heifer was back, but Marilyn-Anne had a cheap, low-tech phone without the ability to send or receive text messages. Terri double-checked to make sure her phone was powered off.

The defense attorney called Samantha Young to the stand. Terri and Dottie inhaled sharply and gaped at each other. Dottie covered her mouth with her hand and closed her eyes. The girl exactly resembled the photos of Carrie Ann taken by Flanagan.

Terri whispered in Dottie's ear, "Isn't that Carrie Ann?"

Dottie nodded and inhaled deeply through her nose.

Her heart racing, Terri watched a lovely young lady with shoulder-length brown hair enter the court. She wore a tailored navy pants suit over a white collared top and low heeled pumps. After the bailiff swore her in, she took her seat in the box and glanced at Blake. After a moment, she directed her attention to the defense attorney.

With his back ram-rod straight, Blake leaned his elbows on the table. Did he recognize who she really was? Terri reminded herself to breathe. She had told Blake Carrie Ann had disappeared after Flanagan located her. She never told Blake she had changed her name.

"Please state your name, age, and occupation for the court."

"My name is Samantha Young. I'm thirty-one and I'm a registered nurse."

Adrenalin flooded Terri's bloodstream. In the stillness of the room, she panted for air. She traded a raised-eyebrow expression with Dottie, who covered her mouth with her hand as if trying to hold back her own panic. How long would it take the prosecutor to discover Carrie Ann's identity as Samantha was a complete lie? What good would it do Blake when he needed the real Carrie Ann to come forward to testify? Maybe the defense attorney was forcing a mistrial. Terri broke into a sweat. She wanted to scream. The truth was being told under the mask of a lie.

"And are you married?" the attorney asked.

Carrie Ann smiled. "Yes, sir."

"Is Young your married name?"

"Yes, sir."

"What were you called before you became Samantha Young?"

She cleared her throat. "Samantha Adams."

Terri had seen lies undo politicians and celebrities when the stupid behavior their lies attempted to cover up would have been forgiven. The court did not forgive. It even had a special legal term for uttering lies in court—*perjury*. This monstrous lie, this false identity snatched out of the air, was transformed into a solid, permanent record, where it could not be forgotten, overlooked, or denied. A mistrial would only grant her more time with Blake, more time for the prosecutor to perfect his case. Terri slumped on the bench. She waited in horror for this big, super-charged, on-the-record lie to explode.

"Did you know Curtis Frank?" the attorney's calm voice flowed.

"Yes." She pursed her lips as if holding back something she wanted to add.

"How did you meet him?"

"He kidnapped me from the mall parking lot in Cleveland, Ohio in early May, nineteen ninety-four." Her voice rang through the courtroom.

Reporters jotted in their notebooks. Spectators murmured and whispered between bowed heads. Dottie dug into her pockets and pulled out a handkerchief to dab her eyes. Hearing about the crime from long ago made it more immediate and frightening than Terri had expected it to. Carrie Ann was a child abducted from a public place. As a teenager, she probably felt safe in her hometown mall parking lot.

"And what happened after that?"

"I was held against my will for six months."

Terri shuddered. All of this testimony will be worthless the moment the court discovers the witness is using a false name. Carrie Ann could go to jail for perjury. She glanced at FBI Special Agent Theron in the front row for his reaction to the witness.

The woman beside Theron whispered and after getting shushed by him, she leaned forward and poked the prosecutor in the back. The prosecutor twisted around. His face paled, his eyes widened, and he spoke to her in an urgent whisper.

Judge Parker said, "Counselor?" as he glared at the prosecutor.

The prosecutor stood. "Excuse me, your honor. I just discovered a witness is in the courtroom, and I was telling her to leave."

The defense attorney crossed his arms while he calmly watched the prosecutor squirm.

Judge Parker said, "Miss Henson? You will be summoned if and when it's your turn again to testify. Until then, you must remain *outside* the courtroom." His tone of voice did not invite discussion or debate.

Sally stood. Pointing at Carrie Ann, she announced, "Your honor, she's a liar. I know for a fact, she ain't Samantha Adams."

Dottie groaned. Terri noticed she had broken into a sweat. Her eyes closed and her lips moved like she was sending up an urgent prayer. Terri's stomach clenched. *There goes the trial. Whatever good Carrie Ann's testimony might have done was rendered useless, the lie exposed.*

The judge gaveled for quiet in the room. Peering over the tops of his glasses he said, "Sally Henson, you are in contempt of this court." To the court officer, he added, "Place her in custody."

Sally gasped. An officer rushed down the aisle and grabbed

Sally's arm. She jerked against his hold, so the officer spun her and handcuffed her hands behind her back. He pulled her out of the courtroom.

Judge Parker addressed the jury. "You will disregard that outburst."

Jurors nodded.

To the defense attorney, the judge said, "You may continue."

Blake's attorney steepled his fingers in front of his chin.

Was he covering a grin? Perhaps because this outburst might be cause for a mistrial or evidence for an appeal.

"Is Samantha Young your legal name?" the defense attorney asked. He dropped his hands to his sides.

Carrie Ann straightened her posture. "It is."

"Did your parents name you Samantha?"

"No, sir. I had my name legally changed."

Terri and Aunt Dottie gave a collective sigh. The threat of Carrie Ann's perjury evaporated, leaving Terri light-headed. Dottie appeared equally relieved.

The attorney faced the jury as he asked the witness, "Why did you change your name?"

"I did it to honor a friend...who died." Carrie Ann raised her chin slightly.

Terri exhaled, finally relaxing on her bench. She grabbed Dottie's hand. Her sweat overpowered her antiperspirant. Terri's shirt stuck to her back. Blake's attorney was not aiming for a mistrial after all. He was playing each move with calculated timing, like a chess master. She wanted to hug him. With fears of a mistrial and perjury behind her, Terri leaned forward in anticipation of the attorney's next move.

"How did you know this friend?" the attorney asked in a bland tone.

"We were both held captive by Curtis Frank."

Terri nodded. He was introducing Curtis Frank's character indirectly.

"How long did you know her?"

Carrie Ann kept her attention on the attorney, speaking loudly enough to carry her voice across the void between the witness box and the attorney's table. "We were friends for five months before she died." Carrie Ann kneaded her hands.

"And when did you start going by the name Samantha?"

"About a month after she died." Carrie Ann took in a deep breath and sighed.

"Did you have any opportunities to escape?" the attorney asked the witness.

"Once, but we had no money so Frank caught us later that day."

"How did he keep you under his control for six months?"

Carrie Ann swallowed. "He made us take pills. He kept us high. He also assigned two older…women to watch us."

"Do you remember the names of these women?"

"The meanest one called herself Sweet Sally." Carrie Ann enunciated clearly as if to rid her mouth of the name. "The other was Evie."

The air conditioner hum was the only sound in the courtroom for a few seconds.

"Samantha," the defense attorney said, "what name did you go by in October of nineteen ninety-four?"

She hesitated as if it would cost part of her soul to say it, as if by speaking the name of that long-lost girl, she might summon her old identity and memories into being. "Carrie Ann Snow."

A collective gasp sounded in the courtroom. Judge Parker jotted something in his notes. The prosecutor remained stoic, his attention focused on the witness.

The defense attorney turned away from Carrie Ann and glanced at the spectators. "Please tell the court what you recall from the night of October twenty-ninth, nineteen-ninety-four."

Carrie Ann's lips became a taut straight line. After inhaling deeply, she said, "I was chained to a bed in the basement of an old farmhouse in North Carolina." She glanced at Blake, who wiped his eyes.

The defense attorney lifted a poster board from beside his table. He placed it on an easel. The larger-than-life photograph featured a smooth, reddish scar circling a bare ankle. A hand-held ruler beside the scar measured it at two-inches.

"Is this photograph of your right ankle?"

Carrie Ann's expression hardened. "Yes, sir."

The prosecutor lifted a metal chain from the evidence table. "And do you recognize this chain?"

"It looks like the kind Frank locked around my ankle."

Two women jurors covered their mouths with their hands. Two others slowly shook their heads. The male jurors appeared stony-faced. Hearing about the chains had been shocking, but seeing them and the scar they left drove a deep impression. The defense attorney dropped the chain on the table. The heavy clanking metal on metal on wood sound caused many of the spectators to flinch. An elderly black male juror scowled at the chain.

The prosecutor plucked two flowered pink sandals from the table. An evidence tag hung from the heel strap. "And do you recognize these sandals, which were found in the basement of the Frank house?"

Samantha's eyes welled. A blink freed tears to roll down her face. "Those are mine."

Terri closed her eyes against the anguish of lost innocence. Such girlish, almost silly-looking sandals exuded the style of a carefree childhood. Terri let go of Carrie Ann, the lost girl. Samantha survived. Samantha was the name of a fresh start and an honored friend.

"At this time, Your Honor, I would like to enter this DNA report into evidence," the defense attorney said. He lifted a few papers from his desk and handed them up to the judge. He examined them and gave them to the bailiff, who gave them to a clerical assistant for tagging.

Judge Parker raised his eyebrows at the prosecutor as if expecting an outburst. The prosecutor picked up his copy and nodded to the judge.

"This report details the DNA extracted from dried blood found on these sandals." The defense attorney nabbed another set of papers from his table. "And this report shows the DNA of our witness," he said, with a wave toward Samantha. "I would like to enter this second DNA report into evidence." He handed it to the judge. After waiting for the second report to be tagged and added to the evidence table, he seized another poster board parked beside his table. He placed it on the easel over the photo of Samantha's ankle.

The poster showed two graphs side by side. He stepped away from the poster then he pivoted back toward it. "According to the DNA reports, the key genetic markers from both these DNA reports match." He paused to glance at the prosecutor. "The identical DNA from the sandals and our witness proves that she was in the basement of the Frank house." He held out a hand toward Samantha. "Please, tell us, Samantha, why did you leave your sandals behind on that cold night in October?"

"Objection as to relevance," the prosecutor said.

Judge Parker eyed the defense attorney.

"State of mind, your Honor," the defense attorney said oh-so politely.

"Objection overruled."

The defense attorney nodded to Samantha.

"I was afraid Curtis was going to make good on his threat to blow up the house."

Conversations erupted in the courtroom. The judge sighed heavily and banged his gavel three times as if symbolically beating the crowd into submission. Terri's blood ran hot and cold. She dreaded Parker, whose fury showed in his set jaw and narrowed eyes. His glare silenced the last of the whisperers.

"Why did you take his threat seriously?" the attorney asked.

"He had red sticks of dynamite and two cans of gasoline tied to the ceiling of the basement. There were wires running from them to the stairway."

"Did he say anything to you about the wires and the gasoline and the dynamite?"

"He told me the wires led to a switch by the front door. He said he could flip the switch on his way out."

The defense attorney nodded and paused. "So what did you do once you were freed from your ankle chain?"

"I ran out of the house." A smile flickered as if she remembered her feelings of freedom.

"Did you speak with the boy who freed you?"

"Yes, sir." Samantha talked to the attorney without glancing at the jury or at Blake, as though they were alone in the room.

"What did you say?"

"I asked where Curtis was and the boy said they were going to take him to the sheriff."

"Which boy was that?"

"The others called him Gator."

"According to previous testimony," the attorney said, "Gideon Clayton is the one with the nickname Gator."

The prosecutor and the judge nodded.

"Did you see the defendant that night?"

"Yes, sir."

"What was his name, do you remember?"

"They called him Boomer."

The attorney held up his hand to Samantha. "For the record, I'll remind the court that we have established the nickname Boomer belonged to the defendant, Elijah Blake Clayton." Turning back to Samantha, he said, "Were you with the defendant and Curtis Frank until Frank's death?"

"Yes, sir."

"How did the defendant behave toward Curtis Frank? Did he threaten him or harm him?"

"No, sir. He helped Curtis sit up so his head wouldn't bounce on the floor of the truck bed."

"Were you present when Mr. Frank died?"

"Yes, sir."

"Please tell the court what you saw."

She explained that she asked the driver to stop the truck so she could pee in the fresh air. While she squatted behind a bush along the road, she heard the boys shouting. Curtis Frank was rolling under a barbed wire fence, and Boomer tried to catch him. The other boys pulled him away from the fence, and they all fell into the ditch. She choked up during her description of the bull's attack.

"How did the defendant react to Mr. Frank's death?"

"He cried. He said they had to get the body out and take it to the sheriff, but the others argued to leave it...that there was no point. Boomer tied a handkerchief to a stick and waved it like a flag while he ran along the fence. The bull chased the flag, so the other guys dragged the body out."

Terri's heart sank in her chest at the thought of Blake taking responsibility for the death. The Felony Murder Rule could have sent Blake to the chair even though an animal killed Curtis Frank.

"I see. Thank you." The attorney faced the judge. "Your Honor, I know it would be irregular, but I would like to temporarily suspend testimony from Mrs. Young and resume it later."

"Approach the bench, both of you." Judge Parker glared down at them.

The prosecutor popped out of his chair and dashed to the judge's bench. The three took turns whispering until the prosecutor nodded.

Judge Parker adjusted his glasses and wrote a note on his pad. He then addressed Samantha. "You may step down and wait where the bailiff directs you until you are called again. You are not to speak with anyone while you wait. Is that clear?"

Samantha stood. "Yes, sir."

The judge leaned away from his microphone to speak to the bailiff. A moment later, Samantha followed the bailiff out a side door.

During the lull, Terri noticed Moose wasn't in his usual seat at the end of the row. She couldn't find him among the spectators. Even when he slouched, he sat so high people grumbled if he sat in front of them. With two small sons, his father in the hospital, and a ranch to run, Moose had shouldered plenty of responsibilities that could call him away from the trial.

The defense attorney said, "Your Honor, I recall Sally Marie Henson to the stand."

Terri waited along with the packed courtroom for news. Minutes later, an officer escorted Sally, no longer handcuffed, to the witness stand. The officer stood off to the side, where he would not block the jurors' view of the witness. He seemed eager to handcuff Sally and remove her again by force.

Judge Parker said, "Miss Hanson, you remain under oath."

"Yes, Your Honor." Sally eased into the witness chair. She eyed the crowd and the jury like an actress about to perform.

The defense attorney's voice rose, "Earlier you called Samantha a liar and said she was not Samantha Adams."

"That's right."

"She says she's Samantha Adams, and you say she isn't." He paced the area in front of his table. "Can you *prove* Samantha isn't who she says she is?"

Smirking, Sweet Sally answered, "You bet I can. She can't be Samantha Adams because Samantha Adams is dead." Her voice rang through the hushed courtroom.

"She looked alive to me," said the attorney.

Terri watched the attorney. He would have been a great snake handler. Calm, deft, and calculated in his movements, he impressed the crowd.

Sweet Sally shook her head and waved a hand. "Samantha Adams died in early October of nineteen ninety-four. Me and Curtis couldn't afford to bury her, on account of she was a runaway we took in. Curtis was scared the cops would blame us, so we buried Samantha Adams in a field behind our motel in Maggie Valley, North Carolina, right between the hotel and a little creek."

"Then who is that woman who claims to be Samantha?" The attorney gave the impression of a man furious at being duped.

"I don't know, but she can't be Samantha." With that, Sweet Sally crossed her arms.

The attorney shook his head. "Oh, dear. I'm sorry to ask, but it's your word against hers. Can you tell me where the real Samantha is buried so I can have this imposter arrested?"

Sweet Sally nodded enthusiastically. "I think I remember." She curled her fingers over the front edge of the witness stand. "I'm pretty sure it was the Stony Creek Motel. I recall there weren't a lot of room between the motel and the creek."

Murmuring in the crowd caused Sweet Sally to look around. Terri marveled at the woman's stupidity. She confessed to helping Curtis bury a runaway, which begged the question—how did the real Samantha die?

"Thank you, so much for your help. I'll have someone check on that right away," he nodded to Special Agent Theron, who eased out of his bench and strode out of the courtroom.

Sweet Sally nodded. Terri shook her head at Sally's monumental stupidity. Sally appeared onboard with the plan to prove the previous witness was a liar. She leaned back in the booth and smiled like she had the world at her beck and call.

"Would you do me one more favor and tell me what caused that poor runaway to die?" The attorney posed as the embodiment of concern.

Sweet Sally's eyes widened. She blinked repeatedly and her mouth fell open, then clamped shut. A smile quivered on one side of her face. "It was so long ago. I'm not sure I remember the details." With one hand, she swatted the air like she was shooing a bug.

The attorney froze in place. After an uncomfortable silence, he said, "Try." His flat tone sounded like a command.

Cornered, she planted her hands on the side railings while she scanned the room, her glance pausing at each exit as if measuring the distance. She slapped her fingers over her mouth and shook her head. "I think she choked on food. I really couldn't be sure. It was so long ago."

"You said that," he said. He stepped back to his chair. "I'm done with this witness."

Sweet Sally hopped out of the witness box.

"One moment, Miss Henson," Judge Parker said. "The prosecutor might have a few questions."

Sweet Sally's head pivoted toward the prosecutor. When he stood, Sally's shoulders slumped. She trudged back to the witness box and collapsed into the chair.

"How thoughtful of you to take in runaways," the prosecutor said. "How many would you say you and Curtis took in over the ten years you were together?"

"Twelve? Maybe thirteen?" her voice squeaked.

"And when you took them in, did you expect them to help out? Say, doing things for you?"

She fidgeted with her hair and her collar. "I suppose we did."

"Such as?"

"Such as what?"

Terri could not tell if Sally said it to stall or if she was truly too stupid to understand the question.

"What kinds of things would the runaways do for you and Curtis?"

"They did whatever we told them to do." Sally squinted at the prosecutor. "With teenagers you have to have rules or they'll run over you." She nodded at the jury.

No juror nodded back.

"Have you stayed in touch with any of them?" the attorney asked.

Sally hissed through her teeth, then said, "No."

"Weren't they grateful for being taken in off the streets?"

"Not near grateful enough." Sally crossed her arms.

"Would you be able to recognize any of them?"

Her face twitched. "I suppose. But I don't recognize that one who calls herself Samantha."

The prosecutor gathered a dozen glossy photos from his table. "I would like to enter these photographs into evidence." He handed them to the judge.

Judge Parker glanced at the defense attorney, who nodded. Seemingly satisfied everything was in order, the judge examined the photos and then handed them to the bailiff.

The photos were logged and tagged and handed back to the prosecutor. He held one eight-by-ten-inch photo in front of Sally. "Do you recognize this young girl?"

"Yes! *That's* Samantha. That's her."

The prosecutor showed the photo from a missing child poster to the jury and the spectators. The name of the child was blacked out. "Let the record show the name of this missing girl is Samantha Adams."

The jurors glanced at one another with eyebrows raised.

"I told you she was a runaway."

The attorney flipped to another photo and held it up toward Sally. "Do you recognize this girl?"

Sally's face blanched. Her eyes widened, showing whites all around her irises. She reared back from the photo. "No. No. No."

"This photo comes from a recording found in the basement of the Frank home." He held the photo up for the jury. They recoiled from it. When the attorney dropped his arms to his sides, the top photo faced the spectators. The photo showed the same teenage girl with a cord tied around her neck. The girl's eyes bulged and her tongue hung out over blue lips.

Even from her bench, Terri flinched at the image of the dead girl's face.

Sally waved her hands in front of her. Gasping, she dropped her head into her hands.

He flipped the photos in the stack one by one, holding them in front of Sally. "You said Samantha Adams died and that you and Curtis buried her."

Sally withdrew her arms and head as if to hide behind the railing of the witness box. Terri suspected the woman was trying to get into the fetal position. Sally's whimpers carried to the back of the courtroom.

The prosecutor raised his voice. "One of the girls you took in has taken on the name of Samantha to honor her."

Sally's head popped up from the witness box. She resembled a feral cat when she grabbed the railings and said, "Carrie Ann! See I told you she wasn't Samantha Adams. She lied, judge, you can't let her get away with that. And you," she said to the attorney, "can't prove anything. I didn't kill that girl." With that, she shot from the witness box and raced out the side door the jury used. The deputy bolted after her.

On her feet, Terri wanted to chase Sally, but other spectators had also jumped up to get a better view of the action, blocking Terri's path. Judge Parker gaveled for order, while the defense attorney stepped up beside the prosecutor. They watched the side door.

Moments later, the deputy who had earlier escorted Sally into the courtroom again brought her back in handcuffs. He was scowling.

The prosecutor said, "Your Honor, I want to remand this witness into custody."

Judge Parker nodded at him.

The Deputy spun Sally around and hauled her by the arm out of the courtroom through the double doors. When the doors opened, Terri caught a glimpse of Theron aiming a satisfied, uninviting smile at Sweet Sally Marie Henson. Beside him stood Nefi wearing a similar smile. Terri stifled a cheer.

On seeing Nefi, Sally shrieked and backed into the Deputy. "She's a witch!"

The double doors swung shut, muting the sounds from outside.

The judge crooked a finger at the prosecutor, then at the defense attorney. They rushed to the front of his bench under his glare. "What do you have to say for yourselves?"

Both men bowed their heads. The prosecutor's voice carried to the back of the room only because the crowd hushed at once. "May we meet in your chambers?"

Judge Parker checked his watch. "Court is adjourned until Monday. I admonish the jury to follow the protocols we discussed earlier." He banged his gavel once.

The bailiff strolled down the center aisle to the judge.

Judge Parker said, "After you escort the jury out, please stay with Mrs. Young until I'm done with these two." He indicated the attorneys with a nod.

While the bailiff led the jury out the side door, Terri pushed through the throng to the front railing that separated her from Blake and his attorney. It was barely four o'clock in the afternoon, too early to recess for the day. She reached the defense table simultaneously with the attorney. Tapping the attorney's arm, she asked, "What's going on?"

"That's up to the judge. He could declare a mistrial." Sweat beaded on the attorney's forehead.

Terri's ribs tightened.

"If the judge declares a mistrial," the attorney whispered, "then maybe we'll get lucky and the prosecutor won't want to refile."

"Has the prosecutor refiled before?" Blake asked.

The attorney swept his papers into his briefcase with trembling hands. "Yes."

. 21 .

Terri was tucked against Blake's side on the couch in their hotel room. She tried to anchor him in comfort to stop him from pacing the room. She used the remote control to switch on the Friday evening news. Were the attorneys in trouble with the judge? A mistrial could mean they'd have to go through this nightmare again. The top news story on the television began by establishing a shot of the Asheville Courthouse that zoomed in on the front door where the FBI escorted out a handcuffed woman. The sight lifted Terri's heart.

"Blake, look!" Terri pointed to the flat screen mounted on the wall.

The broadcast featured Special Agent Theron and Sheriff Ketchum flanking Sweet Sally Henson as they marched her from the courthouse to a waiting black van. Ketchum opened the door for Theron, who put Henson in. Another FBI agent climbed in the back after Henson. The camera caught Theron shaking hands with Ketchum, exchanging a nod, then closing the door. Good old Pete Ketchum had impressed the FBI.

The narrator said, "Today, the FBI arrested Sally Marie Henson for kidnapping and conspiracy to commit murder for her involvement with the late Curtis Frank, who reportedly ran a sex-trafficking ring in the Midwest. FBI Special Agent Theron, who led the Curtis Frank investigation, said Sheriff Peter Ketchum, of

Haywood County, North Carolina, was instrumental in the arrest of Henson. Theron said Sheriff Ketchum, pictured here, and the crime scene investigators were the first to discover that Frank's farm house in Haywood County was rigged with explosives."

Terri said, "Pete took quite a risk going into the old house."

"Not really." Blake draped an arm around Terri.

"And how is that?"

Blake's green eyes twinkled as he smirked. "Bubba disconnected the trigger back in ninety-four. Took him a month of research, but he figured it out."

"Bubba?" Caleb, an accountant by trade. "I've always thought of him as the quiet one."

The room phone rang at the same time as Blake's cell phone, so Terri answered the room phone on the desk. The clock beside the phone read 6:45 p.m. Room service had delivered sandwiches that remained untouched on the sofa table. Anxiety trumped hunger.

"Nefi and I would like you to join us in my room for drinks," Vincent said. He and Nefi had reserved two rooms at the Grove Park Inn and Resort, down the hall.

Terri glanced at Blake, who was nodding with his cell phone to his ear. "Blake's on the phone right now. Can I call you back in a few?"

"Sure."

Blake spoke into his phone. "At eight?"

Terri eased into the sofa where she squeezed the cushioned armrest. Blake's face had gone slack.

"Yes, sir." Blake planted himself beside Terri on the sofa. He tucked his phone in his shirt pocket. "The prosecutor wants to meet with me and my brothers."

"At eight tonight?" *On a Friday night?*

Blake nodded.

The prosecution had already rested. The defense was essentially stalled out until Monday unless Judge Parker declared a mistrial. If the prosecutor offered to settle for life in prison, then it would indicate he believed the jury's sympathy had shifted from the victim to Blake. For what it was worth, withering away in prison might be worse than a swift death by injection. Terri couldn't imagine Blake languishing in a cell. Why did the prosecutor ask for his brothers to be here?

She leaned into Blake's embrace, tucking her head under his chin so her face rested against his warm neck. His cologne wafted upward from his unbuttoned collar. A silent prayer passed between them.

Blake's neck vibrated against Terri's ear while he spoke. "Who called the room?"

"Vincent invited us to his room for drinks." She wanted to hold him close all night, to keep him in the room, suspending time forever.

"Let's go."

Terri sat up, releasing him to stare. She wanted to keep him all to herself for whatever time remained. She dreaded meeting with the attorneys, going to face whatever news they planned to deliver. She suspected the attorneys wanted to wrap up this mess rather than fret about it through the weekend. To them, this was just another day of work, another task to check off their lists. This is Blake's life, and hers was bound to his, heart and mind.

"What? I could use an hour of normal life," Blake said. "Besides it'll take my brothers time to get back here, get their attorneys and whatever."

Terri pinned him down with a smirk. He wanted a distraction, eh? "I could use about fifteen minutes of whatever."

Unbuttoning his shirt, Blake said, "Tell Vincent we'll meet them in twenty."

At the hospital, Moose braced his back against the wall of the corridor in the emergency room. He was spent. *What do I do now?* He ached from the inside out.

The doctor kept talking, but Moose had stopped listening after mention of the word *dead*. The last thing he had heard before the surgeon left was, "I'm so sorry for your loss."

Loss? This wasn't a car, or a horse, or house keys, or even one's mind. This loss had an absolute finality to it. An unrecoverable loss. A flesh and blood loss, like a chunk of his heart.

A buzzing sounded moments before the door from the waiting room opened to admit another poor soul. There was little room for privacy in the emergency room section of the hospital.

"Moose!"

He recognized the voice. "Hey, Butch. How'd you find me?"

"One of the scrub nurses attends my church. Marilyn-Anne told her to call me," Butch said. "The rest of the family's in the waiting room, except for Blake and Terri. We haven't told them yet."

"Good idea. Give Boomer a break." *Lord knows he'll blame himself somehow.* Moose nodded. "Is the trial over?"

"No telling. The judge called the attorneys into his chambers. Looks like they could start up again next week. You won't believe who showed up to—"

"Not now. I don't want to talk about the trial." Moose's phone buzzed in his pocket. There wasn't anyone he wanted to talk to but family, so he let it buzz. He had more urgent things to figure out. *How do I tell my boys?* Moose's throat constricted with the fear they were home alone, forgotten. His mood shifted from grief to panic. He groped for his cell phone. Were they trying to call him?

"What about my boys?"

"I picked them up from school. Dottie's with them."

"Thank you." Moose hugged Bubba. His phone buzzed again. It identified the caller as Lawyer. *Not now.* "What do I do now?"

Bubba took a deep breath. "I'll make the funeral arrangements."

Choked up, Moose nodded. *One less burden to handle.* He was reaching his limit.

"They'll only let one of us back here at a time." Bubba's cell phone clanged like a church bell.

"Send Mama in." He watched Bubba leave. His phone vibrated again, so he dropped it back in his pocket. *Leave a message already!* Nurses passed him in reverent silence. Machinery hummed, people worked, and life went on around him. Moose had a familiarity with emergency rooms. He'd broken a few bones handling horses and playing football. He had scars from stitches to show for taking dares from his friends. Those injuries had earned him bragging rights. This visit to the hospital was worse than any before it. Death hit like a gut punch.

The access door buzzed. Mama gathered speed down the long corridor and collided against Moose to wrap her arms around him as far as they could reach.

Moose's eyes burned. Even Mama's hug couldn't heal him this time. "Mama, I don't know what to do. I don't know what to say."

Mama patted his back and eased from his embrace. After a sniff, she said, "What do you want to do?"

"I want to make her feel better," he said. He longed to do something, to fix the unfixable. "I want her to know how much I love her. I want her to know I'm sorry. It was a girl." He let out a deep breath. He knew his Mama had tried and tried for a girl and Marilyn-Anne had longed for one as well.

Mama's red, puffy eyes stared up at him. Mama understood. "Is she awake?"

"Any minute now." He checked the doorway to the operating room. The nurse had promised to tell him when Marilyn-Anne came out of anesthesia. His phone buzzed again.

Mama planted a soft palm on his chest. "Has Marilyn-Anne ever seen you cry?"

"Of course not."

"Do you feel like crying?"

Moose's throat tingled. "I need to be strong for her." His phone buzzed again and he considered taking it out of his pocket and flinging it against the wall to silence it. Mama didn't tolerate tantrums, so he let the blasted thing chime.

Mama shook her head. "I never taught you that boys shouldn't cry. You picked up that nonsense at school."

"I've never seen Papa cry."

Mama nodded. "He cried the first time he held you." Her eyes welled up.

A small sensation stirred in his heart, like a loosening of a lifetime of pent-up sorrows. He had his mama's permission to cry, and he knew in his soul she wouldn't think less of him for it.

A nurse appeared from the surgery room. "Mr. Clayton? You can see her now."

"I'll be right there," Moose said. He had one last question for Mama. "Why did he cry?"

"Maybe he was overwhelmed by the new experience. Maybe he was tired. I can't tell you what he was thinking, but I felt closer to him at that moment than I did in the four years of marriage before it. It was as if he finally opened a door and let me in his heart."

Moose handed Mama his buzzing phone and left to be with his wife. He let hot tears roll down his face all the way into Marilyn-Anne's embrace.

Twenty-five minutes later, Blake and Terri arrived at Vincent's room. Nefi let them in. Blake followed Terri into the spacious suite. Nefi raised one eyebrow at him.

"What?" Blake asked, rubbing a hand over his face. "Do I have lipstick on me?"

Nefi shook her head. Terri followed Nefi into the spacious

living area that resembled Blake's room except for the two vases of red roses, the champagne on ice and light jazz music.

Blake asked Vincent, "So who sent you the roses?"

Vincent chuckled and popped the cork. He poured four flutes of champagne. He handed them out and kept the last one. "We wanted you to be the first to know."

Blake glanced from Vincent to Nefi and back before he raised his champagne. "Aww, which one of you proposed?"

Terri elbowed him.

As if using her body to point, Nefi leaned against Vincent, who swung his free arm around her.

Blake said, "Congratulations. Have you set a date?"

"We haven't even told relatives, yet," Vincent said.

Smiling, the four clinked their glasses. Blake took a long swig of the cool bubbly liquid. Champagne always tasted like sweet beer to him. It had been months since he'd had anything to celebrate; six months since his wedding. He hoped the marriage of Nefi and Vincent would heal them from the losses in their lives.

Terri set her empty glass on the sofa table and hugged Nefi. After releasing Terri, Nefi held out her left hand, adorned with a brilliant, one-carat, round solitaire diamond. Blake had learned a thing or two about diamonds while he shopped for Terri's ring, so he judged by the ring that Vincent had done his homework as well.

"Wow. In daylight, you could signal aircraft," Terri said.

"Isn't it pretty?" Nefi asked Terri.

Blake answered, "It suits you." *Like gilding a lily, but it makes her happy. Nefi sparkled plenty on her own.*

Nefi faced Blake. "Thank you."

The way she said it, made Blake wonder if she had overheard his thoughts about the lily. He finished his champagne and set the glass on the sofa table. Nefi had spooky intuitions that almost made him believe she could read minds.

As if on a signal, they settled into seats around the sofa table. Vincent and Nefi took the flowered sofa while Blake and Terri found high-back armchairs. Blake had a tenuous hold on his emotions since the day's proceedings. He was exhausted physically, mentally, emotionally. He had learned things were far worse for Carrie Ann than he and his brothers had suspected. Clinging to the noble intent of rescuing Carrie Ann gave him some consolation. It would not be consolation enough for a lifetime in prison, but life wasn't fair.

"I'm sorry we can't stay too long," Terri said.

Blake planted his hands on the armrests of an overstuffed chair. "My brothers and I are meeting with the prosecutor and our attorneys later tonight."

Vincent set down his glass. "That sounds...unusual."

Blake nodded. Just talking about the meeting gave him a chill. Nefi and Vincent were staring at him. For most of his life he believed he had control over his destiny. He always had choices. Sure, he'd made many a bad choice, but the consequences were proportionate. His future or lack of it, was held in the hands of the District Attorney, his own lawyer, a judge, and possibly twelve strangers—all of whom wanted justice. A man was dead and society needed someone to take responsibility for it to give the illusion of justice so all the good people could rest at night.

"Before your meeting," Vincent said, "you might want to re-button your shirt."

Touching his collar, Blake followed the buttons and button holes down with his fingers. He tugged the shirt hem out of his pants. Sure enough, the buttons were off by two, leaving one side lower than the other.

Certainly wouldn't want to humiliate myself. While he straightened up his shirt, he said, "The judge looked steamed when he ordered both lawyers to his chambers."

"What do you think the meeting is about?" Vincent asked.

"All my guesses are fear-based." Blake tucked in his shirt. Dread hovered over him like a cold shadow. "My greatest hope is for a mistrial."

"What's your worst fear?" Nefi asked. She sat on the front edge of the sofa cushion. Her amber-colored eyes bore through him.

Blake was among rock-solid friends, so he spoke openly. "The prosecutor promised them immunity for their testimony, but what if immunity only applies to the kidnapping charge? What if he charges them as accessories in the cover up of the death?"

At 8 p.m. Friday, April 16th, Blake broke into a sweat between his attorney and Moose at the largest, most ornate mahogany conference table he had ever seen. The dark paneled room reminded him of a coffin. The thick burgundy brocade drapes muffled the traffic noise from outside, where Terri and the other wives except Marilyn-Anne waited. Moose looked as grim as a martyr.

Blake unbuttoned his collar and tugged loose his tie. He would straighten himself up again if he was going on a perp walk. Moose, Bubba, Gator, Butch, and their attorneys sat in solemn silence, leaving two empty chairs at one end of the massive inlaid wood surface. No one, *thank the Lord*, had brought Mama. Even if she had wanted to come, she did not belong in the room when the fate of her sons would be played out like cards on the table. The stakes were too high for her heart to handle. She would surely end up in the intensive care unit.

"Who's with Mama?" Blake asked.

Moose said, "She's at the hospital." He glanced at Bubba, Gator, and Butch as if he expected them to agree.

They nodded. Bubba gazed at his own hands. Gator switched off his cell phone and Butch stared at the table top.

There was something his brothers weren't saying.

"Why? Is Papa worse?" Blake had hoped the doctor would keep Papa there as a precautionary measure until the final gavel fell on the trial. *Maybe they want to hide bad news from me, but he's my father, too.*

"No he's fine. She's just visiting," Moose said.

The double doors opened. Charging the room with anxiety, the prosecutor entered with a folder in hand. His gaze swept the room before he sat at the head of the table and laid his hands on the folder.

Blake's chest tightened. Forcing himself to breathe deeply, he squeezed the cushioned leather arms of his chair.

The feel of the chair tethered him to the present. If he fully lived in the moment, would it delay the future? He sighed.

"Thank you, gentlemen, for coming in on your own. In light of today's events in the courtroom, I believe justice would best be served by reconsidering the kidnapping charge against Blake. Without your testimony, I couldn't prove the rest of you were involved in removing Curtis Frank from his property."

"Testimony for which, they were granted immunity," Moose's attorney added in a deep baritone. He planted his soft hands on the polished surface of the table.

The prosecutor opened his folder. "They were granted immunity from prosecution on the kidnapping charge, yes."

Gasps sounded around the table. Blake eyed the papers. His heartbeat drummed in his ears. What was the man up to? Blake forced himself to breathe.

"I would like you and your attorneys to consider a plea deal I've drawn up." He stood and dealt the papers around the table like cards in front of Blake and each of his brothers. "This deal must be accepted by all parties or it will be withdrawn. I'll step outside while you review and discuss it."

After he circled the table, leaving a trail of papers, he left the room.

Terri paced outside the conference room after the District Attorney entered the room, but suddenly he was passing by again on his way out. He acknowledged Terri, Bubba's wife, Gator's wife, and Butch's wife with a congenial smile on his way back down the hall, where he disappeared behind another heavy oak door.

"That was quick." Butch's wife Brittany raised her eyebrows in the direction of the DA. She was the quintessential minister's wife who generally kept her opinions to herself, but was always on hand to help.

Gator's wife, Gina crossed her arms under her ample breasts and said, "I'm betting it's a plea deal. Relax, Brit. They probably have to read the whole thing."

"Give me numbers any day," said Paige, Bubba's wife, a short pixie of a woman. "Legalese is the worst form of writing." She and Bubba were certified public accountants who ran the books for the Clayton Ranch and a number of other small businesses. Normally, April was their busiest time of year, but since the trial, clients had simply asked for extensions on filing their taxes.

Terri slumped in her barely-cushioned chair. Beside her was an empty chair intended for Marilyn-Anne. "Has anyone heard from Marilyn-Anne?"

The other three wives gaped at her, their eyes wide, and mouths hanging open.

Brittany recovered first and planted a warm hand on Terri's forearm. "I'm so sorry. I thought you knew."

Gina's lips formed a tight straight line. She lowered her head.

"It would have been the first Clayton girl in two generations," Paige said. She shook her head as her eyes welled.

Marilyn-Anne was pregnant? Terri felt suddenly stupid.

Brittany said, "She was four months along. We were all excited about finally bringing a girl into the family. Maeve grew up with sisters and she always wanted a girl. We all wanted a girl."

Terri felt hollowed out. Poor Marilyn-Anne! So much tragedy for one family. They didn't deserve a son on trial, a heart attack, a miscarriage, the suspicious glances from their neighbors, and speculation by the media. Looking down, Terri noticed the white and pink baby sweater and knitting needles in Brittany's open purse. When she glanced up, Brittany gave her a weak smile.

Both women sighed.

Silence filled the anxious gaps. Terri strained to eavesdrop on the men behind the heavy doors. A cough. Shuffling papers. No voices. A plea deal would take the death penalty off the table, right? A mistrial would mean they'd have to go through this nightmare again. Terri tried to imagine Blake's choices.

Paige said, "Bubba's probably mouthing the words as he reads."

Gina crossed her legs. "Remington and Colt do that too."

"That's reasonable behavior for six-year-olds. They still sound out their words." Paige shook her head.

All four women sighed. A solemn quiet blanketed them as they prayed.

Blake slid his copy closer to his attorney so they could both read it at once. His heart skipped and shuddered at the complex language and obtuse sentence structures that left him skimming for keywords. He found something meaty in the third paragraph. "Pursuant to acceptance of this agreement, Elijah Blake Clayton will have the charge of kidnapping and the attendant felony murder of Curtis Frank dropped, never to be retried in the courts of the State of North Carolina or in Federal Court." Scanning to the bottom of the page, Blake waited for his attorney to catch up.

He glanced up and saw his brothers and their attorneys hunched over their copies. Bubba's lips moved as he read.

Agonizing moments later, Blake's attorney flipped the page. Where was the dreaded "but"?

Buried in the legalese, Blake found hope. "Pursuant to a unanimous acceptance of this agreement by all the parties listed within...the parties will accept a guilty judgment under North Carolina Statute 14-399, each party will also accept as punishment, a fine of $500, and twenty-four hours of community service to be approved in writing by the Honorable Judge Parker, court of the district.... In addition, Elijah Blake Clayton will pay $5000 in court costs...."

What is North Carolina Statute 14-399?

Lightheaded, Blake took a deep breath and leaned back in his chair. Had he read it right? A fine and community service?

His attorney smiled and patted Blake on the forearm. His eyes stung, blurring his vision. His spirit emerged from the darkness. He could have a future with Terri if his brothers agreed, all for one and one for all, to the plea deal. He waited for their reactions to the deal.

Gator's attorney, the youngest partner of an Asheville law firm, gaped and pointed at the paper in front of him. "Can the DA do that?"

Blake's attorney said, "Judge Parker signed off on the plea."

Blake asked, "Is there a problem?"

"Give him a minute." Blake's attorney leaned his elbows on the table as he nodded at Gator's attorney, who nodded back.

Blake's attorney then addressed the roomful of anxious souls like their study leader helping them cram for a final. "I believe the part of North Carolina Statute fourteen dash three ninety-nine that the esteemed District Attorney names here is part D. It's a class 3 misdemeanor."

From a death-penalty case to a misdemeanor. A measly class 3 misdemeanor at that. Praise God.

"What does it mean?" Moose asked.

"It means Blake doesn't have to die," Bubba said.

"I got that part, thank you," Moose told Bubba.

Blake's attorney opened his chubby hand over the table. "Because Curtis Frank was responsible for his own death, basically the District Attorney is charging you boys with dumping more than fifteen, but less than five hundred pounds of trash in a river."

Stunned expressions of the Clayton brothers transformed into laughter.

Bubba held a pen over the last page of his copy. His attorney stopped him by grabbing his wrist.

"I want to do this," Bubba said with a heavy dose of threat in his voice.

The attorney released Bubba's wrist. "It has to be notarized and witnessed."

Bubba set down his pen and smiled at Blake.

Moose folded his copy so the signature page was on top.

Gator wiped his eyes with a cloth handkerchief. Too overcome to speak, he simply nodded. Blake suspected Gator had carried an enormous burden of guilt for having brought his brothers into the situation in the first place. He had been the one whose sinful nature led to the discovery of Carrie Ann's captivity.

Butch's response sounded like part of a Sunday service. "Praise the Lord for delivering our brother."

Amens rose.

Blake's attorney stood. "Are we in unanimous agreement on the terms?"

Moose answered, "We're all in. Bring on the notary."

Blake's attorney left the room.

Sniffling, Gator said, "I'm so glad we're not going to lose Terri. We needed a vet in the family."

Blake said, "Hey."

"Yeah, yeah," Gator said, waving a handkerchief at Blake, "you too. By the way, you owe Marilyn-Anne for telling off Ernie in front of the whole breakfast crowd at Casey's Diner."

"I thought Mama caused Ernie's change of heart," Blake said.

Gator chuckled. "Casey said Marilyn-Anne told Ernie to get off his butt and do some real investigative reporting."

"She used the B-word in public?" Blake slapped his right hand over his heart. Marilyn-Anne's mama might rise from her grave and wash her mouth with soap.

Moose nodded, one side of his mouth tugged upward. It was a mixed emotion smile that Blake had seen once before on Moose. When Moose's son Noah was five, he asked, "Daddy, is it okay if I love God more than I love you and Mommy?" Hugging Noah, Moose had peered over the boy's head at Blake and asked who took second place. Noah told him it was a tie. Moose gladly accepted second place, even tied with Marilyn-Anne, after God. That same half-smile of pride showed on Moose again.

The prosecutor reentered the room with Blake's attorney and a sharp-eyed elderly black woman who carried a small cherry wood box. The men stood, which startled the woman as the prosecutor introduced Mavis Beacon, notary, and his assistant. He directed the notary to sit at the head of the table. After she sat, so did the men. While Mavis unpackaged her notary seal from a wooden box and velvet cloth, the prosecutor reviewed the conditions of the plea agreement. The brothers lined up in birth order to process their agreements. Moose led the group. His attorney served as a witness as did the prosecutor. Bubba came next, followed by Gator, Butch, and finally, Blake. After gathering up the papers, the prosecutor asked the group to wait while Mavis made copies.

Moose stopped him. "How long do we have to pay the penalty?"

"Ten days." When the prosecutor left the room, the family and their attorneys collapsed into chairs.

Moose pointed to Blake. "You haven't visited Papa, yet."

"I had to stay near the courthouse."

"It's a thirty-minute drive." Moose leaned his elbows on the table.

"I didn't want to stress him." It stung Blake to admit it. He blamed himself for being the greatest source of stress in his father's life and the probable cause of his heart attack.

"*Someone's* got to tell Papa the good news," said Gator.

"Just don't ask him for the money," Bubba said.

Lighter than air, Blake's spirit danced inside. His eyes welled, overflowing when he blinked. He was a free man. Okay, an unemployed free man, but he had family and friends who still loved him. Would Terri forgive him for losing her practice?

The prosecutor carried two canvas sacks marked U.S. Postal Service. He set the small one on the table and then he swung up the larger one, which landed on the table like a body. "You should have these," he said to Blake.

Blake swallowed. "What is this?"

The prosecutor patted the smaller sack. "Public opinion in favor of conviction." He pointed to the larger sack. "And public opinion in favor of declaring you a saint." With that, he smirked and left the room.

Mavis entered, triggering the men to stand. This time, she didn't flinch but simply grinned. She distributed the copies of the signed plea agreements. She stopped in front of Blake and craned her neck up. "I read correspondence as part of my job. My favorites are on top," she said, with a wave toward the large sack.

"Thank you, Mrs. Beacon," Blake said.

She placed her hand lightly on Blake's shoulder and said, "Say hello to Maeve from Bootsie."

Bootsie? Blake nodded.

After the door had closed, Moose's attorney said, "I thought you were exaggerating when you said your mama knows everyone."

Moose shouldered the large sack. "Let's go home."

Blake's attorney picked up the small sack. "I'm going to keep these just in case someone gets upset about the plea. Oh, and let's keep the details of this agreement private, shall we? I doubt the media will bother to look up the statute, so let's not invite them to."

The group unanimously vowed to keep it to themselves.

No matter how the prosecutor announced the plea agreement, some would declare it a back-door deal for a wealthy family. Blake saw it as justice. God had answered his prayer favorably and the District Attorney had Sally in custody. His thoughts drifted back to Carrie Ann. Both times he met her he marveled at her courage. The first time he met her she was a victim and he was a rescuer; the second, she became victor and rescuer. He prayed she would find happiness and peace.

. 22 .

On the Saturday after the trial ended, morning light streamed through trees onto the polished wooden casket strewn with flowers on the outskirts of a small rural town a few states away. Along the east side of the gravesite stood two bush-sized pink bouquets, one from the Clayton family, the other from a woman with the same first name as the deceased.

"...and so we welcome home to rest Samantha Adams, beloved daughter, sister, and friend. May her soul be at peace with God," the robed pastor said, "in the name of the Father, the Son, and the Holy Spirit. Amen."

The assembled replied in unison. "Amen."

Of the fifty people gathered graveside, fifteen stood out as non-family members. Ketchum was the only dark-skinned person present. He wore his a suit instead of his uniform. Other than a few sideways glances, he didn't get much attention.

Two heavy-set, thick-boned men broke from the family group to approach Ketchum and the other strangers who stood on the opposite side of the casket from the family.

The older of the two with glasses and gray hair spoke to Ketchum. "I'm one of Samantha's uncles. May I ask how you knew her?"

Ketchum answered softly, "I'm Sheriff Peter Ketchum, from

North Carolina. And this is Nikolas Theron, special agent with the FBI—"

Samantha's father stepped up between the heavyset men. "These men brought Samantha home."

The relatives relaxed and greeted them with handshakes while Theron's team introduced themselves. The youngest agent shook hands with Samantha's parents and stepped away to wipe his eyes. The rest of the agents remained more stoic, though they cleared their throats often.

Mr. Adams wiped his eyes with a cotton handkerchief. "Thank you again for bringing her back. I'll be able to sleep now my daughter's had a proper burial."

After the FBI team had identified themselves, Samantha's father turned his attention to the couple and a small boy who stood behind Ketchum.

Ketchum said, "Allow me to introduce Mike and Samantha Young and their son, Clayton."

Mrs. Adams gasped. "Are you the girl from the trial?"

All conversations stopped. Heads aimed toward the disturbance.

Samantha said, "Yes, ma'am." Her posture tightened as if bracing for a blow. "Your daughter was my friend."

Mrs. Adams' eyes welled. She grasped Samantha's arm. "I'm glad you're keeping my daughter's name alive. I hope your parents don't mind."

Ketchum relaxed, grateful for the grace of a grieving mother.

Samantha glanced at Special Agent Theron, who had conducted an exhaustive search for them. "My parents passed away a few years back. I never got to see them after I was…taken."

Mrs. Adams pressed her hand to her lips. After a nod, she said, "I'd like you to consider us family."

Samantha flung her arms around Mrs. Adams. "I'd like that very much."

The family gathered around the young couple and the boy to welcome them with hugs and tears. Shared grief united a woman with no parents and parents who lost a child.

Ketchum, Theron, and the FBI task force declined the invitation to the reception. They strolled across the freshly-mown lawn of the cemetery, among the solemn headstones and budding trees, into warming sunlight, toward their rental cars.

"I think your name is perfect for your job," Theron said.

"Yeah, I get that a lot." Ketchum smiled. "What does your name mean?"

"It's Greek. Theron means *hunter*."

"Perfect." Ketchum nodded. "You're like a superhero. Theron the monster catcher."

Theron smiled.

After passing through a gauntlet of family members who warned about not stressing Papa during his recovery, Blake entered the study where his father was sleeping. It was Sunday after all and the family was skipping church because they needed time to themselves. Going to church would have created a disruption and drawn attention to the family instead of God. The room smelled of dusty fur and gun oil. The breakfast tray of half-eaten food idled on the end table beside Papa's roomy leather reclining chair. His father was smaller, almost shrunken in the chair. Blake eased into the leather sofa nearby to watch his father breathe. Papa was too peacefully sleeping to be disturbed, so Blake used his waiting time to choose his words.

No one had allowed Papa to watch television or see a newspaper throughout the trial, so Blake had been elected to break the good news as gently as possible. Blake considered beginning with an apology, but then Papa might think it was a

SOUTH OF JUSTICE

good-bye speech before starting a prison term. The steady rhythm of a ceiling fan lulled Blake into peacefulness. Should he blurt out his plea deal to a lesser charge? About the time he wished he had brought Mama along, Papa sighed and raised his head.

When Papa spotted Blake, he sucked in a breath.

"You gotta stay calm, Papa, or Mama will toss me out."

Papa nodded. A solemn expression came over him as if he was steeling himself for the bad news. "How long can you stay?"

"I'm free. I can stay as long as I want."

Papa's eyes brimmed over. "Thank God." He cleared his throat. "Just tell me what happened."

"The prosecutor downgraded the charge to body dumping. We didn't kill that man, and we didn't kidnap him."

Papa broke into tears and reached out both hands toward Blake, who rose from the sofa and hugged his father's shoulder.

Papa shouted. "I *knew* you didn't kill that man no matter how wicked he was."

Blake sucked in air and patted his father's chest. "Easy Papa."

Mama stepped into the room and cleared her throat.

"I'm fine," Papa said, waving her away.

Mama stood her ground.

Blake retreated to the sofa. He gave Mama his best sheepish grin, but she wasn't impressed enough to move. Papa waved her away again. After a parting glare at both men, she pivoted and left the room.

"Tell me about the night Curtis Frank died."

Blake recounted the night of the rescue then told him about the trial. Papa listened without interruption and after Blake had finished unburdening himself of the last painful months, Papa smiled.

"So justice was served." Papa wiped his eyes with the back of his hands.

"More like somewhere south of justice, but it's over."

"What do you mean south of justice?"

A childhood of lessons from Bible study and Sunday school weighed on Blake's heart. "I can't help but wonder if he'd gone to prison maybe he wouldn't have died unredeemed."

"God knows your heart, son. God knows that dead man's heart, too. He made his choices in life. Seems to me he was choosing evil over God at every turn." Papa shook his head. "You boys saved that girl from a life worse than death. Think about that instead. And let's not ever speak that man's name again." His voice had regained its authority and energy.

"Yes, sir."

On Sunday evening, Terri welcomed the Flanagans into the large foyer of the Clayton mansion. "I'm so glad you could come."

Quinn and Kate Flanagan took turns embracing Terri. "Thanks," Quinn said, "for inviting us to this celebration."

Kate carried a small gift basket from Zabars, a marvelous neighborhood grocery store in Manhattan. A green bottle of Ravida olive oil nestled in the basket beside bread, dipping spices, and smoked salmon—gifts from one cook to another.

"You helped make it happen," Terri said. "The men are outside at the grill swapping stories and the women are in the kitchen."

Noah Clayton, Moose and Marilyn-Anne's oldest boy, ran into the foyer and partway up the staircase, where he aimed his cap gun at the doorway to the living room. Moments later, his younger brother Micah dashed in, shooting wildly.

With the bluster of a five-year-old, Micah pointed his cap gun at Quinn. "Are you a bad guy or a good guy?"

Terri said, "Mr. Quinn Flanagan was Uncle Blake's boss at the FBI."

Noah called down from the stairway. "Micah. Remember your manners."

Micah holstered his cap gun and stuck out his hand. "How do you do, Mr. Quinn?"

Flanagan's hand enveloped Micah's. "I'm pleased to meet you, Micah. Could you direct me to your Uncle Blake?"

"Yes, sir." Micah tugged Quinn by the hand, pulling him from the foyer.

Noah followed. His voice rang off the walls. "Mr. Quinn, Mr. Quinn, did you ever get shot?"

"I did. But I shot back," Quinn's voice faded.

"Mr. Quinn?" Kate Flanagan muttered, shaking her head.

Terri led Kate through the living room to the spacious farmhouse-style kitchen. "It's a southern thing. I don't know why they leave off people's last names. They called me Miss Terri for months, but I've finally been promoted to Aunt Terri." She finally felt she belonged with the Clayton family. Being called Aunt Terri was one of many signs. The dearest sign of acceptance was finding her bed short-sheeted. She confronted family members privately and by the process of elimination, she discovered the perpetrator was none other than Mama Clayton. That knowledge felt as welcoming as a hug.

The scent of baked apple pies filled the house. The moment Kate entered the kitchen, the women paused in their work. The massive kitchen featured a central island with a granite countertop the size of a regular bed laden with steaming pies on racks. Every counter lining the room was covered with mixing bowls, serving bowls full of various salads, vegetable dishes, potato chips, dip, rolls, and other dishes.

"Ladies, this is Kate Flanagan from New York." Terri then pointed out the others to Kate by name. Finally, she said, "And you know Nefi."

From the far side of the island, Nefi waved a pot holder mitten. A swipe of flour graced her chin.

Mama dried her hands on her apron and grabbed Kate by her free hand. "Terri told me what you and your husband did to help

Blake." Her eyes welled. "Thank you. Without that dear girl's testimony, I don't think...." She choked up.

Marilyn-Anne draped an arm around her. "Now, Mama, you told me I can't dwell on the might-have-been." Marilyn-Anne was right. There was enough to worry about without adding all the possibilities. Already back on her feet from her miscarriage, Marilyn-Anne had warned everyone to stop fussing over her. The lost baby girl was buried beside Marilyn-Anne's parents in the smallest casket Terri had ever seen. The headstone was supposed to arrive in two weeks.

Mama nodded and sniffled. "Would you like coffee? I made a fresh pot."

"That would be lovely. What can I do to help?" Kate handed the gift basket to Mama, who thanked her with a huge smile.

"When the men are done making their burnt offerings, we'll move the rest of the food out to the patio," Mama said. "But for now, let me get your coffee." She set the gift basket on the only bare spot on the counter.

Terri resumed her assignment to pluck teabags from a stockpot of boiled water mixed with cups of sugar as directed by Mama. Southerners liked their tea syrupy sweet. Terri was grateful the ladies entrusted her to prepare something for the meal. When she reached for a long-handled slotted spoon to fish out the teabags, she knocked over her own glass of water off the counter. The glass shattered on the tile floor.

"Oh, I'm sorry!" Terri said.

Marilyn-Anne rushed over with a dustpan and broom and cleared away the glass shards.

Sheriff Pete Ketchum arrived with a large planter of tulips he handed to Mama. She in turn handed the flowers off to Bubba's wife, who carried them out to the serving tables. He paused in the kitchen as if assessing whether or not he was welcome to stay. The ladies gave him cool nods.

"I have to say I was surprised you invited me," Ketchum said.

He wore a green polo shirt, chinos, and boat shoes. Terri suspected he had dressed fancier than jeans and a t-shirt to apologize with a show of formality.

Mama told Ketchum, "You followed the law and your conscience when you were tested." She gave him a hearty hug and pushed him toward the back door. "The boys are out back."

Micah wandered into the kitchen and wrapped his arms around Marilyn-Anne's legs. "Where's Papa?"

Marilyn-Anne petted the top of Micah's buzz-cut. "He's outside. Don't climb on him."

Six-year-old twins Remington and Colt burst in through the porch doors. They shouted in unison. "Dinner's ready!"

The women carted out armloads of serving bowls, dishes, baskets of silverware and napkins, steaming pots of beans, pies and more. Terri poured the sweet tea over ice in a three-gallon thermal cooler that sat inside one of the massive double stainless steel sinks. Each sink was deep and wide enough to bathe a toddler. First Terri screwed on the large plastic top, then Nefi hefted it to the serving counter outside. Terri grabbed a tray of glasses and children's plastic cups rattling with ice cubes. She followed Nefi outside.

The men placed trays of grilled hot dogs, barbecue ribs, hamburgers, and brats on the serving tables and stood nearby. With the crowd of family and friends gathered around, a quiet descended. Leaves rustled. Flanagan traded a glance with Ketchum. Terri remembered that at previous meals, Papa Clayton traditionally gave thanks.

Papa's voice broke the stillness. "Samuel, why don't you give the blessing?"

Moose, the firstborn son, closed his eyes and bowed his head. "Dear Lord, thank you for your grace and mercy. Thank you for hearing our prayers and answering them. Thank you for sparing Pa. Thank you for saving our Elijah from that Jezebel. Thank you for your mercy. May you pour out your blessings on Carrie Ann, uh, Samantha wherever she is. Thank you for our family and friends." He peeked up at Ketchum.

Ketchum nodded.

"In Your name we live and believe. Amen." Moose nodded at his father.

The group responded enthusiastically in unison. "Amen."

Immediately after the blessing, people settled into seats at picnic tables on the patio in the afternoon sun and a slight breeze. Ketchum sat at the end of a table with Kate and Quinn Flanagan at each elbow. While Terri approached the table where Blake sat, she noticed Ketchum and Flanagan shake hands. Terri climbed into an empty spot, across from Blake, between Flanagan and Vincent. Nefi, sitting across from Vincent, had a plate piled as high as Blake's. Still young enough to enjoy a fast metabolism, Nefi, and her full plate also attracted Kate Flanagan's amused interest.

Maeve whispered something to Noah, who then dashed to the house.

"When do you start your job?" Kate asked.

Nefi lowered a sauce-covered rib. "Next week. It's my first job ever."

"Behavioral Sciences is lucky to have you." Blake raised his tea glass at her.

Nefi nodded.

"Speaking of work," Flanagan said, pulling a folded envelope from his shirt pocket. "Chief Watson asked me to give this to you."

Blake took the envelope. "Severance pay?"

Flanagan's raised eyebrows challenged Blake to open the envelope. Lowering it to his lap, Blake opened it. His eyes scanned left to right rapidly. One corner of his mouth tugged up into a half grin. Raising his head, he smiled at Terri.

"I will have to discuss it with my wife," Blake handed the letter across the table to Terri. "The chief says I'm welcome to come back. He also offers to write a strong recommendation for me to apply to any field office."

Terri read it in seconds and handed it back. "Congratulations. One of us needs to work. I have airplane expenses you know."

Nefi said, "There are fifty-six field offices. The closest ones are Charlotte and Atlanta. Don't suppose *you'd* want the Atlanta office."

Blake shook his head. Working with Special Agent Nickolas Theron was not an option.

"Puerto Rico has one, but you'd have to speak Spanish." Nefi shook her head as if to dismiss that suggestion.

"What? I'm trainable," Blake said.

Nefi said, "*Buenos dias,* y'all."

"So much for respecting your elders," Blake said.

Noah returned from the kitchen with a small brightly-colored object. He set it down in front of Terri. An orange sippy cup.

"What's this?" Terri asked.

Noah smirked. "House rules."

Nefi and Vincent exchanged a shrug. A moment of silence struck the kids' table. All eyes turned to Terri.

Blake snorted. "You broke a glass?"

From deep in her chest, a laugh bubbled up and burst from Terri. She nodded. She leaned forward to see Maeve's lips twitch, which was a good as a confession about short-sheeting.

Moose's son Noah tapped Flanagan on the arm. "Mr. Quinn. Mr. Quinn. Can I see where you got shot?"

The boys scrambled from the kids' table and huddled close behind Noah. Gator's sons, Remington and Colt, wore matching green polo shirts, blue jeans, and cowboy boots.

Blake chuckled. "Who told the boys about that?"

"They asked why I wasn't your boss anymore." Flanagan stepped out from the picnic table bench and faced the boys. He unbuttoned his collared shirt and pulled up his white t-shirt. Pointing to a spot below his fourth rib on the left, he said, "This is where the bullet entered." He turned his back to them and said, "Can you see where it came out?"

Three small hands examined the larger circular scar on his back, an inch above his belt. The boys *oooohed* and *aaaahed* at it. Noah's eyes widened when he touched the scar.

Flanagan dropped his t-shirt. "So don't play with real guns, okay?"

"Yes, Mr. Quinn," the boys intoned.

Flanagan returned to his spot at the table.

Blake dug his fork into his three-bean salad and left it there. A breeze carried the scent of freshly cut grass down from the pasture. *What a marvelous day to be alive!* He then pulled a small card from his shirt pocket. "Oh, Noah."

The seven-year-old dashed to Blake's side. His eager face glowed in the sun.

Blake pressed the card in Noah's hand. "Thank you. It worked great."

Noah puffed out his chest and tucked the GET OUT OF JAIL Monopoly card in his back pocket. He sounded like his father when he replied, "Glad to help." He strutted back to his seat at the kids' table.

Vincent set down his fork. "That bag of letters from the prosecutor had a letter from Special Agent Albritton."

"Reading other people's mail is a federal crime," Blake said between bites of brownie. Blake failed to mention the letters were already opened by his attorney. Had the attorney even scanned through them?

Vincent continued, "Apparently, when you and your father delivered a horse to Albritton's daughter, you spent two days showing her how to take care of it and how to hitch it up to a cart."

Blake's back straightened. "Oh, man. I remember. The child looked like a little old lady. She had to ride in a cushioned cart because her bones were brittle."

Vincent continued. "She had a rare disease called progeria. The letter said she died of old age at fourteen."

The idea of losing a child that young stung Terri's heart. There are no guarantees in raising a child. While her thoughts of motherhood grew into apprehension, she eyed Blake's mother.

With a grandchild on either side of her, Maeve Clayton, the matriarch of the family, patted the back of her youngest grandson while he told her about his recent horseback ride. Mama Clayton had wanted a girl but raised five boys instead. She seemed content. Her boys had grown into fine men and fathers. Though Blake had not specifically said he wanted to have children, he had not ruled them out. Perhaps now with the trial behind him, they could afford to make long-term plans.

Bubba's voice cut through the other voices. "Walker, I said open your mouth, now!" He held his three-year-old son by the shoulders.

Terri set down her sippy cup in case she had to perform the Heimlich maneuver.

Walker opened his mouth. From the side, Terri saw the soft folds of his chubby neck squish together.

Bubba cringed and spoke in his serious father tone, "Spit it out."

With the family staring at him, Walker spat out a small, live, green tree frog.

"And no, you can't keep it," Bubba said.

Moose said, "Relax, Bubba. He's had his shots."

Terri gasped. All the more reason to want a baby girl. The family resumed eating while Terri's thoughts drifted to the letters from the fan mailbag she pawed through. Neighbors, teachers from grade school, a high-school football coach, Senator Jenkins and Admiral Ramos also sent letters. They had written to the attorneys and the judge, never knowing if Blake would ever read them. The letters were sent out like ripples in the hope to change the tide of forces threatening to drown Blake. By sheer volume, the letters might have moved the heart of the district attorney.

The letters reinforced what Terri already understood—Blake

was in word and deed the man of her dreams, the one to enjoy happily-ever-aftering with. She entered the marriage in love. She endured the trial thanks to hope, love, and faith. Unemployed, but vindicated at last, she could face the unknown future courageously with Blake by her side.

She found happiness in this large, loud, close family. She was truly a Clayton now. No more waiting for happiness. She welcomed it with open arms.

Nefi clinked her metal fork on her glass, waking Terri from her reverie. Soon others joined in, signaling for the Blake and Terri to kiss. Blake stood and leaned over the picnic table, so Terri stood and leaned forward. With his large, warm hands cradling her face, they kissed to applause.

Though normally one to avoid public displays of affection, Terri savored Blake's long, passionate kiss as if sharing the last air on the planet. It had been months since joy bubbled up in her, months since her last major public display of affection. Then, corseted in pounds of crinoline and lace with her hair stiffened into curls, she had kissed for the cameras. Now, comfortable in jeans, a silk shirt, and Roper cowboy boots with her hair down, she kissed for the joy of it. At the wedding, they had spoken their vows, to love and honor one another for the rest of their lives.

Having field-tested those vows, Terri knew she could now happily keep them 'til death.

THE END

Coming Soon

North of the Killing Hand

by Joni M. Fisher

North of the Killing Hand, a prequel to *South of Justice,*
will be released in the fall of 2016.

Here is a preview.

. 1 .

Fourteen-year-old Nefi Jenkins settled into her perch thirty-four feet up a Strangler fig tree, shaded by the canopy of the top branches. From her favorite place she enjoyed a bird's eye view of the Amazon from the Jurua River that wrapped the west and northern boundaries of the tribe's territory, to the denser jungle to the east, and the swamp to the south. Her parents didn't know of this place because they had not asked. Experience had shown her that forgiveness was easier to gain than permission. She did not want to be lectured about every injury and fatality from falls suffered in the history of the tribe.

On a clear day, she could locate other tribes by smoke columns where women cooked at the center of every settlement. At the center of her village, surrounded by a dozen wooden huts with palm frond rooftops, Mali cooked for Nefi's family and her own.

Nefi longed to travel, even just to visit other tribes, but in August the river ran low. Father refused to go out in August because the boat was too heavy to tow, but Nefi believed the real reason was his fear of anaconda that draped themselves on branches over the river like the braided hemp ropes thrown from a ship. Father said there was no anaconda back in the states. He promised to take her there, but every year changed to "next" year.

Nefi sighed. Each year grew longer and this was the longest month of the year.

Birds scattered from trees along the riverbank west of the village. Nefi dug her father's binoculars from her satchel to investigate the disturbance. A human-made bird call sounded. A warning. Moments later the seven other children of the village dashed to their hiding places.

Had the Matis crossed the river to hunt?

She leaned forward to see around leaves into the center of the village where three men with rifles faced Mali. The small elderly woman turned toward Mama and Papa, who walked toward the strangers. The shortest man pointed to Papa. Nefi focused the binocular lenses on the stranger's face. The Pirarucu Man.

What kind of fool comes to trade this time of year? He probably got his boat stuck in the shallow river. City dweller.

The Pirarucu Man pointed to the ground. Mama and Papa knelt. A chill ran up Nefi's spine. He did not seem like a man who would ever ask for prayer. Nefi widened her view to see Mali step toward Mama and Papa. The Pirarucu Man raised his rifle and shot twice. A tiny cloud of smoke puffed from the rifle.

Nefi sucked in a deep breath. Mama and Papa slumped over. A howl roared out of Nefi as if by sound alone she could scare off the Pirarucu Man.

She lost her balance and fell four feet onto a wide branch below, striking hard enough to cut off her scream. Clinging to the branch, she watched Papa's binoculars fall thirty feet before the rare and unmistakable sound of breaking glass marked its impact.

She shimmied to the tree trunk, hugged it, and slid to the next lower branch. The tree blurred, forcing her to blink repeatedly. Her mind spun. Her feet and arms worked on sense memory as her body scrambled down the familiar smooth-skinned fig tree into the cavernous walled folds in the trunk. Gasping and wobbly among tree roots that arched waist-high around her, she rubbed her eyes to clear away the nightmarish images flashing in her mind.

Stepping over the shattered binoculars, she ran. Crashing through knee-high ferns and tree roots, she tore a fresh path back to the village. Her bare feet slapped the hard-packed mud. She trampled ferns and flowers, sending small creatures scuttling out of her way. She panted. Her heartbeat drummed in her ears. Small branches scratched her arms and her face. Stumbling over roots and vines, she groped her way upright and charged on. She raced to her village, to home, to Mama, to Papa, praying the binoculars lied.

The more twenty-one-year-old Vincent Gunnerson thought about his mission, the more heroic it sounded. He and two others were tasked with a privately-funded mission to go to the Brazilian jungle to pick up the fourteen-year-old niece of U.S. Senator Jenkins. The girl's parents had been murdered, leaving her stranded. Four hours into the jungle it seemed a tame assignment.

Vincent was second in a line of three men hiking generally northeast through waist-high brush and towering trees in *Serra Do Divisor* National Park on the Brazilian side of the Amazon rainforest. Ruis Ramos led the way along a worn pathway. Vincent waved off a cloud of gnats, caught the toe of his boot on a tree root, and stumbled. He gasped, inhaled a bug, and then his rifle barrel smacked him in the back of the head. Good thing only Blake saw it.

Being that kind of friend, Blake Clayton laughed.

Vincent spat out the bug.

"Just a walk in the park, eh?" Blake muttered from behind Vincent.

Their leader Ruis Ramos had suggested this mission would be fairly easy.

So far, Vincent believed him. "Did you expect paved roads?"

"I expected something better than a critter trail in a national park."

Ruis called back, "We're almost there."

There being that spot on Ruis's map labeled Queimado Hill. *There* where they were to meet the Brazilian officials for a briefing and to plan their combined search for the girl.

Vincent had accepted the mission immediately though he spoke neither Portuguese nor Spanish. If anyone asked, he was prepared to say he was in it for money, for bragging rights, for something to do before starting college in September, and for a letter of recommendation from Senator Jenkins. Though he would never admit it, his true motive was to be like his father, a man who daily risked his life to save others as an officer in the NYPD. Rescuing a recently orphaned American citizen from the heart of the Amazon rainforest seemed like the most heroic use of the summer.

He didn't know Blake Clayton's reasons for going, but he was glad to have him along. After serving in the Marines with him, Blake was like the older brother Vincent always wanted. At six foot even, age thirty, red-headed with two-hundred and twenty compact pounds of bone, muscle, and integrity; Blake had the soul of a poetic clown. They had separately applied to Berkeley College and were accepted. So why not take on one last mission before starting college?

Ruis, a former U.S. Navy Lieutenant with special operations training, was five foot nine, and thirty years old. Though shorter than Blake and Vincent, Ruis had movie-star good looks and justified confidence. He had assumed leadership of the mission because he spoke Spanish and a smattering of Portuguese. Vincent just knew Ruis was the kind of guy who slept in Kevlar.

The men arrived at a trailhead that opened onto a hilltop. Standing at the peak of Queimado Hill along the bank of the Moa River in Southwestern Brazil, Blake set his backpack on the ground. Vincent followed suit, keeping his M-16A2 rifle hanging from its strap over his shoulder. He walked to the cliff's edge.

Blake approached Ruis. "How do the park rangers know when to meet us?"

Ruis planted a hand on Blake's shoulder. "Let's not call them that."

Blake raised his eyebrows. "Okay."

"IBAMA," Ruis said, "stands for the *Instituto Brasileire do Meio Ambente e dos Recursos Naturais Renovaveis.*"

How anyone got the acronym IBAMA from *that* mystified Vincent. Even in Portuguese the letters didn't add up right.

"This agency is chronically underfunded and outmanned," Ruis added. "It fights poachers, slash-and-burn farmers, squatters, drug runners, fires, illegal loggers, guerillas, and eco-terrorists over an area larger than California and Texas combined. Occasionally they also rescue lost tourists and arbitrate quarrels between tribes." Ruis's hand dropped off Blake's shoulder. "If nothing else, let's respect them for their mortality rate."

When Ruis headed back toward the trailhead, Blake bowed his head.

Vincent didn't believe Blake meant to insult the local officials. If given a few more minutes, he too might have called them park rangers. He strode to the cliff edge to take in the view.

Blake stepped to the cliff edge beside Vincent. The foliage had been thicker on the trail side of the hill than it was looking eastward. From this vantage point, the Amazon terrain had widely-spaced trees. The Adirondacks looked more like a jungle than this. Morning fog rose from the land like steam as if the land itself was sweating, but the breeze at the cliff chilled. It felt like one-hundred percent humidity. The sun glowed with blurry borders through drifting layers of smoky fog.

Ruis's voice caused Vincent and Blake to turn back toward the trailhead. There Ruis greeted two short, solidly-built men in uniform. They shouldered ancient, dusty rifles that Vincent wouldn't trust in a firefight. Everything about the two Brazilians seemed gritty and dust-covered except for their brightly colored IBAMA agency patches.

Ruis introduced Officers Raposo and Machado.

IBAMA Officer Raposo came up beside Vincent and waved his arm out toward the expanse of the sparse forest below. "*Mirante.*"

Vincent scanned the flat valley below. "That's *Mirante*?"

Raposo spoke rapidly with Ruis in Portuguese that sounded like Spanish with a German accent which made Vincent all the more grateful Ruis handled the translation.

Ruis said something that made the IBAMA officers laugh then he said, "*Mirante* means overlook."

Vincent nodded at Ruis. "And a beauty it is."

The two IBAMA officers smiled at the view. Unlike Vincent and Blake, the officers had not broken a sweat. A chorus of trills, twitters, whoops, hoots, whistles, squeaks, squawks, clucks, and chirps sounded as birds and frogs joined in to celebrate the day. Despite the variety of noises from the trees, Vincent couldn't spot a single creature in the dense vegetation.

Ruis handed cold bottles of water to the IBAMA officers. While the officers drank, Ruis told Vincent and Blake, "I'm going to plan our search with these gentlemen. It'll go faster and smoother if I don't have to translate."

Vincent could take a hint. "That works for me."

Blake nodded. Ruis then spread a topographic map on the ground in the center of the clearing. The IBAMA officers each took a knee along the edges of the map.

Vincent used binoculars to scan the area below. "Brazil," he said, lowering his binoculars, "has seven thousand miles of beach."

"Try not to think about it," Blake said.

They were almost too far inland for Vincent's imagination to conjure coconut-oiled women sunning themselves on topless beaches hundreds of miles away. Almost.

Blake sighed. "Maybe we'll see some genuine Indians."

Images of male Indians in loincloths obliterated all fantasies of beach beauties. A flash of color flitted overhead toward the trees. Vincent located it in the canopy where a branch swayed. There in black, gold, and orange glory, a toucan repeatedly snapped his oversized beak. The bird was just like Toucan Sam on the cereal box. His father had loved that cereal.

A squeal from Raposo's satellite radio scared off Toucan Sam. Raposo tuned his radio, allowing a voice to come through weak but clear. The device resembled a gray brick with an antenna, like Vincent's father's first cell phone. Vincent once used to beat in a tent stake. The phone suffered a few scratches and kept on working. Raposo's phone also sported several deep scratches. Perhaps this *was* dad's old phone sold to an agency in a third-world country. Lowering his radio, Officer Raposo spoke to Ruis.

Vincent raised his eyebrows.

Ruis turned toward Vincent and Blake. "Do you want the good news or the bad news?"

Maybe they found the girl. "The good news," Vincent said.

"IBAMA officers have arrived at Nefi's village," Ruis said. "They are interviewing the villagers and searching for evidence."

"And the bad news?" Blake asked.

"The investigating officers will probably be gone by the time we reach the village." Ruis resumed reading the map.

To locate a fourteen-year-old girl in the vast Amazon River basin was a daunting challenge. They were starting out with disadvantages of time and distance. The murders had occurred five days earlier. But how far away was this village? Vincent stepped up behind Ruis to get a better look at the map.

The two IBAMA officers knelt on either side of Ruis around the map. A penciled line ran from *Cruzeiro do Sul*, where they had landed earlier that morning in the southwest part of Brazil, to their present position at Queimado Hill in the *Serra Do Divisor* National Park.

On the map, Officer Raposo swept his hand toward settlements along the Moa River, a tributary to the Jurua River. The Jurua flowed north-northeast into the Solimoes, which emptied into the great Amazon River. Officer Raposo pointed to a settlement on the Jurua River labeled in the smallest letters on the map. He then set his fingertip farther northeast along the river, to an area surrounded by dark green, and then Officer Raposo said the only thing Vincent understood. *Casa* Jenkins.

Of all the places in the Amazon, this area was the least inhabited. On the flight to Brazil, Vincent learned from Ruis that the rivers were the main form of transportation in the rainforest, but because August was winter—the dry season—the shallow Jurua River meandered through six-hundred miles of canyons and flood plains. The river was too low to navigate by boat from their starting point to the smudged fingerprint that marked *casa* Jenkins; however, the river was deeper downstream from the target village to the north. How long would it take to hike *that* far?

Ruis and the IBAMA officers pointed to different spots on the map. Officer Raposo spread his hand over the map on an area west of the Jurua River and spoke in emphatic tones. The other officer had crossed himself before he sat back on his legs. Vincent stepped up to the map. The discussion continued in Portuguese or Spanish, he couldn't tell the difference. The officers gave Ruis one of their gray brick satellite phones. The officers stood.

Both officers shook hands with Ruis, Vincent, and Blake then they headed back down the trail. Apparently the Brazilians and Americans were conducting separate searches. It made sense considering the vast ground they needed to cover.

Ruis pulled a pencil from his shirt pocket. "This," he said, jabbing at a place on the Jurua River, "is where the Jenkins lived. The villagers report that Nefi ran off on August third and left her family's boat behind. In that terrain, she could have traveled anywhere in this area." He drew an eighty-mile-wide circle on the map. "Both officers say she probably headed north along the river. The water is deep enough there for a boat."

"Why did that officer genuflect?" Vincent asked.

"This area on the west side of the river is the Matis tribe territory." Ruis scowled. "Hostiles."

Vincent sighed. "The girl has a two-hundred-mile head start on us."

"How can we catch up?" Blake asked.

Ruis smiled. "I'm hiring a seaplane to take us to Nefi's village."

Blake paled. The poor guy despised flying more than dental work. "Forgive me, Lord. I should not have complained about the hike. So we go back to the park station?" Blake tucked a thumb under the shoulder strap of his backpack.

"The park we just hiked from?" Vincent asked pointing west to the trailhead.

Ruis reached up and gently nudged Vincent's arm southwesterly. Vincent dropped his arm to his side.

Blake shouldered his backpack. "I don't mind going back. I forgot my bug spray."

"The seaplane can pick us up here, tomorrow." Ruis stabbed the map with his pencil to indicate a place downstream on the Moa River a day's hike away.

Vincent crouched by the map, casting his shadow over it.

Ruis tapped the map. "Officer Raposo believes her parents took her to Manaus for immunizations. If she heads for a city, it's the most likely choice. Copies of her description have been transmitted to authorities all over the country. He said he'll contact us if he gets any news."

Vincent resigned himself to a day's hike to the spot on the map where the seaplane would pick them up. He set his expectations low for the reliability of a seaplane in the Amazon. The nearest airport with a mechanic had to be a couple of hundred miles away. Commercial flights were spooky enough, but the idea of riding in a seaplane gave him chills. They were so small, like a car with wings.

Vincent waved his open palm over the north half of Ruis's drawn circle. "So we hike to the pickup point and fly to her village. After that, we follow the trail northeast and look for signs of her?"

Ruis nodded. Vincent and Ruis waited for Blake to weigh in. Blake nodded.

Vincent found encouragement in the fact that a girl raised here should fare okay if left on her own, but where were the men who killed her parents? And why did she leave the village?

Rising to stand, Ruis shook the dirt off his map. He folded it and tucked it in a plastic bag that he stuffed in his shirt pocket.

"I'm sorry to say we don't have any photo of the girl. Based on photos of her parents, she is probably tall for her age." Ruis dug a string of beads from his backpack. He held it up. "Senator Jenkins said this is something the girl should recognize."

Vincent examined the leather and stone bead choker up close. "Looks handmade."

Ruis handed it to Vincent. "Show it when we encounter any girls."

Vincent said, "I'll be glad to." With that he fastened the leather and stone bead choker around his neck for safekeeping.

"Maybe I should take it," Blake said. "We don't want to scare her off. Females trust me." Blake waggled his eyebrows. He had a kind of boyish Southern cowboy charm women responded to, but still....

"She's fourteen," Vincent reminded him. "Can you say jail bait?"

Blake patted Vincent's shoulder. "And you just turned twenty-one. Legal age here too, I bet."

Ruis cleared his throat. His glare sent chills through Vincent. "I have to make a call." He stepped away from Vincent and Blake.

Vincent overheard Ruis arranging for more supplies and the seaplane. Vincent took a swig of water and tucked the bottle back into the pack. After adjusting the straps comfortably over his shoulders, he waited beside Blake for Ruis to finish his call.

Ruis swung his machete up to his shoulder. He then led the way back to the trailhead. Vincent and Blake fell in line behind him. At the mouth of the trail head, Vincent elbowed Blake and cut in front of him, leaving Blake at the end of the line.

They had brought along a few days' worth of food and water. But how long would it take to catch up with the teenager? And why did she leave her village? They were going deeper into the road-less nowhere. They could encounter poachers, guerillas, drug runners, hostile Indians, and who knows what kind of vicious wildlife. Vincent didn't know which he dreaded most, the flight in a seaplane or the idea that their connection to the outside world depended on a technological, hand-me-down relic. The loaner satellite phone seemed a feeble improvement over smoke signals.

About the Author

Author **Joni M. Fisher** is a reformed Yankee with a B.A. in journalism from Indiana University in Bloomington who lives with her husband Maury in central Florida and North Carolina. When she isn't writing, she can be found flying, hiking, writing for aviation magazines, reading, or at church. An active member of the Women's Fiction Writers Association, the Florida Writers Association, and the Romance Writers of America, she is hard at work on her next novel.

Connect with Joni online:

Official website www.jonimfisher.com/books/

Goodreads (Author Page) www.goodreads.com/jonimfisher

Amazon (Author Page) www.amazon.com/author/jonimfisher

Facebook www.facebook.com/jonimfisher

Google+ www.plus.google.com/+JoniMFisher